Girls' Adventure Stories

OF LONG AGO

'*Lucette!*' *gasped Dr Duval.* '*Can I be dreaming?*'

Girls' Adventure Stories

OF LONG AGO

ILLUSTRATED BY WILL NICKLESS

HAMLYN
LONDON · NEW YORK · SYDNEY · TORONTO

First published 1968
Fifth impression 1975
Published by THE HAMLYN PUBLISHING GROUP LIMITED
London: New York: Sydney: Toronto
Astronaut House, Feltham, Middlesex, England.
© Copyright The Hamlyn Publishing Group Limited
ISBN 0 601 07336 3
Printed in Czechoslovakia – JČT
51090/5

Contents

LIST OF ILLUSTRATIONS

Sign of the Hawk

by Renée Frazer

'Halt! What is your business, citizeness?'

The questioner was a burly man in a rough red cap bearing the tricolour cockade of the Revolution. The young girl who had approached the barricade outside the walls of Paris drew her light cloak more closely around her.

'If you please, m'sieur——' she began.

'Hey?' the man's stare became more suspicious. 'There are no messieurs these days, girl—nor fine mesdames, come to that. We are all citizens—and equals—as you should know!'

Shadowed by her hood, the girl's face flushed nervously. 'Forgive me—citizen; I forgot. In our small village, the new order of things is still strange.'

'Ha! If you are a good patriot, it will be wise to remember in future! Take your turn behind the others and see that you have your papers ready for inspection.'

He waved her aside with his musket, pointing to the straggling queue of farm vehicles, coaches and pedestrians waiting to enter the capital; while those who wished to leave were held up for even more stringent questioning.

The girl drew back, mingling with the throng. She looked tired and worried, and her shoes were coated with mud.

There was mud in plenty on the roads of France, in that dark September, for recent heavy rain-storms had added to

9

the misery caused by the fierce uprisings and bloodshed which reached their peak of terror in the autumn of 1792.

To this girl from the country, it all seemed like a nightmare; news travelled slowly in those days, and in the village where she lived with her guardian the more recent events had so far only been rumoured.

She had heard that the angry mobs in Paris, driven by hunger and years of oppression, had disregarded their more moderate leaders and were hunting down the aristocrats—guilty and innocent alike.

Hundreds had been flung into prison—men, women and even young children—while scores of others had fled to escape the fearful Guillotine.

It was said, too, that many quite humble folk had been seized on mere suspicion and denounced to the Commune, the committee now governing France.

The girl's thoughts were checked abruptly by a commotion at the barrier.

A farm wagon laden with produce had been stopped by the citizen guards. The driver, a stolid countryman, was protesting at the delay, but his protests were ignored by the red-capped revolutionaries. They prodded the straw in the cart with their muskets and rummaged among the crates of fruit and vegetables while the ragged onlookers jeered and shouted approval.

'For all we know, citizen, you may be carrying hidden aristocrats—plotting to aid their friends in Paris! They are cunning, those fine seigneurs who were once our masters; many are escaping in borrowed rags—and we know for a fact that someone is aiding them!'

Angry shouts rose from the crowd.

'Death to the accursed aristocrats!'

'And to all those who help them!'

'To the Guillotine with them!'

It was just then that the country girl became aware of a pair of keen eyes watching her closely.

They belonged to a tall, unkempt young fellow lounging by the barrier. Beneath the red woollen cap his face was so begrimed with dirt that it was impossible to guess his real age. A lank mane of tawny hair added to his wild, rather frightening appearance.

He wore a rough leather jerkin, on which was crudely painted the design of a hawk in flight.

The girl's heart pounded nervously; why was the tall youth staring at her in that strange manner? Instinctively she edged away, drawing her cloak tighter to conceal the richly embroidered gown she wore beneath.

What did the young man suspect? Did he guess she was no peasant?

Sudden panic seized the girl. Quickly she dodged among the waiting vehicles till she was momentarily hidden from view.

At that moment she heard the guard at the gate call to the impatient wagon-driver.

'Your papers are in order, citizen. You may proceed! But I warn you, you'll need a special permit if you wish to leave Paris after sunset.'

The carrier merely grunted and whipped up his horse, muttering about the damage done to his wares. Then the wagon rumbled past the barrier and through the city gates.

The young fellow in the leather jacket was vainly scanning the queue.

'She's given me the slip,' he muttered. 'But no matter, unless I am very much mistaken she is Lucette Duval and she'll be making for the house of the Chevalier St. Raymonde.'

He was struck by a sudden thought. 'The wagon! Of course! She must have climbed in while the carrier was talking to the guard.'

And with this thought he turned and made his way towards

the city centre, following the road taken by the wagon only a few minutes before!

A red sunset broke through the overhanging clouds, crimsoning the narrow cobbled streets of Paris as the farm wagon rumbled on its way towards the market.

At every street corner were gathered noisy groups of citizens —men and women with fierce eyes, and pinched, brooding faces. Some wore tattered uniforms; others clung to their rags. But on every head was the now familiar red cap; and nearly every hand clutched some kind of weapon.

Spotting the cart, they surged around it.

'Where do you come from, citizen? What is the news?'

'Come and join us, citizen, if you are a patriot!'

'Share your vegetables with us in return for a good musket!'

They seemed prepared to lay hungry hands on the produce, while the carrier tried vainly to dissuade them.

Then, suddenly, a tall, dishevelled figure shouldered his way through the crush.

'Friends and fellow patriots! We have more important work on hand!' he shouted.

The crowd paused to stare at the newcomer; for there was something about his manner that commanded attention.

They stared at the crimson sign painted on his leather jerkin, then someone shouted:

'It's Red Hawk! He who was in the forefront of the fight, when we raided the Tuileries Palace!'

'So! That was a good day's work, though many accursed aristocrats managed to escape!'

'Hear me, friends!' The youth's voice rang above the clamour. 'I've heard that they're burning down an escaped nobleman's house, in the Place St. Raymonde! Follow me—and there'll be pickings for one and all!'

The crowd needed no more persuasion. In noisy excitement, they surged after the speaker, leaving the street corner deserted.

12

With a grunt of relief, the carrier again cracked his whip, turning his cart down a narrow side street.

'They're all mad!' he muttered. 'Mad with the wrongs they have suffered. 'Tis best to keep a still tongue—*ah! In the name of Liberty, what was that?*'

The sound that caused him to turn sharply, reining in his horse, was strangely like a girl's stifled sob.

And—it came from under the straw in his cart!

The carrier hastily pulled aside the straw. Then he started back with a cry at sight of the slim, cloaked figure now revealed.

'Name of a name!' he exclaimed. 'Who are you, lass? What are you doing in my cart?'

A pair of dark eyes looked up at him.

'M'sieur—citizen, forgive me! The men at the gate stopped me—and I was desperate. This seemed the only way—'

'The only way? Ma foi! Are you mad, girl? Don't you know the penalty you might bring on yourself—and on me?'

'I am sorry, m'sieur. I did not think of the danger I might bring upon you, otherwise I would not have acted so.'

She spoke with a simple dignity, and the carrier, who had a daughter of his own, was touched by her manner.

He looked around quickly, and gave a grunt of relief. The narrow street was deserted.

'What is your name?' he demanded gruffly. 'And why were you so anxious to enter Paris? It is no place, these days, for a young lass like you!'

The girl had climbed down from the cart, and now she stood hesitantly looking up at him.

'I am Lucette Duval,' she said. 'I come from Brittany. I have brought an urgent message for my guardian.'

The man looked at her more keenly. Her voice was gentle and cultured, which was something rarely met with in France since the revolution.

'And who is your guardian? Why is he in Paris?'

'He's a doctor, m'sieur. He learnt that an old friend was seriously ill and came to visit him. That was a week ago. Since then ...' she hesitated ' ... since then, an urgent message has arrived for him—a matter of life and death. He will be at the house of his friend—I must go there!'

The carrier hesitated. 'What is the name of this friend—do you know where he lives?'

'Years ago, my guardian took me to visit him ... I will never forget his kindness, nor his lovely house; but that was long ago and I do not know where to find the house now.'

'The name, lass—the name of this friend your guardian is visiting?' urged the man.

'He is known as the Chevalier St. Raymonde!'

'*What!*' A startling change took place in the carrier's manner; his weather-tanned face turned a greyish shade. 'An aristocrat—and one recently condemned!'

'He is a good man, m'sieur—an old man, who is very ill, and has done no one any harm.'

But the carrier was already preparing to whip up his horse.

'His house stands in the Place St. Raymonde—where you can hear that tumult, over there.' He pointed with his whip. 'But take my advice, lass, and keep away from it. Leave Paris—before you are caught!'

Agitatedly he jerked the reins, and the wagon started to move away.

'I'm sorry, lass,' he called over his shoulder. 'I daren't help you! Leave Paris, while there's still time!'

The girl stood there staring after the wagon—a pale, tense figure in the crimson light. For the glow of the sunset was now mingled with another, more lurid glow.

Fighting back her fears, she broke into a run—in the direction the man had pointed.

'I must find him!' she whispered. 'I must!'

14

The clamour of voices grew louder, and the sound of a drum beating. Then, as she turned a corner, she gave a broken cry.

Before her was a scene that might have struck terror to any heart.

The fine square which she remembered from childhood—the square with the plane trees and the grand white house with its sparkling fountains—all was lit by a great crimson glare.

The St. Raymonde mansion was ablaze! And in the light of this inferno hundreds of figures were singing and dancing around the broken fountains.

As in a nightmare, hardly knowing what she intended to do, Lucette started through the great gates. Her slim figure attracted the attention of a red-haired harridan who was loudly beating a drum. The woman's bony hand shot out, catching the agitated girl by the shoulder.

'Ho, why the tears, citizeness?' she taunted loudly. 'All good patriots should be rejoicing! Come! Let us see you dance!'

Despite her protest, Lucette's hands were seized, and she was dragged into the wild dance around the fountain. Terrified, she struggled to get free—and the cloak was suddenly torn from her shoulders!

'Ho! There's finery for you, citizens!' shrilled the sharp-eyed owner of the drum, pointing to Lucette's gown. 'Such rich attire—enough to buy us bread for weeks! How did the lass come by it—unless she's an aristo!'

'*An aristo!*'

The shout was immediately taken up by the crowd.

'A young aristo—come to spy on us!'

'Denounce her to the Commune! Have her put to the question!'

'No—no! Wait, citizens! There is a surer way to deal with her!'

15

That ringing shout drew all eyes to the speaker. Lucette's heart turned cold as she saw a tall, wild figure shouldering through the mob towards her.

It was the youth she had seen at the barrier, his face even more begrimed than before.

'Make way for Red Hawk!'

Lucette stood her ground, silent and dignified as Red Hawk advanced. He reached her side and the next moment she was plucked from her feet by a pair of powerful arms.

'Make way! Make way! I'll take her to the prison—to La Force—where many others wait to meet our new friend, la Guillotine!'

Loud laughter greeted Red Hawk's grim sally as he strode off with his helpless captive. Away from the crowd he plunged into a maze of narrow side-streets. Then, as the shouts of the crowd died away in the distance he stopped and placed Lucette on her feet.

'Mam'selle, please forgive such discourtesy!' he said, speaking in French but with a trace of an accent.

Lucette gave a start as she looked up into a pair of gravely smiling eyes. But before she could say anything her captor gave a hurried glance up and down the narrow street then led her towards a shuttered shop which bore the sign of a wig-maker.

He knocked three times, and Lucette heard the grating sound of a bolt being withdrawn. Then the door was warily opened.

A plump, motherly woman stood there, lamp in hand.

'Ah—it is you, m'sieur!' she breathed. 'And . . .' she glanced with quick interest at the girl.

'Another victim of the storm, Mère Picard.' The low-voiced reply was not intended for Lucette's ears, but she just caught the words . . . 'arrangements will be made! Meanwhile' . . . he flashed a smile at Lucette . . . 'a good meal, and a change of

'An aristo!' roared the crowd. 'Denounce her to the Commune!'

clothes for the young lady; and for me, a bowl of water, a cake of soap and a comb!'

Lucette accompanied the woman through the darkened shop, with its array of wigs on the shelves and faint smell of powder and perfume. Red Hawk carefully bolted the door, and followed them into a cosy, lamp-lit parlour.

He placed a bundle on a chair, and turned to Lucette with a half humorous smile.

'When you are refreshed, mam'selle,' he said, 'I wish you to change into the costume you will find in that parcel. Please ask no questions now—and try not to worry. All will be done for your safety—and the safety of someone dear to you.'

'You—you know?' Lucette faltered, staring at him.

'More than you imagine, mam'selle. And the rest you shall tell me later. But, meanwhile, I must leave you—as time is short and there is much to be done. I bid you au revoir—but not for long!'

With a gallant bow—strangely incongruous from such a scarecrow figure—he left Lucette alone with her companion.

The woman smiled at her as she pulled up a chair to the small fire.

'You must rest, ma petite,' she said, 'for you look so tired—and you have a long journey ahead of you.'

'Journey?' Lucette echoed, bewildered. 'But, madame, I don't understand! Where am I to go, and who—who is *he?*'

The woman gently shook her head. She was bustling around, laying the table for a meal.

'That I cannot tell you, chérie. Here, in Paris, he is spoken of only as Red Hawk—even among those friends he can trust. Only a few of us know that he is an Englishman to whom many innocent ones owe their lives.'

After supper the mysterious bundle was opened—and Lucette gasped.

'These are clothes for a man!' she exclaimed. 'It is a

uniform! Do I really have to wear it?' she asked uncertainly.

A uniform it was—the uniform of a citizen soldier, complete with red cap and tricolour cockade.

'Red Hawk has a good reason for all he does,' the woman declared firmly. 'Come—we must not keep him waiting!'

Though bewildered, Lucette obediently donned the uniform, which was made for a small man and fitted her perfectly.

A boyish, soldierly figure she made, her dark hair tucked under the red cap. Mère Picard, an expert, pencilled a few lines on the girl's smooth face, making her appear several years older.

Though it seemed like a strange game, Lucette realised the grim meaning behind it.

Outside, in the streets of Paris, danger stalked by day and night—as she knew from her own recent terrifying experience.

'He should return soon, chérie,' Mère Picard said, with an anxious glance at the clock. 'I have never yet known him to fail . . .'

But, as she spoke, there came a rumble of wheels on the cobblestones outside, followed by a tread of heavy feet and a loud knocking at the shop door.

'Open!' exclaimed a stern voice. 'In the name of the Republic!'

White-faced, Lucette stared at Mère Picard as the stern order came again.

'*Open! In the name of the Republic!*'

'I am coming, citizen—have patience!' called Mère Picard; then lowering her voice to a whisper, she added: 'Wait here, chérie—but be ready if I call. And do not be surprised, what-ever may happen—Monsieur assured me that no harm will come to you!'

Calmly she lit a lantern, and went out into the shop; Lucette could hear her pretended grumbling as she unbolted the door. Then the caller's gruff voice sounded more clearly, also the muttering of a great crowd, outside in the street.

'You are Citizeness Picard—widow of Picard, the wig-maker?'

'I am! And what of it? Who are you, citizen?'

'An officer of the Committee of Public Safety! It has been reported that you are harbouring aristos!'

Lucette's heart tightened. Sick with apprehension, she crept to the inner door. She could see Mère Picard in the shop, and the yellow light from the lantern she held revealed the visitor.

He was enveloped in a grey cape and his face was shadowed by a cocked hat, bearing the tricoloured badge. His voice and manner were curt and authoritative.

Lucette glimpsed a coach drawn up in the narrow street, with a postillion holding a flaming torch. An excited mob surrounded it, all staring towards the shop.

Mère Picard had hesitated; but now her reply came clearly:

'The report is untrue, officer! I have nothing to do with traitors! Who is it that accuses me?'

'You have been denounced secretly—and these worthy citizens demand an inquiry. Who is with you in the house?'

Lucette held her breath as the kindly woman again hesitated. Then:

'Only my young nephew—a good patriot and soldier in the National Guard.'

Shouts from the onlookers drowned Lucette's involuntary gasp.

'Let us see him!'

'Bring him out, to prove your words!'

The officer spoke in a low voice to Mère Picard who, with a startled expression, raised her lantern to see his face more clearly. Then she beckoned Lucette who was standing back in the shadows.

'Lucien!' she called clearly. 'Come here, nephew! The

20

officer wishes to speak to you and ask you a few questions.

The girl was seized with panic as she realised the part she was expected to play. But Mère Picard's reassuring glance gave her courage. Heart thumping, she stepped forward into the lantern light.

She was aware of the caller's searching stare, and the avid crowd pressing around the doorway. Among them was the red-haired woman and others who had been in the mob from which she had recently escaped.

They were only prevented from pushing their way into the house by the commanding figure who stood on the step.

'So, young fellow,' he said curtly, staring keenly at Lucette. 'You are a good soldier, and ready to serve the Republic?'

Lucette nodded, not daring to speak.

'That is well! Tonight you shall prove it! You will come with me to hunt down a condemned traitor.'

Again the crowd shouted, this time with hoarse approval.

The man in the grey cape turned to the crowd.

'Enough, good citizens! I have been sent by the Commune to see that justice is done—and it is clear that Mère Picard and her nephew are loyal to the cause. Come, young fellow'—he beckoned Lucette imperatively— 'prove your zeal! There is urgent work to be carried out tonight!'

As in a dream, Lucette heard Mère Picard whisper: 'Courage, ma petite! He who saved you once will help you again!'

Then a musket was thrust into her hand, and she was following the officer to the waiting coach, while the crowd parted to let them through.

Her companion helped her to enter, and slammed the door against the surging onlookers. Leaning from the window, he called to the postillion:

'To the North Barrier—as quickly as possible!'

The whip cracked, and the heavy coach jolted over the cobblestones. Lucette sat bolt upright on the rough horsehair seat, gazing at the dim figure seated opposite. He had removed his cocked hat, and she could just glimpse his lean, clean-shaven features. He was much younger than she had expected.

From his pocket he had taken a bulky sheaf of papers, and now he was studying them. So far he had not spoken a word.

Where was she being taken? What was the real meaning of this ominous night journey? Despite Mère Picard's reassuring words, Lucette felt a growing fear that she was a prisoner— perhaps on her way to be questioned by the dreaded Tribunal ... she had heard tales of innocent folk being trapped like this!

The coach was rumbling over the bridge across the Seine, where a faint mist was rising. Lucette stole a desperate glance towards the door. This was her chance. There were no crowds here and her silent companion seemed intent on his papers ...

But even as she moved, the man leaned forward swiftly, resting a hand on her arm.

'Take care, Mam'selle! Can't let you fall in the river, and catch your death of cold after coming so far!'

Lucette gulped in amazement as she heard the laughter in his voice. She looked up quickly.

'You—Red Hawk!' she faltered.

'S'sh! The coachman's a friend of mine, but you never know what ears might be listening. We must speak softly. There are questions I want you to answer—necessary for your safety.'

Lucette gazed incredulously at those strong, clean-cut features, hardly able to believe the amazing change that had come over the wild, unkempt youth who had rescued her from the angry mob!

He guessed her thoughts and grinned.

'Red Hawk is only one of my disguises,' he said. 'You are

now looking at Citizen Lupin, supposed agent of the Commune—but I owe you an explanation. I doubt if Mère Picard will have told you very much?'

'Only that you are English, m'sieur.'

He nodded. 'There's little need for you to know more. You will have guessed I am involved in helping to save innocent people who have been condemned to the Guillotine; people like the Chevalier St. Raymonde whom your guardian came to visit.'

'You know about that? But what happened to the Chevalier? And Dr. Duval, my guardian-is he safe?'

'They are both safe and in hiding in an old house on the outskirts of the city. The Chevalier was too ill to travel and your guardian refused to leave without him.'

'Then it was you who rescued them?' cried Lucette.

He nodded. 'There were others, too. I left the Chevalier and your guardian in their hands so that I was free to carry out your guardian's request——'

'His request?' echoed Lucette, staring.

'To look out for you, mam'selle Lucette—and to warn you! He had received word that you had left home, and were on your way to the city with a message that had come for him after his departure. I recognised you from his description, but—' she could sense his quizzical glance—'you seemed in a rare hurry to avoid me!'

Lucette was glad that the dim light hid her flush.

'Truly, I—I was afraid of you,' she admitted.

The young man chuckled.

'I'm not surprised! "Red Hawk" is a wild-looking fellow! But I did not intend to startle you—and I congratulate you on your quick wits in taking refuge in that cart. And now—the message. Do you still have it with you, mam'selle?'

Lucette nodded, feeling for the crumpled note which she had, knotted in her kerchief, in a pocket of her borrowed uniform.

She watched him as he scanned it, and saw his features harden. He read the message slowly.

'To Dr. Duval, from a loyal servant of the Chevalier St. Raymonde,' he muttered. 'My master begs you, for your own sake, to stay away from Paris. He has been denounced secretly to the Tribunal. His accuser's name is — 'Red Hawk broke off. Then—' Zounds, I might have guessed it! That black villain, Gaston Lefeur!'

'You know him?' said Lucette, startled by the other's tone.

'*Know him?*' Red Hawk's voice was strangely harsh. 'Aye, that I do! The most treacherous scoundrel in Paris—an ex-aristocrat turned agent for the Commune; he'd betray his closest friend in his greed for power!'

Lucette caught in her breath.

'But what has he against my guardian? Dr. Duval is only a humble physician—why should anyone wish to harm him?'

Before her companion could reply a sharp order rang out, and the coach was brought to a jolting stop.

'You—within there! Show yourselves! Declare your names, and your errand!'

Lucette's heart froze. A face appeared at the window, lit by a flaming torch. The coach door was jerked open.

'You are at the North Barrier, citizens! Your papers giving you permission to leave Paris—I must inspect them.'

With a reassuring glance at the girl, Red Hawk calmly stepped from the coach to confront the guard.

An extra strong patrol manned the North gate, which gave access to the main road to the coast.

Red Hawk produced a document and Lucette held her breath as the official slowly scrutinised it. She guessed the document must have been forged.

Abruptly, the guard looked up.

'You are Citizen Armand Lupin of the Commune, leaving Paris on urgent business for the Republic?' By his tone, the

24

questioner was obviously impressed. 'And—your companion?'

He stared at Lucette who had risen to her feet, musket in hand, trying desperately to look her part as a young Republican soldier.

'I am entitled to an escort,' rejoined Red Hawk, coolly. 'You will find it written there.'

'True. This seems in order, citizen!' The document was duly signed, and handed back. 'You may proceed!'

'*Wait! A word with you, stranger!*'

The cold, smooth voice had come from the shadows; but now its owner stepped into full view. He was almost as tall as Red Hawk but more powerfully built, and dressed entirely in black, relieved only by a tricolour badge of office.

Lucette could see a sallow, aquiline face, marred by a scar across one cheek; and small, restless eyes, as cold and hard as granite.

It was clear from the respectful way the guards treated him that the man in black held a position of some importance.

Lucette looked anxiously at Red Hawk, who stood there calmly, head erect, his cloak wrapped around him. She could not see his face, as his back was turned towards the coach.

'Why this delay, citizen?' he demanded coldly. 'My papers are in order.'

'Undoubtedly!' The man smiled thinly—a mirthless, cruel smile. 'But the exact nature of your errand is not stated. You are bound to reveal it—by the new law!'

Lucette bit her lip. This was a set-back for which even the daring Red Hawk appeared unprepared.

But only for a moment.

Coolly he eyed the man in back.

'I commend your zeal, citizen!' he said dryly. 'As you are so conversant with the law, you will know that it is a crime for an aristocrat who has once fled the country to return under an assumed name? It is a crime punishable by death.'

The other stiffened, his eyes gleaming balefully.

'And what has that to do with your errand, stranger?'

'I am seeking such a one, to bring him to justice! Are you answered, citizen? Or do you wish to delay the course of the law?'

The other's face was like a white mask, and Lucette's blood ran cold as she saw the look in his eyes. It was a mixture of fear and hatred, which passed in a flash.

'Go your way,' he said curtly. 'But—I warn you—steps will be taken to check on your activities!'

Red Hawk bowed briefly, and stepped back into the coach. The door was slammed, and the postillion cracked his whip.

Once again the coach was bowling on its way, the city walls now behind them, the open road ahead.

With an effort, Lucette shook off the bewilderment and secret dread that had held her speechless.

'Who—who was that man?' she faltered. 'And what did he mean by his threat?'

Her companion had been staring out of the window; now he turned with a grim smile.

'That was Gaston Lefeur. Your guardian's enemy—and mine!'

'*Yours?* You mean—he knows you are Red Hawk?'

'I think he suspects. But, you see, Gaston Lefeur must step warily; for if it were known in official quarters that he is an aristocrat it would mean the Guillotine for him.'

'So if he suspects you have guessed his secret he might not be so eager to arrest you?'

Red Hawk nodded. 'That's right. But in that case he will try other methods of silencing me. We must put on all speed, for I think we have not yet finished with Gaston Lefeur.'

He lowered the window and leaned out. He seemed to be listening intently—but all Lucette could hear was the rumble of the four large coach wheels, and the jingle of the harness.

'Where are we going?' she asked.

'Calais,' came the terse response. 'En route for England, Lucette—and safety for you!'

Even as he spoke, another sound made itself heard—the muffled thudding of distant hoofs!'

Lucette caught in her breath, as she saw Red Hawk draw a pistol from under his cloak.

'Jacques!' he called loudly to the postillion. 'Do you hear that?'

'I hear it, m'sieur! They're after us!'

'Pull up at the next bend, man! I'll join you up there! If there's trouble, we'll be ready to meet it!'

The sound of galloping hoofs drew nearer, muffled by the swirling mist.

Red Hawk turned to Lucette.

'Courage, little soldier!' he bantered, with a glance at her uniform. 'Are you ready to obey orders?'

Lucette nodded. 'Tell me what I am to do, Red Hawk!'

'Your orders are to do *nothing*, Lucette—but to remain out of sight whatever happens!'

Then he slipped from the coach and was swallowed up in the mist. Hand trembling, Lucette pulled the blinds and sat motionless, fighting back her gathering fears.

Meanwhile, Red Hawk had joined the coachman. The man's weather-beaten, wrinkled features were swathed in a muffler, and a cocked pistol protruded from his voluminous cape.

'Let them attack if they dare, m'sieur!' he grunted. 'I'd give a lot to come to grips with those devils—'

'All in good time,' said Red Hawk. 'Our task is to protect our young passenger—and bluff may prove surer than bullets!'

The coachman peered doubtfully at his companion.

'Huh! And what is m'sieur's plan?'

'To baffle 'em, Jacques—keep 'em guessing!' Red Hawk peeled off his coat. 'Quickly, now—your cape, hat and whip! For this once I'll be coachman while you hide on the bank with your pistol cocked—just in case my plan goes amiss . . .'

A few minutes later three mounted figures loomed through the fog. At sight of the coach, they drew rein so suddenly that their steaming horses were almost flung on their haunches.

'Hello, there!' shouted a voice. 'What coach is that?'

Red Hawk peered at the newcomers. The two foremost riders wore the uniform of the Republic—one an officer, the other a sergeant. It was the officer who had challenged the supposed coachman.

The third man, dressed in dark, plain clothes, his face hidden by the collar of his coat, remained in the background, motionless on his horse.

'Answer me, fellow!' rapped the officer, riding forward. 'Whose coach is this? We seek the self-styled Armand Lupin, who tricked the guards at the Paris gate with forged credentials!'

Red Hawk stiffened; so the ruse had been discovered. He thought quickly, then—

'Name of a name! So *that* was the rogue whose coach collided with mine at the cross-roads near Gizare? The impudent dog threatened me and refused to pay damages, though I told him I was carrying a sick passenger. The last I saw of the coach, it was heading for Rouen . . .'

Lucette, huddled behind the drawn blinds, held her breath as she listened. Would the young Englishman's cool audacity succeed?

Unable to suppress the temptation, she peeped behind the blinds.

The third man in the party, who appeared to be in command, had dismounted and was walking towards the coach, followed by the armed sergeant.

As they drew near, the yellow light of the lantern revealed the leader's face. Lucette's heart froze as she recognised the man with the scarred face and cruel eyes! Gaston Lefeur!

He was staring at the coach.

'A curious tale, my friend!' he remarked sarcastically. 'The vehicle shows no sign of damage—but doubtless your sick passenger can confirm the story.'

He moved towards the door and Lucette shrank back, numb with despair.

But Red Hawk was looking down at his enemy, seemingly unperturbed.

'Please yourself, citizen,' he grunted, taking a pinch of snuff from a pewter box. 'You know your business best!'

Gaston Lefeur looked up with a sneer.

'And *you* shall know it—to your cost,' he rapped, 'if my suspicions are correct!'

His hand was already on the door when he recoiled with a strangled yell. The pewter snuff-box, hurled with deadly aim, had smothered him with its contents.

Choking, half-blinded, Lefeur shouted to his escort. The sergeant raised his musket, aiming at the supposed coachman —but the bullet flew wide as Red Hawk leaped from the coach, landing squarely on his enemy's shoulders.

Lucette heard the sounds of the fierce struggle as the two rolled on the ground. Quickly she wrenched open the door. She could see the men's figures locked in a desperate struggle and her blood ran cold as she caught the glint of steel.

Lefeur had drawn a dagger!

Her wits sharpened by fear, Lucette snatched off her stout buckled shoe and flung it with all the strength of her arm.

Her aim was true! With a startled grunt, Lefeur dropped his weapon—even as Jacques' burly figure leapt from the bushes, felling the sergeant with a blow from his first.

With one man stunned, and the officer covered by Jacques'

pistol, the tables had been suddenly and dramatically turned.

Lefeur, his sallow face a mask of hatred, was quickly overpowered by Red Hawk, and his wrists tied behind him with his own scarf.

Then Red Hawk turned and picked up the little buckled shoe, handing it to Lucette with a grave smile.

'When you have done with this, little soldier,' he said, 'I'll keep it to remind me that I owe my life to the girl who disobeyed orders!'

Quickly the three men were carried to a barn by the roadside. With a piece of chalk, Red Hawk scrawled a notice on the door:

> *I ride with the storm*
> *I fly o'er the sea—*
> *A foe to the tyrant,*
> *A friend of the free!*
> *The Hawk swoops for justice—*
> *and liberty!*

Once again they were in the coach; and now Jacques drove with urgent haste, for Red Hawk was anxious to reach Calais without further loss of time.

At last, in the pale light of dawn, Lucette caught her first glimpse of the sea. At the quayside, a brig was moored in readiness to set sail on the full tide.

Red Hawk came on board to say goodbye.

'You will find friends waiting to welcome you to England, Lucette,' he said gently. 'Everything will be done to assure your safety—until your guardian can join you.'

'You mean you are going to try to get my guardian to England—and the Chevalier St. Raymonde?'

Red Hawk nodded. 'Both of them. I shall return to Paris at once, to make certain arrangements. Goodbye, then, Lucette. We shall meet again.'

'Oh, I hope so. Good luck, Red Hawk. And—take care!'

A quick smile and he was gone from Lucette's view.

It wasn't till she was alone that Lucette realised that she hadn't really had a clear look at him since they started on this journey together. She couldn't even describe him accurately if she were asked—and yet she seemed to have known him for ages.

She sighed, wondering who he really was . . .

An hour later, as the sun was rising, the brig set its course for England.

Face at the Window

Three days had passed since that desperate flight from France.

In peaceful England, the grim events across the Channel had made little difference to the lives of ordinary folk; though there were uneasy rumours of French spies, and the chance of another war.

Overlooking the Kentish cliffs stood a large, rambling stone house surrounded by a spacious garden. A solid, comfortable house, well-suited to its purpose as set out on a discreet board beside the gate:

DAME THATCHER'S ACADEMY FOR YOUNG LADIES

Near the close of a sultry afternoon, the notes of a harpsichord mingled with the distant cries of the swooping gulls. The music drifted from the open windows of a pleasant, cream-panelled room where the youthful boarders were enjoying an hour of leisure before supper-time.

Sue Manning was at the keyboard of the harpsichord picking out a tune from memory; her companions listened or talked softly together, while engaged in various skilful crafts encouraged by Dame Thatcher. The dame was out at the moment so the girls chatted more than usual.

'Why, Sue, I declare you'll master the harpsichord yet!' laughed plump Belle Challoner, glancing up from her shellwork. 'But that lively air—it's new to me! Is it one you learnt from our visiting teacher?'

'It's a French tune,' Sue said. 'I heard Will Barty whistling it when he came back from his latest voyage.'

'Will Barty? The boy who ran away to sea and then was given a job on shore by your brother, Peter?'

Sue nodded. 'Will looks after our cottage now. I know there were stories about his being wild and all that but he's all right really. Peter likes him, and that's good enough for me.'

Sue spoke with warmth, for she was devoted to her scholarly, rather eccentric elder brother who had looked after her since their parents had died several years previoulsy.

Peter was a naturalist who wrote books to augment a slender income and was often away from home in search of material for his work. In his frequent absences, young Will Barty had proved a friend indeed, taking care of the cottage and doing many private jobs for his new master—'a deuced impractical bookworm' as Peter described himself.

Sue had crossed to the window, and thrown the casement wider, gazing into the autumn dusk.

She could hear the distant murmur of the sea.

'Out there, across the Channel,' she breathed, 'drums are beating, and terror stalks in every street! Will told me so; he has seen it himself. And he told me, too, of a brave young Englishman who is over there risking his life to save innocent victims from prison and the Guillotine! His real name is unknown; but they call him Red Hawk.'

This caused a ripple of interest among her listeners.

'What's he like?'

'Who is he really?'

Sue shrugged. 'Nobody knows, but—'

She broke off at the sound of wheels on the drive.

'Back to work, eveyone—it's Dame Thatcher!'

32

When the worthy dame entered a few minutes later the girls were all hard at work.

'Susan, I wish to see you in my study,' said the dame. 'You other girls will kindly prepare yourselves for supper.'

Sue gulped. A summons to the dame's private sanctum usually meant serious trouble—or bad news!

Heart beating rather quickly, she followed the principal to her room.

It was a large, pleasantly-furnished room, lined with many scholarly books, but brightened with flowers from the dame's own garden.

As they entered, in the half-light, a slim, attractive figure rose quickly from a chair, and dropped a curtsy.

Sue blinked as Dame Thatcher quietly closed the door and stepped across to the young visitor, taking her by the hand.

'Susan,' she said, 'this is Lucette Duval, from France! She is to stay here as a boarder, at the recommendation of a friend of your brother's. As she is a stranger to England—and English customs—I am putting her in your care.'

Sue saw the quick smile in the girl's dark eyes; saw an expressive face framed in jet-black ringlets. As she held out her hand, trying to think of a suitable greeting in French, the other ran forward and flung her arms impulsively round the English girl's neck.

'You are Sue—yes! I hear all about you—and you are going to be my friend!'

The bewildered Sue felt a warm kiss on her cheek, and saw Dame Thatcher smiling in grave approval.

And just then, as she impulsively returned the young French girl's greeting, Sue happened to glance towards the window.

She caught her breath, half believing that what she saw was a strange trick of the twilight.

Pressed against the leaded pane was a white, cruel-looking

face bearing an ugly scar; and, for an instant, a pair of baleful eyes stared straight into her own!

'Is anything wrong, child?'

Sue started, meeting Dame Thatcher's puzzled gaze. Instinctively she stole another glance towards the window—but there was nothing to be seen there now. The leaded panes were blank in the twilight . . . could she have imagined that terrifying face?

'N-no. I must have been day-dreaming . . .' she shook her head, with an unsteady smile. 'For a moment, I—I thought I saw someone outside.'

'Possibly it was Burrows, the gardener. Why, I do declare you've turned quite pale! It is unlike you to be so nervous, Susan—but no doubt it is the excitement of meeting our visitor!'

Lucette was smiling at Sue in a puzzled way, not fully understanding what was being said. Though she had learnt to speak English it was still a foreign tongue to her.

'It's going to be lovely having you here as a friend, Lucette,' Sue said quickly. 'You must be about my age, and we'll have such fun—hem!' She broke off, encountering the dame's admonishing glance. 'I mean, such interesting talks together!'

The principal nodded approvingly.

'Lucette must perfect her English—and you, Susan, certainly need to polish your French! Now please introduce her to the others, and then show her to her room. She will have the small room next to yours and Belle's.'

'Certainly, madam!'

The two girls were at the door when Dame Thatcher called Sue back.

'One moment, Susan! There is something rather important I wish to say to you.'

Puzzled, Sue approached. The dame was scanning a letter she had taken from her desk.

'You realise, Susan,' she said, in a lowered tone, 'that Lucette has only very recently arrived from France?'

Sue nodded, wondering what was to come.

'I gather from your brother's friend that she has suffered many frightening experiences. She may confide in you—but do not worry her with questions, nor allow the other girls to do so. I am relying on you to help her forget . . .'

'Of course—I understand, madam,' nodded Sue. 'I'll do all I can.'

Sue led the way to the room where the other girls were still gathered. 'Now you can meet all your new school friends, Lucette,' she said. 'Girls—this is Lucette Duval from France. She has come here as a boarder.'

'Welcome to England, Lucette!'

Lucette smiled shyly as Belle came forward and shook her warmly by the hand.

'Thank you! You are so kind! You make me very happy to be here at your school. I was told I should find real friends in England,' she added softly. 'And it has happened—just as Red Hawk said . . .'

'Red Hawk!' The excited exclamation burst from Sue, while the rest of the girls stared and whispered. 'You mean, you've actually *seen* him—spoken to him?'

'But, of course!' Lucette's naturally shy expression had given place to an eager warmth. 'It was he who rescued me from danger, and brought me safely to the English ship . . .'

'What's he like?'

'Is he very handsome?'

Lucette flushed and hesitated.

'I—I cannot say, except that he was very gallant. I could not see his face clearly. In France, he is renowned for his daring. And he has—how you say—the motto. Wait—I try to remember . . .'

The room was very warm, despite the open window.

Lucette slipped off her cloak, and put it over a chair as she tried to think back . . .

'Ah, now I remember the words he wrote—listen!'

Quietly she repeated the words Red Hawk had scrawled on the door of the barn:

> *I ride with the storm*
> *I fly o'er the sea—*
> *A foe to the tyrant*
> *A friend of the free!*
> *The hawk swoops for justice—*
> *and liberty!*

A hush followed the unusual recital. The listeners were strangely impressed, and Sue felt a little lump in her throat. Outside the window the bushes rustled—but strangely there was no breeze.

Sue came to earth and smilingly slipped her arm round the new girl.

'Bravo, Lucette!' she exclaimed. 'Come—I'll help you change your things or we'll be late for supper!'

Sue led Lucette to a small, pleasant bedroom adjoining the one she shared with Belle.

Lucette drew a deep breath. Sue noticed, now, how pale and tired she looked.

"Tis so peaceful here, Sue! No shouting crowds outside—no frightening knocks at the door! I—I could be so happy, if only I had good news of my guardian.'

Sue nodded as she helped Lucette change into a sprigged muslin gown—the uniform evening wear for Dame Thatcher's pupils.

Busy with the fasteners she listened with tense interest while Lucette told of her dangerous journey from Paris.

'If you laugh at your worries, Lucette, you'll help to scare them away! No news from your guardian probably means good news—that's what my brother Peter always says, and

36

I'm sure he's right! And now—this will help to bring back the colour to your cheeks—a little recipe of Dame Thatcher's!'

Gaily chattering to keep up the other's spirits, Sue fetched a little cut-glass phial, and drew out the stopper.

'Here, sniff this! A-ha—you see!' she laughed, as Lucette gasped for breath. ''Tis the dame's own smelling-salts distilled from herbs—and I vow you're better already.'

'I feel better since meeting you,' Lucette smiled. 'The Revolution seems far away and I know Red Hawk will keep his promise. I can almost forget my enemy—the man with the scar—'

There was a splintering crash as the smelling-salts bottle slipped from Sue's fingers.

'Oh, the pretty bottle! What a shame!' Lucette, looking in concern at the scattered fragments, did not notice Sue's startled expression. 'It was my fault for brushing against you as I jumped up—yes?'

'No—no, it was just my clumsy fingers!' Sue rejoined, forcing a gay tone. 'Luckily the bottle was mine—and not Dame Thatcher's!'

She was determined not to alarm Lucette by mentioning that strange face she had seen outside the window of the principal's study. But was it coincidence that the face had borne an ugly scar?

Sue's ready imagination visualised all kinds of disturbing possibilities. She decided to broach her suspicions to Dame Thatcher.

It seemed incredible that the dangers about which Lucette had spoken could reach out to peaceful England! And yet—the Channel was not so wide, after all; and ships arriving with fugitives from the Terror might carry enemies, too . . .

Sue made up her mind. At the risk of being chided as a scaremonger, she would go straight to the dame's study. Now!

Leaving Lucette happily brushing her hair, Sue hurried downstairs and knocked at the principal's door. But Dame Thatcher was not in her study.

The supper bell would ring at any minute and Sue would have liked to tell her news before the other girls came down.

As she made her way through the music-room she noticed Lucette's cloak and hood lying across a chair. Instinctively she picked them up, intending to return them to Lucette—but just then she saw that the french-windows had been left ajar.

Perhaps the good dame had stepped out for an evening stroll in the garden as was sometimes her custom?

Slipping Lucette's cloak over her shouders, Sue hurried across the lawn and along the path through the rose-garden.

She believed she could hear footsteps ahead of her, and she quickened her walk to a run.

'Dame Thatcher!' she called softly.

The footsteps halted; a tall figure loomed suddenly from the bushes beside her—a man dressed in black, his face muffled by a scarf.

Sue bit back a scream as he caught her by the arm, peering into her face.

'This is not the girl!'

He spoken in French, but Sue understood the words.

'Who—who are you?' she gasped. 'What are you doing here?'

In reply, a hand was clapped over her mouth.

'Silence!' came the harsh command, this time in English. 'You will not make a sound—or you will regret it! Alfonse!'

Another, more stockily-built man appeared, wearing the rough garments of a seafarer. The tall man gave an order and the other produced a length of rope. It was plain to Sue that they meant to tie her up, while they continued with whatever lawless purpose they had in mind.

Desperately she struggled, managing to free her mouth

from her captor's hand. She took a deep breath and screamed.

'*Help!*' Her clear voice echoed across the grounds. '*Help!*'

Next moment, a scarf muffled her screams. Almost despairing, she tried to break away. She had come some distance from the school, and it was more than possible that her cry had not been heard.

Then, suddenly, her heart leapt. There came pounding footsteps—an answering shout in an English voice.

'Hey! What's amiss here?'

From the bushes plunged a sturdy, fair-haired youth. He swung a stout staff in his hand.

'Out on you, bullies!' he shouted. 'Two of you, maltreating a lass! Two skulls deserve to be cracked!'

Sue slipped free of the scarf. 'Will Barty! Will—look out!'

Sue's gasp of delighted recognition and relief changed to a warning cry. The foreign seaman had drawn a pistol; but ere he could fire he was sent sprawling by a well-aimed blow from the boy's whirling staff.

'And now you, mister—whoever you are!' panted Will, striding towards the tall stranger.

The man reached under his cloak—and a long, murderous blade flashed in the moonlight.

'Back, young dog!' he snarled. 'Or, by thunder, I'll run you through!'

In that tense moment, Sue thought she heard a distant sound of galloping hoofs; but she barely gave it a thought. Her whole attention was fastened on that unequal conflict between a lad armed only with a staff, and a skilled swordsman!

Will Barty, the ex-ship's prentice, had not been seen in the district recently, and there had been rumours that he had gone to sea again. But here he was, bold and grinning as ever, as he parried the darting sword with his oaken stave.

Sue's first impulse was to fling herself at the man—but she realised that an unwary move might precipitate a tragedy.

At the moment, the stranger's sole purpose was clearly to scare the bold youth into letting him pass.

'Out of my way, cur!' he ordered harshly.

'Not while I've an arm to raise, mister—an' a stout stick to belabour a spy!' retorted the boy defiantly, 'You may be a great man among those murderers across the Channel—but this is English soil!'

He sprang aside as he spoke, aiming a blow which would certainly have felled his opponent—if the man had not ducked swiftly.

Next instant, the point of his sword was at Will's throat.

Sue screamed and darted forward, momentarily diverting the foreigner's attention. And in that instant came unlooked-for aid.

Another figure leaped from the bushes—booted and spurred, and wearing a tricolour hat and cape. And his face was concealed by a mask!

'*En garde* you scoundrel!' he cried, drawing a sword. 'Or are you a coward as well as a bully?'

'Well said, sir!' shouted Will, his grin even broader. 'You came just in time!'

The Frenchman drew a hissing breath. Then he lunged fiercely at the masked challenger, who parried swiftly, forcing the other to retreat.

Steel clashed on steel, as the darting blades flashed in the moonlight. Both men were skilled swordsmen, but the man in the mask revealed a cool nonchalance that made his opponent look clumsy. Thrusting and parrying, the duellists disappeared among the trees.

Meanwhile, the dazed seaman had regained his feet and was making his escape, hotly pursued by Will Barty.

In a few minutes the rose-garden was deserted except for Sue.

Till now she had felt stunned by the amazing swiftness of

40

events; but, as her thoughts cleared, she tried to piece together what had happened.

It was clear that the two foreigners must have come for Lucette, and had been momentarily taken in by the fact that Sue was wearing the French girl's hooded cloak.

How Will Barty had arrived so opportunely she could not guess. And as for the masked swordsman whom Will had called 'Sir'—his dramatic intervention couldn't be accounted for in any part of Sue's reckoning.

Will came hurrying back at that moment, a broad grin on his face.

'Zounds, Miss Sue—such goings on!' he exclaimed. 'You've missed a rare sight! Those Frenchies riding off like mad as though the whole King's army was on their tail—instead of one Englishman!'

Then his manner changed.

'But your pardon Miss Sue,' he added remorsefully. 'Here I am joking while you're so pale and shaken. Did those furriners hurt you?'

'No, Will—I'm all right,' Sue rejoined, with a tremulous smile. 'But only thanks to you—and that tall young stranger. Who *is* he, Will?'

'Sorry, Miss Sue—I've sworn not to tell his real name. But over there, in France, they call him—Red Hawk!'

'Red Hawk!' Sue's heart gave a bound, as she stared at the boy in wonder. 'Here—in England? And he's a friend of yours?'

Will coughed, plainly on his guard.

'In a manner of speaking, Miss Sue. I've done some jobs for him—for my work at the cottage leaves me plenty of spare time and Mr. Peter's an easy master.'

'My brother's never mentioned him—I wonder if they've ever met!' breathed Sue, her excitement almost banishing the shock of her startling adventure.

41

Will shook his head—then shrugged his shoulders.

'I wouldn't like to say, miss—but, speakin' of Mr. Peter, I've brought you a message from him. That's how I chanced to hear when you cried out just now.'

'A message from Peter? Where is he?'

'On his way home, Miss Sue—he sent word asking me to give you his love and to say he'll be visiting the school very soon.'

Sue's eyes lit up.

'I must tell Dame Thatcher! And I'll introduce him to Lucette—she's new girl who's just come from France.'

Then her eager smile faded, as she remembered the other, grimmer tidings she had for the young French girl. How could she break the news to Lucette that her dreaded enemy was so near?

But Peter would advise her; she had always confided all her thoughts and her fears to her brother and he never let her down.

Just then there came hurrying footsteps—and into the rose-garden burst the school gardener, armed with a bill-hook. Behind him, carrying an enormous umbrella, bustled Dame Thatcher herself.

'Sue Manning! Goodness gracious—we've all been at our wits' end thinking some harm had come to you after hearing you scream! What are you doing out here? And *you*, young man'—she jabbed the umbrella towards Will—'kindly explain you presence in my grounds!'

'Hem!' Will coughed, dodging nimbly to avoid another vigorous thrust. 'If you please, ma'am . . .'

'I do *not* please!' said the dame sternly. 'I await an explanation!' She swung round. 'From you first, Susan.'

'Will brought a message from my brother, madam,' gulped Sue. 'And—and he bravely helped to drive away two foreigners who were trespassing——'

'Mercy on us all!' the dame threw up her hands. 'Foreigners

in the grounds of my academy! Whatever will happen next!'

Sue seized her chance to speak urgently aside to the bewildered principal.

'I believe the strangers mistook me for Lucette, madam!' she breathed. 'You remember I thought I saw a face outside your study window?'

Quickly Sue repeated the strange story the French girl had told her. The dame's expression became even more grave.

'Good gracious—I had almost forgotten! But what makes you imagine . . .'

'Say nothing of this to the other girls, Susan,' she enjoined. 'I do not wish to spread further alarm. The two men may merely have been ordinary thieves or poachers, taken by surprise—but we cannot ignore the more serious possibilities!'

Beckoning the gardener, she instructed him and the boot-boy to search the grounds thoroughly and to make sure that the gates were padlocked.

Then she turned to Will.

'Young man,' she said, her tone thawing a little, 'it seems I may have spoken hastily. Perhaps I can offer you some refreshment, in return for your timely service . . .'

'Hem—very kind of you, ma'am, but I was only too glad to be of help!' Will doffed his cap with a guarded wink at Sue. 'And now, if you'll excuse me, I'll have to be off to my duties—my best respects to you, ma'am, and to the young ladies!'

He departed, jauntily whistling and twirling his staff. Sue suppressed a smile. Will, who would cheerfully have faced a dozen swordsmen without flinching, was secretly rather scared of the redoubtable Dame Thatcher!

But more serious thoughts returned as she and the principal returned to the school. The other girls, who had been ordered to remain indoors, gathered around them, agog with anxious questions.

'Thank goodnes you're safe, Sue!' gasped plump Belle Challoner. 'We heard such frightening sounds—shouts and galloping hoofs! Cook declared the French had invaded Kent!'

'Twas a false alarm, Belle!' said Sue, lightly, remembering Dame Thatcher's warning. 'Some trepasser in the grounds—but he was chased off by Will Barty.'

Just then, the principal called for silence.

'Come, girls!' she said. 'You are all too ready to listen to foolish gossip! Calm yourselves and file in quietly to supper. Susan—' she beckoned to Sue and spoke in a lowered voice. 'I instructed Lucette to wait for you in my study. Please make sure that she is not alarmed.'

Sue needed no prompting. Quickly she hastened to the study.

Lucette turned from the window as she entered. 'I'm so glad you have come, Sue!' she said. 'I could not find out what had happened, and—and I was afraid . . .'

'Afraid?' Sue gave a quick laugh, slipping her arm around the other's shoulder. 'Come on—there's cold chicken for supper; and I've got some exciting news for you!'

'News?' Lucette smiled eagerly, as they crossed the hall. They could hear the distant chatter of the other girls, already at their evening meal.

'It's a secret, Lucette—but I'll give you three guesses!' Sue intended to tell Lucette that Red Hawk was actually in England! That would give her hope and courage, whatever else might be in store.

But just then the French girl gave a startled gasp.

In the recent excitement, the door leading to the gardens had been left unbolted. Now it swung open—and Sue collided with a tall, cloaked figure who had stepped from the shadows!

'Well!' exclaimed a deep voice, with a hint of laughter. 'Here's a fine welcome, to be sure!'

44

Sue gasped, as she was whirled from her feet in a pair of strong arms.

Lucette was staring wonderingly at the tall young man, who stood there laughingly with Sue in his arms.

He was a scholarly, yet handsome figure, in a travelling-cloak and suit of dark velvet, his boots dusty as though he had travelled far.

He might have been about twenty, though the spectacles he wore made his age difficult to judge. His face was lean and sun-tanned, and his smile was reflected in a pair of searching grey eyes.

''Pon my word, little sister, I vow you've grown since we last met!' he chuckled. 'And that was only a few weeks ago! What have you been doing with yourself—hey? But before you tell me I insist on being introduced to your friend!'

Sue slid from her brother's arms and drew Lucette forward.

'This is Lucette, Peter—Lucette Duval, who's just come from France! Lucette—I want you to meet my big brother!'

Lucette blushed a little shyly as she shook hands; but the young man's quick smile put her at her ease.

'Mam'selle Lucette,' said the young man with a gravity belied by the bantering gleam in his eyes, 'I humbly salute you! In becoming Sue's friend, you have taken on a hazardous task!'

Sue laughed. 'Don't mind Peter. It's just his way of saying that I'm such a hopeless scatter-brain I'm bound to lead you into scrapes!'

'No—no!' Lucette protested, smiling. 'With Sue, I feel—how do you say—so at home. Now she is my friend I am no longer afraid.'

'There!' exclaimed Sue, looking challengingly at her brother. 'What do you say to that?'

Peter raised his eyebrows quizzically.

'Hem! It seems I owe you an apology! But tell me'—

he glanced keenly at his sister—'what was that commotion I heard as I came along a few minutes ago?'

'Oh—just a false alarm!' Sue flashed him a warning glance. 'But here comes Dame Thatcher!'

The bustling arrival of the good dame saved Sue from having to go into details.

Peter stepped forward to greet the principal, who welcomed him with unfeigned pleasure. She had a warm regard for Sue's scholarly, somewhat eccentric brother.

'So you are back from your travels, Mr Manning? And how is the book progressing?' she asked.

'Ah—the book!' Peter looked solemn. 'Slowly but surely, y'know—wouldn't do to rush it. I have been gathering much valuable material.'

'Indeed?' Dame Thatcher looked interested. 'I should very much like to have a copy when it is finished.'

'Hem!' the young man coughed, with a flicker of a smile. 'I shall certainly bear that in mind! Meanwhile——' he changed the subject—'I came to ask a special favour. As I may be away again pretty soon I should like to take Sue and her friend Lucette for a little outing tomorrow—if you will permit them the time off, of course.'

Sue suppressed a little whoop of excitement, while Lucette's eyes sparkled.

'Oh *please!*' exclaimed Sue in eager appeal.

To her relief, Dame Thatcher was smiling benevolently.

'Certainly!' she said. 'As it happens, Mr Manning, your request fits in with the school curriculum! Tomorrow I had planned to give the pupils a practical history lesson by conducting them on a tour of ancient Canterbury. The post-chaise will be calling here at noon and returning in the late evening. During that time Sue and Lucette will be free to join you.'

'Splendid!' said Peter. 'I have no fixed plans. The girls may choose where they wish to go—what they wish to do. I'm sure Sue has plenty of ideas! What would Lucette like to do?'

Sue nodded, with a quick glance at her friend.

'I was telling Lucette about some of our English customs—and she said she would love to go to a fair!'

'Splendid! Let me see, isn't there one in the district now?'

'Yes—in the grounds of the old castle!' exclaimed Sue eagerly. 'Will told me he saw the booths being set up——'

She broke off a little anxiously, for she had noticed Dame Thatcher's pursed lips.

'I do not normally approve of fairs,' said the dame. 'Such odd folk attend them, and one hears of much rowdiness! However, on this occasion, as you girls will be safely escorted——' her manner thawed as she looked at Sue's brother—'I have no objections!'

Sue and Lucette sighed in relief.

Peter grinned.

'The fair it is, then. I'll call for you girls tomorrow in the gig. About noon.'

Sue kissed her brother, and then Lucette came forward and shook hands. Sue noticed that she studied Peter closely in this moment, and that there was a quizzical look on her face as they left the room.

On their way to join the other girls at supper a few minutes later Lucette was very thoughtful.

'Sue,' she said, suddenly. 'Has your brother ever been abroad?'

She looked surprised.

'Peter? I don't think so—he's never mentioned it! But why do you ask?'

'I just wondered. Somehow I felt we'd met before. You're lucky to have such a nice brother.'

Sue smiled. 'I'm glad you like him, Lucette—I know he's taken to you! We'll have so much to talk about when we see him tomorrow!'

The Enemy Strikes

Half-a-mile from the school, on the very brink of the cliffs, stood a quaint, rambling cottage built of flint, with one tall chimney on its slated roof.

It was known locally as the 'Crow's Nest', and it was believed once to have formed part of an ancient inn of that name—the resort of a notorious smugglers' gang.

But the encroaching sea had eaten deeply into the cliffs, and much of the old building had long since been swept away.

Now the cottage stood in a trim garden, the lattice windows on one side looking out across the Channel. Two sides were bounded by a dense thicket which concealed the old stables and out-buildings; while, on the fourth side, a wicket-gate gave access to the lane.

This was Peter Manning's retreat when he happened to be at home; an ideal spot for writing.

Tonight, someone was clearly at home; for smoke came from the tall chimney, and lamp-light glowed warmly behind the leaded panes.

In the oak-beamed kitchen, over a blazing log fire, an iron pot slung on chains exuded an appetising smell of something cooking.

And, stirring the contents, was sturdy Will Barty, coatless and with a cheery grin on his face.

'Reck'n the guv'nor will be nigh famished!' he declared. 'That long journey, and not a bite to eat; but you'd never have known it to see him in action—phew! There's daring and skill to copy, Will, my boy!'

The lad often spoke to himself when on his own.

Will possessed a keen wit and a ready tongue, as well as a pair of hands prepared to tackle almost anything. Fighting, cooking, splicing a rope or firing a cannon—he had been a jack-of-all-trades at sea and ashore. And he had found a friend and master after his own heart in the surprising young owner of the Crow's Nest.

"'Spect he's been up at the school with Miss Sue,' he soliloquised, stirring vigorously. 'Luckily she's never tumbled to his secret! If she knew I reckon she'd insist on packing up and joining him. Aye, she's got plenty of spirit has Sue.'

Just then there came a brisk clip-clop of a horse's hoofs in the lane. Will immediately downed the ladle and sprang to unlatch the door as the rider dismounted at the gate.

'Everything all right, Will?'

'Right as rain, Mr Peter! I left the other lads to keep watch and slipped back to see to the pot. Reck'n you could make short work of a broiled rabbit——'

'Nothing I'd like better, Will! But, first I must see to Toby.' He patted his horse's name. 'By the way—any fresh news?'

Will nodded and gave a cautious glance up and down the lane.

'*The Albatross* berthed an hour ago, and the captain sent a package for you by hand. It's marked "Urgent"!'

'So?' Peter's expression became more serious. 'I'll be with you in a jiffy!'

He stabled his horse, rubbing it down and seeing to its feed before joining Will in the cottage.

The rabbit stew was already on the table and beside the plate was a sealed packet inscribed simply to Monsieur R., c/o *The Albatross*.

Sue's brother ripped it open and scanned the contents; Will saw his hands clench suddenly and the pleasant eyes behind the spectacles grew suddenly hard.

But he sat down to his meal without a word.

The boy knew better than to question him; it was not the first time he had seen that expression on his young master's face—and it had always portended swift action!

But this time Peter calmly finished the savoury stew, and

re-read the letter before speaking of his latest plans.

'Thank you, Will,' he said, 'I needed that excellent supper! Now please draw the curtains and see that the door is bolted. There is work to be done!'

Will promptly obeyed as the young man rose to his feet and began to pace the room, frowning in deep thought.

At length he seemed to come to a decision, for he halted and looked at the boy keenly.

'I've an important task for you, Will—the most important you have carried out for me yet!' he announced gravely.

'Yes, Mr Peter?' Will was immediately alert. 'Just say the word!'

Peter nodded approvingly. 'First, then—I have to leave here almost immediately. When is *The Albatross* due to sail?'

The boy's eyes widened.

'At—at dawn, Mr Peter—but I don't understand! You have only just come back from——'

'I know, Will—and I'd planned to stay for a while, but that has all been changed by this news! The life of a good, brave man is in deadly peril. He has risked everything in our cause and his loss would be a blow to us all—' and he added gruffly to himself— 'especially to a young girl, here in England, whose heart would be broken!'

Will looked at him quickly, hazarding a guess.

'Would that be the young French lady up at the school, sir? I haven't seen her, but I heard she was Miss Sue's friend.'

Peter nodded.

'You're right, Will—and that brings me to your task! I want you to be my deputy here while I'm away—and be ready to guard Sue and Mam'selle Lucette, if ever they need a friend!'

Will flushed with pleasure, squaring his broad shoulders.

'Rely on me, Mr Peter! When do I start?'

'Tomorrow,' said Peter. 'I promised to call for the girls to take them to the fair. I don't want them to be disappointed—

but their safety comes first! Harness Toby, and call at the school by noon—before the post-chaise leaves. I'll give you a note to hand to Dame Thatcher!'

Will grinned, secretly proud at the thought of taking Miss Sue and her friend to the fair! While Peter, a weight taken off his mind, set to work to prepare for his urgent journey.

At midnight they set out for Dover. Young Will drove the gig while Sue's brother sat deep in thought.

But Peter Manning was no longer the neatly-dressed young man who had visited Dame Thatcher's school earlier. True, he still wore a fine cloak, but beneath the cloak he had on a rough leather jerkin. He no longer wore spectacles and his hair was pulled down over his brow.

Even Sue would hardly have recognised him as her brother. But he was clearly well known to the captain and crew of *The Albatross*. They treated him with great respect.

For they knew him as—Red Hawk!

The brig, with sails unfurled, was straining at its moorings, all ready to set out on the dawn tide, but Peter urged Will not to wait.

'Hurry back to the cottage, lad, and get in some sleep!' He smilingly slapped the boy's shoulder. 'Sue and Lucette will want you to look your best tomorrow!'

Will grinned, and then looked more serious.

'About your secret, Mr Peter—isn't it time that Miss Sue was told?'

Peter shook his head.

'It's safer that she shouldn't know, Will; but you have my permission to tell her—if anything serious should happen!'

Then he stepped aboard, a tall, striking figure in the dim light of the ship's lantern, till the boy finally lost sight of him.

With conflicting feelings Will drove back to the cottage, his pride at Peter's trust in him mingled with a foreboding he could not explain.

Dawn was breaking by the time he reached the cottage, and drove the gig round to the tumble-down old stable.

It was too dark to see to unharness Toby, so he groped for the tinder-box and lantern on the shelf.

And just then he thought he heard a footstep behind him, muffled by the straw!

Will turned quickly, groping for the pistol Peter had lent him; but he was a second too late.

A figure stepped from the shadows, and a stunning blow crashed down on the boy's head. He staggered, and collapsed in a crumpled heap . . . then everything went black . . .

When Will dazedly opened his eyes it was to see the morning sunlight and he wondered why he could not move his limbs. Then a stab of recollection brought a groan to his lips.

He was lying on a heap of straw, his hands and feet secured with cord and a scarf tied round his face.

He struggled desperately to free himself—to call for help; but his muffled groans could only be heard by Toby, the horse, restlessly pawing the ground in the stall nearby . . .

The sun rose higher; and at Dame Thatcher's Academy, a mile away, life was beginning to stir.

Sue, as usual, was one of the first to wake. Eyes sparkling, she slipped out of bed and hurried into the next room. Lucette was still sleeping. Her dark hair was spread over the pillow and she moved restlessly, murmuring in her dreams.

As Sue shook her gently by the shoulder, Lucette awoke with a stifled cry, clinging to her friend's arm.

'Lucette—I didn't mean to startle you!' Sue cried.

'Oh, but I'm so glad you woke me!' Lucette shivered. 'I thought I was back again in Paris—but in a gloomy cell; and from the window I could see the carts passing below, all filled with poor prisoners on their way to . . . to . . .'

'It was only a dream,' urged Sue.

'I—I know,' Lucette whispered, 'but—it seemed so real!

I even imagined I could see their faces. One of the prisoners was a tall young man—so strong and kind, and with eyes that seemed to understand. He—oh, Sue—he was *your brother!*'

'Peter?' Sue smiled. 'My scholarly brother is probably having breakfast at his cottage with a book propped beside him—making up for the time he'll lose when he takes us to the fair this afternoon. He's coming for us at noon, remember.'

Noon found the two girls waiting outside the school gates.

The rest of the girls were assembled in the school drive, while Dame Thatcher read a list of instructions concerning correct deportment for the journey to Canterbury.

Just as she finished reading, the Canterbury Mail drew up to the gates with a clatter of hoofs and much shouting and whoa-ing.

The red-faced guard climbed down from his perch, and touched his hat with a respectful grin.

'A good mornin' to ye, ma'am—and 'tis a grand day for a spin! Six seats reserved inside, and five a'top; but——' he checked his list with the party of eager, bright-eyed girls—'I see there's two young ladies extra.'

Dame Thatcher smiled across at Sue and Lucette, who had just joined the group.

'They will not be accompanying us. A friend will be calling for them shortly. And now, please—attention, girls!' She raised her rolled umbrella, like a shepherd's crook, as she beckoned her flock. 'Each girl to her place; and those travelling on top will remember to wrap up well!'

What excitement! The coach was quickly filled, inside and on the roof, with gay gowns and be-flowered bonnets, smiling faces and waving hands.

The dame turned for a final word with Sue and her companion.

'Goodbye, my dears! I wish you a pleasant outing, and a safe return!' She tapped Sue meaningly on the shoulder.

'And remember, Susan—you must be on your best behaviour.'

Then, sedately, she rustled to her place inside the vehicle, with much manoeuvring of her stiff farthingale skirt.

The door was slammed, and the guard tooted his horn; the straining horses answered to the crack of the long whip. Away bowled the coach down the lane, while Sue and Lucette stood waving till it disappeared round the distant bend.

'It would have been nice to have gone with them,' said Lucette, smiling, 'but it will be even nicer to go to the fair with your brother!'

They strolled out of the gate, looking eagerly along the lane in the direction from which Peter's gig should come.

But now the blue sky was clouding over, and the sultry breeze was becoming more noticeable.

'I do wish he would hurry!' Sue exclaimed. 'I'm afraid it's going to rain! Let's walk a little way to meet him. He's bound to be coming from his cottage, so we can't possibly miss him.'

Arms linked, they set out along the leafy lane.

Neither of them noticed a covered vehicle drawn up in a nearby field; nor did they see a pair of bright, beady eyes in a wrinkled face peering through the tangled bushes. The face was that of an old gypsy woman.

'Hey, that's them,' she muttered. 'They're the ones I'm to look for. 'Twill be a simple thing to trick them.'

'Whatever can have happened to Peter?'

Sue spoke lightly but she was becoming more anxious than she would admit.

The girls had reached the cross-roads where, as Sue had expected, they espied a stream of holidaymakers all bound for the Dover Fair.

Some were on foot, many on horseback, others in phaetons or open carriages; but in vain Sue looked for the dapple-grey horse and fast-moving gig in which she had fully expected her brother to meet them.

'Surely he can't have forgotten . . . but, no!' she half smiled, and then frowned. 'Even Peter's not as absent-minded as all that.'

'Perhaps he was tired after his long journey and has over-slept?' suggested Lucette.

Sue's face cleared.

'Of course—you must be right, Lucette! Come on! His cottage isn't far from here!'

Beyond the main road, the lane became even narrower—little more than a bridle-track which skirted the cliffs. Soon the girls came in sight of the quaint flint cottage, its tall chimney stark against the darkening sky.

But no smoke came from the chimney, and the curtains were still drawn. The cottage had a bleak, deserted look which somehow chilled Sue's heart.

Followed by the mystified Lucette, Sue hurried up the path and hammered on the door.

'Peter!' she called. 'Peter! Are you at home?'

But there was no reply; no sound except the rustling of the trees.

'He—he must be out,' whispered Lucette.

'But Peter wouldn't have changed his plans without sending a message,' Sue frowned. 'And then there's Will! He always minds the cottage when my brother's away, and looks after Peter's horse and—goodness! Why didn't I think of that before?'

Darting off, she led the way to the old stable, hidden by the trees.

The door was open, revealing only the trampled straw; neither horse nor gig—nor any sign of life! But on the floor lay a tangled skein of rope, knotted and frayed as though someone had struggled to untie it.

Sue's heart sank as she stared around, though she had no inkling of what could have happened.

Just then Lucette, who had remained by the door, tensed as though listening.

'Hark!'

'What is it?'

'There's someone coming!'

Now they both clearly heard a jangle of harness—a rattle of wheels and a horse's neigh, as a fast-driven vehicle pulled up in the lane!

'Peter!' gasped Sue, her face lighting in relief.

But it wasn't Peter.

A large, covered cart had stopped outside the gate. The sole occupant was a wizened old woman whose age it was hard to guess; for though her face was wrinkled and brown as a nutmeg, her eyes, jet black and watchful, held a glint of subdued fire.

She wore a bright-coloured scarf, swathed around her head like a turban, while from beneath it hung a pair of long, silver ear-rings matching the many glittering bangles which clustered her bony arms.

As the girls stared speechlessly, the woman leaned towards them with a crooked smile, and raised a be-ringed hand to beckon.

'Ma foi—she must be a witch!' Lucette breathed, shrinking back; for, in those days, belief in sorcery was widespread.

But Sue cherished no such fancies.

'She's just a wandering Romany—a gypsy,' she whispered. 'They always come whenever there's a fair. I can't think what she wants with us—but I'll soon find out.'

Sue moved across to the gate, followed by the French girl. The woman called to them.

'Come, my pretty ones—-you need fear nothing from old Zola!'

56

The dry, cackling tones sounded friendly enough, despite the speaker's strange appearance; but Sue was on her guard.

'What is it you want of us?' she asked.

The gypsy gave a mirthless chuckle, shaking her head till her ear-rings rattled.

"Tis well not to trust a stranger, lass—but I come on a friendly errand, while on my way back to the fair. You know not who I am, or the nature of my trade?'

Sue shook her head.

'Ha! You shall learn anon—you and your pretty friend.' The shrewd black eyes darted a glance towards Lucette, who stood rather nervously in the background. 'To help such bonny lasses will be a pleasure!'

'But how can you help us?' Sue asked, puzzled and rather suspicious. 'We are strangers to you.'

'Not quite strangers, dearie. You see, I have come at the behest of your brother——'

'Peter?' cried Sue. 'You mean he sent you with a message?'

The old crone nodded, fumbling beneath her gown.

"Twas as I was setting out early this morning, to obtain certain wares for my trade—a young gentleman hailed me; he was driving a gig, with a dapple-grey horse——'

'Yes, that must have been Peter. But—but where did you meet him?'

'On the road near the quay, my pretty one; he seemed agitated and in great haste. He said he had been away all night on an urgent errand, and had only just returned . . .'

'So *that* is why the cottage is deserted.' Sue's thoughts were in a whirl. 'He had promised to meet us——'

'Aye—so he told me. But he feared he would be delayed . . . He had learnt that I would be passing this way, and asked me to bring word to you.'

'And—the message?'

'That he would meet you at the fair, two hours after noon.'

Sue was no simpleton. Though the old woman's story held a ring of truth—for how else could she know so much?—Sue was not prepared to trust the gypsy on her word alone.

'But what proof have you?' she demanded. 'Who told you my friend and I had come to the cottage—and how were you to recognise me?'

The old crone smiled toothlessly, not resenting the question. She withdrew her bony hand from under her robe.

'By this token, dearie. I showed it to passers-by, and was told that you had been seen hastening in this direction from the cross-roads.'

As she spoke, she unclasped her fingers—revealing a little silver locket, bearing a tiny miniature of Sue herself!

Sue drew a quick breath as she recognised it. It was the locket she had given to Peter—a keepsake which he always carried!

Her doubts were swept aside. The message must be genuine, baffling though it seemed!

How was Sue to have known that the little keepsake had been lost the previous night while her brother was engaged in a duel with an enemy?

*   *   *

Dover Fair! A scene of gay colour as the holiday crowds surged around the booths erected on the sunlit sward within sight of the grim old castle.

It was Lucette's first glimpse of a real English fair. She looked about her with excitement as she and Sue alighted at length from the old gypsy woman's cart.

'Your brother should be here soon, my dear,' the woman said, 'and I have my business to attend to! If ye do not find him speedily, come to my booth; 'tis the big black tent yonder, in the shadow of the castle.'

They watched the vehicle rumble away between the crowded booths and busy stalls till it was lost from view. Then they wandered through the fairground.

Time passed. The time Peter said he would be there came and went with no sign of him. Then a low rumble of thunder brought the first heavy drops of rain.

Suddenly the old gypsy woman was beside them, urging them towards the big black tent as the thunder sounded overhead.

'Hurry, my dears—I have news for you! Come, see who is waiting inside!'

Bewildered, Sue and Lucette stared around, as they were hustled into the tent.

They saw strange groups of figures standing motionless in the shadows; knights in armour, cavaliers—queens in bejewelled robes, a grim headsman with an axe. A painted placard read:

MADAM ZOLA'S WAXWORKS

Sue turned to the old woman, whose wrinkled face was puckered in a sardonic smile. 'Where is my brother?'

'Here, dearie—he waits behind the curtain to surprise you!'

All Sue's earlier suspicions came crowding back. Apart from the old gypsy, they seemed to be alone in the tent.

But even as she stepped back, the curtains were parted and a tall figure stepped towards them, his face shadowed by an enveloping cape.

He was certainly about Peter's height and build—but her brother would never play such a stupid trick as this!

Lucette was staring at the figure, her eyes wide with a dawning dread. Then there came a lightning flash—and Lucette's piercing shriek was drowned by the crash of thunder. She was staring into the scarred, pitiless face that had haunted her since she escaped from France:

'It's a trap!' Sue cried frantically, trying to reach the

French girl. 'Lucette — you must escape —— quickly!'

But old Zola's bony hands held her tightly; and a cloth with a pungent odour was flung over her head.

Struggling desperately, her senses leaving her, Sue dimly heard the man's voice:

'See to her, woman! The English girl is of no account, but might cause trouble . . . The other is to *disappear!* You understand? And it will pay you to keep silent . . .'

And Sue remembered no more.

A tang of seaweed, and the sound of waves lapping on the shingle . . .

Those were Sue's first sensations as consciousness slowly returned. She believed she had awakened from a nightmare; and with a sob of relief she opened her eyes, expecting to see the familiar surroundings of her bedroom at Dame Thatcher's Academy.

Instead, she stared dazedly at a low, uneven roof of chalk, dimly lit by the yellow light of a lantern.

She felt too weak to move; her head was throbbing, and her arms were like lead weights. Surely—surely she must still be dreaming!

This gloomy, narrow cave, with the grey sky visible through a distant opening . . . where was she? What had happened?

Then, as she groped for a fleeting memory, she heard a stifled moan close beside her . . .

The shock was like an icy shower, clearing her numbed mind.

'*Lucette!*' Sue struggled up, staring at the pale figure lying near to her, wrapped in a cloak. 'Lucette!'

The young French girl lay motionless in a heavy, unnatural sleep. The numbing fumes which had overpowered Sue had taken a stronger hold on Lucette, already weakened by shock.

She did not stir as Sue crawled over to her, shaking her gently by the shoulders, calling her name.

60

Then a footstep crunching on the shingle brought Sue whirling round, suddenly tensed.

The old gypsy woman stood there in the cave opening.

'So, you're awake my young lady?' she cackled. 'Well, 'tis of little acount. They'll be here for your friend soon and I'll be on my way.'

'*They?* What—what do you mean?' Sue gasped. 'What is this place? Why have you brought us here?'

'Ask no questions, girl!'

With a threatening gesture, the woman picked up the lantern and retraced her steps to the mouth of the cave.

Sue could hear the faint creak and splash of a boat's oars— a keel grating on the shingle. As the gypsy swung her lantern, there came a shout in a gruff, foreign voice. Heavy footsteps were crunching towards the cave.

Three figures loomed in sight—one tall, and muffled in a dark cloak; the other two obviously seamen, wearing red woollen caps and armed with cutlasses.

The men stepped forward—but now Sue was on her feet, barring their way, face pale and eyes ablaze.

'Don't you dare touch my friend!' she gasped. 'This is England—and there's a law to protect her! I'll—I'll call for help, and bring the coastguards!'

The men hesitated, glancing at their leader.

'Stand aside, girl!' he ordered coldly in English, 'or it'll be the worse for you!'

'No!' cried Sue, despreately flinging her arms round Lucette, as the two sailors came forward.

The tall man seized her by the shoulder, thrusting her towards the old gypsy.

'Here, woman—keep her quiet!' he snarled.

'HELP! HELP!'

Sue's frantic screams echoed through the cave before a bony hand was clasped over her mouth.

Struggling despairingly, she saw the unconscious girl being lifted and carried towards the entrance; but at that moment there came a surprising answer to her cry.

A shout echoed from somewhere above, and there was a rattle of falling chalk and rubble. Next instant, a dishevelled figure landed on his hands and knees outside the cave!

As he started up, flourishing a stout bludgeon, Sue wrenched herself free from old Zola's hold.

'Will!' she cried, overjoyed. '*Oh, quickly!*'

'Miss Sue! Where are you?'

'Never mind me—save Lucette!'

Whirling his club, Will rushed towards the cave, attacking the nearest seaman. The other drew a cutlass, but it was knocked from his hand, and the boy's bunched fist sent the man sprawling.

'Curses on that young meddler—he'll ruin everything!'

Sue's first joy turned to sharp fear, as she saw the tall leader pull a pistol from under his cloak.

'Will—take care!'

Desperately she ran forward, grabbing at the man's arm; but he flung her off, cocked the pistol, and took deliberate aim.

Will, turning to tackle the second sailor, heard Sue's warning cry and realised the peril to the unconscious Lucette.

He sprang deliberately to shield the girl as a shot echoed from the cave; and that gallant action undoubtedly saved his life.

The bullet merely ripped through his jacket, grazing his shoulder; the searing pain spurred him to grapple fiercely with the second ruffian, who had now released his hold on Lucette.

Yet the odds seemed hopeless. The leader had reloaded his pistol, and Sue, running to Will's aid, found her way barred again by the gypsy.

Suddenly came a shouting in the distance—footsteps running on the beach!

Sue's screams were useless—she could not help Lucette now.

Will, flinging off his opponent, sprang quickly to his feet. 'Hurrah!' he shouted. 'This way, lads!'

There came an answering call; and Sue, her heart leaping, saw a group of youths rushing towards them flourishing staves, pitchforks and bludgeons.

The town 'prentices had come to the rescue!

In another minute the enemy would have been routed— but then came the crackle of musket shots, fired from a second boat, just landing on the beach.

In the fading twilight, a dark French cutter, its sails unfurled, could be seen lying off the shore.

'A trap!' shouted Will huskily. 'The cowardly furriners! Quick, Miss Sue—back to the cave! Come on, lads!'

'Lucette!' cried Sue, trying desperately to lift her friend.

But she was dragged aside by a burly sailor; Will, sturdily fighting, was brought down by two others.

Armed only with their primitive weapons, the 'prentices put up a brave struggle. But they were driven back and held, while the unfortunate French girl, still unconscious, was carried down to the boat.

Covered by an array of muskets, the little group on the beach were forced to look helplessly on as the two boats put out to sea.

Sue was sobbing; her mind felt numbed. She could hardly believe what had happened.

She felt a rough hand grip hers; and through her tears she saw Will's face, streaked with blood.

'Don't worry, Miss Sue!' he said. 'They won't get away with this! Some of the lads have gone to warn the coastguards; there'll be a chase! An if that fails . . .'

He stared out to sea, where the dark cutter was just visible sailing swiftly away on the ebb-tide.

'If that fails, Miss Sue,' he added gruffly, 'I'll be off to France myself—to contact Mr. Peter!'

64

'Peter!' gasped Sue, staring. 'You mean—my brother's in France?'

Will nodded, and gripped her hand more firmly.

'The time has come, Mis Sue,' he said, 'when it's right for you to know your brother's secret. He's the brave Englishman you've so often heard of—the one who's risked his life for so many out there . . . I reck'n you know the name.'

Sue's eyes widened incredulously.

'Not . . . not . . .'

'Yes, Miss Sue. Your brother is none other than Red Hawk!'

'Red Hawk!' Sue breathed the name with a thrill of wonder. 'Peter—Peter is Red Hawk! Oh, goodness, how *blind* I've been!'

For a moment, even her distress for Lucette faded into the background; she could think only of her lovable absent-minded bookworm of a brother—suddenly changed into that elusive hero whose deeds had become legendary!

Vaguely she was conscious of Will's strong arm supporting her, helping her up the steep slope from the beach; of a mutter of many voices, of hurrying footsteps and galloping hoofs.

Her first excitement gave place to a sharp stab of pity. Poor Lucette! She had so nearly guessed the truth—that was why she had asked if Peter had been abroad; something about him must have reminded her of Red Hawk.

And now the enemy had struck, in Peter's absence—and Lucette was being taken back to the City of Terror.

They had reached the cliff path now, where a lanky youth was holding the bridle of her brother's dapple-grey horse.

The other prentices had dispersed; some to alert the coast-guards, the rest to their homes to tend sundry wounds and bruises collected in the beach skirmish.

The cold sea-mist was now drifting farther inland, enveloping Sue's shoulders.

'Did you hear that cannon, Miss Sue?' said Will. 'Reck'n 'twas fired by the coastguard-cutter that's gone out after those Frenchies! 'Tis only thanks to the mist they got away—and maybe we'll soon have news!'

He turned aside to speak to the lanky youth; the youth nodded and hurried off on some errand.

Will helped Sue to mount the horse; then, taking the reins, he set out for the cottage.

On the way, he explained how he had been attacked on his return to the cottage; how, next morning, he had managed at length to release himself from his bonds.

But, dazed by the shock, he had collapsed on reaching a friend's house and had not recovered till late in the afternoon.

From his friend, Sam Perkins, he had learnt that the two girls had been seen at the fair with the old gypsy, who was known to be an unscrupulous character. Will had ridden there at once, and picked up the trail, while his friend hurried to contact the other 'prentices.

'And you came in time to save me—though not poor Lucette,' breathed Sue. 'Will, how soon can you get in touch with my brother? Even now, I can hardly believe he is really Red Hawk!'

'I know where to find him, Miss Sue,' Will declared confidently. 'I've been to France with him before.'

Proudly he explained how Peter had chosen him and a few friends to act as couriers—carrying messages, and escorting the refugees once they were safely embarked on their journey to England.

And once he had actually accompanied his young master to Paris in the guise of a dumb French cabin-boy! There he had witnessed one of Red Hawk's daring rescue bids—and had stayed at the wig-maker's shop, where the fugitives were hidden by brave Mère Picard till they could be smuggled to the port.

Later, at the cottage, Will showed her a secret cupboard

containing some of the costumes used by Red Hawk and his youthful helpers.

There was the leather jerkin, with a crimson design—discarded now, since its description was familiar to his enemies.

Here was a deputy's robe and feathered hat; an officer's uniform with a tricolour cockade and, next to it, a French peasant-woman's apron and red bonnet.

To Will's surprise, Sue seemed more interested in the rough jacket and canvas trousers he had worn as cabin-boy. He would have been startled had he guessed the thoughts that were surging through her mind; a reckless purpose which she dared not breathe aloud.

Others were helping Red Hawk in his perilous mission; why should she, his own sister, remain snugly at home?

Her thoughts were interrupted by a loud knocking.

Will hastily closed the secret cupboard, and crossed to the door.

'Who's there?' he called.

'It's Sam!' came the muffled response. 'I've got news!'

'News of Lucette?' Eagerly Sue ran forward as Will admitted his friend. But one look at the messenger's face and her heart sank.

'What's happened?' demanded Will.

The other boy shrugged.

'Those Frenchies escaped under cover of the fog! The coastguards say there's no hope of catching 'em now.'

Will clenched his fists.

'Right! Then there's only one thing for it! It's me for France—and tonight! What's sailin', d'you know?'

The *Dover Maid's* standing by with a cargo for Spain—the captain is always ready to touch in at Calais to help us.'

'So he is! And the tide'll be up in three hours! If you'll help me get the boat out, lad, I'll cut across the bay to save time! Miss Sue'—he turned, with a look of apology on his rugged face—'d'you mind waiting here till the carrier calls for you?'

Sue's heart was beating madly; though not by a flicker of an eyelid did she betray what was in her mind.

'Don't worry about me, Will—I'll be all right!' she declared lightly. 'But first you ought to have those cuts and bruises dressed!'

'Where do you keep your boat, Will?' she asked casually.

'In the cove just below here, Miss Sue—with the luggage I need all tied up in a neat bundle under the tarpaulin! Good-bye, Miss Sue—or "*Au revoir*" —as Mr Peter would say! There's no danger for you now—an' maybe I'll have good news when we meet again!'

Then the boys had gone—and Sue was alone. There was not a minute to lose!

Locking the door and drawing the curtains, she quickly slipped off her rumpled dress and changed into the cabin-boy's outfit last worn by Will. It fitted her fairly well and her hair was tucked neatly away under a woollen cap.

Then she made a bundle of food and a few possessions she might need and sat down to write a note to kindly Dame Thatcher, apologising for the anxiety she might cause and explaining the reason for her action.

Sealing this, she addressed it care of the carrier and pinned it to the cottage door. Then she made her way down to the beach.

Cautiously she descended, fearful that some last-minute hitch might jeopardise her plan. But the narrow strip of beach was quite deserted. Will's boat was there, drawn up on the shingle, a sheet of tarpaulin lashed across the stern and forming a rough shelter for the boy's luggage.

Till now Sue had scarcely paused to think; her plan had been made on the spur of the moment. She was not blind to the dreadful risk it entailed, but her purpose was firm.

For in Sue's blood was that same streak of reckless courage which had changed her scholarly brother into the leader of a desperate cause!

When Will finally launched the boat, the slight extra weight of the unseen passenger under the tarpaulin aroused no suspicions.

Reaching the waiting schooner, the boy climbed aboard to have a word with the captain.

Holding her breath, Sue crept from her hiding-place. Cautiously she climbed the ladder, her small bundle slung on her shoulder.

Her purpose was to wait till the ship was well out at sea and then reveal herself to Will and the captain!

She had just gained the deck when she heard footsteps. Desperately she darted behind one of the ship's lockers and knelt down, scarcely daring to breathe.

The footsteps halted. Then she heard a deep voice—clearly the captain's.

'Calais is out of my way, lad—and there's always a risk. But while I'm master and owner of the *Dover Maid* I'll be proud to be of any service to Red Hawk!'

'Thank 'ee kindly, sir! Then I'll get my baggage aboard!'

Another long, anxious wait; then she heard the bo'sun's whistle—the rattle of the anchor chain; the creak of the rigging as the ship slid out of harbour, rocking on the swell.

They were away—bound for France! The first part of her plan had succeeded—and the rest . . . Sue drew a deep breath. The rest was in the hands of Fate!

Return to Paris

It was near sunset, a few days later. Once again the scene was Paris—and that dim little shop in a side-street owned by widowed Mère Picard.

The kindly woman had just admitted two secret visitors—one, a grey-haired gentleman whose haggard features and sunken eyes revealed the suffering he had recently undergone.

Mère Picard addressed him as Dr. Duval. He was none other than Lucette's guardian—the brave physician who had defied persecution to carry out his duty to a friend.

His companion wore the uniform of an official of the Commune; but he had removed his disguise, and the strong, clear-cut features were those of Peter Manning—alias Red Hawk!

No word was spoken till they reached the cosy parlour, and Mère Picard had closed and bolted the outer door. The elderly doctor, clearly dazed and weak, was led to the chair by the fire.

'I received your message, M'sieur Red Hawk,' said Mère Picard, as she brought them coffee and sandwiches. 'It is wonderful that you have rescued the good doctor when we all feared . . .'

Red Hawk shook his head seriously.

'It was not I, madam, but my willing helpers—and Dr. Duval's own courage! Though badly wounded, he did not murmur at the hardships he was forced to undergo in hiding. His only thought was for his friend, the unfortunate Chevalier.'

Dr. Duval looked up, his face distressed.

'The Chevalier St. Raymonde died of his wounds, madam,' he said gruffly. 'He died in my arms—and it was better that way. Had it not been for Red Hawk, he might have perished in prison—or by that dreaded instrument of vengeance—the Guillotine!'

There were tears in Mère Picard's eyes.

'How long will this Terror last?' she breathed. 'So many innocent folk to suffer for the guilt of others! Thank heaven for those who have been saved, m'sieur—including yourself and your ward.'

The old physician's tired face lit up.

'Ah Lucette! Yes, Red Hawk saw her safely to England.'

He looked up gratefully at the young Englishman whose handsome face appeared unusually grave in the firelight.

'I left her in good hands,' said Peter, quietly, 'but I had hoped that my assistant, young Will Barty, would have been able to send a message through the usual channels. The silence makes me a little uneasy . . .'

He shook himself, with a flicker of his customary smile.

'But I worry needlessly! All arrangements have been made for you to join Lucette in England. You should try to sleep on the journey. That safe but powerful sleeping-draught you prescribed for the Chevalier—you still have some left?'

The doctor nodded, taking a small phial from his pocket.

'I do not need it, my friend—I am able to sleep at will. But it may be of use to someone less fortunate. One dose remains—I shall leave it in Mère Picard's charge . . .'

As the good woman took the phial, there came a sudden rattle of cart-wheels outside. Peter raised a warning finger, and all three were silent, exchanging anxious glances.

They heard the cart pull up. A tense moment passed—then three cautious knocks sounded on the door.

'Ah!' Peter's face lit with relief as he started to his feet. 'That should be Jacques! He may have brought news of the coach that is to meet us outside Paris. But wait here, till I return.'

He hurried from the room and unbolted the outer door. The loyal coachman who had helped him on previous occasions stood outside. In the yard adjoining the shop a covered cart could just be glimpsed.

'Well?' Peter eyed the man questioningly. 'What news, Jacques?'

The other glanced cautiously up and down the narrow street, before replying.

'Strange tidings, M'sieur! Both good—and bad. A coach

is in readiness, and there was no trouble about the papers. They have been approved and stamped for the safe conduct of the doctor and one companion. But . . .'

Jacques looked warily towards the covered cart.

''Tis best for those who brought the tidings to tell you in their own words, M'sieur—two weary travellers I encountered on the way. They are from England.'

'From England!'

Peter caught in his breath as he sprang past Jacques and into the yard.

The cart bore the sign of a miller; and within, seated on a pile of empty sacks, were two travel-stained, youthful figures.

One, Peter recognised at first glance.

'*Will!* What in heaven's name brings you here, lad? What has happened . . .'

He broke off, as the other young traveller turned, snatching off the woollen cap that had concealed a mop of unruly curls.

'*Sue!*' He caught her by the shoulders, half believing her to be an apparition. 'You—here—in France!'

'Oh, Peter—I had to come when I learnt that you were Red Hawk!' gulped Sue, clinging to him. 'Don't blame Will. I tricked him—stowed away on board the ship. When he found me it was too late to turn back . . .'

Peter passed an unsteady hand over his forehead.

'But—I don't understand! What is wrong? Has anything happened to——' he drew a sharp breath— 'to Lucette?'

Sue's words were choked as she tried to answer, but her expression was enough.

The blood drained from Peter's face, his hands clenching.

'Tell me!' he cried: 'Will! I want the whole truth!'

'She was kidnapped, Mr Peter,' said the boy, 'by your enemy—the man with a scar!'

*   *   *

72

Peter was pacing the yard, his face white and grim. He had sent Will indoors to break the news privately to Mère Picard.

Dr. Duval was not to be told while there remained even a glimmer of hope. The blow might prove fatal to the old gentleman, already weakened by illness.

Jacques had departed, too, to make certain urgent new arrangements, at Peter's orders.

Only Sue was left with her brother, watching him as he strode to and fro, his brow furrowed in thought.

Suddenly he halted, as though conscious of Sue's anxious gaze.

'Forgive me, little sister—this is no way for Red Hawk to act!'

'Peter, why did that man Lefeur do this? Why is it so important to him to bring Lucette to France? He can't make a charge against her—it isn't as if she's an aristocrat——'

Peter interrupted her. 'You're wrong, Sue. Lucette *is* an aristocrat. She is connected by birth to the unfortunate Chevalier St. Raymonde. Dr. Duval secretly adopted her and concealed the truth for her own safety.'

'But,' Peter went on, 'Lefeur found out who she really was. Lefeur himself was a cousin of the Chevalier and he knew that if he was ever to inherit the St. Raymonde estates he must first get rid of both the Chevalier and Lucette——'

'So he denounced the Chevalier——'

Peter nodded. 'And he's brought Lucette back in order to denounce her, too. Unless we can track him down very soon——'

Just then, Jacques came hurrying back accompanied by Will.

'News, M'sieur! Lefeur arrived in Paris this morning—with a girl. It is rumoured that she was taken to the Hotel de Ville . . .'

'That means she has been accused before the Committee of Public Safety!' said Peter. 'But there may be a delay before she faces the Tribunal. I'll go there at once, and expose Lefeur as a traitor!'

'You'll risk your life, sir!' gasped Will. 'Let me go with you!'

After some hesitation, Red Hawk agreed.

To denounce his enemy openly would be a rash move. But if he could trace Lucette, a daring rescue bid might be possible —and Will would be a very useful aide!

Sue, who had been an anxious listener, started forward impulsively.

'Peter—is there any way *I* could help?' she asked.

With a quizzical smile, Peter rested a hand on her shoulder.

'Haven't you done enough, my little madcap?' he asked gently.

'No. First you must rest and refresh yourself. Mère Picard will see to that. Then Jacques will take you and Dr. Duval to the coach we have engaged. Fortunately the doctor's papers permit him a companion—and, if questions are asked, you are his granddaughter!'

'I will answer all questions, M'sieur!' put in Jacques. 'You may leave Mam'selle Sue and the old gentleman in my care. But you——'

'Will and I must fend for ourselves,' Peter said. 'If possible, we will overtake you—but your jouney to Calais must not be delayed! A ship has been chartered and will be waiting; my sister and the doctor are to sail for England—whether you hear from me or not!'

Sue fought back her tears when Peter finally embraced her— urging her to take care of herself and the old doctor, and not to worry. Then he and Will departed on their perilous mission.

While Jacques made final arrangements for the journey,

74

Mère Picard fussed over Sue as though she had been her own daughter. A welcome meal, a fresh change of clothes—and a parcel of food to take with her. And, as an afterthought, the motherly woman insisted that Sue should take the little phial entrusted to her by the doctor. 'It may help you to sleep on the journey, my dear, if you become over-tired and anxious. And the doctor assured me it is perfectly safe . . .'

Sue took the phial to please her kindly hostess—though she never dreamed that she would have cause to use it.

She could not foresee the strange workings of fate!

At length Jacques returned to say that all was ready. The old doctor, still in a daze, was helped into the cart; and Sue sat beside him, snugly wrapped in a warm cloak and hood.

Armed with the forged papers, Jacques drove through the noisy streets towards the barrier.

Here they were halted in the queue while the papers were scrutinised.

Suddenly there came a stir in the crowd. There were shouts and jeers as a party of soldiers hustled a luckless prisoner towards the guard-room.

Sue caught a glimpse of a slim, girlish figure in a bedraggled gown, a red scarf tied over her head which partly concealed her face.

'An aristo!' came the shouts.

The escort had difficulty in forcing their way through the crush. Then the guard-room door was opened, and the red glare of a torch fell fully on the pale, tear-stained face of the prisoner.

Sue gave a cry, for she knew that face. *It was Lucette!*

'Lucette!' Sue's shout was almost drowned by the general clamour; but Lucette had heard her.

A look of mingled wonder and hope dawned in the frightened eyes beneath the bedraggled scarf. Then the soldiers roughly hustled their prisoner forward.

Jacques, who was being interrogated by the sentry at the gate, was unable to see clearly what was happening. He made an attempt to return to the cart but his way was barred by the crowd.

Sue did not stop to think: her one impulse was to reach her friend. Slipping from the cart, she tried to squeeze past the jeering onlookers—a conspicuous figure in her cloak and hood among the ragged garments and red caps on every side.

Her chance came as the guards forced back the throng to clear a path for their captive. Ducking between them, Sue flung her arms around the dazed girl.

There were angry shouts, and one of the soldiers endeavoured to drag her away; but Sue stood her ground desperately.

'She's my friend!' she cried. 'What harm has she done? Let her go!'

Her words, spoken in English, were only partly understood.

The corporal in charge lost patience.

'The girl is a crazy foreigner! We've no time to waste! Bring her in with the other for questioning!'

Both girls were seized and pushed through the open doorway amid further shouts and jeers from the crowd. The door clanged behind them.

There was little daylight in the guard-room, which was lit by a smoky lamp. A few guards off duty lounged about, puffing their clay pipes and talking loudly. A hard-faced officer of the Commune was seated at a table before an open register.

The girls were ordered to stand before him.

'Which is the prisoner, Lucette Duval?' he demanded.

'This,' said the corporal, indicating the luckless French girl in her torn gown and red scarf. 'The other is a mad foreigner who claims to be her friend and refuses to leave her.'

'Umph!' The officer eyed Sue sharply. 'And what is *your* name, girl—and business?' he demanded.

Sue gave her name, stating that she had come to Paris

to find her friend which was, in fact, the absolute truth.

The officer scribbled something on a slip of paper and handed it to the corporal.

'Foreign friends of condemned aristos may be held for questioning or deported,' he said curtly. 'Lock her up with the other till the escort arrives!'

The two girls were taken to a gloomy cell containing only a bench, a bare table and a pallet bed. The door was shut and bolted behind them.

With a stifled sob, Lucette flung herself into Sue's arms.

'Oh, how did you come here, Sue? I thought—I thought I was dreaming—but now you too are in danger!'

'S'sh!' Sue tried to comfort her, fighting back her own fears. 'Everything's going to be all right, Lucette! Red Hawk—Peter will save us both!'

'Red Hawk?' Lucette gazed at her wonderingly, new hope in her eyes. '*He* is here, in Paris? And Peter—your brother . . .'

'They are the *same*, Lucette! Peter is Red Hawk!'

Quickly she told the dazed girl all that she had learnt—all that had happened since their fateful parting.

Lucette clasped her hands, eyes shining through her tears.

'I *knew* it!' she whispered. 'I somehow knew from the moment I met your brother that he was, indeed, my brave rescuer! And you——' she impulsively embraced her friend, 'you are as brave as he is! You risked your life to come out here, to find me!'

'Hush!' Sue whispered, for the other was laughing and crying, almost hysterically.

The shock and excitement had been too much for Lucette.

She started to sob again, clinging to Sue.

'Hush, dear—hush!' Sue tried to speak reassuringly. 'When Peter learns what has happened, he'll find a way to come to our help!'

But she could not deceive herself. By the time her brother

managed to trace them, Lucette might already have been removed to some grim prison where rescue would be impossible . . .

Sue's mind was working frantically. Her own position was dangerous enough; but as an English girl with no specific charge against her, it was possible that she would eventually be released.

But Lucette's fate was already sealed.

Unless . . .

Sue drew a quick breath, her pulses racing. There might still be a way—one slender, desperate chance of saving her friend!

She and Lucette were of much the same build; and in the dim light of the guard-room only their contrasting garments had clearly been seen.

Sue was not blind to the terrible risk she would be taking . . . but Lucette's life was at stake. And Sue knew how much the French girl meant to her brother—she was sure Peter was in love with Lucette . . .

Sue made up her mind. Without allowing Lucette to suspect her purpose, she determined to change places with her friend!

And the means were to hand. From her pocket, Sue took the little glass phial containing the powerful sleeping-draught.

'Drink this, Lucette, dear; it will calm you—do you good . . .'

She felt a momentary pang as Lucette trustingly took the phial and raised it to her lips. But it was the only way; Lucette would never have agreed willingly to the plan!

The potent draught was not long in taking effect. Lucette sighed contentedly and allowed Sue to lead her to the bench, her eyelids already drooping.

'I feel so sleepy,' she admitted, 'and—and so safe now with you, my English friend . . .'

Her voice trailed away in another deep sigh; her head fell back on Sue's arm and she sank into a deep sleep.

78

Sue waited for a moment, her heart thumping. There was no time to lose!

Quickly she removed Lucette's ragged gown and crimson head-dress, replacing them by her own hooded cloak. Then she lifted her gently on to the pallet bed.

The red scarf she swathed around her own head, concealing her fair hair and partly concealing her face.

She had barely donned Lucette's ragged gown when there came a sudden commotion from the guard-room. Sue heard voices—and one of them she recognised as Jacques!

'I tell you, citizen officer, there will be trouble if the English girl is not released immediately! See—here are papers signed by a member of the Commune granting her and her grandfather safe conduct from the city.'

More muttering—and then the officer's voice, raised in a sharp order.

'You have bungled, corporal! It is as the good citizen says! Release the English girl—but the other has been denounced, and must be handed over to the prison escort!'

Heavy footsteps approached the cell; bolts were withdrawn! Then the door was opened and the corporal of the guard stood there—with faithful Jacques!

Sue was standing near the pallet bed, her face covered by her hands as though she were sobbing.

She heard the corporal's gasp of surprise.

'Huh! What is this? What ails the English girl?'

'If any harm has come to her . . .' began Jacques, stepping forward—but Sue hastily intervened, seeing that he was about to raise the other girl's hood!

'My—my friend has fainted, m'sieur! It was the distress of finding me here. Please carry her away gently, out into the open!'

Sue's accent was imperfect but it was covered by a pretended sob.

'I will do that, lass! The girl is indeed in need of air.'

The old coachman glanced at the speaker in quick sympathy, but without a trace of recognition. Her tattered gown and red scarf had completely taken him in.

'Come!' said the corporal, shortly. 'We waste time!'

The heavy door clanged, and Sue was alone.

Jacques carried the French girl to the cart and placed her gently inside. Then, still unsuspecting, he drove out into the gathering dusk.

'Now Mam'selle Sue and the old gentleman are safe!' he muttered. 'The coach should be standing by as arranged, and we have only to wait for Red Hawk. But that other poor prisoner they are holding . . . I fear there is no hope for her . . .'

Surely enough, the coach was waiting at the cross-roads, half a league from the city, in charge of another member of Red Hawk's loyal band.

They helped the injured Dr. Duval out of the cart. Though he was still weak the old gentleman's mind was now clear; and he was watching as Jacques lifted the unconscious girl into the coach.

Just then, her hood slipped back—revealing a pale, thin face, framed in jet-black hair!

An incredulous gasp escaped the doctor's lips as he leaned forward.

'Lucette! My little Lucette! Can I be dreaming?'

'Nom du nom!' exclaimed Jacques, grabbing up the coach lantern and holding it to throw a light on the pale face. 'It is no dream! This is Mam'selle Lucette! And the other—that one left behind in the cell . . .'

He passed a hand over his wrinkled features as the sudden realisation came to him.

'That other can only have been *Mam'selle Sue*—Red Hawk's sister! And I heard it said that a secret tribunal will condemn her—to die!'

80

The Last Throw

'The girl is to be taken to the prison of La Force to await her trial! A jailer with the warrant is here now, to escort her . . .'

The grim words reached Sue's ears as she was hustled from her dark cell into the guard-room, where the officer in charge was scanning a paper.

He glanced up at her briefly. In her tattered gown, with the red scarf concealing her hair and obscuring her features, she appeared to be the same girl who had been brought in as a prisoner.

Curtly he ordered the soldiers to take her outside.

Sue's mind felt numbed, after a long, agonising wait. She was scarcely conscious of the muttering crowd—the sea of faces surging in the smoke and glare of the torches carried by the guards. Not for an instant did she regret what she had done.

She was led towards the waiting cart, where a swarthy, red-bearded ruffian in a jailer's uniform was signing a receipt for the young prisoner.

'Where is the escort, fellow?' demanded the officer.

The bearded man grinned sourly, indicating the sturdy driver of the wagon, and pointing to the sword and pistol at his own belt.

'What more should be needed, citizen, to escort a slip of a girl?' he asked.

'I have instructions that she is to be doubly-guarded, in case of a rescue attempt!' said the officer. 'I will let you have two of my own men.'

'As you wish.' The jailer shrugged. 'But hurry! I have other prisoners to collect tonight!'

The corporal and another man were ordered to accompany the young prisoner in the open wagon—similar to the dreadful tumbrils that had conveyed so many victims to the Guillotine.

And so they set out, wheels rattling and jolting over the cobbles.

They had reached one of the more deserted quarters near the river, when the driver turned his horse down a dark side-street.

'Hey!' exclaimed one of the escort. 'This is not the way to La Force prison!'

'It is as good a way as any other!' interposed the jailer, his manner suddenly aggressive. 'Look to your business, comrade —and let the driver mind his own!'

The soldiers exchanged quick glances, clearly suspicious.

'But this street leads *away* from the prison—to the bridge crossing the Seine!'

'What of it?'

'I order you to halt, and turn!' exclaimed the corporal, drawing a pistol.

Next moment, the weapon was knocked from his hand!

With a sweep of his arms, the bearded jailer seized the startled fellow and flung him over the side of the cart, to fall with a thump on to the cobbles.

The other soldier unslung his musket; but he was attacked from behind by the driver. While Sue looked on dazedly, the desperate tussle ended with the jailer and his sturdy helper trussing up both dazed guards with their own belts!

'Phew!' panted the driver, a broad grin on his begrimed features. 'So far, so good, Mr Peter!'

Sue gave an incredulous cry. Then the bearded jailer's arm was around her—and she was looking into her brother's eyes!

'Peter! Oh, Peter—I can't believe it!'

She was laughing through her tears, feeling light-headed and almost faint from shock and relief.

'Peter—you, and Will! But how—how . . .'

82

Peter smiled, holding her tightly, while Will climbed back into the wagon.

'When we discovered that Lucette was to be taken to prison, we had to act quickly!' Peter explained. 'Luckily one of my secret helpers was once a prison turnkey, and he was able to provide me with an old uniform, and blank warrant for the custody of a prisoner. Meanwhile, Will scouted round for a suitable vehicle.'

'I borrowed it from a farrier's yard,' declared Will, grinning.

'We didn't know then, Sue,' put in Peter, gently, 'that my gallant little sister had already decided to risk her own life for her friend!'

While the wagon rumbled towards the Seine bridge, Peter told Sue how he had learnt of her daring exchange. A messenger sent by Jacques had met them as they were on their way to the guard-room, and had blurted out the news.

They had barely time to carry out their audacious manoeuvre, for the real prison wagon was due to arrive at any minute!

'And by now,' concluded Peter, grimly, 'the trick is bound to have been discovered! Thank heaven, the coach with Lucette and Dr. Duval should be safely on its way to Calais; but, if I know Lefeur, he'll have Paris searched for the three of us . . .'

The words had barely left his lips when there came a clatter of approaching hoofs. Two horsemen could be seen spurring across the narrow bridge towards them!

One was a sergeant of the guard, and he was accompanied by a tall man in a dark cloak.

'*Halt!*' rang out a cold, hard voice.

It was Gaston Lefeur.

Instinctively Peter placed himself in front of Sue as Will brought the wagon to a jolting stop.

The two horsemen drew rein a few paces distant. At an

order from his companion the sergeant dismounted, while Lefeur covered the occupants of the wagon with his pistol.

Peter attempted to bluff it out.

'We are in a hurry,' he called.

Lefeur nodded. 'So I see,' he said coldly. 'But you are not leaving Paris yet. In fact, you will never be leaving Paris again if you are the one I suspect you to be.'

He turned to the sergeant.

'Sergeant—seize that bearded scoundrel. I have reason to believe he is the Englishman known as Red Hawk!'

Sue gave an involuntary gasp.

'Courage, Sue!' said Peter, softly. 'Keep behind me! Will—don't make a move—unless I give the word!'

The boy nodded, and Sue remained motionless, her heart pounding.

If Peter was arrested and exposed as Red Hawk she knew he could expect no mercy from the Commune. It would mean certain death for him.

The sergeant was approaching, musket held in readiness. Peter waited—waited for the fellow to come nearer before he made his desperate bid . . . but Lefeur must have sensed what was in his mind for, quite suddenly, he ordered the sergeant back.

'I have remembered how you escaped once before when threatened with arrest, Red Hawk,' he said, 'so I want to remind you first that this time it is different. This time you have the girl with you. If you make one false move I shall shoot her.'

Sue's blood ran cold as Lefeur levelled his gun at her. She heard her brother's sharp intake of breath.

'Now——' Lefeur turned to the sergeant. 'Arrest him.'

Red Hawk shrugged.

'You have won, Lefeur,' he said bitterly. 'Rather than risk the girl's life I give myself up.'

84

He slowly stepped down from the cart, head bowed.

'Peter!' Sue cried, flinging out her arm.

'Don't move, girl!' Lefeur shouted.

The sergeant went forward and prodded Peter with his musket. Peter made no move to resist as he was hustled away from the cart. The sergeant moved round him—and came just a little too close.

Peter acted with incredible speed; the sergeant found himself in a grip of iron, then he was flung forward so that he cannoned into Lefeur's horse.

Lefeur's gun fired, but the bullet went wild as his mount reared.

In that same moment Will leapt from the cart. Even as the sergeant regained his feet, Will was on him, kicking aside his musket and going in with fists flailing.

'That's for Sue!' he yelled. 'And there's one for me—and another for Peter.'

Peter had seized the bridle of Lefeur's horse.

'Coward—assassin! Come down and defend yourself!' he shouted, drawing his sword.

White to the lips, Lefeur hesitated, looking for help from his companion. But the sergeant was lying recumbent on the ground.

Scowling, his eyes narrowed, Lefeur drew his sword and made a sudden desperate lunge at his opponent. But Peter sprang back and then grabbed the other's foot, dragging him from the saddle.

He waited with a grim smile till Lefeur had regained his feet and recovered his weapon.

'*En garde!*' cried Peter, grey eyes glinting, as he leaped into the attack.

Her heart in her mouth, Sue looked on. She had never even dreamt that Peter could handle a sword. Yet here he was, her bookish brother, engaged in a fight with a man who was obviously a master of duelling. And this, she knew, was to be to the death!

Sue felt almost faint as Lefeur lunged expertly. The blade missed Peter by inches, but Lefeur was coming forward all the time, never letting up. He thrust and thrust again, and so savagely that it seemed to Sue that Peter must fall before the fury of the attack.

She glanced at Will who had moved up and now stood beside her, watching the duel with keen interest. Will didn't seem at all put out.

'Will! Peter will be killed,' she cried. 'Lefeur means to kill him.'

Will nodded. 'Aye, he does. But Lefeur's picked the wrong man this time.'

He saw suddenly how distressed she was.

'Everything's going to be all right, Sue,' he said gently. 'I know the way Peter handles things—he's waiting till he gets the measure of his opponent. Any moment now you'll see how expert he is—and so will Lefeur . . . there, what did I tell you!'

Peter had suddenly begun to attack, so that it was now the Frenchman who was on the defensive. Even so, Lefeur was fighting fiercely, using every trick he knew.

But he was driven back to the parapet of the bridge, still fighting desperately. Realising that he was cornered, he made a last frantic bid to regain the advantage.

Leaping on to the parapet, he lunged fiercely down at his opponent. Peter sprang back, and his lightning thrust toppled Lefeur from his balance.

With a cry, the man fell from the parapet . . . and from far below there came a dull splash followed by a long silence.

It was broken at length by Peter, as he turned from the parapet, his face stern and rather pale.

'The account is settled!' he said, gravely. 'It was the only way! Lefeur has met his rightful end—at long last!'

With a sob of relief, Sue started towards her brother; but a wave of faintness swept over her—and she was caught in Will's sturdy arms.

*   *   *

That strange, terrifying adventure in France remained a vivid memory in Sue's mind throughout her life; though the hours immediately following the grim duel on the bridge seemed blurred and dreamlike.

She could vaguely remember being smuggled out of Paris —Peter feigning the role of a peasant, with an invalid sister and a younger brother. Then the long journey to Calais, by coach, with the ever-present fear of pursuit.

Lucette and her guardian were waiting for them at a small post-house, in the charge of a friendly official. There had been a joyous reunion and then—the boat to England.

It was a year later that Sue was bridesmaid at her brother's wedding to Lucette.

Dame Thatcher was present, with several of the girls from the Academy; and, of course, Will Barty was there!

He grinned at Sue when, after the ceremony, she followed the happy couple from the church.

'Mr Peter will be settling down now, Miss Sue,' he whispered, 'and he wants us to keep his secret. There are only a few of us who'll ever know of his daring work in France.'

Sue nodded, glancing proudly at her tall, handsome brother and his pretty young bride.

'That's so like Peter! But to you, Will—and to Lucette and me—he'll always be Red Hawk, secret hero of the Revolution!'

The Wreckers

by Elizabeth Sheppard-Jones

'Mam, Mam! Owen is coming home! Due in Cardiff Docks today or tomorrow. A year, a whole year it is since we last set eyes on him.'

Morfydd burst in through the cottage door and threw her plump arms around the frail shoulders of her mother who sat, as she did all day, by the wood fire that burned brightly in the hearth.

'Hush now, Morfydd fach. Calm yourself, child, and tell me how you have this news of your brother.'

Like all working people in 17th century Wales, they spoke in Welsh. Mrs Roberts' lilting voice was quiet but her eyes shone with the same excitement that lit up her daughter's face.

'I've just seen Twm Pedlar,' replied Morfydd. 'He was in Swansea yesterday and he says the *Fortune* had docked there and was unloading its salt and wine before coming up channel for Cardiff. Twm said Owen was well . . .'

'Did Twm see him—did he see my son?' interrupted Mrs Roberts eagerly.

'No but he had news of him from a sailor he met in the market. There is no doubt it, Mam—no doubt at all.'

Morfydd threw some more wood on the fire. It was November and beginning to get cold—not that it was ever really warm, even in the height of summer, in the little stone cottage, exposed as it was on the top of the cliff to all winds and weather.

'Well, my girl, you must clean and tidy the cottage, get blankets from the chest. Have we food enough? And ale? Owen will not thank us for the milk we drink.'

Mrs Roberts half rose to her feet, her spirit anxious to do what, alas, her body would not let her. She sank back in the chair.

'I'm sorry, Morfydd, that everything is left to you. I do not have the strength of those tiny kittens that were born to Shan Cath in the outhouse last week.'

She tried to smile and Morfydd leapt up from where she had been sitting on the hearth mat which she herself had made from strips of old rag.

'Don't you worry now; I am strong enough for both of us. And you will feel stronger as soon as your eyes have feasted on Owen. He will take care of us; things will be better now and he will have money for good food and warmer clothes for you.'

'Yes, yes, true enough, no doubt; then, like your father, he will be off again. We women cannot compete against that temptress, the Sea. I do not know what it is that takes our men back and back again into her cruel arms.'

'Don't you be thinking of it,' said Morfydd. 'Only think that soon we shall be seeing Owen. Oh, and if I had been a boy, I, too, would have wished to be a sailor. A good life it is, and better than working on this arid land of ours.'

'And a good death, too, think you?'

Mrs Roberts spoke bitterly. She had been widowed two years ago when her husband had been drowned in a storm off the coast of Spain. From then on, her health had gradually declined and Morfydd, only twelve at the time of her father's death, had taken charge of the house and the small holding from which they managed to scratch a living. Owen, three

90

years older than his sister, was already at sea and, although he had said he was willing to come home to look after his mother and sister, Morfydd knew it would break his heart to have to do so and she had forbidden him to mention the matter again.

'Don't speak so, you only distress yourself,' Morfydd comforted her mother. 'Now, how about that ale for Owen. Will you be all right if I take the eggs to Mrs Parry at the Inn? I'll get a jug of ale there and bring it safely back to welcome that rogue of a son of yours.'

'Yes, you do that, but hurry up about it and no stopping in the village to see that gossip-making wench of the blacksmith. There is plenty to do here, even if she has nothing to do in her father's house.'

'Mair means no harm, Mam, good enough heart she has, and good enough friend to me. But I'd not call at the forge today anyway; her Mam will be baking and Mair has to knead the dough for the bread.'

'Glad I am to know she works occasionally,' said Mrs Roberts tartly. 'Off you go then; will you take the dog with you?'

'No, no,' laughed Morfydd. 'Too lazy that Beti for a real walk. Since she gave up working sheep, she cannot even chase a sea-gull.'

Mrs Roberts was cheered by her daughter's gaiety. Indeed, she never ceased to wonder at the zest and high spirits of this blackhaired, blue-eyed Morfydd of hers, whose life was nothing but work and striving to care for an ailing mother, with a very occasional visit to see the friend of whom Mrs Roberts did not altogether approve. She guessed that Morfydd was happy enough with her lot, but God knew why it was so.

'You are a good girl,' she told her. 'Go your way then; mind the eggs and do not spill a drop of that ale. Come back by the woods.'

'But I'll go by the sea-shore,' said Morfydd obstinately.

'That is right, and break the eggs clambering over those rocks of yours,' said Mrs Roberts.

Morfydd didn't argue. She took the eggs to Mrs Parry nearly every week of the year and always went and returned across the Bay of Dunraven, high tide or low tide. Only once, when the tide had been extra high, and she had had to scramble hurriedly across rocks and pebbles to avoid a wetting, had the basket slipped from her grasp and the eggs broken, spreading their golden harvest in a sticky mass over the smooth grey stones. Mrs Parry had forgiven her this long time, and she had never told her mother. Still, she wouldn't risk the ale; woods on the way back, as her mother had said.

She collected the eggs from the little brown hens that scratched in the back yard, and set off along the winding path that led from the cliff top down to the sandy bay where, this afternoon, the sea, far out, glittered quietly in the autumn sunshine.

Morfydd looked behind her once, up at Dunraven Castle— not so much a castle as a great house—perched some way beyond the cottage. There lived Squire Walter Vaughan, a mysterious—and some said wicked—man, a drunkard and a ne'er do well. She looked quickly away from the fine, cold castle, her eyes moving to the south east of the bay where a long rocky promontory pointed out to the sea. This was known locally as Trwyn-y-Wych—Witch's Nose—and Morfydd wrinkled her own small nose as she drew in the lovely, sea-salty air that blew up from the Channel. She loved every bit of these cliffs, rocks, beach and sea with her heart and soul and mind. These, she could have told her mother, had her mother thought to ask, were the reasons for her happiness. How could she ever be bored when the scene around her was ever-changing, the wild things teemed on sea and shore and the humans plied their graceful sailing ships up and down the Severn Sea (as the Welsh called the Bristol Channel), bringing the wines and spices, silks and salt from far-away lands, and taking out the coal and wool and hides. The exotic romantic countries which received these Welsh goods always seemed to Morfydd possessed of every extravagant, but no practical, commodity of their own.

She began to clamber over the rocks, stopping to peer into the rocky pools, dipping her finger occasionally to stir the sea anemones or tickle the scuttling crabs. When she reached the stretch of yellow sand, she looked out to sea and waved vigorously at a craft she saw in the distance. Its sails seemed to wave back gaily. At first, she thought it might be Owen's ship but then she realised it was only a small trader and that with the tide not high until midnight, it was unlikely that a ship of the *Fortune's* size would risk the dangerous Nash sandbank that lay a few miles off shore. It was a clear day on this, the Glamorgan side of the Channel, but a light wind was blowing up from the Somerset coast opposite and a few dark clouds had appeared on the far horizon.

'Pity for England,' thought Morfydd. 'They think we always have rain in Wales but looks like they, not us, have it today all right.'

She picked up a fine-edged pebble and wrote her name laboriously in the sand. She had had no schooling; her name was the only word she could write. She decorated the letters with fronds of sea-weed and stepped back to admire her handiwork. She watched while the tiny waves of the incoming tide slowly washed over, and finally obliterated the clumsy letters.

'You are not always so gentle, you waves,' said Morfydd. 'Mind you stay so and look after Owen for me tonight.'

The gulls, circling and gliding, cried sadly overhead. Ghosts of drowned sailors, it was said. Morfydd shivered. She clapped her hands and shouted at them.

'You birds, you! That's all. Only birds!' She laughed un-surely and, grasping her basket more tightly, she ran across the Bay of Dunraven and up the path that led to the village on the other side. Not an egg was broken as she passed over the basket to Mrs Parry, wife of the man who owned *The Ship and Anchor* Inn.

'Owen's coming home; the *Fortune's* on its way,' said Morfydd breathlessly. She accepted thankfully the mug of buttermilk Mrs Parry offered her.

'The Lord be praised!' said Mrs Parry. 'Storm's brewing though.'

'Oh, I don't think so; fine day it is,' said Morfydd.

'Storm's brewing,' repeated Mrs Parry.

Morfydd refused to be depressed by these words. Mrs Parry was known the length and breadth of South Glamorgan for her pessimism. However, Mrs Parry's next words did strike a chill down her spine.

'A night for the wreckers,' said Mrs Parry.

'Wreckers!' echoed Morfydd. 'But they haven't been out for months.'

The Bristol Channel, with its dangerous currents, difficult tides and innumerable sandbanks, had always been a likely death-trap for sailors in bad weather; and there had always been men on shore to take advantage when ships foundered on the rocks. There were rich cargoes to be salvaged and dead men told no tales when jewellery was snatched from ears and throats and fingers. And, as if this was not bad enough, there were men so wicked they would lure deliberately the ships and sailors to their watery graves. The coast from Car-diff to beyond Swansea was as notorious for its wreckers in the 17th century as it had been for its pirates in the 16th.

A frown creased Morfydd's smooth forehead. 'I could not bear it if harm should come to Owen; and such news would kill my mother.'

94

'There, there,' said Mrs Parry. 'I meant nothing. Forget what I said, child. Weather's fine enough now for certain. No use to those old wreckers if it's a clear moonlit night. And the *Fortune* might well stay in Swansea Dock till tomorrow. Who knows? Not to meet trouble halfway, is it?'

Morfydd's spirits rose again. 'No, no, indeed as you say, Mrs Parry. And Mam told me to ask for a jug of ale for Owen, if you please. We will take it in part payment for the eggs.'

'Spill the lovely liquid you might, girl,' said Mrs Parry, pessimistic as ever. 'Better for Mr Parry to bring it when he rides over to pay rent to Squire Vaughan tomorrow, isn't it? I know you and the way you will run across that beach of yours. How hope you to save the ale?'

'I always save the eggs,' said Morfydd.

'Nearly always,' corrected Mrs Parry.

'Anyway, not to bother Mr Parry, please. Owen might need the ale before tomorrow, or at least very early in the morning. I'll be careful, and I promised Mam I'd go back by the woods; quicker it is that way and not so steep.'

Mrs Parry found a large jug and filled it half full, covering the top with a cloth.

'May I leave the basket?' asked Morfydd. 'I can collect it when I return the jug to you. Owen will be with me then. How he will have grown! A young man now! I can scarce wait to see him, and hear the tales of the wide world he will bring with him. He will teach me things; I shall learn from Owen. Did you know that he can read and write? He has spent much time studying during the long hours at sea. Twm Pedlar told me all about it; Owen's friend told him in Swansea market-place. Do you think it's true? I'm sure it's true; Owen always said one day he would be able to read the Bible. Are you not longing to set eyes on him yourself?'

'Yes, yes,' said Mrs Parry, adding under her breath so Morfydd could not hear, 'if indeed he is alive when I do.'

Dead sailors were a common occurrence to her: a grand-father killed fighting the Spanish Armada; a son, probably dead, not returned from the far East these four years; a brother drowned off France; a fisherman cousin wrecked off these very shores and his body lying on the bed of the Severn Sea. Mrs Parry was not bitter like Mrs Roberts; but maybe it was not surprising that she was a pessimist.

Morfydd, realising that she had been longer from home than she had intended, stopped chattering, said goodbye to the Inn-keeper's wife and took again the path that led down towards the Bay. But, this time, when she reached the bottom, she turned inland towards the valley. She walked slowly and carefully along the foot-path that wound through the copse, thinking idly of Mair. She wished she could have called to see her. Mair had said she was going to carry out a love spell yesterday. She would have taken her vest to the water, soaked it there and carried it back home in her teeth, unwrung —for only thus could the spell hope to be successful—where she would have hung it over a chair before the fire. The figure of Mair's future husband should have appeared, have turned the garment and then disappeared. Morfydd longed to know if this had happened. She knew whose figure Mair hoped to see. Well, in another day, she could see him in person! No use for Mair to deny she had designs on Owen Roberts: everyone knew she expected he would soon carve her a love spoon. Morfydd, too, hoped he would do so, even though there might be objections from their mother. These would be soon overcome; Mair would be a good wife, a loving daughter-in-law—and such fun as a sister-in-law.

At this point in her thoughts, Morfydd was distracted by the sound of voices ahead of her. She moved forward cautiously, hiding behind the trunks of the larger trees. There, in an open space, she glimpsed a group of four men, all known to her. She was about to step forward to greet them when something held her back—providence maybe, or perhaps the fact that one of them, Matt of the Iron Hand, was a man she had never liked nor trusted. It was he who was speaking at this moment. Morfydd craned forward to hear what he was saying.

'The portents are good, men. Look you at the sky, feel the wind blow up . . .'

Morfydd was aware that the wind had increased in force within the last half-hour, the sun was weaker, and the clouds that had been over Somerset earlier that afternoon were now high in the sky, menacing and black.

'There'll be plenty for all,' went on Matt. 'The *Fortune's* well named, boyos.'

At mention of her brother's ship Morfydd was so startled she nearly dropped the jug of ale.

'Is Squire joining us in this?' Huw Parry, simple young nephew of the Inn-keeper, asked the question.

Morfydd wondered if Mrs Parry knew what company he kept; Matt of the Iron Hand had a bad reputation. Perhaps she did know. It had been rumoured that not all the brandy at her husband's Inn was come by legally. Perhaps she had been trying to warn Morfydd because she knew what Huw was up to.

'Walter Vaughan has had his belly full of wrecking,' growled Matt.

The blood in Morfydd's veins ran cold at sound of that dreaded word 'wrecking.'

'We'll leave him out of this tonight,' went on Matt.

'He's Squire; he has legal right to all cargo washed up on his shores.' Morgan Edwards, an employee at the castle, put in a few words on behalf of his lord and master.

'Morgan's right.' Dic Jones, whom Morfydd had always known as a quiet man who wouldn't say boo to a goose, nodded his head. Fancy Dic Jones in on this! Mair had al-

Morfydd craned forward to hear what the men were saying.

ways said he must be up to no good: how did a plain weaver manage to live in such comfort, said Mair, and he with a family of fourteen children.

'Right or not,' snapped Matt, 'Vaughan has no heart for this any more, and if we do the dirty work, we get the reward, see. Leave him out, I say.'

Morfydd recalled the many rumours she had heard about Squire Vaughan. Her mother would never discuss them, saying he was their landlord and it was best not to ask too many questions. But Morfydd had always wondered; she had meant one day to ask Mair who, living in the village, must know, as most of the villagers did, in what way Vaughan was involved with some of the less respectable men of the district. Well, it looked as if she was learning something now. And Mair had once told her that Matt had lost the hand, where now he wore an iron hook, by order of the Squire. Vaughan had been magistrate at the time when Matt had been caught pirating; yet afterwards the ill-assorted pair had appeared to be the best of friends.

'If Squire has lost heart,' Morgan Edwards was saying, 'it is only since that night he organised a wrecking and you, Matt, brought him that hand you had cut off the body of the drowned captain of the ship. Remember that, do you?'

'And it belonged to his own son, Vaughan's long lost son; his ring was still on the finger,' said Dic. 'I was there myself.'

Matt laughed mirthlessly, his huge black beard shaking on his out-thrust chin.

'Aye, I remember,' he cried. 'Revenge is sweet; lost my hand I did by order of that man, and happy moment it was when I placed proof in front of Vaughan that he had drowned his own son.'

Morfydd shuddered. That such a thing could make a man happy! Matt was more evil than his companions, more evil than Squire Vaughan, evil enough though they must be.

'What are the plans for tonight?' asked Morgan Edwards. 'Usual way of luring the ship, is it? And what time do we gather?'

'Usual way,' said Matt. 'It's never failed before. Midnight it'll be; high tide then. But, mark you, if storm has blown itself out before or passes over without breaking, leave it we will until another night when another ship is worth the taking.'

'Pity to miss the *Fortune* though,' said Dic Jones. 'Pity indeed.'

Terrified by what she had already heard, Morfydd longed to run far away from the scene of such frightful plans; but she had to hear more. She must know more that she might help Owen and the *Fortune*. Ships had been wrecked before on the rocks of Dunraven. No use pretending she didn't know that it was not always accidental. Look the other way when it had nothing to do with you. Ask no questions, as her mother was always telling her. So, men drowned: sometimes they drowned when they might have been saved, but it was unlucky to save a drowning man. This time it was different: the life of Owen, the brother whom she loved, was at stake. She could not stand by idly. What was the usual way of luring a ship in order to wreck it? What was the usual way? As if in echo of her unspoken words, Huw Parry spoke.

'How do we lure the ship then, Matt?' he asked.

'Doesn't the boy know?' asked Dic Jones.

'Huw's not been with us before,' said Morgan Edwards.

'He's too soft for the job', said Matt, and turned to Huw. 'We lure the ship in, boy, by tying lights on the horns of the sheep.'

So that was how it was done! Morfydd took a step back; twigs and fallen leaves crackled under her foot but not one of the men looked in her direction. Lights on the horns of the sheep! At last she had something to go on. She must make a plan, must be as bold and cunning as these four conspirators:

100

Matt of the Iron Hand, respectable Morgan Edwards, quiet Dic Jones and silly Huw Parry. Come to think of it, it would be easy enough to be as bold and cunning as silly Huw Parry!

'What do the lights do, Matt?' Huw was asking as Morfydd turned to go.

She heard faintly Matt's rough voice give reply. 'Ships out at sea, boy, think the lights are those on mastheads of other ships; they move in closer, see, believing it safe, not knowing, since they cannot see, that Trwyn-y-Wych is there ready to catch them on the end of her nose.'

Morfydd waited to hear no more; for the rest of the way home, her mind buzzed with ideas for a plan to foil the wreckers. It would need courage and good timing. She would have to act alone, or nearly alone. Her mother's health would stand no shock and there was no one else in whom she could confide, their only neighbour being Squire Vaughan himself and, after what she had heard in the woods, she didn't suppose he would be of much help.

Beti ambled to meet her as she approached the cottage.

'It is you, my Beti, who will have to help me,' said Morfydd, bending to pat the dog's silky coat. Beti wagged her tail and yawned.

It was an effort to act normally in front of her mother, as if nothing had happened, but somehow Morfydd managed to appear her usual, cheerful self. They went to bed before seven o'clock, as soon as it was dark, to save the few precious candles for Owen's homecoming. Morfydd lay wide awake on the truckle bed at the foot of Mrs Robert's larger one, listening to her mother's even breathing and occasional snores. She prayed that the weather might improve, then she herself could rest peacefully. Her prayers were not answered: outside, a gale was already beginning to blow, rattling the shutters on the windows and shaking the ill-fitting doors as if demanding entrance. The storm was increasing steadily.

Four or five hours ticked away slowly on the old kitchen clock before Morfydd rose quietly from her bed and crept out of the cottage. The darkness appeared quite impenetrable; it was as if a black velvet cloth had been tied tightly about her eyes. The wind howled and bellowed across the cliff top, rushing over the edge to meet the screaming waves as they banged on the cruel rocks below. It was too windy for much rain but what there was hit Morfydd's cheeks with painful force. She stood still for a few minutes to let her good country eyes get acclimatised to the dark and then, as soon as she could distinguish it, she went towards the outhouse where Beti and Shan were bedded down together. Shan's kittens stirred in the straw.

'Come you, Beti,' wheedled Morfydd, 'work there is for you to do this night.'

Beti had retired from work when her master, Morfydd's grandfather, had given up sheep farming on the Brecon Beacons and moved to Cardiff to live with his sister. The shepherd had given the dog to his granddaughter, and now Beti spent her days eating, sleeping, teasing Shan and going for occasional short rambles with Morfydd to whom she was devoted. She wagged her tail furiously when she heard Morfydd's voice but at the suggestion of work she rose very reluctantly to her feet. Like all Welsh sheep dogs, Beti had been trained to obey without question whatever orders were given her.

Morfydd took a stave from the corner of the outhouse to help her on her way and, together, girl and dog left the precincts of the cottage and walked across the cliff in the direction of Dunraven Castle. Morfydd was not sure where the wreckers would start their dirty work, but Vaughan had sheep grazing this side of the Bay and these would be the handiest for those lights they had talked about. It was as she had suspected: out there in the darkness there glowed one or two moving lights, like large glow-worms weaving hither and thither. And was it her imagination that not far out on the boiling waters of the sea she could glimpse the tossing shape of a ship that might be named the *Fortune*? Pray God she was not too late.

'Beti! Beti! Herd the sheep, girl.' She gave the two low whistles her grandfather had once taught her, which ordered the dog to move the sheep to lower ground. What if Beti had forgotten what once she knew so well? She didn't appear to be moving. Morfydd repeated the whistles. This time, ears twitching, Beti slunk forward: she quickened her pace, darkness holding no difficulties for her canine sight. She quivered with excitement, smelling the sheep, reminded of old, almost forgotten, times on the Welsh hills. The moving lights, which had gradually increased in number during the last few seconds, quivered and hovered. They began to scatter as Beti reached them: she hurried and harried the sheep, chasing them farther and farther inland, beyond and behind the castle where the ground was lower and quiet invisible to those at sea. Morfydd gave another single whistle, pitched higher, telling Beti to guard the sheep and keep them where they were. As she did so, she heard Huw Parry's voice call out wildly across the cliff top.

'Matt! Morgan! Dic! Help! The sheep, them stupid sheep; crazy they've gone. What to do, boyos!'

There was no reply. He called out again. Morfydd could not restrain a smile. So, they'd left this young simpleton, had they, to cope with the sheep while they, the strong men, had gone down to the beach to deal with the more difficult part of the job. Call away, Huw, they'll not hear you. The four of them together might have beaten Beti at her game and have managed to drive the sheep back to the cliff top; but Huw Parry on his own, never! She sensed he was not far from her, running towards the beach below, hoping to get help. She held out her stave in front of her. With a scream, Huw tripped over it and fell, face down, on the wet grass.

'Who did that?' he sobbed. 'What has happened to me? Who is there? Oh, the good Lord help a poor sinner!'

Morfydd pulled her shawl across her mouth and spoke in a muffled voice. She couldn't have deceived the others, but Huw Parry was easy game.

'Ghost of the last sailor drowned at Dunraven Bay,' she moaned, 'come to haunt you, Huw Parry. Get you gone from here. Turn you round; not to the beach, mind you, or I shall swallow you up.'

She waved her arms and groaned and screeched. Combined with the orchestra of wind, rain and sea it was an effective performance. Huw gave a couple of terrified howls, rose to his feet and fled inland as if the ghosts of all the sailors ever drowned off the coast of Glamorgan were flapping at his heels.

Exhilarated by the success of her plan so far, yet shaking at the effort it had cost her, Morfydd looked once again towards the sea. There was no doubt about it this time; there was a ship lumbering its way up the choppy Channel, its masthead light gleaming faintly, a couple of miles away from the traps laid by rocks and wreckers.

'God go with you, Owen bach, and the rest of the crew of the *Fortune*,' murmured Morfydd.

She waited until she was sure the ship was safely on its way to Cardiff before calling Beti away from the sheep.

'Good girl, Beti, good girl,' she whispered when she felt the dog's cold nose against her hand. 'Home it is now, and a treat for you.'

Head down, shawl clutched tighter round her, she pushed her way back against the angry breath of the giant wind. In the cottage, her mother had not stirred. She should never know, poor soul, Morfydd promised herself, how near she had been to losing Owen that night. She slipped under the rough blankets. Beti hovered uncertainly near the door, knowing that this was usually forbidden territory.

'Here, Beti,' urged Morfydd. 'Treat I promised you.' She patted encouragingly the foot of the bed and Beti, with a snuffle of pleased surprise, jumped up and snuggled down.

Morfydd stretched out a hand and fondled the soft head. 'Not such a lazy old dog, is it? Fine job you and I did tonight.'

She closed her eyes and, while the elements continued to rage unmercifully outside, she dreamt that the wreckers, including Squire Vaughan, were chained on the far tip of Trwyn-y-Wych while she danced on the golden sands of Dunraven Bay, the quiet waters lapping at her feet and the sun shining in a cloudless sky.

Jehane of the Forest

by Joan Aiken

It was half-past five on a grey day in February, in the far-off days when knights in armour valued chivalry more than their lives, and gruesome and dark superstition gripped the country folk of England. Dusk was falling over the two dozen wooden houses that formed the willage of Ware. Pigs, sheep, and oxen were safely shut up, and the dim gleams from rush dips, coming through an occasional chink in a log wall, showed that the good people of the village were indoors too, eating a scanty winter meal of porridge or salt meat.

Only one thing was abroad in the cold twilight. For the last hour a girl had been kneeling crouched in the round hole that formed the entrance to the village bakehouse, hidden in the shadow. When she was quite certain that everybody had gone indoors to supper and that there was no one to see her, she cautiously stood upright, stretching to rid herself of stiffness. It had been warm in the bakehouse and she shivered outside, and pulled her handwoven brown overskirt up over her shoulders. She had no cloak. Then, casting a wary glance back at the houses, she began picking her way as silently as possible down towards the stream which crossed the foot of the village street and meandered away through the meadow.

When she was well away from the buildings she began to call softly, 'Linnet! Linnet!' and then louder, as the babbling of the stream drowned her voice, 'Linnet! *Linnet!*'

It had not been safe to come out before. She knew better than to show herself in broad daylight and provoke a rain of curses and catcalls—'Witch! Witch!' and, very likely, clods, sticks, even stones. Sir Cador, the Lord of the Manor, who lived in the moated grange at the top of the village, was angry, for some reason, if he heard of her being persecuted, and he or Heriot, the bailiff, had sometimes punished stone-throwers, but that did not make the girl any better liked. And Sir Cador was not always at home. When he was away, raiding or fighting against King Arthur's men, the girl was apt to lead a tormented life. There had been one dreadful day, which she still remembered with a shiver, when Wat the Thatcher had suggested ducking her, and a rabble of the worse-natured villagers had dragged her down to the sedge-pool and thrown her in. She could not swim and, after a few struggles, had sunk, weighed down by the folds of her heavy brown dress.

After what seemed a lifetime someone, kinder-hearted than the rest, had exclaimed, 'Give over, lads! She's no witch or she'd not lie like that at pond's bottom. Hoist her out, say I.' And rather unwillingly she had been dragged out again and abandoned to cough herself back to consciousness on the reedy bank. But plenty of people in the village still believed that she really was a witch and that she had somehow managed to trick them by breathing under water.

Since then she had hidden in the bakehouse during the hours of day and gone out only after nightfall.

She crossed the stream, jumping the stepping-stones which were still slippery with ice. Patches of snow lay here and there, for the winter had been late and hard. Such grass as showed was brown and scanty; the villager's beasts, unless vigilantly watched, tended to stray away from the poor, overgrazed meadow and wander into the heath beyond the sedge-pool, and from there into the dangerous forest.

108

Needless to say, no one cared what became of the witch-girl's goat when she loosed it on the common meadow. Let it stray where it pleased, helped on its way by a kick or two. No doubt, being closely connected with the Devil, it would find plenty of friends if it wandered into the fearsome forest known as Darkriding.

'Linnet!' the girl called the goat. 'Linnet! Where are you, my pretty?'

Fear by Night

Biting her lip with anxiety she crossed the heath. It was nearly dark by now, and she stumbled sometimes over brambles or patches of furze. The black line of forest trees came nearer and nearer—she could hear the wind sighing in the treetops, rising sometimes to a moan. When it did this the girl caught her breath in terror and stood still, trembling, until her need to find the strayed goat drove her on again. The forest was full of evil and threats, especially at night; in comparison a few clods and curses from the villagers seemed almost harmless. Dared she go back and ask someone to help her? But no, even if she escaped without a beating, which was unlikely, she knew full well that not a soul in the village would venture into the forest at night—no, not if it was to save his own father.

Muttering a disconnected series of prayers—'Oh heaven, help me. Don't let *It* catch me. Dear Mother of God, please help me find Linnet, *please!* She'll be so frightened and lonely. Kind heaven, don't let the Wanderer hear me—don't let Linnet be very far away,' she hurried on. For a few steps she tried the experiment of walking with her eyes shut—the dark seemed less frightening that way—but it was not a success. She tripped over roots and almost stunned herself by walking into a hawthorn stump.

'Linnet, Linnet!' she whispered—she dared not call aloud among the trees for fear of *who* might hear her.

She had now crossed by gradual stages into the forest itself. Huge oaks grew here and the ground was smoother underfoot. The moon, rising over the village clearing from which she had come, threw light ahead, and she could see the wide, gnarled trunks like giants all round her.

She halted in indecision, wondering which way to go. Then, to her left, she heard a faint sound—was it a cry? She strained her ears. There it came again! Could Linnet have been caught in a thicket?

The girl hurried towards the sound, winding her way among the long, pale, silvery strips of light between the trees. Suddenly she stopped dead, with the back of her hand pressed to her mouth, stifling a gasp of fright. Beyond a great oak something moved and glittered; she caught the flash of moonlight on metal and heard a clink. Then a man groaned, a deep sound of weariness and pain. The girl stood trembling, half resolved to flee back to the village—but, in the end, pity and curiosity urged her forward again. She was certain the voice had been human—not that of demon or monster—and it sounded so despairing and weary that her heart was touched. Like a shadow in her dark dress she stole round the tree until she could see what lay on the other side.

There was a dead horse and a dead man. The man lay with one arm flung over the horse's neck. No, he was not dead, for he moved and groaned again, but he was badly wounded; she could see that his armour was rent and hacked, and a pool of blood had soaked into the dry grass.

Nearby was the little white goat, Linnet, cause of the girl's perilous trip into the forest. She had been nibbling grass uneasily, breaking off every now and then to sniff with disquiet at the stranger who lay so still. When she saw her mistress coming she trotted forward, bleating joyfully, and gave the girl a gentle butt in the side, as if to say, 'Here I am! Well? You came looking for me, didn't you? Why don't you give me a pat?'

Her mistress was too occupied in looking at the wounded man to pay any attention. What could be done with him? He must not be left here to freeze all night, that was plain, but how could she get him back to the village? And, once there, who would take him in? The villagers hated strangers, and so did Sir Cador—it was likely enough that this young knight, for such he seemed, had been robbed and left for dead by some of Sir Cador's men. How could she help him?

He groaned again. All of a sudden she saw that his eyes were open and looking at her in the moonlight.

'Drink!' he said weakly. 'I beg you, give me some drink.'

The girl looked round with desperate indecision. It was a long way to the brook. Then she remembered that Linnet had not been milked since the morning. There was no milking-bowl, but the knight's helmet lay beside him and seemed undamaged.

'Now Linnet,' she whispered. 'Stand still and be a good goat.'

Linnet, who was young and playful, at first seemed inclined to be coquettish, but in the end she allowed herself to be milked into the helmet.

'Here, sir,' the girl said. 'Let me give you a drink of milk.'

She managed to raise his head until he was leaning on her shoulder, and helped him to drink. He swallowed the milk down in great thirsty gulps.

'Good . . . thank you . . .' His voice tailed off, his eyes were closing.

'Sir!' the girl said urgently. 'You cannot go to sleep here, you must not! The forest is a dangerous place. I will try and bandage your wound and then you must come with me.'

She looked around. His cloak and weapons had been taken.

She pulled off his surcoat, which was cut and torn, then struggled to undo his hauberk, gashing her fingers on the ragged edges where the metal had been pierced.

'Leave me, I pray you,' he begged faintly.

'I cannot leave you, sir.'

At last she found the trick of the laces and got the hauberk undone. With strips torn from his surcoat she bandaged the wound in his shoulder and another in his leg. Then she made him drink some more milk.

'Now sir, I beseech you! Make an effort to stand up. Lean on my shoulder.'

Beware 'The Wanderer'

His head kept dropping forward in weariness but she would not leave him be. Half dragging, half pushing, she raised him till he was on his feet, supported by the broken shaft of his spear, with his other hand on her shoulder. It was plain that he hardly knew where he was.

'How the stars do whirl round!' he said wonderingly.

'Come now, sir, please try to walk. If you stay here you will freeze to death.'

'Let me but lie down and sleep again,' he muttered protestingly.

'No sir, there are demons and wild beasts in these woods. Come—first one foot, then the other.' Nagging and urging she forced him along, slowly, slowly, through the trees. Sometimes he was docile and came with her obediently; then, all of a sudden, he would get the idea that he was still engaged in battle, and would shout and struggle.

'Ten against one, you craven rascals!' he cried out. 'Is that how you fight battles in this country? My Queen would be shamed if her knights did so!'

'Sir, sir!' the girl hushed him in alarm. 'You must not shout

112

aloud. The Wanderer might hear you. Come, we must hurry.'

'The Wanderer, child?' He looked at her vaguely, swaying against the spear as she shifted his hand on her shoulder. 'Who is the Wanderer?'

'I must not tell you here!' She glanced warily over her shoulder. They had left the forest now, but it was still close behind. She led the knight forward across the heath. Ahead of them gleamed the sedge-pool, silver in the moonlight. While she dressed his wounds the girl had remembered the fowlers' hut by the pool, empty since old Nol had died last Michaelmas. Nobody was keen to move into it and live so close to the forest, and it had remained empty since then. But the hut was sound and would serve as a shelter where the knight could rest undisturbed.

'Here, sir, that's the way! Only a few more steps now.' Luckily the marshy ground was still firm with frost and bore them up. They crossed to the hummock where the hut stood by a clump of willows. Its door hung ajar, showing a wedge of darkness, and the girl suppressed a tremor as they stumbled through, but there was no one inside. The knight collapsed on to the floor with a groan, half leaning against the wall.

'Wait—' and the girl was outside in a flash, to gather a great armful of dry reeds. She returned and spread them for his bed. He let himself fall sideways on to them and was asleep before she had finished arranging his pillow.

Bread to Bake

Luckily old Nol had left a great stack of firewood, which the villagers had been too lazy, or too superstitious, to touch. The girl was able to kindle a fire in the stone hearth. By its light she could see to pile more reeds round the knight and cover him with the remains of his surcoat. Then she bank- ed the fire with damp earth, to make it last as long as possible, and tiptoed out, closing the door behind her.

Linnet was browsing outside, uneasy and jealous because she had received so little attention. She bleated indignantly and her mistress patted her.

'Hush, Linnet, and come now, we must hurry; see, the moon is nearly halfway up the sky and all tomorrow's bread still to bake.'

Girl and goat ran down to the stream and followed its ice-fringed banks back through the meadow to the stepping-stones near the village bakehouse. Here the protesting Linnet was shut up in a little pen with an armful of marshy fodder. The girl ate a couple of dry crusts and—as she had lost her supper-drink of goat's-milk—washed the bread down with an icy gulp or two from the stream. Then she entered the bakehouse and set to work.

Before she had left on her search for Linnet she had made up the fire in the big, stone-built oven as high as she could pile it with logs of wood. By now these had burned down to a red-hot, glowing pile, which the girl dexterously shovelled out on a long-handled flat spade, until the oven was empty and ready to receive the loaves. These had been left to rise in the warm bakehouse, arranged in rows on a flat metal tray. Each housewife's loaf had its maker's distinctive mark on the side—a cross, a circle, or a twisted lump of dough. The villagers made their own bread, but were obliged to bake it in the communal oven, which, like the mill, belonged to the Lord of the Manor. For every baking of bread they must pay him with a handful of flour, and this was a bitterly unpopular tax; many was the angry glance or hostile word that the girl received as the village women brought or fetched their loaves.

She had long ago given up protesting that she received no profit from the baking; it was simply her work, as it was Wat Thatcher's to keep the house roofs repaired, and she was paid with a few stale loaves and the right to sleep in a corner of the bakery. The Lord of the Manor showed her no other favour; in fact he rather disliked her if looks were anything to go by. Only, he would not allow her to be stoned.

It was hard to keep awake in the warm bakehouse, but very necessary. If she allowed the loaves to burn, her enemies would have every right to beat her black and blue, and would certainly do so. She arranged herself leaning against a sharp sliver of wood, used for testing the bread, so that if she fell asleep it would prick and wake her. Crouched like this she sank into a half doze once or twice but was each time sharply roused. At the end of an hour the bread was baked and put out to be fetched for the village breakfast; then the girl, was free to curl up on a pile of sacking and go to sleep.

She did not sleep for very long. More than two hours before sunrise she was awake. She took her own little loaf of black bread off the corner of the tray. It was still warm and she cradled it comfortingly in her hands as she slipped out into the icy mist that had come up overnight. The mist was a good thing; it prevented her being seen by the few people abroad at that hour as she ran warily down to the stepping-stones and crossed the stream. She carried her wooden clogs in her hand, so as to make no noise; on the far bank she knelt and slipped her felt-shod feet into them.

A flight of duck and snipe rose up, honking, as she crossed the frosty sedges and she longed for a bow; bread was good, no doubt, for a man, but meat would be better. Perhaps it would be possible to catch him some fish . . .

The hut was silent as she approached. She lifted the latch and slipped in cautiously.

They young knight was still sleeping as she had left him. Her first care was to rebuild the fire. In a few minutes she had flames leaping. From a bag over her shoulder she brought out a small iron pot and filled it with water from the brook. While it heated she took off the knight's bandages; he still slept deeply but moaned a little in his sleep. Next she washed the wounds, and with clean rags which she had brought with her bound them up again. Now he woke; gazed at her but his eyes, bright with fever, hardly took her in.

'Drink!' he muttered drowsily.

She had warmed a cup of milk. He drank it, and ate a little bread, sopped in the milk. Then he fell back exhausted on the heap of reeds. Only his eyes followed her wonderingly as she stepped about, rebuilding the fire, putting a cup of water beside him.

'I thought I was in the forest,' he murmured. 'Where is this?'

'A hut.'

'I am not dead?'

'No,' she said, smiling faintly.

He sighed, and his eyes closed. 'I must go now,' she said presently. 'I will come back this evening to cleanse your wounds again and bring food.'

He seemed to accept this, as he had all her help, trustfully and incuriously. But as she reached the door his eyes opened and focused on her fully for the first time.

He saw a thin girl, hollow-cheeked and hollow-eyed. Her black hair was braided back smoothly, and though her brown dress was worn and ragged she bore herself with a certain unconscious pride.

'Who are you?' he asked.

'They call me Jehane,' the girl answered.

'Jehane who? Or Jehane what?'

'Jehane the witch.'

At this moment the early-morning stillness outside was broken by a ragged chorus of shouts and cries that seemed to come from the heath beyond the pool. The girl started and her face became pale.

'I must not linger here or the villagers will find you,' she said. 'Make no sound. Till this evening, then.' Noiseless as

'I must not linger or the villagers will find you.'

a shadow she left the hut and sped away into the mist.

For a few minutes the mist was her friend and concealed her as she left the hut behind her and skirted the pool, running low, like a lapwing, behind the screen of willows. She hoped to take a wide circle over the heath and return to the village unobserved. But now the mist deceived her, falsifying the direction from which the shouts seemed to come. All of a sudden, she walked straight into the midst of a group of men. They parted at sight of her.

'Hey, it's the witch-girl—so she's the cause of the trouble!'

'You might have guessed it, Diccon—isn't she at the root of every trouble?'

'I'll have your skin off you for this, you jade,' growled the man called Diccon, and before Jehane could turn and run he grabbed her by the arm.

'What is it?' she asked, terrified. 'What's the matter?'

'You cast the Evil Eye on his cow, old Crumbock, and now look at her!'

The group divided and she saw that Crumbock, a lean, scraggy red cow, had greedily ventured too near the stream-side while searching for pasturage, and had been caught in a treacherous patch of bog. She was mired up to her shaggy flanks, and so great was her terror that, whenever the men approached to try and pull her out, she only sank deeper in her frantic struggles.

'Throw the girl in the bog too,' suggested someone. 'Maybe that will take off the curse.'

'No, please! I didn't curse her, I swear I didn't!' Jehane struggled unavailingly. 'Let me go!'

'Not likely. We'll give you a taste of bog, see how you enjoy it. One—two—three—'

'Don't! Don't! she gasped. 'Let me go and I—I'll try to get her out for you.'

Wat and several of the men were all for throwing her into

118

the bog, but Diccon wanted his cow back and shouted at her:

'All right, Witch. You put her in, you pull her out!'

'Keep back then—don't frighten her,' said Jehane desperately. 'Have you a rope?'

A rope was flung at her. The men stood at a little distance in a hostile, muttering group. She had half a mind to try and run for it, but saw this would be hopeless; they could easily overtake her. As she hesitated, with the rope in her hand, she caught Crumbock's eye. A sort of message flashed between her and the cow. All animals had an instinctive trust in Jehane; even the wild ones would come to her willingly, which was one of the reasons why she was suspected of witchcraft.

Jehane's Rescue

A strange understanding seemed to spring up between Jehane and the frightened animal. She knelt on a tussock, as near as she could get, and stretched out her hand. Crumbock snorted, but did not move her head, and let the girl's fingers move gently over her muzzle.

'There, there, my beauty,' Jehane said soothingly. 'There, my handsome.'

She turned and called to the men, 'Can you get me a big armful of rushes to lay on the bog?'

'Not I; I'll help no witch,' said Diccon, but a couple of the others found her a heap of stuff, brushwood and bramble. She spread it on the quaking mud and crawled over it to Crumbock.

'See, she's a witch for sure! The bog refuses to suck her down,' grumbled Diccon.

'Blight take your tongue, you ungrateful churl! Can't you see the lass is so thin she hardly weighs more than a bundle of rushes herself? If she was risking her neck to save my beast I'd be a bit more civil,' said Hob, the smith.

'Her neck's forfeit anyway. If she doesn't save the cow I'll see it's the halter or the stake for my fine lady, one or the other.'

Jehane tried to take no notice of the low-muttered talk behind her, but the gist of it came through. She was struggling now, with her arms up to the armpits in icy, evil-smelling mud, to pass the rope underneath the cow.

'That's the way, lass! Aye, you'll do it yet,' called Hob.

At last she had the rope pulled through, and tied it in a firm knot. Then she wriggled back and passed the free end round a gnarled old willow trunk that grew nearby, then tossed the end of the rope to the men.

'Pull on that now,' she told the men, 'while I encourage the cow.'

Hob guffawed. 'Encourage her, girl? Why not sing her a ballad?'

But Jehane talked coaxingly to Crumbock, holding the cow's desperate pleading eyes with her own. 'Come on now, my beauty, take a step. Pull out, girl, the men are on your side. Help yourself! Pull!'

The men—except for Wat Thatcher who stood scornfully apart—heaved together vigorously. At first it seemed as if the bog would never release its victim but finally, between a last jerk of the rope and a wild plunge of her own, Crombock came free with a loud, sucking squelch, and lurched heavily into the midst of her rescuers.

'Ah, I'll be lucky if she doesn't take her death from this,' grumbled Diccon, looking her over gloomily.

'Cheer up, neighbour! Ask thy missus to give her a sup of good hot ale and she'll be right as a trivet.'

'As for *you*,' Diccon suddenly snarled, turning to grab Jehane, who had been trying to shake the worst of the mud off her dress, 'I'll teach you to magic my beasts! You'll get such a beating as you'll remember for many a long say, you devil's brat!'

120

A Knight's Plan

He picked up his cudgel.

'Here, hold hard, neighbour,' protested Hob. 'Who's to say she magicked the cow? She'd not magic and save it both; 'tis not reasonable.'

'Save your breath!' growled Diccon. 'Any man that interferes with me I'll know for a demon-lover and a friend of witches. Maybe you'd like to dance with the jade on Fern Knoll, and go running with the Wanderer in the long nights!'

The men crossed themselves. Hob paled and said hoarsely, 'Nay, you know I—'

Ignoring him, Diccon raised his cudgel.

A voice cried, 'Hold, there! Loose the girl you knave, loose her, I say!'

The men turned, their mouths ajar.

A knight on a richly adorned horse was cantering towards them. He wore handsome armour and a surcoat embroidered with a running bear in red. His shield bore the same device. His vizor was up, exposing a sharp-featured face, with fair hair and a pair of cold blue eyes. Behind him trotted his squire, a boy of sixteen or so.

'Save us,' muttered Wat. ''Tis Sir Cador. I thought he was still away from home.'

'So!' said Sir Cador. 'As usual, you rogues, I find you abusing defenceless orphans instead of tilling your Lord's fields.'

Diccon looked at his feet in a hangdog manner and muttered that the wench had been ill-wishing his cow.

'How so? No—' as Diccon opened his mouth to speak—'*you* tell me.' The knight gestured to Hob.

'My lord, the cow fell in the mire and neighbour Diccon would have it that the girl had magicked her,' Hob spoke up sturdily enough. 'So some of us were for throwing in the girl

121

alongside the beast, but the girl offered to try and get Crum—the animal out. And so she did.'

'How? By witchcraft?'

'No, my lord. By plain good sense,' said Hob, 'and putting a rope round her middle.'

'Nay!' cried half a dozen voices. 'The girl whispered devil's words in the cow's ear, to make her climb out of the bog. 'Tis odds but she'll yield nothing but buttermilk from now on.'

Diccon uttered a fearful oath. 'If she does that—!'

'Enough,' said the Lord of the Manor impatiently. 'I see no witchcraft in all this. And I give fair warning that the next man to lay a hand on the girl will be whipped thrice through the village at the cart's tail. Well, speak! Who yearns for the lash?'

None spoke, but there were some sullen looks. Jehane shivered in her wet dress. Sir Cador looked at her coldly.

'Had you behaved with more discretion, wench, I doubt this foolish trouble need never have come about.'

'My lord—' began Jehane, and stopped.

Sensing the full measure of hate against the girl, Sir Cador came to a decision. 'Squire!' he said.

'My lord?' The young squire drew up alongside on his palfrey.

'Take the girl up before you and bring her to the Manor. Since these blockheads cry Witch if she but crosses the road, we'll see how she does among my lady's tirewomen. And you, villains, back to work before you taste the rope's end on your own account.'

Jehane opened her mouth to protest, but the Squire had yanked her under the armpits and hoisted her on to his saddle bow before she could say a word. And in any case, what was the use? No good telling Sir Cador she was innocent of provocative behaviour, no good objecting to her treatment: he was the Lord of the Manor and could do as he pleased.

The two horsemen trotted away, leaving angry faces and rebellious murmurs behind.

'Ay, he can call us blockheads if he likes—he'll laugh on the other side of his face when he's had that devil's spawn up at the Manor for a week or two. But let her not show her face in the village again, that's all, or she'll get a taste of her own oven. Matters were better in the old Lord's time—*he* didn't protect witches and demons.'

'There weren't any,' Diccon pointed out.

'Just the same, neighbour, the girl baked a tasty loaf of bread—better than old Gathercole used to, half crust, half cinders. Who'll be baker now?'

'If you ask me,' said Diccon, driving his cow towards the meadow with an ill-tempered thwack, 'it's a wonder we haven't all been poisoned long ago.'

Meanwhile Jehane, bumping uncomfortably on the Squire's pommel, suddenly let out a sharp anxious cry.

'My goat! Who will look after my goat if I am not there? They will let it starve! Oh, sir, let me down to go and fetch my poor Linnet!'

'Tush!' said Sir Cador sternly, 'I'll have no more rioting and unruliness in the village such as breaks out whenever you show your face. One of the jack-boys can fetch your goat, it can run with my lady's herd.'

'Thank you, my lord,' murmured Jehane. But the goat had not been her chief worry; what really troubled her was how, if she were cooped up in the moated grange, would she be able to get out and tend the wounded knight in the fowler's hut? But she dared not speak this part of her mind, and it was well for the hurt knight that she kept silent.

In the village street Sir Cador drew rein. 'Ho there!' he called.

People left their tasks—anvil, sawhorse, washtub—and came running. Jehane, crouched on the Squire's saddle-bow, received some black looks, but nothing was said; the villains looked at their lord.

'A dead horse lies in the forest yonder,' Sir Cador said carelessly. 'Has aught been seen of its rider?'

A Kindly Face

No one spoke a word. Faces were blank. At last a man said:

'We venture not into the forest, my lord, for fear of demons. Most likely one of them has made away with him.'

'Ay,' came an agreeing chorus, 'the Wanderer has him for sure. It was wailing in the tree-tops last evening.'

Sir Cador shrugged. 'Perhaps. It is of no importance. He was one of King Arthur's scoundrelly knights.'

He rode on, and the people made haste to get out of his path.

The Squire, who was a good-hearted lad, noticed Jehane's anxious looks.

'Don't worry about your goat, lass,' he said kindly. 'I'll fetch it myself.'

He was rewarded by a brilliant smile.

'Oh, sir! How good you are!'

'You need not call me *sir*,' he said laughing. 'My name's Guy.'

At the Manor, which was a battlemented grange with a moat and portcullis, Jehane was given over to the women servants, who with grumbling and pinches helped her to wash and gave her clean dry clothes—dark-blue gown, a white wimple and hood. Thus equipped she was brought before my Lady Isabel, Sir Cador's wife.

Lady Isabel was handsome but shrewish-looking, with sharp cold eyes and a thin mouth. She was very richly dressed in an ermine cloak over a fur-trimmed velvet surcoat, and she had a high, pointed head-dress ornamented with jewels.

'Save us, what a little bird of ill-omen!' she exclaimed when she saw Jehane. 'I'll have no such sour, pinched faces about me. Set her to work in the kitchen or the laundry, 'tis more suitable labour for her.' And she dismissed the girl from her presence, as if the very sight of her brought uneasy thoughts. Jehane made no objection; indeed, the farther she was sent from Sir Cador and his lady, the better she liked it, since there might be a better chance of slipping out to the knight in the hut. And there was something strange and uncomfortable in Sir Cador's manner towards her, which always made Jehane anxious to be away from him; she had a feeling that he knew more about her than she knew herself, and disliked what he knew. It was he who had sent her to work in the village bakery. Sometimes he rode down to the village to see that she was not molested in her work, but he always seemed more annoyed than pleased to find that she was doing her job properly, and rode away again fast as if her very existence irked him.

She was put to work in the great kitchen and spent the day running hither and thither at the bidding of the cook. There were two fireplaces, one with huge joints turning on spits, one with cauldrons of stew, and a stone oven like that in the bakehouse. As Jehane was well acquainted with baking she was set to watch the loaves and pies, but, as well, she had to chop and stir and baste, wash dishes, fetch and carry.

Once or twice she was sent for herbs to the walled garden of the manor, which lay beyond the moat. Here in the summer grew peas and beans, beetroot, onions, garlic, lettuce, and watercress. Even now there were cabbages and leeks, as well as many healing herbs. Jehane seized the chance to pluck a handful of these—comfrey and horehound, rue, wormwood, and valerian—and slipped them into the satchel she carried at her belt; there were too many people about to risk running off to the fowler's hut at this time of day but she hoped

125

to snatch a chance to visit the wounded Knight later that night.

It began to look as if she would not succeed, however; the evening meal was eaten at five and long before it there was a regular frenzy of activity in the kitchen; the cook called for Jehane if she was out of his sight for a moment.

At last they all sat down to eat at trestle tables in the Great Hall. Sir Cador and Lady Isabel, any visiting knights, the chaplain, seneschal and squires sat at the High Table, with a great silver salt cellar, knives, spoons, a tablecloth and silver plates. The men-at-arms and servants sat at bare tables farther down the hall, according to degree. Jehane found a seat at the very foot, among a gaggle of scuffling little boys, the pages, who could only eat after they had served their lord and lady. The food was better than Jehane had ever tasted in her life, but she had no appetite and could only swallow a few mouthfuls; however she managed to smuggle some bread and cheese and a piece of meat into her satchel, wrapped in a napkin. After supper the whole household gathered round the hearth in the centre of the hall to tell stories and crack some rather mildewy nuts. This was when Jehane had hoped to slip away, but she found, to her dismay, that the drawbridge was raised and the house barred and bolted for the night.

She was standing in a corner wondering what to do when the young Squire, Guy, approached her.

'I came to tell you that your goat is safely shut up in the byre, maiden. I myself made sure that she was fed and milked,' he said.

Her face lit up. 'Oh, sir, may I go and see her?'

'Not till tomorrow,' he told her. 'The farm buildings are beyond the moat.'

Jehane bit her lip with disappointment.

'What is worrying you?' Guy asked kindly. 'Why, there are tears in your eyes! But not over a goat, surely? Are the other servants being unkind to you? It will pass. I remember

126

when I first came here as a page I thought the cuffs and ill-natured remarks would last forever, but I soon found people here are kind enough. It is just their way with newcomers.'

'It is not that,' Jehane said desperately. Dared she tell him the truth? She thought not. 'Oh, sir, you are kind and understanding—the truth is that I cannot endure being cooped up inside walls. I am not used to it. If I could get out, but for an hour! I have a pet hare and some birds that I feed every evening down on the meadow. They will be missing me. I do so long to escape into the free air for a little time. Is there no way out save across the drawbridge?'

Guy looked round him cautiously.

'In truth there is a way,' he said in a low voice. 'I learned it by chance, for the secret is kept by Sir Cador and the chaplain. There is a passage under the moat.'

Jehane's eyes widened. 'A hidden passage!' she breathed.

'Can I trust you?' Guy said. 'You look like a maid who can keep a secret.'

'Oh sir, indeed you can trust me. I will not breathe a word.'

'Come then.'

He led her through a room, where a laughing crowd of pages and waiting-women were playing blind-man's-buff, and into the chapel, dimly lit by tapers burning before the altar.

''Tis here,' he whispered. 'Once when I was a boy playing hide-and-seek I lay hid behind the arras curtains and saw Father Boniface open the trap.'

There were slab tombs set in the stone-paved floor. One of these, instead of an inscription, had a design of leaves and flowers cut in its surface. Guy knelt and pressed on a carved rose. Instantly the slab tilted sideways so that a hole was revealed, and a flight of steps going down.

'Are you afeared?' he asked. 'I will show you the way. He clambered down into the hole and Jehane followed him.

She would not confess it, but she was rather frightened, particularly when he tilted the slab back and they were left in the pitch dark.

'To open it from underneath, find a carven cross at the south-east corner and press upwards, so,' Guy said, and demonstrated. 'Now we go down these steps, under the moat—hold high you skirts for the ground here is somewhat damp—and up another flight of steps.'

Secret Door

The way was longer than Jehane had expected; they seemed to walk along the damp, narrow dark passage for about three hundred yards.

'Where does it come out?' she asked.

'My lady has a little summer pavilion, set in a grove of nut trees in a corner of the garden wall. The outer entrance is cunningly set in the thickness of the pavilion wall. Here we are,' he said, turning to help Jehane up another steep flight of steps. 'And the door is opened by a secret balance in like manner to the one in the chapel.' He opened the door for her and she saw stars shining and smelt the fresh night air.

Guy hesitated. 'Would you wish me to come with you, maiden?' he asked shyly. 'There are wolves and evil men abroad by night—demons, too, from the forest, they say—'

'I am obliged to you but it is not at all needful,' Jehane said quickly. 'I am well-used to go out in the village at night.' She thanked him again heartily for his kindness and was relieved to hear the door shut behind him. He had sounded rather wistful, as if he would enjoy coming with her, but nothing was further from her wishes.

As soon as she was sure he was safely out of eashot she ran like a deer, not in the direction of the village, but across the great fallow field where in the daytime sheep grazed, and over the heath. The moon had just risen, and she was able to find her way to a fallen willow by which she crossed the stream, wider and deeper at this end of the meadow.

She approached the fowler's hut cautiously. No sound came from within. Stealing in, she found the hurt knight dozing. It was plain that the fever had left him. She woke him gently and dressed his wounds with the herbs, then brought out the food she had for him. He submitted to the doctoring with sleepy docility; as he ate he woke up more and began to ask questions.

'What place is this, child?'

'The village of Ware, sir, in the great wood of Darkriding.'

'And whose is the manor?'

'Sir Cador of Stone Guard.'

'Sir Cador,' he repeated musingly. 'Yes, I remember now, His men set on me, ten against one, in the wood yonder, robbed me and left me for dead. But who are you, child? You say they call you Jehane the Witch. Are you truly a witch?'

'No sir,' she said. 'Indeed I know nothing of witchcraft or enchantments. But they call me witch because I have skill with animals, and because I was found in the forest and none knows who my parents were.'

'Found in the forest?' he said curiously. 'Who found you then, child?'

'A holy hermit who lived in a cell far from here in a woodland valley. He reared me until I was twelve years of age and taught me my prayers, and knowledge of herbs and animals. Then he felt a sickness coming on him, so he brought me to Sir Cador, who found me service in the village. But the people of the village would have nothing to do with me; they call me witch and stone me, so that many times I have wished I was back with the good hermit.'

'What became of him?'

'He died,' Jehane said sadly. 'That was four years ago. His cell is empty now and evil creatures throng in the forest for want of his holy prayers to keep them at bay. Indeed, I wonder that you came alone through Darkriding safely as far as you did.'

'I found my fellow-men more perilous than these evil creatures you speak of,' he said smiling. 'What manner of beings are they, child?'

Jehane looked cautiously round and sank her voice to a whisper. 'There are wolves that take on the likeness of men by day but run as wolves at night. And there are women with the faces of fierce birds, and many-headed serpents. But the worst monster of all is the one they call the Wanderer.'

'What is the Wanderer?'

'Its real name is the Mirkindole, but men fear to speak it aloud. It is a huge beast, as large in itself as a whole castle. In clear weather it bides in its lair, but when the tempest blows and the wind is high, then the Mirkindole roams abroad in the forest and its breath is deadly cold.' She shivered.

'What is it like?'

'Black as night,' said Jehane. 'It is covered with a great mat of black fur, so thick and dense that you might think you had seen part of the forest coming towards you, were it not for the eyes, which shine with a fearful pale light. It can fly through the air faster than the swiftest bird, and as it flies it cries out with a loud moaning cry. All who hear its detestable voice near to are in its power and stand as if stunned until it takes them away. And they are never seen again.'

'In truth, a fearful monster,' said the knight. 'Has it made away with many?'

'Many,' Jehane told him. 'The strips of land at the outermost verge of the fields go untilled, for none will venture near the forest of an evening. And the Mirkindole's track has often been seen in the snow where men have vanished.'

'What exactly is the track of this terrible monster like?'

'A single track, like that of a bird, sir, but in size huge and shapeless, as if a tree had been walking through the snow.'

'By the rod,' said the knight, his eyes kindling, 'it would be a proper knightly task to rid the forest of this peril, and such a quest as I have vowed to accomplish for my sovereign lady, Queen Guenevere.'

Jehane looked at him with awe.

'Have you indeed come from Queen Guenevere, sir? Oh, tell me, what is she like?'

The Fairest Lady

The knight said solemnly, 'She is the most valiant and fairest lady that I know living. Her eyes are blue and her hair is the colour of winter birches when the sun shines on them.'

'Oh, how beautiful,' Jehane breathed. 'And King Arthur, you have seen him too?'

'Naturally. It was King Arthur who dubbed me knight.'

He did not add that he had only received his knighthood a couple of months ago and that this was his first Quest. He was a very young knight.

Now she knew he came from King Arthur's court Jehane treated him with even greater respect.

'What is your name, fair sir?'

'I am Sir Huon of High Holding.'

Jehane said the name to herself and liked it. It seemed to suit the young knight, who looked much better now that the fever had left him and he had eaten and slept. His hair, cut short in the knightly fashion, was fair, and his eyes were a clear grey. He was as brown as a berry from living out of doors.

'But sir,' she said, 'if you come from King Arthur's court you are in great danger from my master, Sir Cador, for he hates King Arthur and kills any Knights of the Round Table who 'happen through the forest. You must indeed be careful.'

'So much the greater glory,' said Sir Huon cheerfully. 'As soon as I am healed of my hurts I shall slay the Mirkindole. Then I shall fight Sir Cador and vanquish him and make him pay homage to King Arthur. Or no,' he added, thinking it over, 'I believe it would be better to kill Sir Cador first; then I can use this village as a base for attacking the Mirkindole. What do you say, child?'

Jehane was rather startled. 'But Sir Cador is my lord!'

'A traitor knight who teaches his men to fall on unsuspecting travellers is no good lord for you, child. I shall challenge him to single combat. I wonder if I can stand up yet?'

Sir Huon stood up, but collapsed with a groan and a curse.

'There now, you've started the leg bleeding again,' Jehane scolded him, and rebandaged it carefully. 'I must go now,' she said when she had done, and made up the fire. 'I will come to you again tomorrow, if I can escape unnoticed.'

'Good night, Jehane of the Forest, and may God go with you,' Sir Huon said gravely. He surprised her then by taking her hand and lightly touching it with his lips. 'I wish I could accompany you to protect you from the evil creatures of the night.'

'I shall be all right, sir, never fear,' she answered shyly. 'I am too small for them to notice me.'

Lost Treasure

Shutting the door behind her she darted swiftly across the heath, paused on the meadow to throw a handful of crumbs to her tame hare, and then made her way through the sleeping village to the manor garden. None hindered her entry into the secret passage, nor out into the chapel at the other end. As she dared not risk going to the kitchens at this late hour, she curled up in a corner of the chapel and went to sleep there. Her last waking thought was one of wonder at the fact that she, Jehane, the lowest of the low, should have had her hand kissed by a knight of King Arthur's Court.

For the next few days Jehane managed to slip out each evening unobserved, to take food to Sir Huon and dress his wounds. He chafed bitterly at his inactive life and at the need for secrecy and concealment, but obeyed her command not to go out of the hut, even when he could hobble a little. She knew well that any of the villagers, seeing him, would murder him or haul him off to Sir Cador for the reward that would be forthcoming. Sir Cador did not wish any traveller who had encountered his treatment to escape again to the world beyond the forest.

Jehane found that life at the Manor was not much worse than that in the village; the other servants avoided her and eyed her askance, for rumours of her reputation as a witch had reached them, but apart from stray kicks and pinches they did not actively ill-treat her. Occasionally she felt a sort of chill in her bones and found Lady Isabel's measured glance upon her; there was something of dread in this cold scrutiny and Jehane always made haste to escape from it.

Young Guy, the Squire, was the only person who showed her any friendliness. One of her many tasks was to milk the goats, and he would stroll out and help her.

It was Guy who told her about the lost treasure of Stone Guard.

''Twas sixteen years ago,' said Guy, who was hardly more than that age himself. 'In those days the old Lord, Sir Jerome, was master of the Manor. But Sir Cador envied him his lands, and came with a great band of men to lay siege to Stone Guard. It is said that the seneschal was in Sir Cador's pay, and by night he treacherously let down the drawbridge and raised the portcullis to let in Sir Cador's troop. So they entered swiftly at midnight and surprised the defenders and slew every man, even Sir Jerome and his lady and their children.'

'That was evilly done!' exclaimed Jehane. 'I marvel that you can serve such a master. As for myself, I have no choice, being born here, but you are free.'

Guy shrugged. 'My parents are dead and Sir Cador bought my wardship from my uncle. I have no choice either.'

'But tell about the treasure.'

'They say that Sir Jerome, who was a merry-hearted man, had a great love for jongleurs and troubadours. It happened that a troop of these Egyptians, or travelling minstrels and fortune-tellers, were at Stone Guard on the night when Sir Cador attacked. One of these a woman, swifter and more cunning than her fellows, escaped the general slaughter and made her way out through the secret passage. With her she took a casket containing the treasure of the manor, and it is said that Sir Cador was wondrous wroth when he found it had gone, and that with all his killing he had won for himself nothing but bare stone walls.'

'What was in the casket?'

'Oh,' said Guy, 'tales vary, but all agree there was a gold goblet, set with rubies, and a jewelled diadem, and a silver cross, wondrously chased, and a jewelled girdle, which, it is said, can only be worn by the true lady of Stone Guard.'

'Why so?'

'If one should try it on who is not the true lady, the girdle refuses to stay fastened, but the clasp unlooses and the girdle falls to the ground. They say, too, that besides these treasures there was another, the greatest treasure of them all, but no man knows what is was.'

'I wonder what it could have been,' said Jehane. 'And I wonder what became of the treasure.'

'Doubtless it is scattered widely enough after sixteen years,' sighed Guy. A horn sounded from the courtyard. 'It is the summons for a sortie,' he said, scrambled off the hayrack where he had been sitting, and ran to join Sir Cador's horsemen.

Almost every day Sir Cador led his men out on a raiding party through the forest, and rare was the sortie that did not provide money and arms from some luckless traveller or party of merchants. Men had good cause to fear a journey through the Forest of Darkriding.

Jehane had much to tell Sir Huon that night when she went to tend his wounds. She repeated the story of the treasure, and Sir Cador's surprise attack on Stone Guard.

'That was a foul and treacherous deed, to approach thus secretly by night and not in fair and open battle!' Sir Huon said. 'Truly it would be ridding the world of a pest to slice Sir Cador's head from off his shoulders, and I vow I will try to do it.'

'You must gain more strength yet awhile,' Jehane said anxiously, watching as he limped impatiently about the hut. 'Sir Cador is a renowned fighter, who has slain many knights in his time.'

She was much troubled by Sir Huon's vow, first because she feared he would be killed, and secondly, because though she realised that Sir Cador had committed many villainies, yet he had always been a protector to her, if without any apparent liking or kindness.

The Hermit's Prophecy

But an evening two weeks later was to teach her something new about Sir Cador.

The weather, which had been fine and frosty since the attack on Sir Huon, had suddenly broken, and a wild wind had been blowing for two days, with flurries of rain. Towards evening the gale rose even higher, moaning and howling through the trees, until the villagers went shuddering indoors, bolting and barring their houses against the menace of the

Mirkindole, who roamed abroad in such weather.

Jehane, terrified yet steadfast, had performed her usual errand to Sir Huon at top speed, running through the dark wet fields with her hood pulled well over her head and her fingers in her ears, for fear she should hear the dread voice of the Mirkindole calling her to its lair. Weak with relief she returned to the Manor and slipped back along the secret passage to curl herself, as usual, in a shadowy corner of the chapel. But she could not sleep; she lay trembling and wakeful, listening to the wind, wondering if Sir Huon would be safe in the small wooden hut so near to the forest. And presently her thoughts were disturbed by the sound of low voices nearby. It was Sir Cador and his lady! But why should they be talking thus privily and apart in the chapel, instead of among their men and maidens in the warm, well-lit hall?

'The churls in the village are rebellious,' said Sir Cador. 'They have been grumbling to Heriot the bailiff. It seems that the Mirkindole has claimed four more victims in the last two days.'

'What of it?' said Lady Isabel carelessly. 'Why should we be troubled?'

'Heriot says they are on the brink of a revolt against me if I do not find some means of putting an end to this scourge.'

'You will not go out against the Mirkindole?' Lady Isabel said anxiously.

'Not I! Do you take me for a fool? But the villagers say I am to blame because we are harbouring the witch-girl, Jehane, at the Manor. They say she summons the Mirkindole to the village.'

'In that case have her put to death,' his wife said. 'I have always detested the black-browed, sour-favoured jade ever since I first laid eyes on her. Have her burnt at the stake.'

Jehane, listening, turned deadly cold, and clenched her teeth to prevent their chattering.

'No, I dare not,' said Sir Cador. 'You remember what the hermit of the wood said when he brought her to me: "Guard her well, for should she come to her death at your hands, so surely you yourself shall die!"

'True,' said Lady Isabel thoughtfully. 'Yet he was only a doddering old man, and he himself is long since dead. Maybe the prophecy was naught but foolishness. Leave matters to me, husband: I will work out a plan. I long to be rid of the girl.'

'I am with you there,' said Sir Cador. 'I know not why, but the very thought of her gives me an ague in my bones.' He shivered as the wind howled outside. 'Come, let us go back to the fire.'

The door shut behind them and Jehane was left alone, trembling in the darkness.

Next day a pair of gipsies came riding to the Manor on brightly-bedizened mules. Sir Cador had not the old lord's love for minstrels and entertainers, but he suffered them to be admitted if they had goods for sale. This pair carried all manner of fairings, ribbons and laces, brooches and bangles, silks and satins and beads. The women servants were agog to buy, and even Lady Isabel condescended to have the Egyptians summoned before her.

Jehane, scattering fresh rushes on the floor, heard Lady Isabel bargaining for a length of red sarsenet and a bale of gauze, a pair of silver buckles and some scented, gold-embroidered gloves, and paying with a handful of silver coins. Then she saw Lady Isabel murmur something into the gipsy-woman's ear, and another purchase changed hands—a tiny phial, no bigger than her little finger.

'Does the gracious lady wish her fortune told?' the gipsy asked.

'No!' Lady Isabel snapped. 'I place scant faith in prophecies and predictions! You can tell the fortunes of my tirewomen if they are so credulous, but such nonsense is not for me.'

'But one moment longer,' said the gipsy. 'Since the gracious lady has bought so liberally of our wares, I make her a gift of this girdle, which has many sovereign healing properties.' And she gave Lady Isabel a beautiful girdle, curiously wrought with gold and precious stones, before curtseying, turning her back, and walking swiftly over to the curious, chattering crowd of women-servants who eagerly surrounded her and started chaffering for her goods.

Jehane, however, saw Lady Isabel gird the beautiful belt round her fur-trimmed silk gown. The buckle slipped, and the belt fell to her feet. With an angry exclamation she stooped, picked it up, and put it on again. The same thing happened.

'Alison!' she called sharply. 'Help me fasten this girdle.'

''Tis a faulty catch, maybe,' said her tirewoman, hastening to help her. 'Let me try, my lady.'

But her efforts were no more successful; each time Lady Isabel put the girdle on, it slipped off her again.

'The thing is bewitched!' she exclaimed resentfully. 'Let the gipsy be brought back!'

But the gipsy-woman, having sold the last of her wares, had joined her man at the great gate and left the Manor. On her way through the hall she paused and looked searchingly at Jehane.

'You have a lucky face, my young maiden,' she said. 'What will you give me to tell your fortune?'

'I have no money to pay you, mother,' Jehane said regretfully. 'All I can give you is this bunch of sweet herbs.'

'For that I will read you a warning, child. Avoid the kind word and the cold heart, beware the brimming cup and the rushing wind. If you are in need, say a prayer at the resting-place of your first friend. And forget not the old Egyptian—it may be we shall meet again.'

She passed out and mounted her mule.

Jehane gazed after her, strangely impressed by this woman, who, though old and wrinkled, was upright and swift-moving, whose eyes were as bright as the jewels that dangled from her ears, and whose black ringlets were unmarred by any hint of white.

Lady Isabel was enraged by the trick girdle. She would have despatched Sir Cador to fetch back the gipsy and beat her soundly, had he not been away on a raiding party. When he came back she was full of angry complaints.

'Plainly there is some spell on the girdle,' Sir Cador said. 'Why do you not lay it on the altar all night, my lady? Perhaps the holy influence will rid it of evil magic.'

This seemed good advice and Lady Isabel followed it, for she was longing to wear the beautiful jewelled belt.

A Death Potion

At supper that evening Jehane was taking her meal among the pages at the foot of the bottom table when Alison, the tirewoman, came to her with an unusually aimiable expression twisted on to her sharp, sallow face.

'My lady thinks you have been looking something pale and tired these last few days, maiden. She sends you this cordial, made with many healing herbs, to restore the roses to your cheeks.'

'It—it is very kind of her ladyship,' stammered Jehane, taking the goblet automatically. It contained a red liquid with a strong aromatic scent. 'I do not deserve her notice.' 'No *that* you don't!' snapped the maid, turning on her heel. 'Wondrous times, indeed, when any common kitchen slut may be doctored by the lady of the manor!'

Jehane's eyes were drawn in mysterious fascination to the brimming cup. She thought of the gipsy's warning—had the woman guessed Lady Isabel's intention? What did the drink contain? Could she, without arousing too much attention, tip it among the rushes under the table? But at present everyone's eyes were on her. It would be best to wait for a few minutes, to try and make the spill seem accidental. She pretended to eat hungrily, moving the cup a little to one side.

Presently she was forgotten again; the other servants turned back to their supper. She moved her hand casually towards the cup, looking in a different direction. Then something about it caught the corner of her eye and she turned swiftly. The page who sat beside her grinned impudently.

He was a pestilent, spoilt little brat named Godric, whom everyone detested because he shirked his tasks and bore tales .bout the others.

'It was *so* kind of Lady Isabel to send me the drink,' Godric said, smirking. 'The roses in my cheeks have been wilting these two weeks and more. I found it a mighty nice potion, I can tell you!'

The cup was empty; the boy's mouth and chin were splashed red from the haste with which he had gulped down the drink. Godric had solved Jehane's problem.

'May it do you as much good as it would me,' she said coldly.

After supper Godric became extremely sleepy, and the last she saw of him was curled up, snoring among the rushes. Next morning he was dead, but this Jehane did not know until many days later.

That evening Sir Huon declared that on the morrow he would be well enough to take up arms once more.

'I have trespassed on your kindness long enough, dear Jehane,' he said. 'Well I know the trouble and danger you have had, to visit me secretly and bring me food and medicines. Never knight had kinder lady. When I have achieved my Quest and return to my lady Queen Guenevere I shall beg her to send for you. It is a foul shame that so beautiful and brave a maiden should spend her life in so evil a place.'

Then Jehane told him of the talk she had overheard last night between Sir Cador and his lady, and of the goblet of drink and Godric's curiously deep sleep.

Sir Huon turned pale with anger.

'The vile wretches!' he exclaimed. 'He and his wife are serpents of the same litter. Stone Guard will be a sweeter place without the pair of them. Tomorrow I challenge Sir Cador to mortal combat. But first, Jehane, I must beg a last boon of you. Before I can fight I must needs find me a horse and armour—can you help me achieve this?'

'What you ask is difficult,' said Jehane. She cudgelled her brains. Perhaps Guy could help—yes, that was it, she would take Guy into her confidence and ask his advice.

'I will see what I can do,' she promised.

'I like not your returning to Stone Guard tonight,' Sir Huon said, frowning doubtfully.

'I shall be on the alert, never fear,' she told him, though inwardly she felt less bold.

Magic Girdle

When she reached the Manor, all seemed quiet enough. The chapel was silent and shadowed, with three tapers burning before the altar. Something gleamed below them; inquisitively stealing nearer Jehane saw that it was the gipsy's jewelled girdle.

She felt a strange urge to pick it up and examine it. Never in all her life had she seen a thing of such beauty, for it was wondrously wrought, heavy with gold and precious stones; the fastening was a curious one, three slender gold prongs set close together at either end of the belt, each prong with a ruby in its head. Although she had never seen the girdle before that day, it seemed queerly familiar, and even her hands seemed accustomed to the weight and feel and shape of it.

'I wonder how these prongs fasten together?' she thought dreamily, and without pausing to reflect, tried it round her waist. It fitted exactly, and the six spikes of the fastening slid together like the fingers of clasped hands, until the red jewels flashed together in one line.

She felt as if she had been wearing it all her life.

Then something, some little sound, made her turn towards the door that led from the chapel into the hall. Lady Isabel was standing there, her face a white mask of rage, her eyes darkly dilated. Her breath came in a little hiss.

'You!' she whispered. 'You—vile—*slave!* What are you doing here? How dare you put on that girdle?'

Jehane stood white and speechless, in utter consternation.

'Ho there!' Lady Isabel called, turning her head sharply. 'Mar! Jake! Kat! Jocelin! Alison! Come here and bind this insolent jade who has dared take my girdle!'

A crowd of servants came running. They surrounded Jehane jostling and buffeting her; in a moment her hands were dragged together behind her back and tied with painful force.

'Now take that girdle off her!' commanded Lady Isabel.

Here they encountered a difficulty; the girdle would not unclasp.

First the women tried, then the men, bruising and hurting Jehane in the process. Her side was cut, her tunic torn.

'Seems like it won't budge, my lady,' panted Jocelin, the steward.

'Fools! Do I have to soil my hands with touching the girl myself?'

With a look of repulsion Lady Isabel finally approached and tugged at the girdle, but her attempt to remove it was as fruitless as those of the servants.

'It's bewitched, my lady!' said Alison, stating an obvious truth.

142

'Ay, that's it. The girl's put a spell on the belt.'

'She's a witch, everyone knows that.'

'Yes, and what's more,' exclaimed the maid called Kat, 'she put a spell on young Godric the page, my lady; he stole her drink at supper so she ill-wished him and since that time the lad's been asleep and can't be waked; he lies like one in a swoon.'

'What shall we do with her, my lady?'

'See if a beating will make her leave go of the girdle,' decided Lady Isabel coldly.

Jehane was hustled out into the courtyard, where they tied her to a post and laid on her with a will until she sagged, fainting against the ropes. But still the belt could not be undone.

'It comes from the devil and so does she!' snarled the exasperated steward, reporting failure to his mistress. She reflected a little and said:

'Very well. If the belt is some devil's artifice, as I begin to believe, I wish no part of it. Let it stay on her.'

'What shall we do with her, mistress? Shall we make a bonfire and burn her?'

'No,' said Lady Isabel. 'Sir Cador does not wish her death to lie at his hands. Take her out over a mule's back and tie her to a stake on the heath; she belongs to the devil, so let the Mirkindole come and claim his own, then perhaps he will stop molesting poor honest folks.'

This seemed to everyone a clever and masterly plan, and they applauded Lady Isabel's wisdom, as she had intended. Jehane was flung roughly over a mule's back, the drawbridge was let down, and a noisy crowd, carrying dozens of torches to give them bravery in the black night, escorted her through the village.

They made such a noise that people came yawning to their doors to inquire what the devil was afoot.

"Tis the witch-girl, neighbours, being taken to her reward

at last. Speed her on her way with our blessing!' they cried.

Some of the peasants hurried after to join in the fun by throwing clods and rotten eggs.

Hob the smith staggered out, rubbing his eyes.

Then he saw Jehane strapped limply over the mule, battered and draggled, with her black hair streaming loose. Only the jewels in her belt glittered defiantly. Hob gaped. 'What devil's work is this, friends?' he asked, and a dozen people told him. He said nothing, but silently returned to his forge for a keen pike-blade, and followed the crowd.

When they had tied her to a thorn-tree on the heath, their appetite for vengeance grew rapidly cooler. The night was dark and rainy, the wind rising.

'Let us be off, friends,' called Jocelin. 'Leave the witch to her master—we don't want him to find us here and snap up the wrong mouthful!'

They scampered back to the village, even faster than they had come, congratulating themselves on a good evening's work. Only Wat Thatcher, who had always cherished a special grudge against Jehane, whispered to Diccon his neighbour:

'Do you and I come out at dawn, friend, to see if the Mirkin-dole has truly done our work for us. If not—' he made a significant gesture with his knife, and Diccon nodded.

When the shouting had died away and the last torch had been quenched, a dark figure stole from behind the hawthorn and set to loosing Jehane's bonds.

She was beginning to stir faintly, as the rain and the fresh wind revived her.

'Who is it? Oh, where am I!'

She looked dimly down at the man who knelt before her, working the rope free and rubbing warmth back into her chilled ankles. It was Hob.

'Oh, my lady, my lady!' he quavered. 'Why did you not tell me your true rank months agone? I should have guessed—I

144

should have guessed! With your mother's dark eyes looking out of that face of yours, and your father's proud way of walking—devil fly away with Hob for a purblind old fool! That I, your mother's groom, should have seen you and not known you—well-a, well-a-day!'

'Why, who am I?' said Jehane, bewildered still from her faint, looking down at the kneeling Hob.

'Her very own way of speaking!' he exclaimed, but at this moment his words were broken short by a fist which knocked him over backwards and an angry voice which exclaimed:

'What are you doing to her, knave? Loose her this instant!'

The Mirkindole

It was Sir Huon, very out of breath, very much in earnest, armed with nothing but a billet of wood.

'Doing? What the devil do you think I am doing?' muttered Hob resentfully, struggling up. 'She is my true liege lady and I'm trying to help her after those scum from the Manor have nearly made mincemeat of her.'

'I cry your pardon—I mistook your intent,' Sir Huon jerked out—he was still very puffed after running from the hut. He helped Hob undo the rest of the ropes. Jehanc was so weak and exhausted that she sank down on the wet grass.

'Best you come back to my house and my old woman shall make you a warm posset my lady—' Hob began.

'No, Hob, it would be madness,' Jehane said faintly. 'If Lady Isabel knew you had given me shelter she would have you strung up to the nearest tree. I'll stay with Sir Huon tonight and then try to make my way through the forest to some safe refuge.'

'Madam,' said Hob earnestly, 'so soon as the people of the village know that your father's daughter is alive, every man of them will be for you, heart and soul—'

'My father?' Jehane began, but Sir Huon interrupted sharply.

'What is that sound?'

They had been too absorbed to notice its beginning and now it seemed to fill the night—a mournful, wild, rushing cry, like the wind in the trees but a thousand times more dread and piercing. 'Stop your ears!' gasped Jehane, her cupping hands over the sides of her head.

The sound grew and grew till it seemed to sweep by them like the blade of some mighty scythe, and they felt a whirling buffet of wind; the sky darkened to pitch-black and the trees flattened like grassblades as the Mirkindole clove the air above them. Then gradually the fearful cry died away, the trees and bushes righted themselves; and the wood was silent, save for the frightened cheeping of birds wakened from sleep.

'Merciful heaven, what an escape!' whispered Jehane. 'I have never heard the Mirkindole so close! Quick, let us come to the hut. Hob, you come too—'

Hob made no answer. The moon drifted from behind a cloud and lit the spot where they stood, but there was no sign of him; only the pike-blade he had brought gleamed brightly on the grass and, nearby, one huge, misshapen footprint as big as a knight's shield was scored deeply into the hard ground.

'Hob! Hob, where are you? Hob!'

There was no reply; not the faintest sound or cry to indicate how Hob had been swept away. Jehane, who had remained dry-eyed and steadfast under blows and curses, burst into a bitter storm of tears.

'Oh Hob, poor Hob! He was always kind to me—why did he have to be taken?'

Sir Huon snatched up the pike-blade and made to follow the Mirkindole but there was no telling which way to go. 'Where is its lair?' he cried to Jehane.

'They say it lies a d-day's journey to westwards.' Jehane's voice wavered and Sir Huon turned to her remorsefully.

'Forgive me, child—I was so bewildered by the passing of the monster that I forgot your plight. You are in sore plight. I will carry you to the hut.'

He did so, and there built up the fire and gave her a warm drink, tending her hurts as gently as ever she had his, while she told what had happened to her. Together they puzzled over the mystery of the girdle and old Hob's words.

'Do you think I can be Sir Jerome's daughter?' Jehane asked.

'Truly I believe so.' He settled Jehane on the bed of rushes and himself lay across the door.

'I wish I could see the gipsy again,' Jehane said sleepily.

'We will find her. But first I follow the Mirkindole to its den to rescue Hob, if it be possible.'

'And I come too. After all, if what he said is true, Hob was my mother's man.'

'Sleep, then. We rise early.'

They were wakened, before dawn, by voices, and, looking cautiously out through a chink, saw Wat and Diccon reconnoitre the thorn tree, discover the Mirkindole's footprint, and run back to the village with the joyful news that the witch had been carried off.

Huon and Jehane waited no longer. They ate the remains of the bread and cheese that she had brought last night, and set off westwards into the forest.

'On our way,' said Jehane, 'we shall pass the cell of my good old master the hermit, and that is well, for the gipsy told me that if I was in need I should say a prayer at the resting-place of my first friend. We can say a prayer for poor Hob.'

'Truly we are in need,' said Sir Huon. 'I doubt if ever knight and lady set out on a quest so ragged and ill-armed.'

Nonetheless, as it was a fine spring morning, with birds clamorous and leaves budding on the trees, they could not be too down-hearted. The sun shone warmly upon them and they went forward hand in hand talking so hard that they chanced on the hermitage unaware.

It was a safe, sheltered place, half cave, half chapel, set in the side of a little valley. A stream ran bubbling past the entrance and hazel thickets screened it closely. Jehane's face grew soft with recollection as she told Sir Huon about her childhood here, and the kind old man who had cared for her.

They knelt and prayed for the hermit's soul, and for poor Hob, and for Sir Huon's success against the Mirkindole. Then Jehane took Sir Huon to see her own little room, another cave in the cliffside. Great was their astonishment at finding there a suit of mail, with a sword and shield, spear and helmet. The armour was black, the shield, and the three plumes of the helmet, white. A gold-embroidered surcoat hung nearby, and below it ran a legend:

'This is the harness of Sir Jerome, Lord of Stone Guard, foully murdered. Here shall it hang, and no man may touch it, save that brave knight who shall avenge its owner, and succour his daughter the Lady Jehane, and deliver his people from the fell and ravening Mirkindole.'

A Noble Quest

While they were wondering at these words, Jehane suddenly laid her hand on Sir Huon's arm. She had heard the thud of a horse's hoofs outside.

They looked at one another in startled disquiet. They heard the rider dismount; his stirrup clinked; then the horse was still and steps went into the chapel. There was a silence, followed by the sound of weeping.

Jehane laid her finger on her lips and stole forth to where

148

she could see into the chapel. Then her eyes widened. 'Guy!' she exclaimed.

Guy indeed it was, weeping before the altar as if his heart would break. He turned in amazement at her voice.

'Jehane!' he gasped. 'Am I dreaming?'

It took some time to convince him that she was herself, in very substance, and had not been taken by the Mirkindole, but as he heard her story his face brightened wonderfully. Sir Huon came out and was made known, and Guy knelt to do him honour. They told him their intention to seek out the Mirkindole in its den, and he was fired with enthusiasm.

'Oh sir!' he cried, 'may I come with you? May I be your squire? It is a noble quest. I will give you my horse—indeed, he is Sir Cador's best charger. When I heard this morning about Je—about the Lady Jehane, I was so mazed with grief and rage that I ran to the stable and took the first beast I came to, intending to seek the court of King Arthur and cry for vengeance.'

'Come with us and welcome,' Sir Huon said. So Guy helped him put on the black armour, which fitted as if it had been made for him. There was no device on the shield, 'and that is well,' said Sir Huon. 'So it shall remain until I have proved myself.'

Meanwhile Jehane went up to the head of the valley where she whistled on her fingers as shrilly as any ploughboy. Presently came the sound of cantering hoofbeats.

'Ah,' she said smiling. 'I wondered if they would remember. Always in the winter I used to feed them, until they were so tame they came to my whistle.'

Huon and Guy watched in wonder as a troop of forest ponies burst out of the thicket and surrounded Jehane, nuzzling her and making much of her. 'Faithful friends,' she said happily, 'you remember your old playfellow, do you? But I have no bread to give you today.'

She fondled and patted them, presently picking out two, a handsome bay and a slender white pony.

'These will serve Guy and me,' she said. So they were mounted and equipped. Guy had a bow and his dagger with him, Jehane too brought out a bow and sheaf of arrows with which, long ago, she had been wont to practise shooting in the forest.

Guy and Jehane sat their horses bareback, but this was no hardship to them, bred and born in Darkriding both. Their hearts rose high as they rode forward to the west and their horses' hoofs thudded valiantly like drum beats before battle.

The Monster Attacks

All day they rode, stopping once only to eat a few provisions that Guy had brought for his journey.

Towards nightfall they came to a dismal part of the forest all set about with rock and bramble. Tall pine trees sighed overhead, and the air was uncannily cold, thick, and dank with a chill and noisome mist.

'It is my guess that we are nearing the Mirkindole's lair,' shivered Jehane. The way here lay downhill, through a long, narrow, rocky gully, its farther end shrouded in mist and darkness. The cold, as they advanced, became more and more deadly.

Sir Huon reflected. 'We need a plan of attack,' he said. 'The Mirkindole flies or leaps in great bounds, so it may be out and over us before we can stop it. To guard against this chance, I want each of you two to mount the sides of the gully and wait here, with bent bows, while I go on to prick the monster out of its lair.'

Jehane would have objected to this order, suspecting, in part correctly, that Sir Huon wanted her to remain in a place of safety. But as Guy automatically obeyed his leader she had no choice but to follow suit.

'Shall I kindle a fire?' she suggested. 'They say that some-times the Mirkindole kills by cold. Perhaps it hates heat—in any case, a fire will hearten us.'

'That is a good plan,' approved Sir Huon. 'Perhaps the light of the fire will rouse it.'

In the end they decided to have two fires, one on either side of the ravine. And Guy suggested that they should stuff their ears with moss, lest the dreadful cry of the Mirkindole cause them to fall into a swoon.

When the fires were kindled, and burned brightly, Sir Huon set himself ready for battle. He closed the vizor of his helmet, swung his shield into position, gripped his spear, and clapped spurs to his horse, which started off at a gallop down the gully.

Then the watchers began to hear, even through the stuffing in their ears, the detestable wailing cry of the Mirkindole, so they had come to the right place. Tense with anxiety they waited, straining their eyes to try and see through the swirling wreaths of mist.

The wailing grew louder and louder, until it seemed impos-sible that the world could contain any more sound; they were dazed and deafened, but still it grew. Suddenly like a huge black cloud the Mirkindole rose up from its lair at the bottom of the gully. It hove in the air, its one leg sweeping in circles below it like a battering-ram. Of the Mirkindole's shape, little could be seen: it was huge, it was covered with a coat of blackness, it had two luminous, menacing eyes that glared defiance at Sir Huon. Having risen high above the gully, it came whistling down on him. His horse bucked and screamed, but he held it grimly, stood in his stirrups, and darted his spear high and true into the midst of the whirling blackness. Then, and not a moment too soon, he kicked his right foot from the stirrup and slid round under the horse's belly, just in time to escape the great flailing foot of the Mirkindole which passed within a hair's breadth of the saddle, and struck the horse. It fell, but Sir Huon leapt to safety some distance away.

Meanwhile the Mirkindole hurtled on up the gully, rose, fetched round in a circle, and returned to its lair, wailing hideously, with Sir Huon's spear somewhere in the core of its body. Both Guy and Jehane discharged their shafts at it as if flew by, but each shot went wide because of the monster's speed.

It settled into the mouth of its den again, wounded, but not to death. Its mouth gaped open, breathing out a murderous cold fog. Sir Huon ran down the gully until the monster's mouth was directly in front of him like a cave of icy, wet black leather. Its great tongue roved out at him; he could see the teeth like icicles above. Steadfast in his aim, he leapt on the tongue and thrust his sword right into the Mirkindole's gullet; then slipped back just before the teeth clashed down.

With a screech like ripping leather the Mirkindole shot upwards and hovered, this time directly over the knight. Its leg swung wildly, like a mad pendulum.

Jehane and Guy raced along the sides of the gully. Both discharged arrows, both found their mark. But Jehane's second shaft was a flaming one; she had thrust it into the blaze before firing it. Like a shooting star it streaked straight into the heart of the Mirkindole's darkness.

With an unearthly wheezing gasp the monster rocked in mid-air, rose, twirled, and sped away, shrinking and burning before their eyes, until it resembled nothing so much as a whirling black rag of ash. The leg twisted off and fell with a thump on the ground. The Mirkindole was no more.

Hob's Revelation

For a moment they could hardly believe it; the end had come so suddenly. Then Jehane and Guy ran down the gully to Sir Huon. He was reeling in an ague of cold from the monster's breath, and had to be led back to the fire and warmed before he could speak.

They lit a great bonfire before the Mirkindole's den, and all night long one or another of them kept feeding it with branches. By morning the cold was somewhat abated and they were able to venture in. It was a grisly place, lined with icicles and scattered with bones of animals and men, but to their joy they found Hob unhurt. At first they thought he was dead, but he was merely rigid with cold, and after they had rubbed him before the fire and given him a hot drink, made of melted ice and forest herbs, he recovered and wept with joy to see Jehane once more.

'For you are truly my dear lady,' he said. 'As soon as I saw you in that girdle, which your lady mother used to wear, I wondered where my eyes had been all these years. You are the living image of her.'

'But how can I have escaped when Sir Cador sacked Stone Guard and killed all the people?' Jehane said.

'You were only a babe then, madam. It's my guess—I was away from home at the time, rounding up a drove of forest horses, that's how I won clear—it's my guess your sainted mother must have entrusted you to the gipsy-women, along with the casket of jewels.'

'Of course!' Jehane exclaimed. 'And she left me with the hermit.'

'You go to King Arthur now, my lady,' Hob said earnestly, 'and claim your rights.'

'We are already bound there,' Sir Huon told him. 'I vowed the fruits of my first quest to my sovereign lady Queen Guenevere, so I shall give her the Mirkindole's foot. Then I shall ask my lord King Arthur's permission to fight the cause of the Lady Jehane against Sir Cador and restore her inheritance.'

'Ay, that's it,' said Hob approvingly. 'And meanwhile I'll be stirring up the village people, the miserable numbskulls;

153

I long to see their faces when they hear who 'tis they've been miscalling and abusing. But what can I take 'em, madam, as a token that my story's a true one?'

'I will give you the girdle,' Jehane said. 'It is the only thing of my mother's that I have, and some of them must have seen her wearing it.'

'But can you undo it, my lady?'

'Oh yes, *I* can undo it,' said Jehane calmly. 'It was only those others who failed, when they tried to take it by force.'

Hob set off at once to return home, for he said he could not endure to think of his poor old wife's sorrow, believing him eaten by the Mirkindole.

The others journeyed slowly on westwards towards Camelot, where King Arthur held his court.

Conveying the Mirkindole's foot proved an awkward business; it was too large and heavy to carry. The horses had a most violent fear of it, too, whinnying and struggling if it was brought near them.

At last Guy devised a kind of litter made strongly of branches and slung between Sir Huon's charger—which had recovered from its buffet—and the bay pony. After two days' journeying thus, they came to the forest village of Yaffle Tarn, where the people were so overjoyed to hear the deadly Mirkindole was dead that they kept the travellers for a day, feasting them and pressing gifts on them of food and clothes, saddles for their horses, and a cart pulled by a stout cob to carry their trophy.

So they were able to press on more swiftly, and now it was only two days' journey to Camelot.

The last night they spent in the forest was at Gaylord's Ride, where again they were honoured with feasting and much merry making.

Next morning when they rose to continue on their way, the cart with the Mirkindole's foot in it was missing. Not a soul in the village knew where it had gone. Sir Huon's brow grew

154

dark with anger at having his trophy thus treacherously stolen, and it might have gone hard with the people of Gaylord's Ride, whether innocent or no, had not Jehane, who had cantered her pony on to the end of the village, returned with news.

'There are tracks in the wet earth,' she told Sir Huon and Guy. 'Someone has taken our cart that way not long ago. Let us ride fast and overtake them.'

'Bless you, child,' said Sir Huon, 'for keeping me from injustice to our hosts.'

They pressed on at a hot pace towards Camelot, for that was where the tracks were leading, and shortly before dusk reached King Arthur's castle.

It was a fine, heart-stirring sight to see. The gate was raised, the towers were glittering white, and the King's standard flew from the battlements. Knights were coming and going in splendid armour, with plumes dancing and pennants fluttering. Troops of men-at-arms were exercising, bowmen were shooting at targets, squires were tilting at the quintain.

Lovely ladies, most richly dressed, rode with their knights or watched them performing feats of arms. And all the time poor people with grievances, or any in trouble or distress went up to the castle to tell their wrongs to the King, and came away with Knights of the Round Table who had sworn to fight in their cause.

Jehane and Guy were somewhat timid at the thought of presenting themselves, dusty and travel-stained as they were, before the King and Queen, but Sir Huon bade them be of good heart. They left their horses with a page and made their way to the Great Hall, where a trumpeter announced them with a flourish:

'Sir Huon of High Holding and his squire! The Lady Jehane of Stone Guard!'

A silence fell as they walked forward to where King Arthur and Queen Guenevere sat, robed in scarlet.

155

Then Jehane exclaimed under her breath, 'Look! Look who is there!'

A knight stood before King Arthur. He had his back to them but they heard his voice:

'And so, my lord King, I slew the dreadful Mirkindole and cut off its foot, the which I bring to you in token of loyal allegiance. And in return I ask your support against my villeins who have risen against me and thrust me out of my own Manor of Stone Guard. And I ask you to help me find and punish the witch known as Jehane of the Forest, who has evilly led my people on to rebellion and turned their hearts against me, with a false knight, Sir Huon, and my own squire Guy who has been enticed away from me with spells and black magic.'

He made a deep bow and a lady who stood beside him, all robed in black cried loudly, 'Behold the Mirkindole's foot!' and twitched a silken covering off the foot, which up till now they had taken to be a table in front of Queen Guenevere.

Everybody lapped politely and there were a few cheers, but not many, since Sir Cador was not a knight of the Round Table, and moreover his reputation was very evil.

Sir Huon stepped forward and cried in a loud voice.

'Lies, foul lies, my lord King! It was not he who slew the Mirkindole, but I, helped by the good squire Guy and the Lady Jehane, who is no witch but the rightful lady of Stone Guard, and whose father was treacherously slain by Sir Cador.'

'He speaks truly,' said Jehane and Guy together.

King Arthur considered, with his chin on his fist. He was a splendid-looking King, with hair the colour of red gold and the most piercing blue eyes Jehane had ever seen. Presently he said:

'We are more inclined to believe Sir Huon, who is our own good knight, and has been known to us from childhood. But it behoves us to judge fairly in this thing. Are there any other witnesses?'

156

'Yes!' cried the back-clad woman shrilly—she was Lady Isabel—'I was with Sir Cador when he slew the Mirkindole. And in token that I am the true Lady of Stone Guard I wear this magic girdle!'

'How did she come by that?' muttered Sir Huon, thunderstruck. 'Can they have taken it from Hob? And why does it not fall from her false body?'

But the quick-witted Guy whispered, 'See, it is not properly fastened. She has tied the ends together with a silver thread.' Pretending to examine the girdle, he stepped towards Lady Isabel and, swift as thought, cut the silver lacing with his dagger.

Then they saw a marvel, for the enchanted girdle fell to the floor and like a snake began to wriggle until it reached the feet of Jehane. She reached out and picked it up, whereupon it at once coiled round her waist.

A Duel

'Behold the true Lady of Stone Guard!' shouted Sir Huon, while Lady Isabel, pale with rage and shame, covered her face with her hands, and King Arthur said coldly, 'In faith, madam, the girdle seems to know better than you where stands its true owner.'

Lady Isabel turned and slunk from the Court, casting a look of spite and hatred at Sir Huon and Jehane as she went. And from that time they never saw her more.

Then Sir Huon fell on one knee before the King and said, 'Sir, I beg leave to challenge this false knight Sir Cador to a joust, the outcome of which shall prove which of us twain is the liar.'

Sir Cador's eyes gleamed. King Arthur said doubtfully, 'Sir Cador is known to us by renown as a cunning and experienced fighter, while you, Sir Huon, are young and untried.

'*Behold the true Lady of Stone Guard!*' *exclaimed Sir Huon.*

It were no shame to you if another of my knights should take him on—Sir Lancelot, for instance.'

Jehane clasped her hands together anxiously. But Sir Huon said firmly;

'No, my lord King. He has abused and slandered the name of the Lady Jehane, whom I hope to make my wife, and he has stolen the glory and the trophy of my fight with the Mirkindole. This is my proper quarrel.'

'Very well,' said King Arthur. 'You may fight at noon tomorrow. In the meantime we will forget all quarrels in feasting and good-fellowship.'

So they passed the evening merrily. The Queen, a noble-looking lady with eyes that smiled even when her face was grave, and a laugh like the music of a moorland brook, led Jehane away and robed her according to her station, in a white silk robe and a blue brocaded tunic, richly embroidered with pearls. She asked to hear the whole story, and Jehane told it her from start to finish.

'It is the most wondrous tale that ever I heard,' said Queen Guenevere. 'And happy I am that Sir Huon has won himself a lady of such rare spirit and beauty, for he is my favourite of all my young knights.' She kissed the blushing Jehane on both cheeks and braided up her hair with pearls until when Jehane looked into the Queen's silver mirror she hardly recognised the splendid image that she saw there.

Next day at noon they all assembled in the lists beyond the castle moat. This was a fair open field, with galleries all round for the many spectators who had come to watch the combat, and a covered pavilion for the ladies, where Jehane sat at the Queen's knee.

The heralds blew a blast on their trumpets and the marshals of the field led the two knights to their stations. Sir Cador wore a suit of steel armour, richly chased with gold, and a jousting helm with a black plume. His shield bore the device of a black bear of the forest with the words 'Gare L'Ours.' Sir Huon still had on Sir Jerome's armour from the hermitage, with the plain white shield, but he had put on his own jousting helm and carried Jehane's sleeve as a crest. Each knight was armed with sword and spear.

Queen Guenevere dropped a handkerchief and they feutred their lances, set spurs to their horses, and met in the centre of the lists with a crash like thunder, shivering their spears to the handles on each other's shields. The trumpets sounded again, and they reined back their horses and retired once more to the ends of the lists, where they were given fresh spears.

Once more the Queen gave the signal and they galloped together. This time Sir Cador, hoping to unhorse Huon, held his spear sideways and swung it round with a whirling motion. But while he did this Sir Huon had directed the point of his spear to the bars of Sir Cador's vizor and hit it fairly before the other's lance had a chance to reach him. One of Sir Cador's stirrups broke and he was borne violently backwards and hurled to the ground.

Sir Huon leapt nimbly from his horse, waving his sword and calling on his opponent to surrender. But Sir Cador neither spoke nor stirred. When the marshals cut the laces of his casque and undid his hauberk they found that he was dead—slain fighting for his own worthless cause as he had sent so many poor travellers to their deaths.

As the heralds were proclaiming Sir Huon the victor a dusty figure rushed into the lists. It was Hob. He was eager to tell how Sir Cador, out of vengeance for Hob's proclaiming Jehane to be the true owner of Stone Guard, had set upon him and taken the girdle from him. Then the people had risen against Sir Cador and Lady Isabel, charging them with the death of Godric, among others, and they had fled from Stone Guard by night.

'The people are all agog to have you back, my lady, and show their changed hearts and good will,' said Hob to Jehane.

So Huon and Jehane were married; King Arthur gave away the bride and Guy stood in attendance. After their wedding-feast they rode back with Guy and Hob through the forest to receive the allegiance of Jehane's shamefaced people.

On the way they stopped at the hermitage, and whom should they meet there but the gipsy-woman.

'Ah, my pretty lady, I find you in better case than last time we met,' said the gipsy. 'Rich in love, rich in lands, and a husband with a strong arm to boot—' and she nodded towards the picture of the Mirkindole, rampant on Sir Huon's shield—'said I not that you had a lucky face? Can you spare a bit of silver now to have the old gipsy-woman tell your fortune?'

'Willingly, dear mother,' said Jehane, giving her a handful of coins. 'But you don't need to tell my fortune. We are going to be happy all the days of our life.'

'Then I will give you a wedding present instead,' said the gipsy, and she opened a door, cunningly hidden in the rock wall of the chapel, and brought out an iron casket. It contained treasures—a ruby-studded gold goblet and a jewelled crown and a carved silver cross. 'Here you are, lady dear—' tis the lost treasure of Stone Guard, given to me by your mother when she trusted your young life to my hands.'

As they exclaimed at the jewels the gipsy left them, passing with her swift noiseless stride through the thickness of the hazel coppice. When they looked up she had gone.

So they rode happily on, among the green leaves of spring and the songs of birds, to take possession of Stone Guard. And from that day, with the strong arm of Sir Huon to vanquish evil, there were no more evil deeds or foul monsters in the Forest of Darkriding, but wise rule, and peaceful living, and happiness throughout its green and murmuring glades.

A Lamp for Elizabeth

by Kathleen O' Farrell

They were all up on Vicarage Hill, making tossy-balls of cowslips, when Elizabeth had her great idea. The year was eighteen hundred and fifty. The sun was shining, and the cowslips smelt as cool and creamy and fresh as the farm butter which Adam Barleycorn delivered to their home every week. They made Elizabeth think of Lucy—Lucy had been so clever at making tossy-balls. She had been two years older than Elizabeth and they had been the greatest of friends as well as sisters. Elizabeth knew that she would always remember Lucy when cowslip time came around.

It seemed all wrong that Lucy shouldn't be here with them now, with Robin and Elizabeth and Mary Anne and little Charlotte. But then a great many things were wrong, things which Mama and Papa and Miss Russell, the governess, seemed to take for granted. They would shake their heads and sigh regretfully, but when Elizabeth asked why someone didn't *do* something, they would tell her to stop bothering her pretty little head. Even Mr Bradley the vicar, who wrote letters to *The Times*, was shocked to hear that Elizabeth read the newspapers. He would suggest to her, in his kindly, ineffectual way, that she would be better employed with her flower-pressing or her cross-stitch embroidery.

And now Elizabeth, fourteen years old and with a mind of her own, stood up in the cowslip field, a defiant little figure in her striped silk dress of grey and white with the broad bands of cherry-coloured ribbon on the wide sleeves. Her grey eyes shone with determination under the neatly ringletted hair.

'I've made up my mind,' declared Elizabeth Fairfax. 'I'm going to ask Mama and Papa if I can train to be a nurse!'

'A nurse!' Miss Russell, thin, very genteel, dressed all in drab brown save for the one demure pink rose on her bonnet, threw up her hands in horror. 'But my dear Miss Elizabeth, your parents would never permit such a thing! A young lady like you! A refined young lady!'

Mary Anne and little Charlotte, pretty and fairylike in their white muslin frocks with wide blue sashes, stared at their elder sister in disbelief. As for Robin, an impudent young scamp then half-way up an oak tree, he laughed the idea to scorn. As though Elizabeth could ever bring herself to do such unpleasant work! Why, none of his sisters had been brought up to be useful—girls of their class never were. With Papa a well-to-do merchant there was no need for his daughters to earn their own living. As long as they grew up graceful and charming, able to sketch a little, play a little music, perhaps know how to make jams and jellies in the still-room, they would eventually be married to young men from a similar background. Robin was glad that he was a boy, with a life of adventure ahead of him. He had made up his mind to be a soldier, and although everyone said an army career was hard and rigorous and that the food was dreadful, at least it would be exciting.

Miss Russell felt rather nervous and not a little guilty after Elizabeth had made her announcement. She hoped she would not be blamed for the young girl's strange ambition. Why, she would be the very last person to foster such unlady-like ideas! It must be because of poor dear Lucy, she told herself sadly. They had been so close, Lucy and Elizabeth, and since her sister's death Elizabeth had never been quite the same. But there, thought Miss Russell with resignation, life was like that. Everyone had their share of sorrow—had not she, herself, lost an adored baby brother?

But perhaps it was just a young girl's whim, soon to be forgotten. Miss Russell brightened as she escorted her youthful charges down the hill and into the valley. Here the lovely old house stood, the house of warm red brick, set among orchards and formal gardens gay with spring flowers. Around its little towers and turrets fan-tail pigeons fluttered, and Elizabeth gazed at the familar sight with eyes full of love.

But she did not forget her resolve, and after family prayers that evening she repeated her intention to her parents. They were just as horrified as she had expected.

'But my dear child,' cried Mama, 'nice young ladies don't become nurses! It's quite unheard of?'

'Perhaps they don't,' agreed Elizabeth quietly. 'But *I* want to. Just as soon as I'm old enough I want to train in one of the London hospitals. Oh, I know what you're thinking— you're thinking it's because of Lucy, and in a way you're right. I was very good at nursing Lucy, wasn't I, Mama? And I'd be good with other people, too, I know I would. I don't care how horrible the hospitals are . . .'

Mrs Fairfax, tall, elegant, imposing in her black silk crinoline gown, was an awe-inspiring person to the servants, but no match for her eldest daughter. Oh dear, she thought, gazing into those determined grey eyes, Elizabeth is going to be a rebel. 'Whatever will Papa say?' she asked weakly.

'Papa will understand,' said Elizabeth.

And when it came to the test, Mr Fairfax was no more able to withstand his child's pleadings than his wife had been. In the end he gave his consent to what he called her 'ridiculous and unseemly plan', secretly hoping that by the time Elizabeth was old enough to go, the novelty of the idea would have worn off.

But weeks, months, years passed by and Elizabeth's determination did not change. As soon as she was old enough she left her pleasant, comfortable Surrey home to begin her training in a big London hospital.

Her parents, who were really very tolerant for those days, gave her their blessing and a small Bible to take with her. Miss Russell gave her a little embroidered pin-cushion, and Mary Anne and Charlotte each gave her a handkerchief they had stitched, with her initials in the corner. As for Robin, he had nothing to bestow on her, but he flung his arms around her neck and whispered: 'Good for you, Lizzie!' He was the only one who ever called her that—and afterwards her cheek felt damp.

Elizabeth started work.

It was just as hard and just as grim as everyone had warned her, and unbelievably exhausting. Why, even Fanny and Rose, the maids at home, didn't work as hard as this! Sometimes she felt like running away from it all, from the floors covered in stained sawdust, the scenes of pain and distress, and the dreadful smell of disease and death which some of the skeleton-like patients seemed to bring in with them. Why had she not stayed in Surrey, in that gracious old house, to pass her days in pleasant girlish pursuits with Mary Anne and Charlotte? Her fellow nurses were mostly rough, uneducated girls, with big red hands and loud voices. Sometimes they had too much to drink and sang noisy tavern songs, and sometimes they poked fun at Elizabeth because of her ladylike manners and soft voice. At such times she felt unbearably lonely, but there was usually someone to come to her rescue, perhaps an older woman who had an inborn respect for the country gentry.

One day there was an air of excitement in the wards, and extra beds were prepared. Elizabeth, enquiring what was afoot, was appalled at the answer she received. 'Why, don't you know?' cried a stalwart girl called Polly Jenkins. 'There's a public hanging today! A murderer is going to dance on air. Oh, it will be a grand sight, with him in his white dunce's cap, and all the prison officers lined up like soldiers, and the hangman all in black! There'll be hundreds there to watch the fun, and some of them will get trampled on in the crush—they always do. We're always extra busy when there's a hanging.'

The very thought of it made Elizabeth feel quite sick, and when, a little later on, a number of badly injured sightseers were carried into the hospital, she felt torn between pity and disgust. There were even women amongst them, one of them with a tiny baby only a few weeks old. How bleak and empty their lives must be, she thought, gazing at their pallid faces, for them to derive pleasure from seeing some poor wretch die!

'Don't take it to heart, dearie,' whispered one of the older, kinder nurses, as she folded up threadbare clothes. 'There's only three that are goners—we'll save all the rest. Sometimes there's a dozen or more killed in the crsuh.'

But hospital life wasn't always harsh and ugly. True, the training was almost non-existent, but Elizabeth applied herself so whole-heartedly to her work, anxious to learn all she possibly could about medicine, dressings, and the different forms of treatment, that she had little time left in which to pine or cherish regrets. And what wonderful satisfaction there was in nursing someone back to health! It might be a child, homesick and terrified, or a frightened old woman, or the harrassed father of a large family, but whoever it was Elizabeth's gentle care and soft voice soon banished fear. More than once she knew quite well that she had dragged someone back from the very edge of the grave.

Once there was a young girl who bore an almost uncanny resemblance to Lucy. Because she had the same delicate

167

prettiness, the same violet eyes and long black hair, Elizabeth felt a special responsibility towards her. She even gave up her precious free time so that she could sit with this favourite patient—the young girl seemed so lonely and had so few visitors that nobody thought it strange. But the day came when she walked out, fit and well again, and Elizabeth felt a stab of grief. 'If only I could have done as much for Lucy!' she thought longingly. 'If only I could have known then as much as I do now!'

When she went home on holiday her parents remarked how thin and pale she was, how tired too! But they could not deny that she seemed happy. 'Though how you can endure such a life is quite beyond my comprehension,' sighed Mrs Fairfax. She shook her head in its exquisite lace cap, and lifted the lid of the silver muffin-dish. 'Don't go back, Elizabeth dear. Stay here, where you belong.'

But, delightful though her home was, with its carpeted floors, its trellised wallpaper, its parlour full of china ornaments and stuffed birds, and Rose and Fanny in smiling attendance, Elizabeth knew she wouldn't stay. 'I think I was born to be a nurse,' she declared. 'The work is hard, but it is full of compensations.'

When she returned to London her parents sighed and Mary Anne and little Charlotte wept, but soon after that there was something else to occupy their minds—something which filled them with even worse forebodings. Because Robin the only boy, achieved his ambition of becoming a soldier, and not long afterwards was sent to the Crimea.

Elizabeth was not quite sure what all the trouble was about. She only knew that England, France and Turkey had declared war on Russia, and that it was a very terrible war indeed, with young Englishmen being killed in their thousands, or dying of disease and hunger and cold. The Crimea was a long way away, and until now she had never even heard of it, but suddenly it was on everyone's lips and its very name brought shudder. And somewhere out there, a newly commissioned officer in a brave red coat, tight trousers, and tall black hat, was a boy called Robin; a boy who, only two summers before, had begged Adam Barleycorn for rides on his hay-cart.

'Pray God he will be all right,' murmured Mrs Fairfax, as disturbing news of the war gradually filtered through. 'If only we could hear from him! Just a few lines to let us know how he fares!'

But no news came of Robin. Weeks passed, and Elizabeth, busy in her London hospital, was terribly afraid. Surely nothing dreadful could happen to Robin! He was so young, so touching in his pride and delight at being a soldier . . . But they said that conditions out in the Crimea were quite unspeakable. They said that half the soldiers wounded in battle never recovered!

If only the Crimea weren't so far away, so out of reach!

And then, in the midst of her distress, Elizabeth began to hear and read of a wonderful woman. She was a nurse, of great experience and wisdom and compassion, and was called Miss Florence Nightingale. Disgusted and dismayed by all the shocking reports she had heard about hospitals in the Crimea, Miss Nightingale had agreed to go out there to try to put things right.

Florence Nightingale! Every single thing about this woman filled Elizabeth with admiration. More than anything else in the world, she longed to meet her. And then one day a fantastic idea occurred to her. Miss Nightingale was recruiting nurses to take with her. Why shouldn't she, Elizabeth Fairfax, be one of those to go?

At first the notion seemed too absurd, too presumptious, even to such a dedicated girl as Elizabeth. For all her middle-class background she felt too small, too humble, too ignorant.

Her schooling, under the timid Miss Russell, had been slight to say the least, and her nursing knowledge had been gleaned as she worked—she had no text book information from which she could draw.

Notwithstanding all this, however, one October morning found her making her way to Miss Nightingale's small, private hospital in Upper Harley Street.

Elizabeth was asked to wait, and as she sat in the small panelled room her heart was beating wildly. What a dreadful mistake this was! To come like this, uninvited and without an appointment, calmly asking to see the lady of whom all England was talking! She, Elizabeth Fairfax, only two years out of the schoolroom . . .

It seemed as though she sat there for hours. And then, just as her spirits were at their lowers ebb, the door opened and a woman came in. She was a tall woman, straight and slender, and although her clothes were simple, they were elegant and good. She had brown hair, grey eyes, and a pink and white complexion, and although she wasn't really beautiful there was a great charm about her. Elizabeth stood up, instinctively dropping a little curtsey. Then she introduced herself.

'And why do you wish to see me?' asked Miss Nightingale.

She looked at Elizabeth with misgivings. Yet another starry-eyed little creature, she thought sadly, coming here to offer herself as a ministering angel. Her keen eyes noticed Elizabeth's delicate wrists, her air of breeding, the quality of her dress and mantle.

'If you please, Ma'am,' said Elizabeth quietly, 'I would like to go with you to the Crimea.'

'Sit down,' commanded Miss Nightingale, taking a chair opposite Elizabeth's. 'Now, let me hear you reasons.'

She waited patiently for the torrent of words which she felt sure would come. Why did her task have to be so difficult? It seemed as though she must choose between strong, rough,

170

uneducated women, too insensitive to care about the conditions abroad, and young girls like this one—small, almost fragile in appearance, and totally unfitted for service in hospitals like Scutari.

But the outburst of sentiment did not come.

'I think, Ma'am,' said Elizabeth, 'you would find me of some use.'

The very simplicity of the words caused Miss Nightingale to look at her young visitor with new respect. She noticed then the quiet determination in her eyes, the almost obstinate tilt of her head. 'Tell me about yourself,' she said, with interest. 'Where do you come from, and what nursing experience have you had?'

So Elizabeth told her all there was to tell starting with Lucy's long illness. And as she talked a warmth crept into her voice; all her nervousness vanished. At long last she was talking to someone who really understood.

'And what do your parents think of this latest idea?' asked Miss Nightingale, when the girl had finished.

Elizabeth flushed. 'They—they are not enthusiastic,' she had to admit. Then added, truthfully: 'Except in one respect, Ma'am. They hope I may hear news of my brother, who has been fighting in the Crimea for many weeks now, and from whom they have heard nothing.'

'I see,' said Miss Nightingale slowly. But she still hesitated. She had made up her mind that only the strongest, most capable, most unsentimental nurses should accompany her on her arduous mission, and this girl, for all her fine qualities, was very young, very small too. How would she stand up to the dreadful conditions prevailing at Scutari?

As though reading her thoughts, Elizabeth stood up.

'I'm sorry to have troubled you, Ma'am,' she said, with great dignity for one so young. She began moving towards the door.

171

And suddenly Miss Nightingale saw another girl, a girl very much like this one—well-brought-up, dedicated, fighting for the right to follow her chosen career: the girl she herself had once been . . .

'Wait,' she commanded. 'Please wait, Miss Fairfax. Do you know, I believe what you said earlier is true. I really think I may find you of some use.'

And so it came about that Elizabeth's wish came true. A few days later, in October 1854, she said goodbye to her parents and sisters, and the staff of the hopital where she had worked, and started the long journey to Scutari. There were thirty-seven other nurses in the party, of whom eighteen were nuns, some Anglican, some Roman Catholics. At first Elizabeth was very excited. It was the first time she had crossed the sea, and when they reached Boulogne the fisher-folk gave them a wonderful welcome—it seemed they knew all about Miss Nightingale's mission! But after that the journey became tedious and tiring beyond belief. In fact it was almost a nightmare. It took them two whole weeks to reach the military hospital at Scutari, and the last part of the journey was by rowing-boat. How glad they all were when they at last saw the big hospital loom up before them! It was a square yellow building, with a courtyard in the middle and a tower at each corner.

But once they set foot inside, their hearts sank. It was, if possible, even worse than they had been led to believe. Even Elizabeth, for all her zeal and determination, was horrified. There were no beds in the wards. The wounded men lay on palliasses, which were rough canvas bags filled with straw, and there were not even sufficient of these to go round. There were no blankets or sheets, not even bandages, and the whole place was filthy and alive with insects. No wonder the patients looked as if all hope had gone. They lay there in their blood-stained uniforms, with no nurses except a few old Chelsea pensioners, who shuffled around in a pathetic attempt to help.

But, shocked and disgusted though everyone was, Miss Nightingale did not waste time on idle words. In a strange way it was almost as though she enjoyed the challenge, for, despite her weariness after the long journey, she immediately began to get everyone organised. She issued orders in a firm, clear voice, and made everyone else as eager to put things right as she was herself.

'First,' said Miss Nightingale, 'we must set to work and make extra palliasses so that every patient has a mattress to lie on. Then we must scrub out every ward.'

And so they set to work, and not a moment too soon, because the very day after they arrived the battle of Inkerman was fought, and still more wounded men were brought in.

As the nurses passed amongst them it was wonderful to see the pleasure light up the men's faces. The nuns, of course, wore their usual habits, but the other nurses wore little caps and long dark gowns and each had a scarf with SCUTARI embroidered on it tied across her chest. It was not an attractive uniform, but to the men they seemed like angels.

The doctors, however, were not at all pleased or grateful, nor were the army authorities. They resented the coming of the nurses and looked upon their help as interference. Some of them would not even admit that there was anything wrong with the hospital. They were rude and sarcastic, especially about Miss Nightingale, and Elizabeth felt hurt and angry when she overheard their spiteful remarks. How cruel they were, how unfair! But she was too busy to brood over the injustice of the situation. They all worked each day from dawn till dusk, had very poor food, and lived in cold, miserable quarters without any comfort at all.

But gradually, very gradually, things improved. The wards became cleaner, brighter places, bandages were procured, the men were washed and cared for properly, and even the food grew more appetizing. And as the atmosphere in the hospital became happier, more cheerful, so fewer men died.

Elizabeth, the smallest and the youngest of the nurses, was a great favourite with the men. As she hurried to and fro along the wards she must have reminded many of them of a little sister, or perhaps a sweetheart, back home in England. The gentle nuns were a little remote, and some of the older women, despite their good nature, rather rough and uncouth, but in Elizabeth the men found a youthful sweetness and gravity which touched them and won their affection.

But never, for one moment, did she win the love and esteem which was accorded to Florence Nightingale. Because, for all her insistence on discipline, order, and obedience, the men openly adored her. They knew full well that but for her many of them would be in their graves, and they made no secret of their admiration. As for Florence, she in turn respected them. Many a time she was heard to comment on their bravery, their quiet heroism.

Every evening, when all the patients were settled down for the night, Florence would take her lamp and tour the wards. That was how she came to be known as The Lady with the Lamp. It was said that many a man, lying awake in the darkness, would try to kiss her shadow on the wall as she passed by, and an American poet called Longfellow wrote a poem about her which became very popular indeed.

'Lo, in that house of misery
A Lady with a Lamp I see
Pass through the glimmering gloom
And flit from room to room.
And slow, as in a dream of bliss,
The speechless sufferer turns to kiss
Her shadow, as it falls
Upon the darkening walls . . .'

Despite the satisfaction which her work brought her, Elizabeth was sadly disappointed at not hearing any news of her brother. Many a time she made enquiries of the men who were brought in, but no one had any tidings of a Captain Fairfax. Slowly hope died within her. So many young men had fallen on the battlefield, many more had been taken prisoner; while others, sick and wounded, had not survived the Black Sea crossing to reach the hospital.

And, as her last hopes for Robin faded, so a dreadful tiredness came over Elizabeth. She was, after all, very young, and the long hours and strenuous work had overtaxed her strength. There was little or no relaxation—how *could* she ever relax when there was so much to be done on all sides? And then home-sickness crept in. She began to lie awake at night, weary though she was, thinking with a terrible longing of her home and family. It all seemed so very far away . . . The old red house in the hollow, with its circling pigeons, its leaping log fires, its candlelight, and warm friendly atmosphere . . . Mama, so correct, but always so sweet and gracious in her hooped gown; and Papa, bearded and rather stern to look at, but so kind and jolly when he romped with his young daughters . . . And dear Mary Anne and Charlotte! They would be stitching samplers this wintry weather, and going for walks with Miss Russell in their high-button boots, little hands folded inside fur muffs.

Elizabeth had never loved them all so much before, or wanted them quite so badly. Suddenly she felt as if she could not bear to stay at Scutari for one more day . . .

Dejectedly, she sought an interview with Miss Nightingale.

'If you please, Ma'am,' she said in a flat little voice, 'I wish to be sent home.'

Miss Nightingale stared at her in disbelief.

'*What* did you say, Elizabeth?'

'I wish to go home, Ma'am.' Elizabeth could not meet her

eyes. 'Several other nurses have gone home,' she added, with a slight touch of defiance.

'*They* were unsuitable,' said Florence Nightingale. 'But you, Elizabeth . . . I did not expect this from you!'

'I'm sorry, Ma'am.' Elizabeth lifted her head now, and her eyes were full of pleading. 'It's just that I'm so tired . . .'

'Bless you, child, so am I!' Miss Nightingale laid a gentle hand on the girl's shoulder. 'We're all tired, almost beyond endurance. But we can't give way to it—there just isn't time! Why, we've been warned to expect another batch of patients at any moment—a bunch of men, sick and starved and well-nigh dead, who managed to escape from a Russian prison camp!'

Elizabeth shook off her weariness. She busied herself with making new palliasses, thinking only of those grey-faced men who would be arriving at any minute. Miss Nightingale was in the kitchen, ordering a special broth to be made for them— they would be too weak to take ordinary invalid food, she said. And then the pathetic little party arrived, young men with old faces and eyes sunk into their heads from sheer despair.

And among them was Captain Fairfax . . .

'Oh, Robin! Robin! My dear old Robin!'

At first he did not know her. He lay there, so deep in apathy that her words failed to reach him. How little remained of that laughing, impudent boy who had once climbed trees on Vicarage Hill! Oh Robin, thought Elizabeth, cradling his head in her arm, you didn't bargain for anything like this when you dreamed of swashbuckling adventures . . .

Then the hot broth was brought in, and this time Captain Fairfax showed a spark of interest.

Very gently Elizabeth raised the cup to his lips, and to her joy he managed to take a little. The glazed look left his eyes. He stared at her, first in astonishment, then in such delight that tears began to roll unheeded down Elizabeth's cheeks.

'Lizzie!' he whispered. 'Lizzie, is it really you?'

But Elizabeth's happiness was short-lived. After that moment of recognition Robin seemed to retreat from her, into a vague, shadowy world in which she had no part. All day long he lay there, tossing and turning restlessly, unable to sleep. Now and then he moaned and muttered to himself, as though his spirit were trapped in some terrible nightmare from which he could not escape. And Elizabeth was frightened, more frightened than she had ever been in her whole life.

'Oh, Miss Nightingale,' she cried, 'we *will* be able to save him, won't we? It would be too cruel if he were to die now . . .'

'We will do all that is humanly possible,' Florence assured her. Her voice was full of compassion. 'If only he could sleep . . . A good, sound sleep would make all the difference in the world to him.'

Elizabeth prayed silently all that day as she went about her duties. Surely God had not restored her brother to her only to snatch him away again? She thought of Mama and Papa, far away in England, waiting with heavy hearts for news of their only son. And of Mary Anne and little Charlotte, who adored their big handsome brother.

The day dragged by, and there was scarcely any change in Robin. He still tossed and turned in delirium. As for Elizabeth, she was almost sick with uncertainty and dread. How would she ever get through the night, she wondered? All those long hours of darkness and suspense . . .

And then, after supper, an unusual and rather wonderful thing happened.

'Will you take my lamp, Elizabeth,' said Miss Nightingale, in a matter-of-fact tone, 'and walk through the wards for me tonight? Just to make sure that all is well. There is a young drummer-boy I must watch over. I fear he will not last the night . . .'

'Lizzie!' he whispered. 'Is it really you?'

So Elizabeth took the lamp. Despite her anxiety she could not help feeling proud as she went up and down the long wards. This lamp, she sensed, was a symbol of all Florence Nightingale stood for, comfort and kindness and gentleness and courage, and an unswerving devotion to duty. Perhaps deep down, she knew even then that the light from it would go on shining far into the future . . .

Many of the men were sleeping, but those who were unable to sleep, who tossed restlessly on their rough mattresses, managed to smile at the little figure, so solemn and demure in her long dark dress and little cap. But under the calm exterior Elizabeth was in a torment of anxiety. Slowly, her heart thumping wildly, she approached the palliasse where her brother lay.

How still, he was! There was scarcely any movement now, under the rough blankets. A prayer on her lips, Elizabeth bent over him.

And then, by the soft, pale light of the lamp she saw that he was sleeping peacefully, that there was a faint colour in his cheeks. 'He's going to get well!' she thought, and her heart sang with joy. Unable to help herself, and to the astonishment of the young officer on the opposite bed, she knelt and kissed her brother on the forehead. Then, gathering up her skirts and raising the lamp aloft, she carried on, serenely, happily down the ward.

Highland Escape

by Judy Thomas

'Rhona! Rhona! Where are you, lass?'

As the urgent shout came echoing across the hillside, Rhona Ross sat up quickly.

All the morning she had been tending her father's few sheep, and she had just finished her frugal mid-day meal. How wonderful it had been to lie back against the warm heather then—in fact, she had almost been lulled to sleep.

But who was it who now called to her with such compulsion? What had happened to disturb the peace of Tannock Isle?

As Rhona came to her feet she saw the dishevelled figure of a man suddenly appear among the rocks above her.

The moment he caught sight of her he waved, and then he was bounding over the rocks towards her.

With what speed he moved! For this was Wild Geordie. It was said on Tannock Isle that even the swiftest deer was no swifter than he was.

A look of apprehension came into Rhona's eyes.

'Wild Geordie!' she murmured. 'Why should he seek me out in such haste?'

She had known Wild Geordie all her life, and always she had mistrusted him, for she knew him to be both clever and unscrupulous.

Many a time she had seen him smile when all the time his eyes had been as cold as ice itself.

Wild Geordie jumped to a stop in front of her, and for a second or two then he was so breathless that speech was beyond him.

'What is it, Geordie?' Rhona demanded. 'Why do you look so alarmed?'

In answer he turned to point beyond the hilltop.

'The Englishmen have come to Tannock Isle,' he gasped. 'Even now Redcoat soldiers are landing on the beach.'

It was the last thing in the world Rhona had expected to hear.

'English Redcoats on—on Tannock Isle?' she exclaimed, in great bewilderment. 'But—but why should English soldiers come here?'

Wild Geordie frowned down at her impatiently.

'You waste time, lass!' he snapped. 'You father must be warned. Run you with all speed to the village and tell him that Redcoat soldiers have landed on Tannock. But look! See for yourself!'

Seizing Rhona's arm, he led her over the rocks and both of them crouched down on the edge of the cliff.

In front of Rhona now was a great expanse of sea. Looking down into the tiny bay, her eyes opened wide when she saw a large ship riding at anchor.

It was an English man-of-war!

More alarming still—on the beach were a number of red-coated soldiers, and a boat that had just left the ship was filled with them!

The Redcoats had indeed come to Tannock!

But why—why?

'Big Hugh—your father—must be warned at once,' Wild Geordie snapped. 'The whole island must be warned. Hurry, lass!'

Rhona pulled her tartan shawl closer about her head. Like the other inhabitants of this island off the west coast of Scotland, she knew that there was much trouble on the Mainland.

She had heard of the Scottish prince who had come from France, and how men had immediately christened him "Bonnie Prince Charlie".

She had heard stories of his triumphant entry into Edinburgh, and of how he had been crowned king.

Heard, too, of his march into England. That had not been so triumphant.

For it was only a very short while ago that one or two islanders who had left to join Bonnie Prince Charlie had returned to Tannock.

They spoke of a terrible defeat at Culloden, and of how the young Scottish prince was a fugitive—hiding in remote districts where the heather was thickest.

It was said that there were Redcoats in every glen, and that the enormous sum of thirty thousand pounds had been placed upon the head of the daring young prince.

But Tannock was so far away from the Mainland. Why should Redcoats come to such a small island?

And why was Wild Geordie so anxious that she should warn her father? Perhaps he thought they would bring trouble to Big Hugh Ross.

Rhona raced away, and not once did she think to glance behind her. Had she done so, she might have seen the look of triumph that spread over Wild Geordie's face.

She would have seen, too, that he stood bolt upright on the edge of the cliff and that he waved his arms as though signalling to someone on the beach below him.

'My plan succeeds well,' he muttered to himself. 'Soon it is I who will rule on Tannock Isle and not Big Hugh Ross.'

Rhona's heart was beating fast as she raced towards the village. She was remembering now how tired and worried her father—Big Hugh Ross—had been these last few days.

She knew that on two nights in succession he had secretly

left the village when everyone thought him soundly asleep.

Could it be that the coming of the Redcoats had some special significance to her father?

Rhona was out of breath when she came upon the huddle of stone-built cottages which made up the largest village on Tannock. To her relief she found her father at home. He looked at her in the greatest surprise.

'What brings you home so early, lass?' he demanded.

'Wild Geordie sent me to you!' Rhona gasped. 'There is a big ship in the bay and it has brought many English Redcoats to Tannock. I've seen them with my own eyes.'

Her father's face changed in a flash. Deep lines of anxiety appeared on his brow.

'Then all is lost!' he gasped. 'Nothing can save him now, lass——'

Rhona's face mirrored his own anxiety—and surprise, too. Him?

'Of whom do you speak, father?' she asked quietly. 'Who is it that must be saved——'

He interrupted her, looking at her closely.

'You are the only one who can leave the village in safety now, Rhona,' he said. 'No one is likely to suspect a girl. You must help him! If inquiries are made about you, I can truthfully say it is your work to tend my sheep down in the glen.'

He caught her arm.

'There is no time for explanations, Rhona,' he went on quickly. 'I only have time to give you instructions. You are one of the few people on Tannock who know the way to Eagle's Cave and who also know its secret. It is to Eagle's Cave that you must go now.'

His voice dropped to a whisper.

'When you reach the cave you will find a young man hiding there,' he went on. 'He is one who sought my protection some few days ago.'

184

Rhona's eyes widened incredulously and he nodded gravely in confirmation.

'You will tell him that you have come from me and are to lead him to Stormpoint Cove, because the Redcoats have come to Tannock Isle,' he instructed. 'At the cove your Uncle Fergus will be waiting in secret with a boat.'

Suddenly Big Hugh's face became a little less anxious.

'Everything fits,' he said. 'Should the Redcoats inquire about you, I will tell them that you have gone on a visit to your Uncle Fergus at Stormpoint. By the time the Redcoats get to Stormpoint the man we have befriended will be far out to sea.'

Rhona was led to the doorway of the cottage.

'There are no signs of the Redcoats yet,' Big Hugh said. 'You should get to the Eagle's Cave without being seen.'

'Your message shall be delivered, father,' Rhona said, with quiet loyalty. 'I will make quite sure of that.'

His arm went about her shoulders.

'Every blessing go with ye, little lass,' he said.

Then Rhona started to run again, with her tartan shawl pulled closely about her head. And as she ran she pondered her father's words.

Who could the young man be who waited for her up in the Eagle's Cave? But it would not be long before she knew.

She made her way towards the glen beyond the village. Then, as she reached it, she turned her head to see if anyone was following her. No one was in sight. But Rhona knew she must be sure.

She lay flat among the heather and crawled forward until she was peering down the whole length of the glen.

Immediately her heart leapt into her mouth.

For someone was moving amongst the heather—a wild, dishevelled figure who ran in a quick, loping way. Even at a distance Rhona recognised Wild Geordie.

And suddenly, far beyond Wild Geordie, Rhona caught a glimpse of something that drove all the colour from her face. It was the gleam of a Redcoat!

Rhona remembered again how she had always distrusted Wild Geordie. He had only recently returned to Tannock after a long absence, when he had lived on the Scottish Mainland.

It was said he had even spent some months in England.

All at once Rhona saw Wild Geordie's trickery.

Wild Geordie must have had some knowledge of her father's secret. He had had a purpose in sending her to warn Big Hugh Ross about the coming of the Redcoats.

He had probably guessed that Big Hugh would immediately send out a messenger, and Wild Geordie had evidently decided to follow after that messenger, with the Redcoats.

Suddenly Rhona's heart was racing and her eyes were bright with a new excitement.

If the Redcoats wanted the man in the cave, he must be someone of great importance!

The young man in the cave must be none other than Bonnie Prince Charlie himself!

'Bonnie Prince Charlie!'

Rhona spoke the words in a hushed whisper. How often during the last year or so she had heard her father and the islanders talk of the young prince who had come from France to be Scotland's rightful king!

So Bonnie Prince Charlie had come to Tannock! And only she, a mere girl, could help her prince now.

Despite Wild Geordie, she would still find a way to warn him. But if she took the usual path she would never shake off her followers.

'The marsh,' Rhona told herself quickly. 'I must cross the marsh now.'

Suddenly she was full of confidence. She was her father's

messenger and her father's message must be delivered. Wild Geordie should discover she was not an easy one to trick.

'It is Wild Geordie who will soon be in trouble,' she told herself. 'He has wasted his time in following after me.'

She went racing on then and not once did she turn her head.

And presently she came to a wide expanse of brilliant green turf—turf that was of far too bright a green.

For that green turf marked the dreaded Marsh of Tannock!

Stretching across the verdant expanse was the twisting line of white-painted sticks Rhona had seen so often.

They were set at very wide intervals, and the only safe way to cross the marsh was to keep in a dead straight line with every stick.

Tentatively Rhona stretched out her foot and began to walk across. Presently the green turf was all about her and she felt her bare feet sink to the ankles.

But directly ahead of her was the first of the white sticks. Coming to it she deliberately pulled it up and, running forward now, she took the stick with her.

Straight to the next stick she ran, and this one she also pulled up.

'Wild Geordie will never follow after me now,' she told herself. 'He'll not dare to cross the marsh with the guidesticks missing.'

Satisfied that her plan would succeed, she ran on. Only when she had reached solid ground on the other side did she throw down her bundle of white sticks.

She told herself that no one would cross Tannock Marsh again until the sticks were replaced.

With the afternoon sun slowly sinking towards the west, Rhona turned towards the hills. She was convinced that there was no longer any danger, but she still took advantage of all the cover she could find.

Finally she was scrambling along a narrow rocky ledge.

Suddenly it turned abruptly, and there, in front of her, was the dark opening of a cave.

'I'm the daughter of Big Hugh Ross,' she called, and her voice echoed hollowly inside the cave. 'I bring a message from my father.'

Only then did someone move; a young man in a ragged tartan kilt slowly emerged into the daylight.

His jacket was torn and frayed, yet he held himself with such dignity that one might almost have imagined he was dressed in rich garments.

Quietly the young man spoke.

'Greetings, little maid,' he said, and his voice was proud and cultured. 'But Big Hugh should know that I do not let any lady endanger her life on my behalf.'

Rhona could scarcely take her eyes from that tanned, handsome face. This young man indeed held himself like a prince.

Rhona was quite sure that this was the prince who had won all Scottish hearts—Bonnie Prince Charlie!

Rhona's eyes were wide and star-like. She made a low curtsey.

'Your—your Highness—sire—there is no danger for me,' she faltered, for she did not know how to adress the young man who had been crowned Kind of Scotland. 'But there is danger for you. There are Redcoats on Tannock!'

Quickly she told him all that had happened that day. And her heart saddened as she saw how tired and weary he looked.

'I would not bring trouble upon the good people of Tannock,' he said slowly. 'Rather would I give myself up——'

'No, no!' Rhona cried, 'for you are our own rightful Scottish prince. I know the secret path to Stormpoint Cove and there my uncle is waiting for you.'

All at once he was smiling at her.

'You are indeed your father's true daughter,' he said.

But with startling suddenness he broke off and Rhona watched in alarm the way his eyes darkened and his hand flashed inside his frayed pocket.

Then her own hand flew to her mouth. For the figure of Wild Geordie was standing in the cave opening!

In spite of her precautions he had found his way here!

Suddenly Wild Geordie placed two fingers to his mouth and he gave a shrill whistle that went ringing down the hillside.

Rhona knew then that, in all certainty, there must be Redcoats close behind him.

Were They Trapped?

Rhona listened in alarm as Wild Geordie's shrill whistle echoed and re-echoed through the cave.

Outside, its echo was picked up by the rocky crags and tossed to and fro like a shuttlecock.

'He is sending a signal to the English soldiers,' breathed Rhona. 'We are trapped!'

Suddenly her view of Wild Geordie was cut off as Bonnie Prince Charlie stepped in front of her. Despite the gloom inside the cave, she caught the gleam of steel as he plucked a dagger from beneath his travel-stained tunic.

In that moment Rhona suddenly lost all her fear of Wild Geordie. All fear of the Redcoats vanished as well.

It was Scotland's rightful king who was standing protectingly in front of her.

For one long moment then the Royal fugitive and Wild Geordie stood staring one at the other. And Rhona couldn't help but wonder that a man born and bred on Tannock Isle could act like this.

For the sake of English money Wild Geordie was prepared to sacrifice his rightful king!

But her heart was hammering.

Another second now and the cave might be full of Redcoats.

But suddenly Wild Geordie whirled on his heel. He gave one last yell of triumph and then he rushed away from the cave mouth.

Rhona's senses whirled. Wild Geordie must have been alone after all. The soldiers were not here yet.

Quickly the prince turned. There was worry on his fine features as he looked at Rhona.

'This may mean danger for you,' he said quietly. 'That is the last thing I would wish——'

'Sire, the soldiers would not harm me,' Rhona said quickly. 'I will look outside the cave and see where they are.'

She jumped away from him before he could protest and went to the mouth of the cave.

There was no one to be seen on the narrow ledge outside, and, despite the sharp command of Prince Charlie, Rhona ventured along the ledge to the corner.

She saw Wild Geordie far ahead of her, racing along the narrow path, and Rhona breathed her relief. Then there was no immediate danger to be anticipated from the English soldiers.

It would be some considerable time yet before they followed Wild Geordie back up that narrow ledge.

Breathlessly she returned to the cave.

'Wild Geordie was all alone,' she gasped. 'The Redcoats must have feared the climb—they must be waiting for him in the glen below.'

Suddenly her eyes were full of confidence.

'Do you know the secret of Eagle's Cave, sire?' she asked quickly. 'Because of it we shall be far on our journey before Wild Geordie can return with the Redcoats.'

'I know the secret, little Rhona,' he said. 'It was the first thing your father pointed out to me when he brought me here.'

Rhona thrilled at the sound of her name. Never in her wildest dreams had she ever imagined that one day a monarch of Scotland would call her by her Christian name!

Once again Bonnie Prince Charlie was smiling.

'There's something that must be settled between us,' he said, 'before we set out to Stormpoint Cove. We shall be on our way before the sun sets, and it may be we shall be stopped on the road and questioned.'

He smiled wryly.

'When I landed on this island I had become used to calling myself Charlie Tamson—Charlie Tamson I must remain. If we are met and questioned, you must say you have met me upon the road by accident. You are on your way to Stormpoint Cove to visit your uncle and you are only showing me the way because that is the place to which I asked to be directed.'

Suddenly he took both of her hands in his own.

'So,' he said, 'I am no longer your Prince Charlie. From this moment I am poor, ragged Charlie Tamson. And because we are to be companions of the road you must learn to call me "Charlie".'

Rhona's cheeks flushed. He actually admitted he was Prince Charlie! But how—how could she possibly call her prince by his Christian name?

Everything in her rebelled against the idea. The clan spirit was strong within her, and she would not dare to call her own clan chieftain by his first name.

Yet Bonnie Prince Charlie was a thousand times more removed above her than any clan chieftain.

'I—I can't sire,' she faltered, and her cheeks were burning. 'My—my tongue wouldn't be able to say the words——'

Suddenly his cheery laughter filled the cave and all in a flash Rhona saw him as she knew he must have appeared during those wonderful weeks when he was being fêted in Edinburgh.

No wonder the Scots had been so quick to christen him 'Bonnie Prince Charlie!'

'I am your prince, little Rhona,' he said gently, 'and my slightest wish must be your command. And my wish is that you learn to call me Charlie. Do you say the word now.'

Never in all her life before had Rhona attempted a task so difficult. Twice the word choked in her throat.

'Ch—Charlie!' she managed at last.

Again he laughed boyishly, and he shook his head.

'That will never do,' he objected. 'Far better that you call me "sire" than to call me by my name in such a way. I pray that you think of me as being your true friend—one you have known all your life. To please me, you must try again.'

Rhona bit her lip. She remembered that time was pressing. By now Wild Geordie would be signalling to the Redcoats. Perhaps they were already climbing towards the cave.

And there was something about the smile on the prince's face that brought an answering smile to her own eyes.

'Charlie!' she said, and this time she said the word naturally.

Then she was suddenly very serious indeed.

'Let us delay no longer,' she urged. 'I shan't consider we're safe until we're out of the cave.'

The laughter faded from Prince Charlie's eyes.

'It is later on that we must fear danger,' he said. 'When the Redcoats arrive outside the cave they will probably content themselves for a long time by firing volleys of shot into it.'

He took her by the hand.

'Come, little cousin,' he said.

Hand-in-hand they walked slowly into the utter darkness at the rear of the cave.

It was Rhona's outstretched hand which first touched the rock wall.

'Here are the steps,' she whispered. 'Do you please continue to hold my hand, sire.'

The secret of the Eagle's Cave had been known to the Ross family for generations. No one knew who had originally cut those steps which led steeply up to the rocky ground high above the cave, but Rhona was very glad of them now.

'Do not worry,' Prince Charlie said. 'In order to make perfectly sure of the way of escape, three times already have I climbed these steep steps.'

The two of them climbed up and up through the chimney-like structure, stumbling sometimes in the darkness.

Presently a tiny square of light showed high above their heads. They continued to climb, and soon it was quite easy for them to see the hole, overgrown with grasses and weeds, which would enable them to reach the open again.

Finally, breathless with exertion, they climbed out to a high rock plateau far above the entrance to the Eagle's Cave.

Bonnie Prince Charlie turned to smile at Rhona.

'You are a lass after my own heart,' he said. 'Few grown men would have climbed that narrow chimney as quickly as you did.'

Rhona felt herself flush with pleasure.

'Before we depart,' the prince went on, 'I would fain see what is happening outside the cave.'

He went striding forward and suddenly Rhona realised the danger he was walking into.

If he stood on the edge of the plateau he would make a perfect target against the skyline and perhaps a musket shot from below might reach him!

But, just as she was about to shout a warning, Bonnie Prince Charlie went down on his hands and knees. Lying flat, he peered over the edge.

After a few moments he turned and beckoned to Rhona. She crawled forward just as the prince had done, and soon they were lying side by side.

They looked down at the cave opening below. Once again

she heard his boyish, carefree chuckle, which delighted her.

'It is just as I said it would be,' he commented. 'See, little Rhona, they are about to fire now.'

Rhona's eyes widened as she saw the circle of Redcoats crouched behind protective boulders some little distance away from the mouth of the cave. Suddenly there was a flash of flame and then the sound of musket shots came to her.

The Redcoats were indeed firing into the cave.

The two lay still and watched until half a dozen volleys had been fired. It was then, for the first time, that Rhona caught sight of Wild Geordie.

He had been lying on the extreme right of the soldiers and now she saw that he was creeping away.

Was Wild Geordie going so that he should not be seen and afterwards be denounced?

Was he stealing away so that the islanders should never learn that he was the man who had betrayed their prince to his enemies?

But suddenly Rhona's heart was beating suffocatingly. Instead of continuing along the narrow path, Wild Geordie had started to climb the rock-face far to the right of the cave.

He was coming towards them!

'Wild Geordie must suspect that there is another way out of the cave,' she whispered quickly to her prince. 'Perhaps he has heard rumours of the secret of Eagle's Cave. See where he climbs the cliff-face now. If he succeeds in climbing to this spot, he'll see the opening behind us and know that we've escaped. He'll come hurrying after us.'

'Then we must leave at once,' Prince Charlie said, frowning. 'It is my fault that we have tarried so long.'

Again Rhona led the way across the uneven rocky ground, crouching low so that they should not be seen.

The sun was close to the edge of the distant sea when they came to a long, winding glen.

'We must cross the burn before dark, sire—I—I mean Charlie,' Rhona faltered. 'It will be hard to find the beginning of the secret way to Stormpoint if it is dark.'

Bonnie Prince Charlie nodded in agreement. It was good to feel the soft heather under her bare feet as she trudged along, Rhona thought. Several times she glanced behind her, but she saw no sign of any following figure.

Had Wild Geordie succeeded in climbing the rock-face—had he found the opening above the cave? If so, he must already be following after them.

They walked out of the glen, and beyond it they came to one of the few island roads. They breasted a slight slope, and there, some little distance in front of them, was the burn.

It had always been a fast-moving river, but now it was more like a raging torrent.

The spring sun had melted the snow on the hills and all the water was tumbling down into the burn.

But it was not the sight of the river that made Rhona's eyes become wide with alarm. Another, far greater problem had presented itself.

There, on the bridge that spanned the burn, was a group of Redcoats!

They had evidently tried to drive a wagon across the bridge and it had come to grief. One now lay on its side, half in and half out of the burn.

There were Redcoats in front, and, perhaps only a short distance behind, Wild Geordie was running to spread the alarm!

With a start of dismay, Rhona realised that her prince was trapped.

She turned to him in despair.

'Sire,' she blurted, 'the only way to Stormpoint Cove is across that bridge, but how dare we cross it with the Redcoats there?'

In Uncle Fergus' Cottage

With fear clutching at her heart Rhona stood there.

Any moment she expected to see the running figure of Wild Geordie—to hear the shout that would warn the Redcoats at the burn.

But one realisation above all smote her. Instead of leading him to safety, perhaps she had only led her prince to his captivity.

'We must not stay here,' she gasped, suddenly recovering. 'Any moment we may be seen!'

Almost simultaneously the two ran a few yards, crouching into a heather-filled hollow at the roadside, which had caught their notice.

They had not been seen, they realised, but the hollow was no hiding-place if Wild Geordie came running along the road behind them.

As they crouched there Rhona's mind was working at top speed. Every moment that Bonnie Prince Charlie remained upon Tannock Island spelled danger for him.

'We must go forward, sire—Charlie,' she breathed. 'If we wait until tomorrow the Redcoats will probably be at Stormpoint Cove. Our only hope is to get to Uncle Fergus tonight.'

He turned and looked at her.

'I've learned to know these English soldiers, little cousin,' he stated. 'If they fail to right that wagon tonight they will not leave it—men will be left on guard over it all through the night. But there is a way——'

Rhona gave him a quick glance. What was coming now?

Ever since Bonnie Prince Charlie's arrival in Scotland with only a handful of men beside him she had heard stories of his reckless courage.

'What way, sire?' Rhona whispered. Even now she found it difficult to utter his Christian name. 'I would take any risk.'

Suddenly his eyes gleamed with excitement and courage.

'Suppose we go forward?' Prince Charlie said. 'We look like ordinary Highland folk, and perhaps they will let us cross the bridge without question. After all, no Redcoat would dream that Bonnie Prince Charlie would ever walk up to him.'

For a moment Rhona gasped at the boldness of such a venture. Then she considered.

'You speak truly, sire,' she said. 'We will say that you are my fisherman cousin, Charlie Tamson. What English soldier would suspect a fisherman?'

She saw him gaze long and hard at the distant bridge, where the Redcoats were grouped, trying to haul their wagon out of the water.

'Maybe I can do more than just pass them by,' he went on, and again there was a chuckle in his voice.

Suddenly he was on his feet and holding out his hand.

'Come, litttle cousin,' he said. 'We will face those Redcoats unafraid.'

And so, together, Rhona and Prince Charlie walked down the narrow road. Rhona kept her head high, though her heart was beating wildly.

But there was something about her companion that was very reassuring. As he walked forward, slouching a little, he was whistling softly to himself, just as though he were but a ragged island youth without a care in the world.

They were almost up to the bridge before they were seen. Suddenly a perspiring sergeant, who had been hauling upon one of the ropes attached to the overturned wagon, turned.

'Halt, there!' he shouted.

He came striding up to stare suspiciously at them.

'What are you doing on this lonely road?' the sergeant demanded. 'Who are you?'

Prince Charlie touched his tam-o'-shanter, and he spoke

with a broad accent that was both charming and authentic.

'I am Charlie Tamson, of Tannock,' he answered. 'All folks know Charlie Tamson, the fisherman. This lassie is ma wee cousin.'

The sergeant's suspicions seemed to increase.

'A fisherman,' he scoffed. 'You haven't the hands of a fisherman!'

Rhona caught her breath, but Prince Charlie smiled in rather a boastful way.

'Yet these hands could shift yon wagon,' he said. 'Why have ye no' sent a man into the burn to place his shoulders underneath the wagon's side?'

The sergeant gave him an angry glance, and there was still suspicion in it.

'I can't order a man to risk his life in that raging torrent,' he snapped. 'But if you're the strong fisherman you say you are—which I doubt—why not shift the wagon yourself?'

Prince Charlie looked at him.

'If you make it worth my while I will go into the burn,' he said in a deceptively wheedling voice.

The sergeant laughed unbelievingly. Then his hand went into his pocket and he brought out a fistful of small coins.

'If you enter the stream,' he snapped, 'and if we right the wagon as a result, this money is yours.'

Prince Charlie grinned and touched his forehead politely. Then, with a half-smile at Rhona, he walked calmly to the edge of the torrent.

Rhona's heart was in her mouth as she saw him take hold of one of the wagon wheels and slowly lower himself into the stream. When he had established a firm foothold the bitterly cold water was right up to his armpits.

Rhona saw him squeeze underneath the wagon's side until the swelling waters were almost lapping against his chin.

'Heave you now!' he called to the sergeant.

198

The Prince was courting disaster — would the Redcoats guess his identity?

Once again the soldiers pulled upon the ropes and Rhona saw the great strain that came into the prince's face. Slowly the wagon began to come up out of the water until, with a lurch, it was back on its four wheels again.

'Bring up the horses,' yelled the sergeant. 'We can drag it clear now.'

It was the sergeant himself who reached out a helping hand to drag Prince Charlie from the grip of the burn!

Rhona could only look at him and marvel. He had performed a feat of strength that few of the islanders she knew could have equalled.

And as the prince stood there with the water dripping from him, the sergeant clapped him heartily on the back, all suspicion gone.

'You Scots are truly a tough race,' he said in grudging admiration. 'I promised you a reward and here it is.'

Prince Charlie took the coins and slid them into one of his tattered pockets.

Then he turned to Rhona beside him.

'Come, cousin,' he said, still with his broad accent. 'Unless we hurry it may be dark before we reach home.'

They crossed the bridge as two horses were being harnessed to the wagon. The soldiers were so busy that they took no further notice of the two.

'That was wonderful, sire!' Rhona breathed, her face aglow with admiration.

Now her only fear was that Wild Geordie might come dashing up to the bridge. If he had indeed followed them then he could not be very far away.

The moment they were out of sight she caught at Prince Charlie's arm.

'Let us hurry, sire,' she said. 'Wild Geordie may be following.'

He smiled down at her.

'There's nothing I desire more than to run, little Rhona,' he said. 'Only by running can I dry myself out of this damp cold. Come!'

So the two sped across the heather, trying to keep low and out of sight as much as possible.

Although darkness came down quickly, Rhona had no difficulty in finding the secret path to Stormpoint Cove.

Because of the darkness they could no longer hurry. Rhona knew how easy it would be to lose the path. If that happened they might wander about all night and never find it again.

Nothing could save them from the Redcoats then!

By this time the alarm must have been raised. Surely Wild Geordie must have reached the burn before dark.

How angry the English sergeant would be when he discovered he had let Bonnie Prince Charlie slip through his fingers.

He would be more anxious than anyone else now to capture the Royal fugitive.

Thus raced Rhona's thoughts.

If only Stormpoint Cove were not so far away!

But as they eventually approached the cove, Rhona felt conscious of a great sense of loss.

A few more minutes and she would be parting from her prince.

Yet she must do all she could to hasten his going. Only when a boat had carried him away from Tannock would her task be complete, and she could feel that he had a chance of getting safety back to France.

And now they were actually at Stormpoint Cove!

'I am here right on time,' Prince Charlie whispered. 'I must give the signal now.'

Next moment the penetrating cry of a sea-bird escaped his lips. It was a perfect imitation.

They waited, but the cove was strangely silent.

Several times the cry escaped the prince's lips. Yet the cove remained silent—no answering cry came to them out of the darkness.

Suddenly Rhona felt apprehensive.

'Something must have gone wrong,' Prince Charlie murmured.

He stood with his head thrust forward as though his eyes were trying to pierce through the dark blanket of the night.

'The boat was to be moored alongside the Black Pillar,' he said. 'Will you take me to it, little Rhona?'

Despite the darkness, Rhona led him confidently across the soft sand. They came to the Black Pillar—a lonely needle of rock that stood a yard or so out from the water's edge.

Rhona stared in surprise and alarm.

Her uncle's boat was not moored there!

'Perhaps Uncle Fergus sleeps,' Rhona suggested—a trace of hope still remained. 'Let me hurry to his cottage and——'

Her companion caught her arm as she half-turned away.

'It would not be wise to go to his cottage,' said Prince Charlie. 'The Redcoats may be waiting for us.'

Again he gave the cry of the sea-bird and still there was no answer. Rhona felt herself tremble just a little. Perhaps Redcoats, covered by the darkness, were already closing in on them.

And before many more hours it would be dawn!

'We must not stand here any longer,' Rhona cautioned. 'It would be best to go back to the glen and wait till dawn.'

And so they made their way back to the glen nearby. How slowly the hours till dawn dragged past. But at last the sky began to lighten in the East.

When the sun came up they were sheltered in the glen, which ran right down to the cove. Nothing moved and there was no sign of any boat upon the sea.

Rhona breathed her relief. Then the Redcoats had not yet

arrived at the glen. Her uncle's lonely cottage was in plain view now. Surely he must be home and asleep.

'Do you stay here,' she whispered to her companion. 'I will go to the cottage. Perhaps Uncle is there.'

'Take good care of yourself, little Rhona,' Prince Charlie said.

Rhona crawled a long way through the furrows between the patches of heather before she risked coming to her feet. Trying to show no sense of hurry, she went slowly towards the cottage.

Coming to the doorway and peering inside, Rhona saw that the cottage had been turned topsy-turvy, as though in a search. But of her uncle there was no sign.

Suddenly her eyes widened. In the hard-trodden earth before the open hearth she saw that a cross—the cross of St Andrew—hand been marked.

Her uncle must have made that sign—it was a warning to any islander who might enter that cottage that danger was close at hand.

Her uncle must have seen the coming of the Redcoats and had made his escape in time! Rhona was sure of it.

Going back to the doorway, she called to Prince Charlie.

He came striding through the heather towards her. He looked at the wrecked furniture and he bit his lip.

'No wonder your uncle failed to keep the rendezvous,' he said. 'Some time yesterday the Redcoats must have been here.'

Suddenly Rhona realised how tired she was. For twenty-four hours she had had no sleep. Now that they had entered the cottage unseen they were safe for the time being.

'But this is a place to hide for the moment,' Rhona said. 'The Redcoats will not come back yet awhile.'

She looked up at the low ceiling of the room.

'Would you lift me up to the ceiling, sire?' she asked.

She could not sustain the habit of calling her prince 'Charlie'.

He gazed at her in perplexity, and then his strong arms were about her and she was lifted as though she were no heavier than a feather.

She pressed her hands against the wooden ceiling and a square began to lift.

'This is a lonely glen,' Rhona explained, 'and sometimes smugglers come here. My uncle's father built this cottage and added a secret loft where he could hide whenever danger threatened. We shall be safe here.'

He helped her through the opening and then he reached up to grip the edge. Easily he swung himself up, to find that there was dry bracken there—bracken that was designed to serve as a bed.

The prince stood before her, smiling.

'Now, little Rhona,' he said, 'you are tired, and you must sleep. But I feel quite wide awake, so it is I who will prepare our meal.'

Rhona tried to protest. She could not let her own prince—Scotland's prince—wait upon her. But he laughed aside all her protests.

He cooked the simple meal in the cottage kitchen and then brought it up to Rhona.

Together they sat in the secret loft, eating hungrily.

But suddenly, to Rhona's alarm, she heard a sound outside the cottage. A few moments later and there were heavy footsteps of men on the stone floor below.

Next came a voice that struck fear to her heart.

It was the voice of Wild Geordie himself. A voice that rang with triumph.

'The birds have been here!' he exclaimed. 'They could have flown but a few moments ago. See—this pot in which oatmeal had been cooked is still warm. We've come to the end of our search at last.'

Escape by Sea

In that first moment Rhona almost gave the prince and herself up for lost.

Now that the Redcoats were in the glen they were surely trapped—sooner or later they must be discovered.

She trembled as she thought of Wild Geordie. Suppose he knew the secret of their hiding-place?

'No—that cannot be so,' she decided quickly, an instant later. 'Uncle Fergus would never trust a man like Wild Geordie with the secret of his cottage.'

But she couldn't take her eyes from the trapdoor in the centre of the loft floor. Would Wild Geordie discover it?

Prince Charlie's hand clasped her own firmly. Once again Rhona marvelled that he could sit so still and breathe so evenly when his enemies were within a few yards of him.

Rhona heard a sharp voice.

'They cannot have left the glen,' it exclaimed. 'If they're hiding amongst the heather, we shall find them. With luck we will soon be sharing thirty thousand golden coins amongst us.'

'Then why do we waste time?' another voice demanded. 'The sooner we capture the Stuart the sooner we leave this bleak island.'

There were the sounds of the men tramping out of the cottage and the door slamming behind them. Rhona listened for a moment or two more and then quietly she crawled to one side of the loft.

Her fingers fumbled at the stonework and she pressed a knob. A small square of stone slid out of its place.

'My uncle's spy-hole,' she whispered.

Prince Charlie was already at her side. Through the small opening they had a view of the glen and also of the small stretch of beach.

The Redcoats were spreading out in a long line across the glen to the right of the cottage, and Wild Geordie was with them.

Prince Charlie spoke then.

'We dare not tarry here longer, little Rhona,' he said. 'When the Redcoats fail to find us, they will return to the cottage and may discover our hiding-place——'

He stopped. Suddenly Rhona realised that something had excited him.

'Beyond that farther rock, the Black Pillar, Rhona!' he said quickly. 'Do I not see the bows of a small rowing-boat?'

Rhona had already seen one long-boat pulled far up on the beach—the one that had brought the Redcoats to the glen.

But the Black Pillar was much closer to her, and Rhona's eyes grew bright when she also saw the bows of a small boat.

''Tis my uncle's boat,' she gasped. 'Perhaps he is waiting for us after all—as he promised he would be!'

Prince Charlie stared again at the Redcoat soldiers.

'It was your uncle's task to row me to the Island of Rhos,' he said quietly. 'There several powerful chieftains await my coming and they have already made arrangements to get me to the island of Skye and then to France.'

'I've been to the Island of Rhos,' Rhona said. 'If you look out to sea, you can just see it, sire.'

There was a morning haze overhanging the sea so that the island was nothing more than a small smudge on the horizon.

The prince's voice was grim with determination.

'We must take a chance, little Rhona,' he said. 'We must leave the cottage now and try to get to your uncle's boat. The headland will hide us from the view of the Redcoats and, with luck, we shall get to sea without being seen.'

Prince Charlie carefully lifted the trapdoor and dropped down.

He reached up to swing Rhona down beside him, and for a moment both of them stood in the doorway, watching the Redcoats beating at the heather with swords and muskets.

'Come!' Prince Charlie said then.

They dodged behind the cottage and Rhona pointed.

'This path will lead us down the cliff to the boat,' she breathed.

They were almost at the edge of the cliff when Rhona pulled up. Her uncle's boat was in clear view now, but there was no sign of her uncle.

And Rhona knew then that there was something she must do.

'I must go back to the cottage, sire,' she gasped. 'My uncle may be in hiding close by, and I must leave a message in the cottage which will tell him that both of us are safe. Do you go down to the beach, sire, and make sure of the boat.'

Prince Charlie started to protest, but Rhona had hurried away.

Reaching the cottage, she crept round it with the greatst caution and, to her relief, she saw that the Redcoats had moved on much farther up the glen.

Entering the cottage, she took a stick and with it she drew a circle around the cross of St. Andrew that her uncle had marked on the floor in front of the fireplace.

Inside the circle she now marked the two letters 'R' and 'C'. If her uncle saw that circle and the two letters he would know that the prince and his niece had left Tannock Island.

Her work done, Rhona moved quickly to the doorway.

But suddenly, with a gasp of alarm, she pulled up and all colour fled from her face.

Someone had stepped forward to bar her way.

Heart beating madly, Rhona raised her eyes to the figure in front of her.

'I knew you weren't far away,' a voice exulted. 'I thought something might bring you back and I kept a watch over the cottage. So I've got my hands on you at last, Rhona Ross!'

And, with a triumphant grin, Wild Geordie gripped Rhona tightly by the arm.

'Where is the vagabond prince?' he demanded. 'Where is he hiding?'

Rhona tried to fight down her fear. She might have been captured, but Prince Chralie was still free. He might still have time to make good his escape.

'I don't know what you're talking about,' she managed to say. 'I —I came here to visit my uncle——'

He shook her.

'You waste your time, 'he snapped. 'Have I not followed you and the Stuart Prince across the island? For the last time—where is he hiding?'

Rhona's eyes remained steadfast.

'I cannot tell you,' she said.

She shivered a little at the angry look that came into his eyes. But then her heart leapt.

A figure came running around the cottage. A familiar figure!

'The Stuart himself!' Wild Geordie exclaimed in triumph, and he flung Rhona to one side.

Her eyes were wide with alarm. Why, oh why, had the prince returned for her? He had come unarmed, and now Wild Geordie was advancing with upflung claymore.

As though in a daze Rhona saw Prince Charlie leap to one side, and then for a moment she thought he had stumbled and that he was going to fall.

But when he straightened himself there was a length of wood in his hand and he flung it up to parry the stroke of the claymore.

Rhona saw the bright steel slide away from the stick, and then Prince Charlie had jumped forward to grip Wild Geordie's sword wrist.

Next moment the sword had fallen from Wild Geordie's fingers. At once the young prince had seized him and flung him with all his strength across the room.

Wild Geordie hit his head against the wall and slid, dazed, towards the ground.

'Are you all right?' Prince Charlie asked Rhona anxiously, turning. 'It came back to see what had kept you so long.'

Breathlessly, Rhona nodded.

'Then come,' said the prince. 'We have no time to waste.'

With her hand in that of the prince, Rhona raced at speed along the cliff path.

And suddenly, from behind them, she heard shouting.

Wild Geordie had recovered!

'To me! To me!' he was yelling. 'The Stuart is here!'

Down the steep incline of the cliff Rhona and the prince scrambled, and Rhona saw that her uncle's boat was already in the water!

As she clambered over the bows Prince Charlie pushed it into deeper water and came leaping aboard himself.

'Take you the tiller!' he gasped.

Once again Rhona marvelled at the prince's amazing strength as he grasped the oars and sent the boat shooting through the water.

They were beyond the bay before the Redcoats reached the sands. Turning her head, Rhona saw that the English soldiers were now angrily hauling upon their boat and dragging it down to the water.

The gesticulating figure of Wild Geordie was prominent among them.

Rhona looked out to sea, pale with anxiety. But then she saw there was a deepening haze, and at once her eyes grew relieved.

'They'll not find us now,' she said. 'An island fog is sweeping down upon us.'

Prince Charlie still rowed with might and main, but Rhona realised that unless they reached the fog-bank quickly the long-boat would catch up with them. In the long-boat there were many rowers.

Then, almost without warning, tiny wreaths of mist were about her. She caught one last glimpse of the long-boat and—there was nothing more to be seen.

They had reached the bank of fog in time!

Even so, it was a long time before Prince Charlie relaxed a little.

'We shall come safely to the Island of Rhos now,' he smiled. 'One might as well seek for a needle in a haystack as try to find a boat in this fog.'

Noon came and went, but the fog was as thick as ever. As time went on Rhona realised that the sun must be sinking towards the horizon.

She knew another fear now. Suppose she had not steered a straight course?

When the fog lifted they might find themselves far out at sea and beyond all sight of land.

In that case they might row aimlessly for days without sighting one of the islands!

Presently Rhona was conscious of a cold wind against her cheeks.

She saw open patches and, suddenly, the fog was lifting. It was still daylight, but the sun was beginning to set.

Then, as she stood up, Rhona's heart was thudding with relief. She had caught sight of a smudge to the east of her. It must be Rhos Island!

The fog had only just dispersed in time. Another few minutes and they would have missed Rhos Island.

'We have had luck,' Prince Charlie said. 'We may yet reach the island before dark.'

Once again he bent to the oars. Slowly but surely the island came nearer and nearer. It seemed as if the boat was moving with greater speed than ever before.

'It is a strong current that helps me,' Prince Charlie smiled at her.

Soon the island was towering in front of them.

Prince Charlie looked over his shoulder.

'Try to steer us between the two cliffs, little Rhona,' he advised. 'It is our only hope.'

The evening twilight was almost gone as they passed close to one of the headlands. Ahead of her Rhona saw how the waves were crashing upon a tiny stretch of beach.

Suddenly the boat was almost swamped by a great surge of foaming water. There was a sudden grinding sound and Rhona gasped in dismay.

It could only mean that a hole had been torn in the boat by a hidden rock!

But a wave picked up the boat and swept in, broadside on, against the stretch of beach. Rhona tumbled out, and was gripped by strong arms. She staggered on the wet sand, Prince Charlie beside her.

Then they scrambled up beyond the reach of the sea and Rhona saw that the waves were splintering the small boat to pieces.

Rhona and Prince Charlie looked about. How narrow had been their escape! This was a very tiny bay and they had the steep side of the cliff before them.

It would be very difficult to obtain a hand-hold or foot-hold on that sheer surface.

And, with a catch of her breath, Rhona saw something else.

The high-water mark was high up on the cliffs and soon the incoming tide would rush over the tiny beach and completely submerge it.

She looked at Prince Charlie and saw that he, too, was

staring at the frowning cliffs. Did he realise the danger?

If there were no way of climbing the cliff the sea would sweep in relentlessly upon them!

The Parting

'Unless we find a way to the top of the cliff we shall be over-whelmed by the tide!'

Rhona turned quickly as Bonnie Prince Charlie spoke.

He had realised their danger.

If they could not climb the cliff the sea would pick them up and sweep them out into the bay.

The strongest swimmer in the world would have no chance against the fierce currents that swept round Rhos Island.

'The tide will be in within two hours,' the prince went on. 'Long before that time I must reach the cliff top and find some way of getting help to you.'

Rhona looked towards the place where she had last seen the small, ruined boat.

There was no sign at all of it now, but here and there she saw a tossing plank that had once been part of the tiny craft.

Bonnie Prince Charlie was already in action, however. He walked slowly along the bottom of the cliff face and his eyes were studying every inch of the surface.

'This looks the likeliest place,' he said at last.

He turned to take both Rhona's hands.

'You have been so brave,' he said, 'that it pains me I have to test your courage further. But I shall not fail you. Wait here for me and I shall return.'

He gave her hands a reassuring squeeze and then he was scrambling upwards. Two or three yards he managed with ease before he had to search about for further hand-holds and foot-holds.

As Rhona watched, her concern for him was tinged with

admiration. He seemed very nimble and agile and the steep cliff appeared to present few difficulties.

He was moving quickly now and Rhona knew real hope. Soon he would be beyond the high-water mark. Once he reached the top she knew he would lose no time in running to the nearest habitation and obtaining help.

But then, just as he was climbing over the high-water mark, the prince appeared to lose his hold.

Rhona caught her breath in alarm. The prince's grasp had slipped and he was falling!

She stood then, pale-faced, completely helpless to do anything. But as he fell he managed to twist himself to one side. A moment later, his body struck a narrow ledge!

Rhoma, relieved, gazed upwards. She expected now to see him scramble back to his feet.

But he continued to lie on the ledge and he gave no sign of any movement!

She caught in her breath. What had happened? Was her prince injured? If so, it was up to her to try to find help.

A desperate light flashed into Rhona's eyes. Could she possibly climb the cliff?

But already her fingers were seeking hand-holds. She started from where the prince had started and slowly but surely she began to climb.

Then, when she was still two yards away from the ledge, Rhona knew that she could go no farther. Above her the rock was like polished glass. How Prince Charlie had managed she could not fathom. He must indeed be a wonderful climber.

But what to do? Could she rouse him?

'Sire! Sire!' she called. 'Sire!'

She tried to shift her grip and the fear came to her that she would go crashing down. Already she could feel her fingers going numb and the rock was cutting into her bare feet.

'Sire!' she called again, but still there was no reply.

She almost gave up hope. Surely nothing could save her. She was trapped—then she started. Something had slapped against the rock face only a few inches away.

For one second Rhona doubted the evidence of her eyes. A rope was dangling in front of her!

Then her fingers closed over it and the fell of the coarse fibre gave her a new feeling of security. For the moment she did not pause to wonder where it could have come from. Rescue was at hand.

And suddenly a movement above made her look up. Prince Charlie was carefully scrambling to his feet.

With his back planted firmly against the cliff wall he reached out, took hold of the rope and pulled her up towards him.

When she was standing on the ledge alongside him he knotted the rope about her waist.

'That rope means there are friends above, little Rhona,' he smiled. 'My coming was expected and a constant watch has been kept for me. Your cries were heard and it is fortunate that I recovered in time to aid you but a little, my brave Rhona.'

Rhona looked up at him. Her heart was thudding with relief at her incredible escape—but now she was staring in concern at Prince Charlie.

'But you're hurt!' she gasped.

He rubbed the back of his head and his smile became a little rueful.

'I was merely stunned by the fall,' he said. 'I am lucky it was no worse.'

He gave a shout then and he waved one arm. Instantly the rope grew tight about Rhona and a moment later she was swinging away from the cliff face.

Up and up she went and then welcoming hands at the top pulled her to safety.

Rhona's eyes glowed with gratitude as she stared at the two

roughly dressed island men who had helped her to safety.

They untied the rope and lowered it back over the cliff. Then they heaved on it to bring up the prince.

At long last he came scrambling over the edge. Disentangling himself from the rope, he pulled himself to his full height and looked at the two men who had saved his life.

'Your help came in the very nick of time,' he said. 'My deepest thanks to you.'

Both men went down upon one knee and bent their heads over the prince's outstretched hand.

'For days we've watched for your coming,' one of them said. 'It is our pride to serve you.'

The other nodded his head.

'We had to come slowly, by creeping through the heather,' he said. 'The Redcoats are all over the island and our every movement is watched.'

'What of the men who are gathered here to meet me?' the prince asked quietly. 'Where are they? Are they safe?'

The first speaker bowed.

'They await your coming with great anxiety, sire,' he said. 'We were told to give you the message that they await you at the Castle of Rhos.'

'Thank you,' replied Bonnie Prince Charlie. 'Then Rhona and I will haste now to the Castle of Rhos. There I can hold conference with my kinsmen—and my gallant Rhona will get the food and sleep she so badly needs.'

Now the prince gripped the hands of the two island men warmly.

'Return you now to your homes,' he said. 'The thanks of your prince go with you. But one more thing I ask of you——'

'Anything, sire, anything,' replied his loyal countrymen.

'That you have a boat ready in the morning,' he finished quietly. 'I wish you to row little Rhona back to Tannock Isle!'

Then, turning on his heel, the prince put his arm around Rhona's slim shoulders.

'Before very long, little cousin,' he said gently, 'you shall eat and sleep.'

And bidding farewell to the men who had saved their lives, the two went stumbling away over the heather towards the Castle of Rhos.

Its outline stood gauntly against the sky and Rhona knew that it must be a good three miles distant. How glad she was of the prince's strong arm to support her.

On they walked, and soon they reached a narrow glen.

Suddenly Rhona found herself gripping Prince Charlie's hand in agitation.

'Listen, sire!' she cried. 'I hear the sound of marching!'

And all at once they saw flashes of red through the trees.

'There is a line of Redcoats marching towards us!' cried the prince. 'We must hide, quickly.'

And taking Rhona by the hand he pulled her off the path along which they walked. Together the two darted behind the bushes and trees at the banked side.

Just in time!

A line of Redcoats came marching along the path which they had just left.

Rhona's heart thudded as the soldiers strode by, but not once did they look round. At last the Redcoats disappeared from view and it was safe to resume their journey.

'We were lucky, sire,' breathed Rhona.

'Indeed,' agreed the prince. 'But we must be on our guard the whole time. The isle is full of Redcoats.'

As soon as they were certain the Redcoats were far away, they again took to the path. They climbed out of the glen, and the Castle of Rhos loomed before them.

It was almost in ruins. Rhona knew it had been destroyed in one of the clan battles during her grandfather's time.

They hurried towards it and the prince thumped on the heavy door that remained with his fists.

Silently the bolts were withdrawn and they passed through.

An islander was there, waiting for them.

'You have arrived safely, sire!' he breathed in relief.

He led Rhona and the prince to another door—and this he tapped upon three times. Bolts were withdrawn, the door slowly swung open, and Rhona found herself looking into a well-furnished chamber.

Six men, who had been seated at a table with their plaid shawls wrapped close, jumped to their feet as Rhona and the Bonnie Prince entered.

They removed their bonnets and bent before the prince to kiss his hand.

Rhona stood by marvelling. She knew that these were Scottish chieftains rendering homage to their king.

One of the chieftains began to speak.

'We feared that you would never come, sire,' he said. 'Our plans are made, and the ship sails tomorrow. We could not have held the ship after tomorrow, but now there should be no danger. We——'

Prince Charlie held up a hand.

'Our conference must wait for a little while, gentlemen,' he said. 'I have with me a young maid from the Island of Tannock—a maid to whom I owe both my life and liberty. My first thought, gentlemen, must be for the bravest little girl in the whole of the Western Isles, Rhona Ross.'

Everybody turned to Rhona, and they bowed.

One of the chieftains clapped his hands. Then the door opened and a serving man came in.

'Black Angus here will see to the maid,' the chieftain said. 'Food is waiting to be served and she may rest in the room beyond.'

Rhona was taken into a small room beyond the big chamber

and here a steaming bowl of food was quickly placed before her.

Only then did she realise how hungry she was!

And when she had eaten, how wonderful it was to lie down on the bed of reeds prepared in one corner. Rhona knew a feeling of luxury, before she fell asleep.

Rhona's sleep that night was the deep, dreamless sleep of one who was truly exhausted.

She awoke next morning to the sound of voices and immediately she was sitting up. Prince Charlie's voice came clearly to her ears.

'Then everything is arranged, gentlemen,' he said. 'I thank you for all the risks you have taken on my behalf. I shall go to Skye in order to pick up a boat that shall carry me to France. It is with regret I shall leave my own dear land, but I leave you, promising that one day I will return.'

The door suddenly swung open and Rhona found herself blinking in the light.

'The little maid is awake,' a voice announced.

Prince Charlie beckoned Rhona into the council chamber.

'I am glad you have awakened early, little Rhona,' he said. 'My stay on Rhos must be short. I shall spend a few hours in sleep and then I shall go to join a ship. But first I have tried to make sure of your safety.'

He placed his hands upon her shoulders.

'All my life I shall remember my little cousin,' he said. 'Perhaps one day I shall come back to reward her. But now, this is the hour of our parting. Already the two men who saved our lives yesterday await you with a boat and they will take you back to Tannock Island.'

Just for a moment there was dismay in Rhona's eyes. She had forgotten that the parting must be so soon——'

'I will take you through the secret passage myself,' the prince went on. 'My kinsmen have told me about it. It is fortunate

218

for there is less risk of your being seen by Redcoats.'

A great slab of stone was pushed to one side and the prince directed Rhona to climb through the opening. He followed after her and they found themselves in a narrow passage.

Someone handed the prince a lighted torch through the opening and then, with his arm about Rhona's shoulders, he was slowly walking forward.

After a while, a speck of light showed ahead and Rhona realised they were coming out to the open air.

'We dare not tarry,' the prince said. 'For the moment it is goodbye, little Rhona. Never, as long as I live, will I forget you.'

And suddenly the prince had taken Rhona's hand and he had bent his head over it.

Rhona stood there trembling, yet she knew a wonderful pride.

Her hand had been kissed by Bonnie Prince Charlie!

'The path leads straight down to the bay,' the prince said. 'You have a long walk before you, little Rhona. Every blessing go with you.'

He turned abruptly and the darkness of the secret passage swallowed him up.

Rhona walked along like a person treading upon air. The wonderful words the prince had spoken kept ringing in her ears.

'Never, as long as I live, will I forget you.' Her prince had said that to her!

Suddenly she was jerked back to reality. It seemed to her that somewhere close behind she had heard footsteps. For the moment she thought that her imagination was playing tricks.

Rhona stopped dead, and she heard the unmistakable sound of two quick steps before everything became silent.

Then someone was following her. Who? It must be some-one who suspected her link with Prince Charlie!

Taken Before the Redocats

'Why am I being followed?' Rhona whispered to herself nervously.

Was it a red-coated English soldier behind her, or a friendly islander whose work began early in the day?

Rhona had to fight down a surge of alarm. It was an almost overwhelming impulse that came over her to take to her heels and run as she had never run before.

She was fleet of foot, and down in the bay a boat was waiting. If she could once get aboard that boat the two men who were waiting for her would not waste a moment in rowing away from the island.

'I dare not run,' Rhona told herself. 'If I start to run now it'll be a sign that I'm afraid.'

She started to walk forward again, and all the time she could hear the unmistakable sound of footsteps behind her.

What could she do? If she were caught and questioned she must have some ready explanation. What explanation could she give for being abroad so early on this lonely part of the island?

She looked inland and she saw how the dew was glistening on the heather. The sight of it gave her an idea and immediately she turned away from the path.

A few moments later she was stooping to pick a small spring flower. Moving on, she picked another and then another.

But all the time she was straining her ears. Her curiosity was overwhelming; she wanted so much to turn her head in order to discover who her follower might be. Yet she knew that she must show no curiosity.

Directly behind her the footsteps stopped again. She knew that the unknown person had stopped to stare at her.

As she plucked a flower now her fingers were trembling, her heart was hammering. She expected at any moment to hear the heather crunch under heavy footsteps and to feel hand upon her shoulder.

But still no denouncement, no command came. As she bent to pick yet another flower Rhona began to hum one of the lilting songs of the islands.

All at once she realised that the sound of the unknown person's footsteps was becoming fainter and fainter.

Whoever it was who had stood to stare at her was now walking on. Perhaps the danger was over.

'But I must go on picking flowers; that must seem to be my only purpose,' Rhona told herself.

When she came slowly back to the path, Rhona had quite a large posy in her hands. Still fighting down the temptation to hurry, she continued along the cliff path. She knew added fear now.

Suppose the two men waiting for her had grown alarmed at her failure to appear? They might not wish to be seen near a boat once the sun was in the sky.

The path took a sharp turn, and beyond it was a large, flat-faced boulder. To this a large sheet of paper had been stuck. Rhona gasped as she read it.

PROCLAMATION

TAKE NOTICE THAT A HANDSOME REWARD IS OFFERED FOR ANY INFORMATION LEADING TO THE CAPTURE OF THE REBEL, CHARLES STUART. ANY PERSON KNOWING OF THE SAID CHARLES STUART'S WHEREABOUTS AND REFUSING TO DIVULGE SUCH INFORMATION WILL BE TAKEN AND TRIED AS A TRAITOR. THIS BY ORDER OF HIS MAJESTY'S GOVERNMENT;

Rhona held her head a little higher.

This was the first proclamation concerning Bonnie Prince

Charlie that she had seen. Yet Rhona had no fears. She knew that no reward, no matter how big, would cause any true Scotsman to betray his rightful prince.

And then again Rhona caught her breath. For close behind her she had heard the sound of heavy footsteps. Without warning a voice spoke.

'This is the lass I saw before dawn on the North Cliff,' it said.

Fighting down that urge to take to flight, Rhona forced herself to turn naturally. She was looking at a roughly dressed individual and behind him were two red-coated soldiers.

The roughly dressed man spoke again and Rhona knew from his speech that he did not belong to Rhos Island. This was a great relief to her, for had he been one of the islanders, he would have known that she was not a native of Rhos.

'You appear very interested in that proclamation, lass,' he said, a hint of accusation in his voice.

Rhona did not flinch.

'It is the first time I have seen such a thing,' she said. 'Naturally I was interested.'

The man's face grew darker still.

'Why are you abroad at this early hour of the morning?' he demanded.

Rhona widened her eyes a little.

'Is it forbidden to pick flowers?' she asked.

The man gave an angry, impatient gesture.

'No one picks flowers before dawn,' he snapped. 'You had some reason for being up on North Cliff, and——'

One of the Redcoats interrupted him.

'We waste time,' he snapped. 'If this is the girl we seek, then she must be taken before the captain.'

His fingers closed firmly about Rhona's arm.

'Come,' he said. 'If you have nothing to hide then no harm will come to you.'

222

As she was led down the path Rhona knew the worst fear of all.

The Redcoats had been given orders to search for her. They must know that she had arrived at the island in the company of Bonnie Prince Charlie.

Only of one thing was she sure. No matter what happened she would breathe no word that could endanger her prince.

She was taken to a large cottage on the outskirts of the village. Half a dozen Redcoats were grouped about it and all of them stared at her with great curiosity. The soldier holding Rhona's arm piloted her inside.

'You will await the coming of the captain,' he said sharply.

Rhona stood there, still holding her posy of flowers and trying desperately hard to keep herself from trembling.

She wondered how much the Redcoats knew. The chances were that someone had crossed from Tannock Isle during the night and had told of how Prince Charlie had escaped by boat.

They would have told of the girl who had been in the boat with him. It might be that Wild Geordie himself had crossed to Rhos Island.

The voices of the soldiers came to her.

'I tell you we waste our time,' someone said. 'Charles Stuart lies at the bottom of the sea.'

Instantly Rhona was listening intently.

'You can't be sure of that,' another voice objected.

'I'm as sure as needs be,' answered the first moice. 'Did I not see a boat being swept towards the island last night, a boat containing a man and a girl? That boat was swept into the North Bay and a little later we saw wreckage out to sea.'

There were murmurs of assent.

'We know that the beach in the bay is covered at high tide and that there's no way of climbing the cliffs,' went on another voice.

'The man and the girl in that boat had no chance at all to escape.'

That speech gave Rhona new hope—but it also hardened her resolution.

More than ever now she must be careful not to betray herself. She must let them continue to think that Bonnie Prince Charlie was dead.

She heard the rattle of arms outside the cottage and then the door opened. An English captain appeared and he gave Rhona a long, searching look.

'So this is the girl!' he snapped.

Seating himself at the rough table, he spoke in a voice that made Rhona jump.

'Who are you and where do you come from?' he demanded.

Rhona stood, tightly clutching her posy of flowers.

'I am related to the Widow McCann, who lives at Scarr Point,' Rhona answered clearly.

Scarr Point was right at the other end of the island and the aged Widow McCann was indeed a very distant relative of Big Hugh Ross, her father.

The captain's face became sterner still.

'If your people live at Scarr Point,' he snapped, 'what were you doing on the North Cliff before dawn this morning!'

Rhona looked at him wide-eyed and she held up her flowers.

'I was picking flowers,' she answered. 'Only on North Cliff can you find flowers like these.'

She realised that her answer had only made him the more suspicious.

'That's nonsense, my girl!' he rapped at her. 'No one goes gathering flowers during the night.'

'I didn't gather them in the night,' Rhona answered. 'I gathered them just before the dawn. Flowers can cure rheumatism if you gather them with the dew still upon them. Look!'

She pointed to tiny drops of water which still clung to some of the flowers.

The captain was looking slightly bewildered now.

'That's why I came so early to gather the flowers', Rhona went on. 'The Widow McCann has rheumatism in both her arms, but it is said the dew-wet flowers will ease the pain.'

It was certainly true that the Widow McCann had rheumatism! But a sneering smile crossed the captain's face.

'The heads of you islanders are full of crazy ideas,' he mocked Quickly he leaned forward.

'Tell me,' he snapped, 'what do you know of the man, Charles Stuart?'

Rhona shook her head at him.

'No man of the name of Stuart lives upon Rhos Island,' she answered.

'I speak of the man who dared to get himself crowned King of Scotland,' the captain said.

Rhona's eyes remained wide.

'But the King of Scotland lives in a place called London,' she answered. 'That's what I have been told.'

The captain gave an impatient gesture. Then once again he barked a question at her.

'What brought you here from the Island of Tannock?' he demanded.

That was when Rhona let some of her flowers fall. While stooping to pick them up she forced into her voice a note of anger.

'Tannock!' she cried, bluffing desperately. 'Do you dare to suggest that I come from the Island of Tannock? There are all sorts of wild tales about that place! No one from Rhos would set foot upon Tannock without a claymore in his hand. That you—that—you——'

The captian slammed his fist down upon the table.

'Enough of this nonsense!' he shouted. 'The man who made

me waste my time over this girl shall be punished! It is obvious she knows nothing of Charles Stuart. Take her away!'

In spite of her overwhelming relief, Rhona managed to keep her face expressionless.

She had succeeded in tricking the captain; he no longer had any suspicions of her.

And that afternoon Bonnie Prince Charlie was leaving secretly for the Island of Skye!

The soldier who had been standing behind her took hold of her arm.

'Come,' he said.

But, even as Rhona took a step forward, the door of the cottage was violently flung open. Despite herself she couldn't prevent the cry that burst from her.

It was Wild Geordie who stood framed in the doorway—the one man who could prove that she was the girl who had helped Bonnie Prince Charlie!

Rhona's Daring Trick

'Wild Geordie!' Rhona breathed. Just for a moment the room whirled about her and she feared that she was going to faint.

Only a moment before and she had been so pleased with herself—and now, with the appearance of Wild Geordie, the danger to her prince was greater than ever before.

Wild Geordie would identify her and he would explain that she had left Tannock Island with Bonnie Prince Charlie. The Redcoats would immediately realise that the fugitive prince was somewhere in hiding on the island.

The search for him would be intensified at once!

Yet, even in her alarm, Rhona noticed something strange about Wild Geordie. There was no excitement in his face, but only blank dismay.

'So you've got the girl!' he snapped at the Redcoat captain.

226

'I suppose you've got the man Stuart as well and I've lost the reward.'

The captain came leaping to his feet.

'Hold that girl!' he snapped at the soldier who had been about to lead Rhona away.

Then he turned upon Wild Geordie.

'What do you know of this girl?' he demanded. 'And what do you know of Charles Stuart?'

Instantly the other's eyes narrowed.

'Tell me first if the man Stuart is a prisoner,' he said quickly.

'At the moment we do not know if Charles Stuart is alive or dead,' the captain said. 'If you have any information concerning him, I'll see to it that you'll get your share of the reward.'

Wild Geordie came farther into the room.

'I am the man who discovered that the Pretender was hiding on Tannock Island,' he said. 'This girl is Rhona Ross, the daughter of Big Hugh Ross. She is the girl who took warning to the Pretender, and who led him across the island during the night.'

A smile crossed the man's features.

'It was I who discovered their hiding-place and it was I who followed after them with the Redcoats when they left Tannock.'

He shook his head.

'The man Stuart would have been captured there and then,' he went on. 'But we ran into a sea fog and after that we saw no further sign of his boat. I knew he was making for this island and I landed at the turn of the tide this morning.'

The captain looked back at Rhona.

'I congratulate you, young lady,' he said. 'You played the part of a simpleton to perfection. If this man had not appeared, I should have let you go and sent in a report that Charles Stuart had been drowned in the North Bay.'

His brows came down in a heavy frown; then he continued.

'You were seen on the North Cliff at dawn this morning.' he went on. 'That is the reason I was so interested in you. You see, during the last few days several figures have been seen on North Cliff, but each time, when my men have investigated, the figures have disappeared.'

The Redcoat frowned.

'I have become convinced that there is some secret hiding-place near the North Cliff. It is probably something to do with the old castle. We've searched the place a dozen times, yet I'm still convinced that somewhere inside it is a secret room. And inside that room Charles Stuart is probably hiding at this present moment.'

Rhona could only stare back at him. She knew that her face was white and that the panic in her eyes must be evident.

The captain's guesses were very near the truth, and Rhona could not conceal her emotion as she thought of Prince Charlie's possible capture.

But the captain had turned back to Wild Geordie and did not notice her white, strained face.

'You are a man of the islands,' he snapped. 'Do you know aught of this secret hiding-place?'

Wild Geordie shook his head then.

'I'm a man of Tannock,' he said, 'and there's no friendship between Tannock and the Island of Rhos. I know nothing of this island.'

At that moment the door opened again and a younger officer appeared. Clicking his heels, he smartly saluted.

'Well,' the captain demanded, 'has that ship cleared the harbour yet?'

'No, sir,' was the reply. 'Your orders were carried out and the ship was searched from stem to stern. We made absolutely sure that no one could be hidden aboard her and then I gave the captain permission to sail. He flew into a rage at once.'

228

'Because you gave him permission to sail?' the captain queried, surprised.

'In a way—yes, sir,' the other officer replied. 'It appears that his coxswain went ashore last night in order to visit some relatives on the island. The man has not yet returned and therefore the captain is unable to sail.'

He shook his head.

'These waters are strange to him and he says he cannot navigate them without the advice of the missing man. Never have I known a captain to be in such a fearful rage.'

An excited gleam came into the captain's eyes and suddenly he snapped finger and thumb together.

'I think I understand!' he said quietly. 'I think I see the whole plot. We have searched the ship and given her permission to sail—but it appears that the coxswain is missing. You can take it from me that when the coxswain does appear it will be none other than the Pretender, Charles Stuart.'

All in a flash Rhona knew that the captain had jumped to the right conclusion. She remembered some of the conversation she had overheard in the old castle when Bonnie Prince Charlie and the chieftains had been in conference.

They had talked of the prince going away on a ship. Possibly it was this one.

The captain was smiling now.

'This matter is going to be quite easy after all,' he said, turning to the other officer. 'You will have you men stationed at the quayside and they will behave as though they have no further interest in the ship.'

Then his voice hardened.

'But the moment the missing coxswain arrives he must be arrested, together with all who may be with him, and brought immediately before me.'

Wild Geordie had listened to all that had been happening in silence, but now he took a step forward and thrust himself before the captain. His face was dark with anger as he spoke.

'And what about me?' he asked. 'Will I get my reward?'

'You'll get your fair share,' the captain said, looking at him with a certain amount of distaste.

Once again he turned to Rhona and it seemed to her that his glance was a little kinder.

'You played your part very well indeed, young lady,' he said with reluctant admiration. 'I should be angry with you, yet I cannot help but admire your loyalty. It seems to me that Charles Stuart has a gift for choosing loyal friends. But I am afraid you've failed, my dear.

'And you still know too much of our plans to be given your freedom,' he went on. 'For the moment I must keep you here. When the Pretender has been captured you shall be brought before me again and then I'll decide what is to be done with you.'

He looked at the soldier.

'Lock her up in the outbuilding,' he ordered. 'And see that there's a sentry on duty outside.'

'Yes, sir,' the soldier answered.

Again Rhona's arm was grasped and she was taken out of the room.

Some considerable distance away was a small stone building —a building that had been intended for use as a store-room. But the moment she was pushed inside Rhona realised it made a perfect prison.

There was a table and chair inside the room, and light was admitted only from a small, strongly barred window.

Swinging the heavy door shut behind him, the sentry left the building. With a sinking heart Rhona heard the key turn in the lock.

She was now a helpless prisoner—but far worse than that was her knowledge that soon Bonnie Prince Charlie must share the same fate.

'If only there were some way of warning him!'

Rhona spoke the thought aloud, but even as she did so it seemed a foolish thing to say. What hope could there be of her escaping from her prison?

Desperately she tried to marshal her thoughts. She tried to remember everything she had overheard in the secret room at the castle. She thought again about her parting from the prince.

He had told her that he was going to snatch a few hours' sleep and then a ship would carry him away from the island.

The more she thought about it the more convinced she became that the English captain had jumped to the right conclusion. The coxswain who, later on, would try to board the ship, would indeed be Bonnie Prince Charlie.

In desperation Rhona looked at the window. But quickly she realised that escape was quite impossible that way.

Peering through the window she saw that outside was a tumbled mass of rocks. If only she could get amongst them it would be so easy to hide.

She dropped down from the table.

Time and time again her gaze strayed to the window. Once or twice the door quivered and she knew that the soldier must be leaning against it.

There must be some way to get out. There must——
Suddenly she checked her scattered thoughts.

An idea had come to her, startling and daring.

'I can but try,' she told herself.

Having thought of a plan she wasted no time at all. Her first action was to tear a jagged strip from her tartan shawl. Climbing on the table again, she let the strip of material wind itself round one of the bars.

Stepping down from the table, Rhona stood for a minute to listen. Again the door rattled and she knew that the sentry was still leaning against it.

Taking a deep breath, Rhona lifted the table and flung it down with all her strength. And at the moment it crashed to the stone floor, she fled across the tiny room to flatten herself against the wall alongside the door.

She heard a startled exclamation and then the sound of a key turning in a lock. The door crashed open and Rhona was hidden from sight behind it.

'What's happening in here?' demanded an angry voice. 'What——'

The sentry had taken two steps inside the room, and now he was staring open-mouthed at the strip of tartan fluttering at the window.

'She's got out!' he gasped. 'I—I don't know how, but somehow she must have squeezed through the bars. Or did she manage to loosen one?'

Angrily, he knelt on the table in order to examine the window bars.

And in that same moment Rhona was around the door and pulling it after her. The instant it clicked shut she made no mistake in turning the heavy key.

Quickly, then, she dodged to the side of the small building and was soon lost to sight amongst the shielding rocks.

She had made her escape!

Mistaken for a Traitor

'Thank goodness, I've escaped!' breathed Rhona. 'But—but how am I to warn Bonnie Prince Charlie?'

Heart thumping, she crouched down among the rocks.

Already the soldier within the outhouse was beginning to shout for help. But, owing to the thickness of the stone walls, the sound of it was very muffled.

It was lucky, too, that the small window faced away from the village.

232

Rhona had a good view of the cottage where she had been questioned. Two or three soldiers were standing in front of it and not once did they turn their heads to look towards the outhouse.

Evidently no echo of the prisoner's shouting carried to them.

Satisfied now that no one had seen her escape, Rhona slid away between the rocks. Slowly she made her way down the slight slope that led to the tiny village.

It was from behind a big, protecting boulder that she obtained her first real view of the bay. There in the very centre of it a large, three-masted ship was riding at anchor.

Rhona gazed at it with conflicting emotions. That very ship was the one which had meant escape for Bonnie Prince Charlie, and perhaps a safe voyage to France. But now——

Unless something were done, and done quickly, that ship would be a trap for the fugitive prince.

As she watched, Rhona saw a small rowing-boat containing two men pull away from the quayside. It was obviously heading for the ship.

It was the sight of that boat that gave Rhona her idea.

Knowing not a moment must be wasted, she wrapped her shawl tightly about her head, so that her hair was completely covered.

The chances were that the Redcoats in the village would not give her a second glance, but would take it for granted that she was just one of the island girls.

Her bare feet raced over the rough ground now. On the quayside a number of Redcoats were lounging about and they appeared indifferent to anything happening about them.

But Rhona knew that this was only acting on their part— they wanted the islanders to think that they had lost all interest in the ship out in the bay.

Again Rhona looked at the small rowing-boat; it had

nearly reached the towering side of the ship.

Right at the end of the quay Rhona saw a sergeant and at once she ran in his direction.

Now she must try her desperate bluff.

With a dramatic gesture she flung out an arm.

'That rowing-boat!' she gasped. 'Do you know the men in it?'

He looked down at her from under heavy brows.

'Of course I know the men in it,' he snapped. 'They're two sailors from that ship yonder—they've just been ashore to pay a call at the village shop.'

That was when Rhona's voice became so high-pitched that she knew it must have penetrated to the cottages around.

'Don't you realise you may have been tricked!' she cried, and her voice was full of excitement. 'Two sailors did come off that ship and they did go into the shop. But isn't it possible that two completely different men came out of the shop?'

Roughly the sergeant caught at her arm.

'What are you trying to tell me?' he demanded.

Rhona sensed that all the lounging soldiers had suddenly become alert.

'There might have been two men waiting for the sailors in the shop,' she went on, her voice charged with excitement. 'It could have been those two men who walked out of the shop and climbed into the boat.'

She drew a deep breath.

'Why—it is common knowledge that the prince is going to impersonate the ship's coxswain!' she exclaimed in her loudest voice yet.

In her excitement she stamped her foot.

'Don't you understand?' she cried. 'One of the men in that boat may be Bonnie Prince Charlie! As you know, there is a great reward——'

The sergeant swung round, to stare at the ship with rounded

eyes. The two men who had rowed out were even now climbing a rope ladder.

The sergeant went into quick action then. Rhona's daring bluff had completely tricked him!

'Down to the boats!' he shouted. 'We've got to get aboard that ship before she has a chance to hoist her sails. A large slice of the reward goes to the man who first claps his hand on the shoulder of Bonnie Prince Charlie!'

The Redcoats couldn't get down to the boats quickly enough.

The one who jumped in first of all seized the oars and the two boats were already moving as the last soldiers jumped aboard.

Rhona stood alone on the quayside; all her attention was concentrated upon the ship.

She was trembling—but with hope, not fear. Nothing could stop Bonnie Prince Charlie being warned now of the danger which had threatened him.

That was why she had raised her voice so high—she had wanted her announcement that the prince was going to impersonate the coxswain to be heard by the villagers.

There was every chance that one of the villagers would know of the prince's hiding-place and that he would lose no time in carrying the tidings to the prince.

The ship would be searched, but the Redcoats would fail to find Prince Charlie!

At the same time Prince Charlie would know that his plan for leaving the island by the ship had failed and so he would remain in hiding.

Rhona saw the two boats draw alongside the ship and she saw the Redcoats go scrambling up the rope ladder. Only then did she become conscious of movement about her.

Suddenly she realised that she was the centre of a ring of people—staring at her with white, angry faces.

Then a tall figure of a man came to stand beside her. In a flash the end of his plaid shawl was thrown over her head and shoulders and at the same time his arm went about her angrily.

'You will come with us,' the man said in a grim voice. 'You shall learn in what manner the people of Rhos deal with a traitor.'

Rhona made no attempt to struggle. At that moment she was incapable of feeling any sensation of fear. All she could think of was that she had saved Bonnie Prince Charlie.

Some of the islanders had followed Rhona and her captor. Suddenly the latter stopped in his stride.

'Only Iain is to come with me,' he snapped. 'The rest of you go home.'

And now Rhona, realising her position, tried to protest. But again and again she was silenced.

For some considerable distance the two men walked along the coast. Finally, Rhona was placed upon her feet and helped to climb a very steep cliff path.

When they reached the top of the path, the two men turned to look down into the bay.

'The Redcoats are leaving the ship,' growled the man Iain.

Rhona, watching, too, saw the Redcoats clamber down into the two boats and the boats pull away.

'They have no prisoner with them,' observed Rhona's captor, 'and see—the ship is about to sail.'

They waited until the ship actually began to move and then, her captor's strong arm about her, Rhona was led inland.

Down a narrow, gloomy glen she was taken and finally she was shepherded into a dark cave.

'Keep you guard over her, Iain,' her captor said. 'I must find out what has really happened.'

'I can tell you everything——' began Rhona.

'Silence!' snapped Iain. 'We have no love of traitors!'

All of a sudden the fire left Rhona and she felt more tired

236

than she had ever felt before. She could argue no longer.

With a sigh she sank down, exhausted, on a heap of dry bracken and almost before she knew it her eyes were closed and she was fast asleep.

For since her first meeting with Bonnie Prince Charlie, Rhona had tried her strength severely. Nevertheless, it was a shock to her when, awakened by a gentle shaking, she opened her eyes to realise that night had come.

It was the voice of her tall captor that sounded in her ears.

'You must tarry here no longer,' he said. 'The time has come for you to leave.'

Suddenly Rhona gasped. There was no longer an angry glint in Iain's eyes. He was smiling at her kindly.

'We have done you an injustice,' he said quietly. 'But now we know the truth.'

Rhona gazed at him, wide-eyed. Why did her captor no longer believe she was a traitor?

But there was no time to ask questions now. Firmly Iain pulled Rhona to her feet and directed her to follow him.

It was one of the darkest nights Rhona ever remembered and she had no idea in what direction the Rhos islander led her. There was not even a star in the sky to give her an idea.

Sometimes they followed a rough path, while at others they were tramping over the uneven tufts of heather.

Suddenly, directly ahead of them, there was a shout of alarm—a shout in an English voice. At the same time came the sound of several musket shots and then Scottish voices raised in anger.

'Down!' hissed Rhona's guardian. 'Down!'

Next moment and Rhona was lying full length in the heather. There was more shouting, there were more musket shots, and she heard the unmistakable ring of steel against steel.

Somewhere, not far ahead of her, a pitched battle was being fought.

How long she lay in the heather Rhona never afterwards knew. Slowly but surely the noise of shouting and clanging steel grew fainter and fainter until at last there was no sound at all to be heard.

'Come,' the man Iain said then.

They went stumbling on, and once again she was half-carried down a steep cliff path. At the bottom of it she was released, however.

'Do you wait here,' the Scotsman said quietly. 'If you try to climb that path by yourself, you will only tumble into the sea.'

As Rhona waited, every nerve in her body was tense. How did the man know that she had spoken of Prince Charlie's plans in order to save him from an ambush?

Only one person could know that—Bonnie Prince Charlie himself! Her captors must have met Prince Charlie, while she was sleeping in the cave!

A murmur of voices came to Rhona, but she could make nothing of the words that were said. And then her captor had returned. He led her across a strip of sand and there, at the water's edge, she saw a small boat.

In the stern a figure was standing, cloak flapping in a rising wind.

Without any warning, Rhona was swung off her feet and lifted bodily into the boat.

As she lay in the bottom of the boat the tall islander bent to push it into deep water, and the figure in the stern steered the boat out to sea with a single oar.

Rhona watched him, feeling that the situation was beyond her. Why had she been placed in this boat—where was she being taken?

But then for the first time her unknown companion spoke and his voice caused Rhona's heart to give a leap of unbelievable joy.

238

'I fear, little cousin,' he said gently, 'that we embark upon a most dangerous voyage.'

The man in the boat was Bonnie Prince Charlie!

They were together again! But into what new peril were they going now?

The British Ship

'Sire!' Rhona gasped. 'You are here—safe! All day long I've lived in fear that you'd be captured.'

A sudden lightning flash split the darkness asunder and for one fleeting moment she saw him clearly. And she saw that he was smiling at her.

'Had it not been for you, Rhona,' he said, 'I would have been made prisoner many hours ago. You do not have to explain why you raised the alarm that I was on the ship. I know that you did it to prevent me from walking into a trap.

'Luckily,' he added, 'I met your captors and was able to tell them you were no traitor.'

Another mighty gust of wind rocked the frail craft, and Rhona saw the prince pull powerfully at the oars. Not until there was a momentary lull did he speak again.

'Even then I was almost captured,' he went on. 'When I was being guided down to this boat we were attacked by a body of Redcoats. However, we were able to put them to rout——'

The roar of the wind swept the rest of his words away from her. He continued to pull powerfully at the oars.

'I could not leave you on Rhos Island, little cousin,' he said then. 'Ever since you raised the false alarm the Redcoats have been searching every nook and cranny for you.'

He smiled gently at her.

'I knew your only hope of safety was to leave the island

with me. Otherwise I would never have risked you in a storm such as this will be.'

A tremendous gust of wind tore at the boat and, despite the prince's efforts, it was almost caught in the trough of a mighty wave.

Somehow he managed to pull the boat around so that it successfully climbed the wave. Suddenly water was swirling about Rhona's bare feet.

'Under the stern seat, you will find a baling can,' Prince Charlie shouted above the storm. 'And pin your shawl tight with this brooch, otherwise it will be whipped from your head.'

Next moment Rhona was holding a magnificent brooch in her fingers. Even in the darkness she realised that it was studded with jewels and that it was an object of great value.

But now its value was of no consequence—it was only its usefulness that mattered. Quickly she pinned her shawl tight and reached for the baling can.

Rhona knew she must try to empty the boat before the next great wave beat down upon it.

This wasn't the first time that she'd been caught at sea in a small boat, so baling was nothing new to her. But now she baled with greater strength than ever before—for she knew that their very lives depended on it.

Even if they had wanted to speak now it was impossible. The howling wind drowned all else. And the prince's every effort was concentrated on keeping the frail craft head on into the storm.

The lightning flashed and the thunder rolled, and time itself ceased to have any meaning for Rhona. Her body and her limbs began to ache with the strain, but she knew she dare not stop.

It seemed to Rhona that she had been baling for hours on end when suddenly she became aware that she could hear the creaking of the prince's oars. This meant the wind must have lost something of its fury.

She realised then that for a few minutes she had heard no crash of thunder and had seen no lightning flashes. The storm must be abating.

The seas were still running high, but now that the wind was dying down the mountainous waves would die down, too.

Presently she found that she could lay down the baling can. Now there was no longer any swirling water inside the boat.

They were going to ride the storm after all!

How wonderful it was to sit back upon the stern seat and to relax for a moment.

Bonnie Prince Charlie spoke then—in a strange, hoarse voice that she hardly recognised as his.

'I must rest for a moment, little cousin,' he said. 'I fear me that——'

His voice tailed off as he suddenly slid forward and lay prone in the bottom of the boat.

'Sire! Sire!' Rhona cried in alarm, seizing the ends of the oars before they slipped over the sides.

She bent down in an attempt to lift him up. Then another gasp escaped her and she gazed wide-eyed at her hand. There was blood on it!

In that moment Rhona remembered how she had lain in the heather and listened to the firing of muskets and the clanging of steel.

Prince Charlie had told her that on his way to the boat he'd been attacked by the Redcoats. In the battle he must have been wounded—and yet he had toiled at the oars all night.

Never had Rhona known such courage and determination. No wonder the whole Scottish nation had been prepared to follow this brave young prince.

But now nature had taken her due; he was completely unconscious.

At that moment the dark clouds above suddenly broke and immediately there was a pale light over the sea. It was a sign that dawn was almost at hand.

A cry escaped Rhona then. To the right of her was the indistinct outline of a ship. It was a small schooner—heading in the direction of their boat.

Suddenly Rhona was standing up and frantically waving her shawl about her head. There were men on the ship—men who would be able to attend to the prince's wound.

It didn't matter whether the ship was manned by friends or enemies. The only thing that did matter was that Bonnie Prince Charlie should be taken on board so that he might receive care and attention.

There was one dreadful moment when Rhona thought the vessel was going to veer away from her. Then its bows swung towards her again and she knew that she had been seen.

Seizing the oars herself now, Rhona began to pull towards the oncoming ship. She drew nearer the black side of the schooner, and as she did so she saw faces staring down at her.

'My cousin is ill!' she shouted with the full force of her lungs. 'I—I can't lift him up.'

Two agile sailors came swarming over the side of the schooner. Their first task was to lift Rhona up so that her hands could be grasped by the men left on the deck.

Then a rope was passed underneath Bonnie Prince Charlie's arms and, still unconscious, he was pulled on board.

A stocky man came to stand in front of Rhona and she realised instinctively that he must be the captain—and knew, too, by his accent that he was English. She must be careful!

'How came you to be so far at sea in weather such as this?' he demanded.

Rhona forced herself to speak naturally.

'The storm drove us away from our island,' she answered.

'I suppose your companion got knocked about by the storm,'

the captain said. 'We'd better get him below, so he can rest.'

Both Rhona and Bonnie Prince Charlie were drenched to the skin. But so were the captain of the schooner and his crew.

It appeared that the vessel had taken a very severe buffeting in the storm and had shipped a vast quantity of water.

The prince was placed upon a rough bunk and the captain looked down at him, aided by the light of a storm lantern. For the first time Rhona saw the prince's wound.

There was a jagged cut along the temple.

"'Tis a pretty severe blow he has received,' the captain said. 'He suffers but from concussion. He needs only rest.'

Rhona gave a gasp of relief.

And the crew had very little time to devote to Rhona and the prince now.

The ship had been damaged and it was necessary to get the damage repaired as quickly as possible. So Rhona and the prince were left alone and Rhona's first task was to bathe the cut.

She realised soon that her prince was sleeping the sleep of utter exhaustion.

It was then that she remembered the brooch he'd given her.

Her hand went up to her shawl, but she discovered that it was lying loose over her shoulders. Of the brooch there was no sign.

Yet she was sure that the shawl had been pinned tight about her head when she'd been hoisted up on board.

'The brooch!' she gasped. 'It may betray us!'

She had only caught a momentary glimpse of the brooch, but she knew it to be a valuable one. Such a brooch would never be used by a girl of the islands to pin her shawl.

Suppose the brooch had fallen on deck—suppose it had been picked up? It might be the one thing that would give them away.

Rhona knew that she must try to make sure. Venturing up

to the deck, she saw that the sun was now high above the horizon and the schooner was sailing over an almost placid sea.

The sailors were still so busy that nobody took any notice of her. Very carefully she looked along the deck. But there was no sign of the brooch.

She had just decided to give up looking for it, when a step sounded behind her and she turned to see the captain smiling down at her.

He asked after her cousin and Rhona told him that he still slept.

He looked towards the west then.

'You must remain with us a day and a night,' he said. 'It will take me that time to reach a port where I can drop anchor. I will set you and your cousin ashore at the tiny village of Helier on the Scottish coast.'

Immediately Rhona was reassured.

She had no fear of the people she would find at the village of Helier. She knew nothing about the place at all, but she did know that no true Scotsman or Scotswoman would ever prove traitor to Bonnie Prince Charlie.

'You'll be needing food and sleep,' the captain said. 'Food is already being prepared.'

Rhona ate quite a good meal and at last she curled up on a bunk that was actually dry.

When she awoke it was almost dark and her first thought was for the prince. She went to his bunk and saw that he was still asleep.

'He's been awake for several hours,' one of the sailors told her, 'but he was too weak to do much talking. After this second sleep he'll probably be as right as rain.'

Rhona remained close by.

Once or twice during the night she dozed and then she became aware that it was growing light outside.

Rhona lost no time in going up to the deck.

244

Swiftly she realised that the ship had anchored in a very wide bay.

And all in a flash her eyes were wide with suspicion.

She was not looking at a tiny fishing village—she was looking at a town of some considerable size.

Why had the captain dropped anchor here instead of near a tiny fishing village, as he had said formerly?

A murmur of voices came to her from behind the big centre mast.

She recognised the captain's voice.

'I have no doubts at all,' she heard him say. 'The brooch I picked up is sufficient proof for me!'

Then her heart quickened as the captain's next words came to her.

'In less than a quarter of an hour I shall return with a Redcoat captain and then we shall know, beyond any shadow of doubt, whether our wounded passenger is indeed the Pretender, Charles Stuart!'

On Dry Land Again.

Rhona's heart seemed to stand still. Surely all was lost now. The English captain had discovered his passenger's identity!

All because of her own carelessness—all because she had dropped the wonderful brooch the prince had given her.

Furthermore, the prince was still weak from his wound. Even if he had fully recovered, he was little better than a prisoner on board now.

Rhona clenched her hands. They had come so far together —they had surmounted so many difficulties. Surely they could not admit defeat now?

If the prince were captured by Redcoats, she knew she would never forgive herself for as long as she lived.

'The prince must be told at once.'

That was Rhona's first impulse, to hurry below deck and warn Bonnie Prince Charlie of his peril. But she realised that any abrupt movement on her part might attract attention to her.

And so, though she chafed at the delay, she forced herself to remain within the shadow of the tall mast.

In the grey light of the early dawn, she caught a glimpse of the captain as he went over the ship's side and then the creak of oars came to her.

The captain was on his way to the shore. Within the next quarter of an hour the news would be known to all the Redcoats.

When the boat returned to the ship it would be filled with soldiers.

But now was her chance to warn her prince.

Down the narrow companionway flew Rhona and she sighed in relief at seeing the prince sitting up in his bunk.

His eyes were bright again and he gave her a welcoming smile.

'It seems I have slept like a log for nearly twenty-four hours,' he began. 'And now I am——'

'Sire! Sire!' Rhona had to interrupt. 'There's great danger. The captain of this ship knows who you are, and even now he's on his way to bring Redcoats here!'

In a flash the prince was out of the bunk.

'Thank goodness, I am feeling better,' he stated. 'They will not take me easily, little cousin.'

Rhona's heart almost failed her. Somehow she knew that Prince Charlie had no intention of being taken without putting up a great fight. But suppose he were badly hurt?

Surely there must be something she could do—something even in the short time that remained.

And then, a quick gasp escaping her, Rhona remembered something she had seen on deck.

246

'There is a chance, sire!' she gasped. 'Even now we may be able to escape.'

Breathlessly she explained and a glow came to the prince's eyes.

''Tis both a sound and a bold idea, Rhona,' he murmured. 'More than ever do you place me in your debt. No harm will come to you, for I shall be very close at hand.'

Again Rhona climbed the companionway. Surveying the deck she saw that the crew were gathered in the bows of the schooner. Evidently they were staring after the captain's boat.

Nobody saw Rhona stoop over a heavy sack of ballast. Quietly she dragged it to the side of the ship, and it needed all her strength to lift it up upon the rail.

The moment she had the sack balanced Rhona cried out as though in panic.

'Jump for it, sire! 'Tis your only hope! Jump!'

She heard startled gasps from the men in the bows and then Rhona pushed hard at the sack. It toppled over and hit the sea with a mighty, resounding splash.

Instantly pandemonium reigned upon the decks.

'I heard him go over!' somebody shouted. 'He'll escape us yet!'

'Into the boats!' roared another voice. 'We'll pick him up within a few yards!'

Rhona, crouching back in the shadow of the mast, saw the men go scrambling over the side into the boats below.

But there was one member of the crew who remained behind. And before Rhona could hush him, Prince Charlie opened his mouth to speak.

'So far so good, little cousin,' the prince whispered with a smile.

Desperately Rhona gestured—but it was too late.

The man standing at the ship's side must have possessed very keen hearing. Suddenly he whirled round and Rhona knew he'd caught sight of the prince.

'So you tried to trick us!' he cried as he came leaping forward. 'That's my luck! Now I shall capture you unaided and the reward will be all mine.'

Rhona saw the glint of a dagger he had pulled from his belt. But Bonnie Prince Charlie had already jumped into action.

Even as the seaman leaped forward with the dagger upthrust, the prince dived underneath the blow. He took his attacker about the knees and brought him crashing down to the deck.

It seemed to Rhona, during that struggle, that her heart would never stop pounding. At any moment she feared the other seamen would return and come swarming over the ship's side. But more than ever she feared the dagger that the remaining seaman held.

Over and over the two men rolled, locked in fierce combat.

Thoughts of the huge reward gave the seaman added strength—but Prince Charlie was fighting for his freedom.

Then Rhona saw her prince seize the other man's knife-arm. With incredible skill he wrested the knife from the seaman. It was only the work of a moment for him to land a punch that stunned the Englishman then.

'Our plan has worked, little cousin!' cried the prince leaping to his feet. 'The schooner is ours!'

Rhona's heart throbbed with relief. But then she heard the sound of angry comments coming faintly from the open sea ahead.

'We're pulling in the wrong direction!' came a voice. 'I see no sign of a swimmer.'

Bonnie Prince Charlie stood motionless for a moment and Rhona saw he was staring towards the distant houses on the shore. Clearly he was thinking of the danger there.

'There is but one thing to do, Rhona,' he said then. 'If we can but gain a little time we shall be safe—and get away.'

He ran forward to the bows and Rhona saw him lean far over the ship's side.

With the seaman's dagger he was severing the taut anchor rope, and it was light enough for Rhona to see the strands fray apart, and hear the snap as they parted.

Instantly the schooner began to swing round with the tide.

Bonnie Prince Charlie's arm went about Rhona's shoulders.

'We must hope the tide will carry us across the bay, little cousin,' he said quietly.

It seemed that a very strong current had the schooner in its grip. In fact, it had moved some considerable distance before the first cries of alarm were raised.

'Look to the schooner! It's adrift!'

The sound of distant, excited shouting came to Rhona from the quayside. But now her thoughts were alive with the thought of a new peril.

As far as she could tell the schooner was being carried down towards a mighty headland!

As Rhona watched she felt her legs go weak.

But for once luck was with them!

Suddenly the schooner heeled over as though caught in the grip of another current. And now the bows actually swung away from the great mass of rock.

They were going to clear the headland after all!

But there was still danger. By this time the alarm would have been raised, and many boats would be putting off from the shore.

If they remained on board then nothing could save the prince from capture.

Rhona studied the sea ahead and she judged that the schooner would only miss the headland by a matter of a few yards. That was when she pointed to a hatch cover.

'There is no lifeboat, sire,' she said quickly, 'but that hatch cover could serve us as a raft. If we launch it just beyond the headland and leap on to it, we may not be seen. Then your enemies will waste valuable time catching the schooner!'

Prince Charlie smiled his admiration.

'A sound idea, little cousin!' he exclaimed. 'And when the Englishmen catch their schooner, they will find no one but yonder stunned seaman on board!'

It took all Prince Charlie's great strength to get the wooden hatch cover over the side of the schooner. But he managed to do it just as they swung round the huge headland.

'Now, sire,' Rhona gasped. 'Now is our chance.'

The cover was slid over the side and it floated perfectly. Rhona lowered herself down to it and then the cover rocked violently as the prince landed alongside her.

Somehow they managed to keep their balance; and, slowly circling, the flat piece of wood was swung around the headland and out of sight of the bay.

'They will not know that we have left the schooner,' Prince Charlie said, his eyes bright with relief.

He had thought to bring a thin plank of wood with him and this he now used as a paddle.

Ahead of them Rhona saw a strip of beach and beyond it a heather-covered gully. Once they reached that heather without being seen, they might yet win to safety.

Thanks to Prince Charlie's strength the raft made good progress, and the moment it was in shallow water they slid off and waded on to the beach.

Reaching the heather, they travelled only a few yards and then flung themselves flat.

They saw now that the schooner was moving farther and farther out to sea. A few moments later the first of the pursuing boats came into sight and then in quick succession half a dozen more.

Not one of the boats turned towards the tiny beach—they all continued after the schooner.

'Come, little Rhona!' the prince whispered.'We must away.'

Even now Rhona could scarcely believe that they had escaped. But, turning her head, she saw that the boats were still making for the distant schooner.

It might be an hour or more before the crew succeeded in gaining her. Only then would they discover that Rhona and Prince Charlie were not on board.

Rhona wondered if the captain was in one of the boats. Perhaps the alarm of the drifting schooner had been raised before he had landed on the beach.

In that case, his first thought would have been for the safety of his ship. It might be that the Redcoats at the town still had no knowledge that Prince Charlie was in the vicinity.

The prince led the way up a long slope and Rhona began to strain her eyes. In what part of Scotland had they landed? Were they upon the Mainland or upon yet another island?

Owing to the storm and to her sleep aboard the schooner Rhona had no means of telling how far they had travelled.

On and on the two plodded now. Two hours later and they came to a ridge of very high ground.

To one side of her Rhona could see the wide sweep of the sea, but on the other side there was nothing but bleak heather-covered countryside.

She still could not tell whether or not they had reached the Mainland.

But Prince Charlie was also staring intently about him and now he gave vent to a sudden exclamation.

'Maybe the fates have been kind to us after all, little cousin,' he said quietly.

Quickly he unbuttoned his jacket and then his fingers were feeling along the inside of it. To Rhona's great surprise she saw him tear away a few stitches and reach inside the lining for something that was hidden there.

He drew out a thin sheet of crumpled paper.

For a few moments he studied it and then once again he intently surveyed his surroundings. He nodded his head in evident satisfaction.

'This is luck indeed, little cousin,' he commented.

He looked at the paper again and pointed to two distant mountain peaks. At the same time he held out the sheet of paper so that Rhona could see the rough map that had been drawn upon it.

'This map was drawn by your father, little cousin,' he went on, 'and it was given to me by him. It shows the escape route that he worked out. Surely luck was with us when the English ship took us aboard after the storm. The ship has brought us to the very place I hoped to reach!'

Again he looked at the two distant peaks.

'We are upon the Island of South Uist, Rhona', he went on. 'And upon this island I have many faithful friends. Escape for me now, little cousin, may be a very simple matter.'

Rhona clasped her hands in joy.

How wonderful if she could be a witness of the moment when Prince Charlie boarded a French ship—a ship that would carry him away to freedom again!

'Where will you find your friends, sire?' Rhona queried.

He smiled at her.

'On this slip of paper a certain inn is marked,' he told her. 'There a young Scotswoman—one Flora Macdonald—even now awaiting my arrival. My instructions are to trust myself entirely to her.'

But there was fear in Rhona's eyes once again as she looked about her now. Suppose after all the English captain had been able to raise the alarm?

In that case, by this time, every Redcoat on the island would have started to search for the fugitives and they might not be able to visit the inn.

'Sire! For your safety we must go at once!' she gasped.

But Prince Charlie shook his head. He had another idea.

'Not yet, little cousin. A cave is marked upon this map—a cave where we shall be safe from all the Redcoats in Scotland. We must seek this cave at once, for I am not as fully recovered from my wounds as I imagined.'

He smiled wryly.

'Even though our time is so short, I must rest, little cousin, before I set out to find the inn where Flora Macdonald awaits me.'

Rhona realised it was the best thing to do.

As they walked on Prince Charlie several times consulted his map. And presently they were following a path amongst the heather that was little more than a deer track.

They were climbing most of the time, but Rhona realised that the track was bringing them nearer again to the sea.

Presently Prince Charlie was forcing his way through dense bushes until all further progress was prevented by a high wall of rock. But here the prince parted two bushes and beyond Rhona saw the narrow entrance to a cave.

'I have to thank your father, little cousin,' Prince Charlie said, 'for the very clear instructions he gave me. Here for the time being we shall be safe.'

There was even a little trickle of water at the side of the cave and because of it they were able to quench their thirst.

It was then, as she explored, Rhona saw a small package resting upon a ledge. A cry of delight escaped her when she opened it, to find a small quantity of oatmeal and a few strips of dried venison.

'Your friends have anticipated your coming, sire,' she said. 'They have left a little food here, so that we shall not go hungry.'

The prince looked at her.

'It is as well, Rhona,' he said slowly. 'My strength is almost gone. At the moment I could not possibly make the journey to the inn. But by morning I shall have recovered and then we will continue on our way. Rest you also, for no one will find us in such a safe hiding-place as this.'

He laid himself down inside the cave and almost at once he was asleep.

Rhona sat a few yards away, her back resting against the wall of the cave. She must keep watch.

But her long walk across the island had tired her more than she realised. She tried to keep awake, but, despite herself, her eyes closed.

How long she slept Rhona never afterwards knew. But suddenly she was wide awake. At the other side of the cave the prince also sat up quickly.

For from somewhere outside had come the loud report of a musket.

Rhona gasped. Could it be that the Redcoats had found their trail—that they were even now on their way to the cave?

Oh, why had she not keept awake?

She was the first at the cave entrance. Carefully she parted the bushes and then she stilled her breathing for a moment.

There were indeed many Redcoats below the cave. Even as she caught sight of them one soldier lifted his musket and fired.

Had she been seen—had the shot been directed at her?

But then, just below her, Rhona heard a crashing amongst the bushes. She caught sight of magnificent wide-spread antlers and, next moment, an enormous stag burst into view.

The Redcoats were stag-hunting!

But once again Rhona held her breath and she knew alarmed dismay.

The stag was coming directly towards the cave. The conviction came to her that the magnificent animal knew of the cave—that it was one in which it had probably sheltered many a time.

Now it was going to use the cave as a refuge from its enemies.

Unwittingly the magnificent stag was going to betray Bonnie Prince Charlie.

In Disguise

Rhona suddenly realised the prince was at her side.

'Our luck has turned for the worse, little cousin,' he said gravely. 'Our presence here will frighten the stag, but the moment it hesitates it will present a good target. The Redcoats will hurry to the spot and nothing can prevent the cave from being discovered then.'

There was another musket shot, but the bullet evidently missed its mark, for the magnificent stag came charging on, climbing higher and higher all the while.

Now Rhona realised there was only one thing that she could do. In order to save her prince, she must take a tremendous risk.

'It is scarcely likely, sire,' she said quickly, 'that the Redcoats know of our presence upon the island. If they were searching for us, they would not be chasing after a stag. And if they do not know that you are on the island, they will not be suspicious of me.'

Before he could question her, before he could even guess at her plan, Rhona had thrust the bushes aside and then darted out of the cave.

Immediately she went scrambling down the slope in front of her and she made all the noise she could.

The stag heard her at once. Flinging up its antlers the big animal came to a stop. Then, catching sight of Rhona, it swung away at a tangent.

From one of the Redcoats came a cry.

''Tis an island maid!' he shouted. 'Do not fire yet. She has tried to head off the stag for us!'

But Rhona had meant exactly the opposite. She meant to save the stag, as well as the prince.

The big animal was racing along the slope now, getting farther and farther away from the cave and heading for a wood. After it the English soldiers stumbled and quite a number of them fired their muskets.

But in their haste their aim was poor and the big stag raced on, plunging out of sight into the wood. It seemed to Rhona that her plan had succeeded. The Redcoats were racing along below her and it appeared that not one of them had as much as a glance to spare for her.

Only at the last moment did she spot the straggler—a Redcoat who limped. He was slowly climbing towards her.

Almost, in the first flash of panic, Rhona turned to flee. But common sense told her that such an action on her part would be dangerous.

If the English soldiers did not know about the landing of Bonnie Prince Charlie, she had nothing to fear.

The English soldier came slowly towards her.

'Never have I hated anything as much as I hate these islands of yours,' he groaned. 'A man cannot stir a step along your rough paths without risking his limbs.'

He lifted his right leg in order to rub his ankle tenderly.

'I am lucky that I have only wrenched my ankle,' he went on. 'That is why I cannot keep up with the others.'

He looked very curiously at Rhona then and once again she knew alarm.

'Who are you?' he demanded. 'Why does a maid like you wander alone in this forsaken countryside?'

It needed all Rhona's will-power to keep her voice steady.

'It is my job to attend my father's sheep and cattle upon the hillside,' she told him.

That was certainly true!

He shrugged at her explanation.

"'Tis a job to which you are very welcome, missy,' he said. 'I only live now for the day when Charles Stuart shall be captured. In these islands we live on nothing but porridge and fish and I like neither.'

The sound of a musket shot came to him and then an angry shouting. Instantly his face darkened.

'They must have lost the stag!' he cried. 'But we must catch it. We promised ourselves to eat of meat tonight. And that is a feast I have no intention of missing.'

With that he went hobbling on and Rhona was left alone. She smiled a little to herself now. The Redcoats would not catch the stag—it was as elusive as the prince.

She stood looking after the man until he had disappeared from sight. Even so, she took the precaution of going back to the cave by a very roundabout route. In the entrance she found Prince Charlie waiting for her.

'Once again I owe my safety to you, cousin,' he said. 'You make my debt to you a greater one than I shall ever be able to repay. I tell you, little Rhona, that when I saw the stag heading for the cave I gave myself up for lost.'

Rhona had meant to insist that they should leave the cave at once—but one look at the prince's drawn, tired face made her change her mind immediately.

The prince was still weak because of his wound. He dare not venture out into the open now, especially as Redcoats were so near at hand.

'What worries you, little cousin?' Prince Charlie demanded.

Rhona bit her lip for a moment.

'This cave is no longer a safe hiding-place, sire,' she said slowly. 'Those soldiers evidently did not know that you had landed upon the island. But when they return to their camp they will learn the news. And some of them are bound to remember the girl who headed off the stag.'

He nodded his head.

'Which means that Redcoats will come flocking back to this glen,' he said. 'Maybe we'd better leave at once—'

But in taking a step forward he staggered and almost fell. Rhona took hold of his coat sleeve.

'It will take the soldiers time to return to their camp,' she said quietly. 'They may not hear the news before the sun is down. In that case they will not come back until dawn.'

She parted the bushes at the cave entrance and looked up and down the now deserted glen. She tried to comfort herself.

Even if the Redcoats did return it was unlikely that they would find the cave, especially if the prince never ventured near the entrance.

But now Rhona wondered if he was going to be really ill. In that case he would need help—help that a mere girl would be unable to give him.

Surely the wise thing to do was to make contact with Flora Macdonald as quickly as possible? The chances were that she would know of men who would be only too anxious to help their prince.

Resolutely Rhona turned to Bonnie Prince Charlie.

'Tell me where to find this inn, sire,' she pleaded. 'I will go there, I will meet this Flora Macdonald and tell her that you are hiding in this cave. It may be that she will immediately send a trustworthy man to escort you across the island.'

He looked at her and he shook his head.

'Already you've taken many risks on my behalf, little cousin,' he hold her. 'But this is one risk that I dare not let you take. If you venture forth alone then you are bound to be captured.'

He smiled gently.

'Already it must be known,' he went on, 'that you have landed on this island with me. That means that every Redcoat will have been given your description. The soldiers will be searching for you as eagerly as they search for me.'

But Rhona's eyes were shining, for she had already thought of a plan.

'I think I can make sure, sire,' she said confidently, 'that no Redcoat will recognise me as the maid from Tannock Isle.'

Her eyes fastened for a moment upon the silk neckerchief which the prince wore about his throat.

'I would beg the loan of your neckerchief, sire,' she went on. 'And when you gave me the brooch I saw that you had a few other pieces of jewellery. Among them, I believe, was a pair of heavy earrings. May I borrow those, too, sire?'

He looked at her for a moment and then he slowly pulled off his scarf. Then out of his picket he took two heavy gold earrings—earrings that would only be worn by a man. For it was the fashion of the age for many men to wear earrings.

Rhona took the scarf and the earrings.

'And one other thing, sire,' she said quietly. 'Do you lend me you dirk as well.'

He did so and, promising to return in a few moments, Rhona left the cave.

Slowly she made her way through the bushes, till she came to a patch of damp-looking peat. Here she used the prince's dirk to dig up a slab of turf. From the underneath of it oozed a thick, yellow liquid.

Squeezing the peat between her hands, so that they would become covered with the yellow liquid, Rhona rubbed her hands over her face and neck. Then she used the yellow liquid to stain her hands and her arms.

This done, she fastened the heavy rings to her ears and finally pulled the scarf over her head, and knotted it beneath her chin, so that her hair was completely hidden.

When she took off her plaid shawl, she no longer looked like a girl of the islands. Anyone seeing her would have taken her for one of the many dark-skinned gipsies that roamed the Western Highlands.

Going back to the cave, she parted the bushes. As she entered it, the prince, who had been lying down, jumped to his feet.

'Who are you?' he gasped. 'How came you to find this place——'

He broke off as realisation came to him.

'Rhona!' he gasped. 'For a moment I did not recognise you!'

Rhona smiled her satisfaction, for she knew now that her disguise was a good one.

'It is safe for me to venture abroad now, sire,' she said. 'No one will take any notice of a gipsy girl. As I walk along, I will break off twigs from the bushes and make myself a basket, such as is always carried by gipsies.'

He gazed at her for a long moment.

'It still distresses me that you must venture forth alone,' he said quietly. 'But I am weaker than I thought.'

From the lining of his jacket he took the map sketched by Big Hugh Ross. And, as Rhona looked over his shoulder, he traced out the route she was to follow.

'You have a long journey in front of you, little cousin,' he said. 'You cannot possibly hope to reach the inn until late tomorrow.'

'I'll make the fastest speed possible,' Rhona assured him.

His strong fingers closed over her hands for a moment.

'May the fates go with you, my brave little cousin,' he said his soft voice a little husky.

Cautiously then Rhona slipped out of the cave, leaving her plaid shawl behind her. She made her way forward swiftly and presently came to the end of the glen.

She saw no sign of the Redcoats. They must still be in vain pursuit of the stag.

As she walked along, Rhona broke off many twigs and her nimble fingers set to work making a basket. When at last it hung upon her arm, her gipsy disguise was quite complete.

Twice that afternoon Rhona saw roving bands of Redcoats. Each time she took to the heather for, despite her disguise, she did not want to come in contact with them if it could be avioded.

She had memorised the route on the roughly drawn map and she was positive that she was going in the right direction.

When twilight came she saw a crofter's cottage far ahead of her. She walked towards it, wondering if she dared beg shelter for the night.

But soon she was able to see that it was a tumble-down, deserted cottage and this was a great relief to her.

Before the last rays of the sun faded from the sky, Rhona had made herself a bed of dry heather inside the cottage. She was asleep the moment she lay down and it was the rays of the early morning sun that awakened her.

She had brought a little of the oatmeal from the cave, and by mixing it with some water she was able to make a meal for herself.

Then, once again, she set out on her way.

Several times during that morning the sight of red uniforms caused Rhona to go into hiding. But noon came and she was still safe.

And it was during the afternoon that Rhona found herself walking along a rough cart track. Her heart thudded with excitement. If she had followed her instructions correctly this track would lead her to the inn where Flora Macdonald was awaiting news of Bonnie Prince Charlie.

Rhona rounded a sharp bend—and then her eyes shone with delight. Here indeed was a large inn! Eagerly Rhona looked at the huge yard at the back of it, surrounded by a cluster of outbuildings.

Without a doubt this was the inn she sought.

But suddenly Rhona gave a gasp and all colour left her

face. In the yard at the back and around the inn she saw several splashes of red. The place was filled with Redcoats!

Surely if the English soldiers had taken possession of the inn her task of reaching Flora Macdonald would be impossible.

At The Inn

Flora Macdonald may not even be at the inn now! Rhona thought frantically. Suppose she has come under suspicion? Suppose she has been taken away by the Redcoats?

But then her eyes were gleaming with determination.

'I—I must find out!' she told herself.

All she could do now was trust to her disguise. She made sure that the neckerchief was firmly knotted under her chin, that the earrings were still in place.

Then, basket dangling from her arm, Rhona walked slowly towards the inn.

There were several soldiers in the yard but none took any notice of her as she opened the gate.

From one long building she heard the sound of horses and outside its door she saw two soldiers. One of them was engaged in cleaning the mud from a tall pair of riding-boots, while the other was holding up an officer's great-coat, also brushing mud from it.

On a barrow at the man's side rested an officer's three-cornered hat, with a red plume fastened to one side of it.

The voice of the soldier cleaning the boots carried to Rhona.

'When Captain Lawson rode in he'd been in the saddle for a full twenty-four hours,' he said wonderingly. 'Never before have I seen a man so tired. It is a sure thing he will sleep the clock round before we set eyes on him again.'

The other worked hard at the long great-coat.

'Never before have I seen a man so bespattered with mud,' he remarked.

Ears alert, Rhona crossed the yard and tapped upon the back door of the inn. It was opened by a maid-servant about the same age as herself.

'Let me tell your fortune,' Rhona pleaded. 'Willingly I will do so, if you give me a scrap of something to eat.'

The maid-servant looked at Rhona and then she looked over her shoulder at the English soldiers.

'Now more than ever before I would like to have my fortune told,' she said anxiously. 'Because of those Redcoats I go in fear of arrest, for they find fault so quickly. Come you inside.'

Rhona entered a low-ceilinged, smoke-blackened kitchen. A huge pot was simmering over the fire in the great open hearth and from this the maid-servant filled a basin with stew.

'Do you eat,' she invited.

Rhona was glad to do so, for she had not eaten for many hours and felt weak with hunger.

The maid-servant seated herself on a stool at the other side of the table.

'For two days now I have lived in fear,' she confided to Rhona. 'No sooner did I arrive here with my mistress, Flora Macdonald, than the Redcoats swooped down upon the inn. Ever since we have been prisoners.'

She looked about her as though fearful of being overheard.

'The Redcoats believe that my mistress has come to this island,' she whispered, 'in order to seek out Prince Charlie. Thas is why I am afraid and why I would like to know if my fortune is good or bad.'

Rhona hoped that her intense interest did not betray itself. So Flora Macdonald was still at the inn—and already under suspicion!

How would she be able to get in touch with Flora? With so many Redcoats about it seemed impossible. Yet she must find a way.

'I would know my fortune,' the maid-servant said, the

moment Rhona had finished her meal. 'Will you tell it now?'

Back on Tannock Isle it had always been said that Rhona's. grandmother was gifted with the second sight. Indeed, it was her grandmother who had taught Rhona how to read a person's hand.

And so, taking the maid-servant's hand, Rhona told her fortune from the signs her grandmother had taught her to look for.

'I see a long and happy life ahead of you,' she said at the end. 'You have nothing to fear from the Redcoats.'

The maid-servant gazed at Rhona in tremendous relief.

But just then Rhona heard the stamping of hoofs in the yard. Evidently a horseman had just ridden up.

Suddenly the door was flung open, and for a moment Rhona could hardly believe her eyes.

But when the full realisation of the newcomer's identity struck her, she quickly lowered her head.

The man who burst so unceremoniously into the inn kitchen was none other than Wild Geordie!

Then the traitor from Tannock Isle had followed after her from Rhos Island!

Would Wild Geordie succeed in penetrating her disguise? Breathlessly, Rhona sat there.

Then an inner door opened and a redcoated sergeant entered. He stared hard at Wild Geordie.

'Are you the man we were told to expect?' he demanded.

'I am that man,' Wild Geordie told him. 'I have travelled on the heels of the prince ever since his escape from Tannock Isle. I followed him to the Island of Rhos and now I have come to Uist.'

He slapped one fist into the other.

'I know that the prince has landed here,' he went on. 'And he is still accompanied by the girl who helped him escape from Tannock Isle. I know, too, that the prince has friends upon

Would Wild Geordie succeed in penetrating Rhona's disguise?

this island and that arrangements have already been made to take him as quickly as possible to the Isle of Skye.'

An angry scowl crossed his features.

'If the Pretender is allowed to escape to Skye,' he cried, 'then in all certainty he will slip through our fingers. The moment he reaches Skye, he will be hurried to the mainland and there a French ship will be waiting to carry him away.'

Wild Geordie's face was dark.

'I have been sent here, for I have seen the prince at close quarters and I know exactly how he is dressed. Moreover, the girl who travels with him is also well known to me.'

The sergeant turned on his heel.

'You had better see Captain Lawson at once,' he rapped.

Wild Geordie followed him through the inner door and he gave not a glance at the two girls seated at the table.

Never had Rhona known such tremendous relief. Wild Geordie had stood within a few yards of her but, because of her disguise, he had failed to recognise her!

How was she to get in contact with Flora Macdonald, though? And even if she did succeed in making contact, how would Flora be able to get away from the inn?

Rhona knew she must somehow stay at the inn, watching for a chance to meet this friend of Bonnie Prince Charlie.

She looked at the maid-servant.

'I am a long way from my home,' she said quietly, 'and I do not like the idea of spending the night lying out in the heather. Do you know of some place here where I could sleep?'

The other smiled at once.

'I would like to help you, because you have chased away my fears of the Redcoats,' she said gratefully.

Getting to her feet, she took down a small lantern which stood above the wide chimney.

'There is plenty of straw in the loft above the stables,' she said. 'You can sleep there in secret, but early tomorrow you

266

must leave, otherwise I shall be in trouble with the inn keeper.'

Tremulously, Rhona smiled her thanks at the maid-servant's kindness.

When she stepped out into the inn yard she realised that darkness had come. The other girl led her to the stables and pushed open the door. Holding the lantern above her head, she pointed to a ladder.

'That is the way to the loft,' she said.

'You—you are very good,' Rhona replied huskily. 'My thanks——'

But suddenly something caught her attention and she stopped. She was gazing at an officer's great-coat and three-cornered hat which hung behind the stable door.

They were the hat and coat that the soldiers had been cleaning when she had entered the yard!

And the sight of them now sent an audacious plan spinning through Rhona's brain.

Just for a moment she hesitated. Dare she take the maid-servant into her confidence? Surely there was no risk, for the girl was an island girl like herself.

Surely she, too, would want to do all in her power to help the fugitive prince.

'The soldiers are right about your mistress,' Rhona said, quickly coming to a decision. 'She does seek to get in touch with Bonnie Prince Charlie, and I have come from the prince. With your help it may be possible for your mistress to leave the inn so that I may guide her to the prince.'

The maid-servant stared at her, wide-eyed.

'What would you have me do?' she asked breathlessly.

Rhona pointed to the hat and coat hanging behind the door.

'Do you think you could smuggle those to your mistress?' she asked. 'Could you get them into her room without anyone seeing them?'

'I—I think so,' the other answered. 'I can at least try.'

Quickly then Rhona outlined the rest of her plan and the eyes of the maid-servant grew wider and wider.

"Tis a great risk to take,' she said at the end. 'But, for the sake of the prince, who has suffered and lost so much, I will do my best to help you. If I succeed I know that my mistress will be pleased.'

She took down the great-coat and the officer's hat and peered out of the doorway.

'There is no one in sight,' she murmured. 'If I use the back staircase, it is very unlikely that anyone will see me entering my mistress's room.'

The maid-servant went hurrying back across the yard, taking the uniform coat and hat with her, and the door of the inn closed behind her.

Rhona's eyes shone as she thought of the girl's loyalty.

But now she had no intention of sleep. Leaving the stable, she crept towards the far end of the yard. Only then did the yard gate come into sight, and with a catch of her breath Rhona saw that a sentry was on duty.

But that sentry didn't see the slight figure which slid over the wall and immediately vanished into the darkness beyond the gate.

In the darkness Rhona waited. Had Flora Macdonald received her message? Would she take the tremendous risk that Rhona had asked her to take?

'She must—she must!' Rhona told herself. 'Only by taking it can she hope to meet the prince now.'

The minutes dragged by and still Rhona waited. And then, suddenly, the back door of the inn opened and for a moment the figure of a Redcoat officer was sharply outlined against the light from inside the kitchen.

The kitchen door swung to and the officer came walking slowly across the yard and headed for the gates.

268

Rhona held her breath. Could her plan possibly succeed?

The sentry heard the sound of approaching footsteps and he caught sight of the red plume on the officer's hat. Instantly his musket went to his shoulder and his hand came across in a salute.

The officer acknowledged the salute and, walking past the sentry, opened the gate and strode out into the darkness of the narrow lane.

The figure in officer's uniform came slowly through the darkness towards Rhona, leaving the sentry still on duty at the gate beyond.

'Miss Macdonald,' Rhona breathed. 'Is it you, Miss Macdonald?'

The figure reached out to take hold of her arm.

'I am Flora Macdonald,' a quiet voice said. 'And thanks to you I have at last escaped from that inn.'

In that moment Rhona felt her beart rejoicing. Her plan had indeed succeeded!

When sending the great-coat and hat to Flora Macdonald she had suggested she should wear them to escape from the inn.

And Flora Macdonald had walked straight past the sentry without being recognised.

Gazing at her in the darkness Rhona realised that she could only be a few years older than herself.

'Let us not talk now,' Flora Macdonald said. 'Let us hurry on. Soon we shall come to a path with which I am very familiar and when we reach it I will get rid of this hat and great-coat.'

But little did they realise there was someone else who had lurked in the darkness at the back of the inn.

As Rhona and Flora Macdonald walked on, a dark figure moved silently behind them.

If she had seen him, Rhona would have experienced overwhelming alarm. For it was Wild Geordie who followed after the two girls—his face alight with triumph.

'Wild Geordie's luck has turned at last,' he murmured. 'Rhona Ross was foolish to think that she could trick the keen eyes of such a one as myself. The moment I entered the inn kitchen, I know who she was.'

He rubbed his hands together in infinite satisfaction.

'How wise I was to keep my knowledge to myself,' he exulted. 'Unknown to the Redcoats, Flora Macdonald has left the inn and now, guided by Rhona Ross, she goes to meet the prince. The two girls are now leading me straight to him.'

He loosened the dirk he carried in his belt.

'Wild Geordie will yet become the richest man in the islands,' he muttered in satisfaction. 'For now the prince will be taken by me alone and I shall gain the whole of the reward.'

He smiled. And ahead of him Rhona and her companion walked on into the darkness—to meet the prince.

Where was the Prince?

All through the night Rhona and Flora Macdonald walked side by side.

Almost as soon as they had taken to a narrow path Flora had got rid of the heavy great-coat and hat and dropped them out of sight into a gully and, unhampered, she was able to lead Rhona across the island.

She told Rhona that she knew this part of the island well.

It was the home of her brother, Angus Macdonald. In fact, it was on a short cut that would bring them out at the prince's cave that Flora led Rhona.

No sooner did dawn begin to streak the sky than Rhona was looking over her shoulder. Her great fear was that she might see glimpses of red behind her.

Perhaps the escape of Flora Macdonald had been discovered almost at once and now the Redcoats had set out in immediate pursuit!

Slowly the morning mists lifted and as far as Rhona could tell nothing moved amongst the heather behind them.

For the first time she saw her companion clearly. As she had guessed, Flora Macdonald was only a few years older than herself.

Rhona marvelled at the girl's bravery. Despite the fact that the Redcoats were already suspicious of her she was risking her liberty in her efforts to get in touch with the prince.

An hour after dawn they climbed a steep slope and then Rhona found herself looking down a long glen. She stared incredulously.

For this was below where the secret cave was situated. She had never imagined that she could have returned to it so quickly.

'This—this is it!' she gasped. 'The cave stands high upon the right-hand side.'

Flora smiled at her gently.

'I know,' she said. 'Did not I tell you that we were taking a short cut? But let us still hurry, for all our plans will go wrong if the prince does not arrive at my brother's house today.'

With a wildly beating heart Rhona climbed the last few yards to the cave. Had the prince recovered his strength? The chances were they would find him asleep, for it was still very early in the morning.

It was Rhona who parted the bushes and who stepped first into the cave. Flora Macdonald followed close behind her.

'Sire,' Rhona began excitedly. 'Sire, I have brought Flora Macdonald——'

She broke off. Her eyes had become accustomed to the gloom and she saw the cave was empty!

'He—he is not here!' Flora gasped in sudden dismay.

Just for a moment Rhona knew a great alarm. Had the prince been captured during her absence?

Then, lying on the ledge where she had found the small

package of food, she saw not only her own plaid shawl, but the bonnet and plaid that belonged to the prince.

'See!' she cried excitedly. 'The prince has left his bonnet and plaid behind him. He cannot be far away.'

But Flora was clasping her hands.

'He would not take the risk of leaving the cave himself,' she murmured.

Despite her fears, Rhona smiled.

'I am not sure,' she said quietly. 'He is one who hates to be inactive. If he had recovered his strength, he would hate to lie cooped up in this cave. I think we shall find that he has only ventured abroad in order to obtain some exercise.'

Flora looked at her anxiously.

'I trust you are right,' she commented. 'I trust, too, that the prince will not keep us waiting long. If we do not reach my brother's house today, we shall miss the boat that is waiting to take us across to Skye.'

She clasped her hands.

'If that happens the prince may never get another chance to leave this island.'

It was then that somewhere nearby a twig snapped. Instantly both girls swung round.

'The prince!' Rhona gasped in great relief. 'He must be coming now!'

The bushes parted and a bare-headed figure stepped into view. In his hands was a drawn claymore.

At sight of him a scream almost rose in Rhona's throat and she shrank back against the wall of the cave.

The man who had parted the bushes was not Bonnie Prince Charlie.

It was Wild Geordie!

Flora Macdonald also shrank back in dismay.

But in that first moment Wild Geordie had no eyes for the two girls. He leaned forward as his gaze probed into every nook and cranny of the small cave—but he found nothing.

'The prince,' he snapped, 'what have you done with the prince?'

It was Rhona who found words to answer him.

'The prince is not here,' she said.

Immediately Wild Geordie's face was full of anger.

'So once again you have deceived me, Rhona Ross,' he cried. 'Evidently Wild Geordie wasn't quite as clever as he thought he was. You must have realised that I recognised you at the inn—you must have known that I was following you.'

His knuckles showed white as he gripped his claymore.

'So you led Wild Geordie on a wild goose chase!' he exclaimed. 'You brought me to this cave because you knew I would think that the prince was hiding here.'

For one moment Rhona feared that he was going to leap towards them.

'But you cannot hope to save the prince,' he went on. 'Now that I've shown myself to you, I will see to it that you do not escape me again. I shall take both of you to the English camp, and there the English will make you tell what you know of the prince.'

There was a thoughtful gleam in his eyes now.

'When you have told where the prince is,' he went on, "it will be because you were captured by me. And so I shall still be able to claim some reward for the capture of Charles Stuart.'

Rhona reached out to pick up her plaid. As she did so, Wild Geordie saw the bonnet and plaid of the prince.

'Do you hand that bonnet and plaid to me,' he rapped. 'That is a finer bonnet than any I have ever worn. That plaid, too, will look far better upon me than it ever looked upon the false Stuart.'

He snatched the bonnet and plaid from Rhona and quickly he pulled them on.

'And now,' he said, 'we make for the English camp. You will walk quickly in front of me.'

Rhona looked at Flora Macdonald. A wild desire to try to escape had come upon her. But she knew she would never be able to out-distance Wild Geordie. And if she tried to run away she might endanger her companion.

Flora reached out to take Rhona's hand.

'The more they waste their time with us the better,' she said softly. 'Every minute so wasted must be a minute gained for our prince.'

And so, side by side, Rhona and Flora Macdonald started away from the cave, with Wild Geordie striding along close behind them.

As they drew nearer to the coast, however, Rhona was quick to see that Flora's eyes were never still.

She evidently hoped that she might be seen and recognised by some of the islanders and that they would come to her rescue.

On and on they walked, and it was all familiar ground to Rhona now.

She was being taken to the port where the English schooner had dropped anchor.

'But Prince Charlie is still free,' she kept comforting herself. 'By now he may be on the other side of the island. Perhaps already he has found a ship to take him away.'

Presently they were climbing a path that led to the cliff edge. When they reached it, Rhona knew they would be in sight of the port.

'Hurry!' Wild Geordie suddenly snapped. 'You waste my time!'

Rhona stole a glance at her companion's face, and saw Flora looked worried and pre-occupied.

Angus Macdonald was waiting for her to bring the prince to catch his ship today.

274

Rhona tried to fight down her own fears. In one thing at least they had succeeded.

Bonnie Prince Charlie was still at large, and no matter how much they were questioned, they would not give him away!

Not that they could—for neither knew anything of the prince's present whereabouts.

Near to the edge of the cliff the path took a sharp turn. The two girls rounded it—and then, without warning, a dark shadow stepped from behind a projecting boulder.

'Hold!'

It was a voice full of command, and the sound of it forced a cry from Rhona's lips.

It was Bonnie Prince Charlie himself who had stepped between Wild Geordie and his two prisoners!

A Disappointment

Rhona saw the sun flash upon the steel of the claymore the prince held in his hand.

Somehow, since parting from Rhona, he had succeeded in arming himself!

'Hold!' he cried again. 'We are well met, my Tannock Traitor!'

Wild Geordie answered the command with a shout of anger.

'The Pretender!' he cried. 'Wild Geordie's luck still holds. It's the whole reward I'll now be claiming—not a paltry share!'

Suddenly, Wild Geordie's clamyore was flashing in the early morning sun.

The two girls scrambled farther up the path, and now Rhona could see the port. And right at the foot of the path was a large camp where many Redcoats were stirring.

But she gave those things only a fleeting glimpse.

Her heart was full of fear—fear for her prince.

She knew Wild Geordie's strength; men had talked about his skill as a swordsman at Tannock Island.

But in the same moment Rhona remembered the prince's prowess with the sword. Once before he had overcome Wild Geordie when he, the prince, had been unarmed.

Clang!

The heavy claymores struck together, and in that first minute Rhona feared for the outcome.

For cleverly Wild Geordie manoeuvred his way until he was standing between the two girls and the prince.

Then, parrying his opponent's thrusts, he moved to higher ground, thus gaining a great advantage. He attacked with such force that the prince was forced to give a dozen paces at least.

With their hearts in their mouths, Rhona and Flora Macdonald watched.

They knew that the prince must still be weak from his wound——

But suddenly the prince was attacking, and now it was Wild Geordie who gave ground.

Slowly, a step at a time, he backed higher up the path until both Rhona and Flora were compelled to move farther away from the tussle.

It was Rhona who pulled Flora to one side.

'If we stand here,' she gasped, 'we'll be in full view of the Redcoat camp.'

There was no longer triumph in Wild Geordie's face—only alarm. But still he fought.

Now back and back he was forced, however, until he was standing right at the top of the path in full view of the camp.

Then Rhona realised the added danger.

The Redcoats had seen Wild Geordie and a number of them were racing towards the cliff path.

It seemed as if they would be hemmed in from all sides. They were helpless to save themselves.

'Sire! Sire!' Rhona gasped. 'You have been seen—the Redcoats climb the path!'

Even as she spoke the first word, the prince jerked Wild Geordie's claymore out of his grasp. It circled in the air and disappeared from sight over the edge of the cliff.

With his man disarmed, the prince stepped back a pace in order to look in the direction where Rhona was pointing.

In that moment Wild Geordie stooped and picked up a heavy stone. With a treacherous smile he lifted it to his shoulder to hurl at the prince.

But something made him pause.

One of the Redcoats on the cliff was pointing—pointing to Wild Geordie, and a great, triumphant cry came from him.

"'Tis the Pretender himself! We have him at last!'

Rhona caught her breath. Was there hope yet? The Redcoats must have recognised the bonnet and the plaid Wild Georgie was wearing.

But they were taking it for granted that the wearer was none other than Bonnie Prince Charlie!

The prince jumped quickly to one side. Abruptly Wild Geordie turned, but as he did so he struck his heel against a stone on the cliff edge.

Suddenly he was tottering backwards. He struggled wildly to recover his balance, but the piece of rock he was holding proved his undoing.

As he tripped, he clutched the heavy stone to his chest, and the weight of it bore him backwards.

There was one cry, and then Wild Geordie disappeared from sight over the edge of the cliff.

With a gasp, Rhona turned away her head.

Then, from below, came another shout.

'The Pretender has gone over the cliff! He has fallen into the sea!'

Rhona's dismay turned to a tremendous relief. Wild

Geordie had landed in the sea. And for the moment they were safe!

The Redcoats, believing it was the prince who had fallen, would put to sea in the hope of picking him up. It was unlikely that any of them would now make for the cliff top.

And then Flora Macdonald was speaking urgently.

'They have not seen us, sire,' she gasped. 'They saw only Wild Geordie. Because he was wearing your garments they think that he was the prince. They will not seek after us yet. Never again shall we have such a chance as this. Come! Let us follow this gully!'

With Flora taking the lead, and with the prince bringing up the rear they went scrambling down a narrow gully.

At the bottom Rhona could not help the sigh of relief which escaped her when she saw that no one was scrambling after them.

But if Rhona had looked over the cliff she would have seen that Wild Geordie was already a danger. It was some time before his head broke the surface of the sea. When it did the traitor from Tannock Isle started to swim strongly.

Straight for the beach he went and here many Redcoats were lined up to await him. The moment he waded ashore several hands gripped him firmly.

But immediately there were cries of dismay and anger.

''Tis not the Pretender after all!'

Wild Geordie scowled at them.

'You waste your time with me!' he snapped. 'The Pretender seeks safety inland. 'Twas the Pretender I fought with on top of the cliff—had I not tripped and fallen he would be my prisoner now.'

And then he actually laughed.

'But Wild Geordie can still bide his time,' he muttered. 'Does he not know the plans made for the Pretender by Hugh Ross of Tannock Isle? Only Wild Geordie knows where Flora

278

Macdonald will seek a boat to carry her and the false Stuart to Skye.'

His voice became urgent and he turned to the men.

'Take me to your captain—quickly!' he rapped. 'I have much to tell him.'

And, with the troops, he hurried away.

Meantime, Rhona and her two companions were hurrying, too. But Flora's eyes remained anxious as they pressed on.

'We still have a long way to go,' she breathlessly explained. 'We shall not be safe now until we reach my brother's house. Do you keep close behind me for, should we be seen, we dare not hope to escape again.'

Soon they were walking across a part of the island that Rhona had not seen before.

Confident at last that there was no immediate danger, they slowed down their pace a little. The prince fell into step alongside Rhona.

'I should not have left the cave this morning, little cousin,' he told her. 'Once again my impatience has brought danger to my friends.'

He looked very concerned indeed.

'A night's rest worked wonders,' he went on. 'And yesterday morning I was myself again. Still I remained in the cave all day.'

He shrugged his shoulders.

'But this morning I could remain inactive no longer. As there was no one to be seen and, as I did not expect you back so soon, I thought it safe to venture forth.'

'We feared you were captured, sire,' said Rhona.

'I came upon a crofter's cottage,' he explained. 'And there I was given a meal and, thank goodness, I was also asked to accept this claymore as a gift.'

Once again his face showed deep concern.

'Luck was indeed with me this morning, little cousin,' he

went on. 'As I started to climb towards the cave, I saw you and your companion walking away from it followed by a man who was wearing my bonnet and plaid. I knew at once you were in trouble and so I followed after you.'

Prince Charlie paused.

'Not until you'd almost reached the coast did I get my chance to get ahead of you. What happened then you know.'

Rhona looked at him with glowing eyes.

'Your sudden appearance on the cliff path, sire, was the most wonderful thing that ever happened!' she breathed.

He looked down at her.

'But you have a story to tell, too, little cousin,' he said.

Quickly, Rhona told of her adventures at the inn and how Flora had succeeded in escaping from under the very eyes of the Redcoats.

Bonnie Prince Charlie looked at Flora, who was walking on ahead.

'The Scots are a brave race,' he said. 'Methinks that their women folk are fully the equal of the men where bravery is concerned.'

At that wonderful compliment the colour flooded Rhona's cheeks.

They continued on, but every few minutes Rhona could not resist the impulse to look behind her.

For her mind was still full of Wild Geordie. He had fallen into the sea, but Rhona knew the traitor to be the strong swimmer he was.

As soon as the Redcoats saw him, one glance would tell them that he was not Bonnie Prince Charlie.

The moment that fact was known, the Redcoats would flock to the cliff-top, hoping to find the trail of the man who had been with Wild Geordie when he fell over the cliff. So Rhona thought.

The sun was high in the sky when a sudden exclamation

escaped Rhona. **Once again** she had turned to look behind her.

For, some distance away, she had seen the sun glint upon shining equipment.

'The Redcoats follow after us!' she gasped.

The horizon was so clear that they were able to pick out the moving figures of a large party of Redcoats.

'They are too far away to worry us now,' Flora Macdonald said quietly. 'Within half an hour we shall reach my brother's house. There, sire, you will be safe.'

But it seemed that the shocks of that day were not finished.

They came to the head of a wide glen and it was Flora Macdonald who now pulled up with a gasp of consternation. Both the prince and Rhona hurried to her side.

Half-way down the glen they saw a large stone-built house, with a narrow ribbon of road which wound by it.

But they also saw the Redcoats who were camped at the roadside!

'Look!' Flora gasped. 'They road is guarded on both sides of the house. There are sentries, too, up on the brae itself.'

With alarmed eyes she looked at the prince.

'My brother and his household must have become suspects, sire,' she said. 'The house is surrounded by Redcoats and we cannot approach it without being seen.'

The prince's eyes had narrowed.

'Then I shall be denied the pleasure of calling upon your brother,' he said quietly. 'We must travel on to the coast as we are.'

Flora shook her head.

'We cannot go on,' she said positively. 'Ahead of us lies the most desolate part of the island and there is only one Pass that leads to the coast. That Pass must already be very well guarded.'

Flora trembled as she spoke.

'And because of the Redcoats behind us, we dare not try to retrace our steps.'

Rhona looked round her with a deep sense of dismay. She had come so far in her travels with the prince now—had overcome so many difficulties. Yet it seemed that all was lost.

'If we could only get to the house!' Flora said. 'Even with the Redcoats surrounding it you would be safe, sire. And my brother's plans are already made for conveying you secretly to the coast.'

She pointed to a jagged scar in the hillside some distance ahead—a scar that led right down to the wall of the house.

'If a sentry had not been posted up on the brae,' Flora went on, 'we could have used that gully and got to the house without being seen. But that one sentry can see almost the whole length of the gully.'

Rhona looked at the solitary Redcoat. Only one soldier stood between the prince and comparative safety.

Rhona looked at the soldiers who were camped at the roadside. If only she were still disguised as a gipsy!

But early that morning she had washed the stain from her face.

Nevertheless, she turned quickly to Flora Macdonald.

'Do you change your plaid shawl with mine,' she said. 'If I walk down the road alone, nobody will take much notice of a solitary island girl wearing the Macdonald tartan.'

Rhona's eyes were glowing with excitement now.

'The soldiers will probably let me go on to the house. If I can have but a few words with your brother, Flora, I think I shall be able to take the sentry's attention away from the gully.'

Quickly she explained the plan she had in mind. Then, before she had finished, Flora Macdonald was taking the plaid shawl from her shoulders.

'You think quickly, Rhona,' she said with a smile. 'Such

a simple plan as yours might well be successful. Let's try it!'

And so the solitary figure of a girl wearing the Macdonald tartan appeared on the road.

Rhona forced herself to walk along slowly. But as she passed a large tent her heart thudded.

Then it gave a great jump. A Redcoat sergeant stepped out in front of her!

'What is your business upon this road, missy?' he demanded.

Rhona tried to look at him with wide-eyed surprise.

'I go to the house of Angus Macdonald,' she answered quietly. 'He often gives away food to poor crofting families and I hope that he may have some food for me.'

The sergeant smiled.

'It's a wonder to me how you people manage to live at all upon these barren islands,' he said. 'I hope Angus Macdonald may have food to give you.'

And Rhona was allowed to continue on her way.

Her breath came quicker in her relief.

So far her plan had succeeded. Could she hope that the rest of it would succeed also?

She knew that unless it did, all hope must be abandoned for the prince's escape.

Her Plan in Full

A heavy bell hung before the house of Angus Macdonald, and when Rhona pulled upon it the door was opened by a tall maid-servant.

She looked at Rhona inquiringly.

'I would speak with Angus Macdonald,' Rhona said quietly. 'I have a message from his sister.'

The maid-servant's eyes widened for a moment and then she reached out almost to drag Rhona inside. It seemed she could not close the door quickly enough.

'Come with me,' she said breathlessly. 'This way, please.'

She led the way into a large room where Angus Macdonald and his family were seated at their mid-day meal. As soon as the maid-servant gave Rhona's message Angus Macdonald came jumping to his feet.

Rhona recognised him at once from his likeness to his sister.

How anxious he looked!

'What news of Flora?' he asked huskily. 'Has she fallen into the hands of the Redcoats?'

'She is hiding at the top of the brae,' Rhona answered quietly. 'She fears to approach the house because there is someone with her.'

Immediately there was a tense silence inside the room.

'You mean the—the prince?' Angus Macdonald asked, his voice shaking.

Rhona nodded her head.

Quickly Angus Macdonald crossed to one of the windows and he peered out.

'I don't know what has gone wrong,' he said as he turned back. 'This morning, without warning, Redcoats appeared all about the house. I knew when I saw them it could only mean that they'd discovered that I'd been in touch with Prince Charlie.'

He clenched his hands.

'I feared for my brave sister, too,' he said. 'I knew when she went out to meet the prince that she was risking arrest.'

He shook his head.

'If only the prince had arrived here two days ago!' he went on worriedly. 'I could have got him to the coast without any difficulty then. As it is now—I know not what to do.'

Rhona looked out of the window.

'If he stays upon the brae,' she said, 'he must be captured.'

She looked quickly then at Flora Macdonald's brother.

'Suppose the prince comes to the house unseen,' she prompted, 'what would happen then?'

'If he comes to the house unseen,' Angus Macdonald told her, 'I can hide him away. If the Redcoats search for him then they would have to pull the house down stone by stone before finding him.'

'Then,' Rhona said quickly, 'I have a plan.'

Once again she outlined the idea she had told to the prince and Flora Macdonald.

'The English Redcoats have a great love of food,' she said. 'Every time I have spoken to one of them they have complained bitterly about our poor island fare. I am sure that food—especially meat—will tempt a Redcoat more than anything else.'

Angus Macdonald looked at her, and there was admiration in his eyes.

'Our prince is very lucky in his helpers,' he said. 'But let us waste no further time.'

A few minutes later Rhona slipped out of a side door. She was carrying a cloth-covered basin which had been filled with venison stew.

No sooner was she outside the wall of the house than she clambered down into the gully. After that, bending low, she started upon the long ascent.

Up on the hillside a sentry was slowly striding to and fro. Hearing a sudden sound behind him he spun round and his eyes widened at sight of Rhona.

'How did you get here without my seeing you?' he demanded gruffly.

Rhona pointed to the gully.

'I climbed the gully from the house,' she said.

As she spoke she uncovered the basin so that the sentry had the full benefit of its appetising aroma.

'I saw you up here on the hillside, and I thought that

perhaps you'd be hungry. I have brought you this meal.'

The sentry looked quickly about him and then he seated himself upon a flat-topped boulder.

'Venison stew!' he whispered hungrily. 'It is many days since I last sat down to a dish of meat. What you have brought to me, missy, is very, very welcome.'

He took the basin and quickly he began to eat.

Rhona seated herself at his side so that she obstructed his view of the gully.

'All my life I have lived upon these islands,' she said. 'I know nothing of the outer world. Tell me of this England from which you come. Is it true that many of its cities are bigger than some of our islands?'

He was too busy eating for a while to answer her.

'I come from London,' he said at last. 'The largest city in the whole world. Would that I were back there again!'

Immediately Rhona was playing for time—asking him all the questions she could think of.

He told her of the great Tower of London and of the great palace of Whitehall.

'Yes,' he laughed, 'it was not so long ago that there was great panic in Whitehall. Had the Pretender not turned back when his army reached Derby he might today be king in Whitehall.'

Out of the corner of her eyes Rhona watched the gully. She held her breath as she saw first Flora and then the prince go by.

The soldier went on eating and talking and he saw nothing at all.

By the time the basin was empty Rhona knew that both Flora and the prince had reached the house unseen.

She made to rise, her heart singing—but suddenly, behind them, there was a sudden rolling of loose pebbles and the sound of a sharp, authoritative voice: 'Stand to attention!'

The basin fell from the soldier's lap, to shatter into pieces as he leapt up. He spun around to face an angry Redcoat captain.

But the appearance of the captain had an even greater effect upon Rhona than upon the sentry. She stared at him in sheer disbelief.

For she was looking at the captain she had last seen upon Rhos Island.

'So', he said curtly, 'we meet again.'

He bit his lip for a moment.

'I did not expect to find you upon the hillside,' he went on.

'I came up here to discover why my sentry was no longer pacing out his beat.'

He looked at the shattered basin, and then he looked towards the gully. Immediately his eyes were full of enlightenment.

'So!' he exclaimed. 'It was not kindness that caused you to bring food to my sentry. While the foolish man's attention was taken with satisfying his hunger, somebody slipped down the gully on his way to the house. I do not need to wonder who that somebody was.'

And then the captain was smiling.

'So, after all,' he dryly commented, 'you have made my task easy for me. If I search the house of Angus Macdonald I know now that I shall find the Pretender, Charles Stuart.'

Lifting a whistle to his lips, he blew three loud blasts.

Rhona went hot and then cold.

She knew that the whistles were a signal that the house of Angus Macdonald was to be raided.

The soldiers would burst into it only a few minutes after the prince himself had entered it.

With a sudden gasp Rhona spun upon her heel and went rushing into the gully. The sentry would have darted after her, but the captain stayed him.

'Let her go,' he said quietly. 'She can be rounded up later. It is the Pretender we want.'

Down the gully Rhona flew, across the yard and into the house. In the dining-room she found an anxious group gathered about Prince Charlie and Flora.

'Those whistles,' Angus Macdonald gasped. 'What do they mean?'

Rhona fought to get her breath.

'The Redcoats know that the prince has entered the house,' she said. 'Even now they are running here to search for him—'

A cry of utter dismay escaped Angus Macdonald.

'Then all is lost!' he gasped. 'We have no time to open the secret hiding-place. If we start to open it now the Redcoats will surprise us when it is only half open.'

Rhona also looked about her in utter consternation. She couldn't stand by and let her prince be captured as easily as this.

There must be something they could do—some trick they could play.

And then—an idea came to her.

'There is only one thing to be done!' she gasped. 'It may yet give us time!'

Quickly she explained her plan.

Only a few moments later there was a loud knocking at the outer door. It suddenly crashed open, and there was the sound of heavy footsteps on the flagstones in the hall.

The door of the dining-room was flung wide and the Redcoat captain strode in with half a dozen soldiers at his heels.

He saw Angus Macdonald and his family seated at the dining table, and with them Rhona and Flora Macdonald.

It seemed that they were in the middle of their meal.

A tall maid-servant was serving at table—a maid-servant who turned away as the soldiers burst in and who walked slowly to the nearest window. Leaning her elbows upon the sill, she stood looking out, but no one noticed her movements.

Meanwhile, Angus Macdonald came to his feet.

'Is it English manners to invade the privacy of a Scottish gentleman's home in this way?' he demanded.

Angrily the captain stared at him. His eyes had a steely glint in them as they swept the room.

'You know why I am here,' he snapped in answer. 'I seek the Pretender, Charles Stuart.'

Angus Macdonald looked at him and shook his head.

'You waste your time,' he snapped.

The Redcoat captain took a step nearer to him.

'The Pretender is in this house,', he stated firmly. 'Only a few moments ago he came down the gully from the hillside. He seized his opportunity when the attention of my sentry was occupied by that girl.'

He pointed to Rhona.

Angus Macdonald shrugged his shoulders.

'There seems to be some mistake,' he said coldly. 'It was my sister here who came down the gully.'

The captain stared at Flora Macdonald. And she coolly returned his gaze.

'Why should your sister enter your house in such a secret way?' he wanted to know.

Again Angus Macdonald shrugged.

'My sister approached the house this morning,' he stated, 'and she was surprised to see it surrounded by Redcoats.'

He paused for a moment, weighing his words carefully.

'Fearing that something had happened to me—fearing that your soldiers might prevent her coming to the house—she decided to enter it secretly. That is why her friend engaged your sentry in conversation.'

'When she came down the gully the prince was with her,' the Redcoat captain insisted. 'We have been warned to keep an eye upon Flora Macdonald.'

He gazed round the rather bare room and saw there was no place where a man could have been hidden away.

'It is obvious that I waste my time in this room,' he snapped. 'But I know that somewhere in this house the Pretender is hidden. I'm telling you that he will not remain hidden long.'

He spun upon his heel.

'Come,' he rapped.

He flung himself out of the room, and the file of soldiers followed after him.

Only then did the tall maid-servant turn back from the window. She was wearing a long gown to which a hood was attached and the hood had been pulled over her hair.

But underneath that hood was the face of Prince Charlie!

It had been Rhona's idea that he should don one of the maid's biggest dresses and pretend to be waiting at the table.

The Redcoat captain and his soldiers had not given him as much as a glance.

'Quickly now,' Angus Macdonald said urgently. 'I need the help of every one of you.'

He moved hurriedly to a huge sideboard which stood against an inner wall.

Without the help of the prince they could not have moved the sideboard at all. But now they managed easily.

As one end of it came away from the wall Rhona gave a gasp. There was the opening of a secret place behind it.

'Quickly, sire,' Angus Macdonald gasped. 'Quickly!'

The prince squeezed himself between the sideboard and the wall, and then he had disappeared into the secret opening.

It was all the others could do then to push the huge sideboard back into place. When it had been done they went back to their seats at the table.

When the discomfited Redcoat captain returned to the room some half an hour later, the whole of the house had been ransacked from top to bottom.

'Well,' Angus Macdonald greeted him. 'Your search did not benefit you after all.'

The captain scowled.

'Maybe you spoke the truth about your sister,' he said, 'but I know that plans have been made for the Pretender to come to this house. I know, too, that you have made plans to spirit him away this evening.'

He laughed then, and he looked straight at Flora Macdonald.

'Within an hour or so,' he went on, 'I know that you are expecting a coach—a coach that you have ordered to convey you down to the coast where a boat is waiting to take you to your father's home on the Isle of Skye.'

The captain gave a grim smile.

'I am fully aware that you had planned the Pretender should travel with you.'

He shook his head.

'I have taken it upon myself to cancel your instructions about the coach,' he went on. 'A coach will arrive here soon, but it will be a coach which I have ordered, and it will be driven by a man that I trust.'

The captain drew a deep breath.

'Furthermore, dear lady, that you may not be tempted to risk your liberty by getting in touch with the Pretender, I have decided to travel with you on the coach and to see you safe aboard the ship that will take you to Skye.'

Angus Macdonald and his sister stood perfectly still and only Rhona saw the great consternation that showed in her eyes for a moment.

It seemed that—in spite of everything—the English captain still had the power to bring all their plans to naught.

'One other thing,' the Redcoat captain went on, 'I shall quarter men in this house until such time as the Pretender is captured. If there is still a chance that you have him hidden here then you may take it from me that he will never escape.'

With those final, shattering words he made his departure.

When Rhona entered the hall of the house some little while later she saw that two soldiers were on guard inside it.

He had kept his word!

She found her opportunity of speaking to Flora in private.

'What will happen about the prince now?' Rhona whispered.

Flora clasped her hands.

'The prince must leave with me this afternoon,' she said. 'If he fails to go aboard the boat that will take him to Skye, then all will be lost. Unless he travels with me, he will not be able to get to the ship, which is waiting to take him to France. That ship is his very last hope.'

Yet it seemed to Rhona then that the prince's attempt to escape was doomed to failure.

Now that the English captain was travelling with Flora that night, it would be utterly impossible for the prince to travel with her.

Thus he must indeed miss the boat that would take him to the Isle of Skye.

And he couldn't remain a prisoner behind the great dresser for any length of time. He would need food and water, and it was a most difficult task to pull the huge piece of furniture away from the wall.

With soldiers quartered in the house, who were on the alert day and night, the hiding-place must be soon discovered.

Never in her life had Rhona felt so helpless. Always before she had been able to think of something to do whenever danger had threatened her prince.

But now she could think of nothing.

She was again in the dining-room when she heard the sound of hoofs. Crossing to the window she looked out and she saw a great lumbering coach turn into the yard.

On the box was seated a bewigged driver wearing a coat edged with tarnished gold lace.

Rhona looked at the coach and suddenly there was a sparkle of excitement in her eyes. Quickly she turned to the white-faced Flora.

'All is not yet lost!' she cried. 'Maybe it is good fortune and not bad that the English captain intends to travel with you. Because of that the prince may still leave your brother's house in safety.'

Journey by Coach

Flora Macdonald's voice was desperate.

'You speak of the impossible, Rhona. 'Tis out of the question that the prince should travel with me now.'

But the excitement had only deepened in Rhona's eyes.

'There is still a chance,' she insisted. 'Our prince is brave, and there is no risk that he fears to take. Has not his audacity carried him safely through many a peril already?'

Quickly then Rhona explained the plan that had come into her mind.

For a moment Flora hesitated, but as she looked out of the window at the coach hope suddenly replaced the despairing expression in her eyes.

'My brother must be told at once,' she said then.

Angus Macdonald came quickly at his sister's call, and once again Rhona explained. At the end he frowned.

''Twill mean a great risk for the prince,' he said, 'but methinks it is a risk that he must take.'

Once again Flora Macdonald's face became full of anxiety.

'But what of you, Angus?' she inquired. 'If Rhona's plan succeeds it will soon be known that you sheltered the prince in your house. It will mean certain arrest for you.'

Angus Macdonald shook his head.

'Do not worry about me, my sister', he said. 'If the prince gets safely away, then I shall be well able to look after myself. Tonight I shall slip away unseen from this house and not all the Redcoats in the world will be able to stop me.'

He smiled confidently.

'When it becomes known that the prince has sailed for France,' he went on, 'the Redcoats will soon leave the islands. When they have gone I shall return. But we waste time.'

Spinning upon his heel he clapped his hands and the tall maid-servant made her appearance.

Angus Macdonald gave her quick instructions and instantly she set about the task of placing wooden platters upon the long wooden table.

'Do you seat yourselves at the table,' Angus Macdonald commanded Rhona and Flora. 'You must eat before you start upon your long journey.'

Crossing to the huge sideboard, he picked up a small bell and started to ring it. It was a signal to the household that a meal was being served.

As everyone in the house sat at the same table, all the servants came flocking in.

But Angus Macdonald beckoned two tall islanders to him before they could seat themselves at the table.

They listened intently to him as he spoke, and at the end their expressions hadn't changed.

Quietly both men moved to the wall near the door and one of them detached a wide plaid from his shoulder.

The maid-servant filled the platters with food and the rest of the household started to eat. But for once Rhona was so worried that she had no appetite at all.

Would things turn out as she had anticipated? And, if so, would her plan succeed?

Perhaps she was demanding too much of the prince— perhaps she was asking him to take too great a risk.

Suddenly, in the midst of her frantic thoughts, the door was flung open and the Redcoat captain appeared. He was already attired for the journey.

He spoke angrily.

'The coach has arrived,' he snapped. 'If we are to reach the coast before nightfall it is necessary that we leave at once. I have no intention of being caught upon the mires you call roads after dark.'

Angus Macdonald stood up at the head of the table.

'My sister travels upon a long journey,' he said. 'If the winds are contrary their voyage to Skye may take a very long time. Thus I think it necessary that she should eat well before her journey starts.'

Then Angus beckoned to the captain cordially.

'And I invite you, sir, to partake of our Scottish hospitality.'

Angrily the Redcoat captain came walking farther into the room.

'You knew the coach was expected,' he snapped. 'You should have eaten long before this. I insist that we leave at once—'

That was the moment when the door closed quietly behind the Redcoat captain.

At the same time one of the servants stepped quickly forward.

His plaid went over the captain's head, to be drawn so tightly about his mouth that he was unable to utter a sound.

Then the captain felt the point of a dirk pressing into the small of his back.

'If you wish to remain safe,' Angus Macdonald said quietly, 'you'll make no attempt to struggle.'

Half choked as he was, the Redcoat was incapable of putting up any real resistance. Quickly he was relieved of his long great-coat and his sword.

It was Rhona who picked up the cockaded hat which had

been knocked to the floor when the plaid had been flung over his head.

This done, the Redcoat's arms and legs were tied and then he was securely gagged.

'Now,' Angus Macdonald said tersely.

The whole household helped to pull away the huge sideboard from the wall.

Rhona's excitement was so intense that her breath came in quick gasps. At any moment she expected Redcoat soldiers to burst in, in search of their captain.

But the sideboard was pulled away from the wall, and at Angus Macdonald's whisper the prince came quickly out of the secret hiding-place.

He looked on in surprise as the English captain was carried behind the sideboard and thrust into the hiding-place he had just vacated.

'Quickly, sire,' Angus Macdonald said. 'There is not a moment to lose. If all goes well you'll be leaving this house within a few minutes.'

Rapidly he explained Rhona's plan, and at the end the prince's eyes were glowing with excitement.

'I have said it before,' he stated, 'and I must say it again. One of the luckiest things that ever happened to me was my meeting with Rhona Ross on Tannock Isle.'

Quickly then the prince was pulling on the officer's great-coat. He buckled the long sword about him and then he carefully pulled down the cockaded hat well over his eyes.

It was just as well that he was of the same build as the Redcoat captain.

In fact, it was the realisation of this that had caused the plan to form in Rhona's mind.

'One of my men will take you out by the back door, sire,' Angus Macdonald said. 'If you walk quickly round the side of the house you should be able to get to the coach without

296

having to pass any of the Redcoat soldiers. My sister and Rhona will leave the house immediately you have reached the coach.'

Bonnie Prince Charlie paused only to fervently thank Angus Macdonald for the great risk he had run in offering him sanctuary.

A minute later the door was quietly opened and the prince followed one of the servants out of the room.

The two minutes that followed then were perhaps the worst of all. Everybody in the room feared to hear a wild shout signifying that the prince had been seen and recognised.

They all stared at Angus Macdonald, who had stationed himself near the window.

'The prince is at the coach now,' he suddenly whispered. 'Do you hurry, sister.'

Hearts thudding, Flora Macdonald and Rhona left the room, pulling their plaid shawls about their heads as they did so. They passed two soldiers who were stationed in the hall and then they were out in the open.

The bewigged coachman still sat upon the driving-seat and the prince, in his officer's uniform, stood alongside the vehicle.

The moment Rhona and Flora appeared he pulled the door open.

As they climbed inside he bowed respectfully, and then quickly he followed after them.

'Make good speed, driver,' he said.

The whip cracked and the horses strained at the traces. The vehicle began to lumber towards the yard gate.

Here a sentry was on duty. Would he look into the coach? Rhona wondered frantically.

But at sight of the moving vehicle the sentry came to attention, and he remained at attention as the coach went by him and turned into the narrow roadway.

Only then, as the heavy vehicle began to gather speed, did Rhona breathe easily once again.

Her plan had succeeded!

With ordinary luck now the prince would be well on his way to safety.

Once more he was heading for the coast and for the boat that would start him back on his long journey to France.

On and on lumbered the coach and then Rhona saw they were approaching a very narrow valley. She knew it must be the Pass that Flora had told her about—the only Pass that led to the coast.

Flora had also said that this Pass was bound to be guarded by Redcoats, Rhona remembered.

Suppose some of the soldiers insisted upon looking into the coach—suppose that they knew the English captain by sight?

In that case, in the very moment of success, her plan might still fail.

Even as the thought came to Rhona she heard a loud shout.

'Halt! In the king's name!'

The coach stopped with such a jerk that Rhona was nearly flung forward out of the seat.

She gasped then, for the prince had leant over to pull down the window.

At sight of the cockaded officer's hat, however, the soldier who had stopped the coach smartly saluted.

'I travel on the trail of Charles Stuart, the Pretender,' the prince rapped coldly. 'You delay me at your peril.'

The soldier saluted once again, and then he stepped back from the coach.

'I have no wish to delay you, captain,' he said.

The coach moved on, and the prince sank back into his seat. Never had Rhona admired him so much as she did at that moment.

In all the emergencies they had encountered since leaving Tannock Isle she had never once found the prince thrown off his guard for long.

Out of the Pass the coach jolted, and then it was moving over very flat countryside. Several times the prince looked out of the window and finally he spoke.

'The time has come for me to deal with the coachman,' he said quietly. 'We dare not let him drive us to the place where we are to be met.'

Leaning out of the window then he called to the driver to pull up. As the man obeyed, the prince opened the door and then jumped down to the roadway.

'Do you step down from your box', he commanded. 'There is something wrong with the back of this coach.'

The driver clambered down from his seat and he followed the figure in the Redcoat uniform to the back of the coach.

'What is amiss?' he gruffly demanded. 'I thought the coach was travelling very well indeed.'

Slowly then the prince turned.

'There is nothing amiss,' he said quickly.

The driver stared at him and immediately he gave a violent start. Utter amazement came into his eyes.

'You're not Captain Lawson,' he burts out. 'Why, you must be—'

The prince finished the sentence for him.

'Yes,' he said. 'I am Charles Stuart, whom some men call the Pretender.'

As quick as a flash the driver's hand flew to the knife thrust into his belt. But he was given no chance to drew it.

The prince immediately leapt at him.

His reaction was so sudden that the other was caught off balance. He reeled back to fall alongside the coach.

There at the roadside a tremendous tussle took place. But Rhona had little doubt of the outcome for she knew that the prince was a man of exceptional strength and agility.

It was indeed the prince who at last scrambled to his feet while the coach driver remained lying in the roadway.

'He has but lost his senses for a little while,' Prince Charlie said quietly, 'otherwise he is not hurt. He will recover soon and can walk back to yonder village we passed.'

Prince Charlie stepped forward to close the door of the coach.

'We press on,' he smiled. 'No one will interfere with a Redcoat captain who drives a coach.'

But first Prince Charlie dragged the stunned man to the side of the road out of harm's way.

He climbed into the driving-seat and a few minutes later the coach was travelling at the fastest speed yet.

Inside the big vehicle Rhona and Flora exchanged relieved glances.

'The worst is over,' Flora said quietly. 'Ahead of us loyal friends are waiting who will make sure that we reach the Isle of Skye in safety. I do not fear then that anything will prevent our prince getting a safe passage to France.'

On and on the coach lumbered and just before the last of the twilight faded Rhona caught sight of the sea far ahead.

Eagerly Flora leaned out of the window and gave instructions to the prince.

'That headland is our destination, sire,' she said as she pointed ahead. 'Do you halt the coach when we reach it. There we must await the signal.'

The prince nodded his thanks.

It was quite dark when the horses started up a steep slope. They only made it with difficulty and Rhona realised that they must have arrived at the headland.

The coach stopped and instantly Flora was clambering out. Rhona followed after her.

It seemed to her there was a steep bush-covered slope in

front of her—a slope that led right down to the sea.

'We have arrived above Black Cove,' Flora said quietly. 'If all has gone well a boat is waiting there ready to set sail for Skye. But first we must await the signal.'

The three of them stood together in the darkness. And perhaps for Rhona those were the tensest moments of the whole adventure.

They had come so close to succeeding. Surely nothing could go wrong now?

Suddenly Flora caught Rhona's arm.

'Look!' she gasped.

Far below them Rhona saw a swinging light. Thrice it swung and then there was only darkness again.

Someone far down in the cove had swung a lantern three times.

''Tis the signal,' Flora cried excitedly. 'Do you light one of the carriage lanterns, sire, and then swing it once in reply.'

Inside the coach the prince used a tinderbox in order to light the lantern. Then stepping out, he swung it in a long arc before placing the lantern back inside the coach.

'We wait now,' Flora said happily. 'They will come to us to guide us down to the beach.'

That was the moment when the clouds parted and a bright moon sailed into a patch of clear sky. Rhona found herself looking down a bush-covered slope.

She saw the strip of beach at the bottom and also at one end what appeared to be a fisherman's cottage.

She saw, too, the rowing boat that had been pulled up on the sand just out of reach of the water.

It was as she heard the two gasps of her companions that she noticed the big ship riding at anchor inside the cove.

Rhona remembered the ship she had seen off Tannock Isle. This was a man-o'-war!

She gave an alarmed cry.

Why sould a man-o'-war be riding at anchor in the cove?

Could it mean that there was to be no escape for the prince after all—that in spite of everything it was his enemies who were waiting for him?

Wild Geordie Again

'Sire! Sire! Ous plans must be known! There should be no warship in the cove! It must be your enemies who gave us the signal!'

There was great fear in Flora Macdonald's voice.

As she spoke she half-turned as though intending to run back to the coach. But the prince reached out to take her arm.

'Hold!' he said quietly. 'It may be that all is well—that things are far better than we anticipated.'

He spoke with such quiet confidence that for a moment Rhona's fears were stilled.

Then the prince was pointing to the great warship.

'That is no English man-o'-war that rides at anchor,' he said quietly. 'That it a French warship. I have seen too many French warships not to instantly recognise their design.'

'If—if only you can be sure, sire!' Flora gasped.

'I am sure,' he told her. 'It must be, Flora, that your loyal friends from Skye have somehow made contact with that French ship. It is probably a French ship sent to the islands especially to seek me out.'

The prince smiled reassuringly.

'Your friends would naturally tell the French captain of their plans, and they would direct him to this cove.'

Suddenly his voice was full of eagerness.

'Perhaps my travels are indeed over for the moment,' he said. 'If that ship does wait for me then by dawn I shall be well on my way to France!'

All the while Rhona had been staring at him. And now she knew a further cause for alarm.

'Your disguise, sire,' she gasped. 'You are still dressed as a Redcoat officer! If friends are climbing towards us they may think on seeing you that they are walking into a trap and may open fire.'

Instantly the prince started to unbutton the great-coat.

'It is well that I still have you to think for me, little cousin,' he joked. 'I had indeed forgotten that I was in disguise.'

He flung the captain's hat and the great-coat into the coach behind him, retaining only the long sword.

The moon had drifted behind a fine bank of clouds so that it was almost pitch dark again.

Rhona stared down the slope, but no sound came to her. And still she was uneasy.

How could they make sure that the men who must be climbing towards them were indeed friends? Impulsively she turned to the prince.

'Do you let me go down the slope a little way, sire,' she breathed. 'It will give me a chance to see who approaches. If Flora comes with me she will know at once whether they are friends or foes. Should they be foes, then I will whistle to warn you.'

He smiled at her.

'Would your whistle travel far, little cousin?' he wanted to know.

Rhona answered him very confidently indeed.

'On Tannock Isle,' she answered, 'my father's dogs wander far in quest of straying sheep. I have been taught to whistle so that the sound will carry from one end of the glen to the other.'

He nodded his head then.

'It would perhaps be better,' he said, 'if both of you left me at this moment. If it should be foes who come this way, then it would be best for me to attract all their attention. If I must once again flee then I shall flee quicker alone. And it will give you a chance to find some hiding-place for yourself.'

Then he smiled again.

'But I am still sure,' he went on, 'that the presence of a French ship in the cove means that I shall soon be talking to friends.'

Rhona gazed down the slope again and still she heard no sound. Reaching out then she took Flora's hand.

'Come,' she whispered.

There was just sufficient moonlight to allow her to pick a way amongst the bushes.

Bending low and trying to make no sound both girls descended about a third of the way down the slope.

It was then, ahead of her, Rhona saw something move.

Instantly she pulled her companion down behind a bush.

Once again the moon sailed into a clear patch of sky.

Only a few yards to the side of them they could see two men coming quietly through the bushes. At sight of them Rhona's eyes opened wide. Never before had she seen two men so well dressed.

Flora's whisper sounded in her ear.

'We have nothing to fear,' Flora said. 'From their dress I know these two men to be French.'

The two men went on silently climbing, and at a safe distance the two girls followed after them.

They saw the two men step out to the roadway, and they saw them doff their hats in an elaborate gesture as they bowed low.

Rhona heard their voices speaking a strange lauguage. Again Flora spoke reassuringly.

'All is well,' she said. 'They speak in French to the prince.'

Prince Charlie and the two men were deep in conversation as the two girls came out of the bushes. Never before had

304

Rhona heard anyone speak so quickly. She was amazed!

She wondered how the prince could possibly understand what was being said!

The prince turned and beckoned to them.

'All is well, my sweet cousin,' he said. 'Yonder ship awaits but to convey me to safety.'

He introduced the two girls to the Frenchmen. And their names sounded very strange in Rhona's ears.

'It is just as I expected,' Bonnie Prince Charlie said. 'The French ship was cruising off the islands when it was hailed by a boat from Skye.'

He nodded towards the two Frenchmen.

'They were told that the boat was on its way to pick up Mistress Macdonald and myself. Naturally the French ship sailed for the cove at once.'

One of the Frenchmen spoke in English then, but with so pronounced an accent that Rhona could scarcely understand him.

'We have no time to waste, sire,' he said. 'We know that out at sea an English man-o'-war is searching for us. If we are to make safe passage back to France, sire, we must be out to sea long before dawn.'

Impulsively the prince turned to the two girls.

'I cannot leave,' he said quietly, 'until I am assured of the safety of my two companions. But for them the Redcoats would have captured me days ago.'

Again the Frenchman spoke quickly.

'Everything has been arranged,' he said. 'The two ladies have but to go to the cottage on the beach where the fisherman awaits them. He will take them to the next cove where the boat from Skye is waiting.'

The other Frenchman spoke then.

'Please to hurry, sire.' he said. 'At any moment we may have a bright moon in a clear sky. If an English warship sees us at anchor inside the cove we may not be able to make our escape.'

Prince Charlie reached out to take the arms of the two girls.

'You shall see me safely aboard the boat which waits at the beach,' he said.

Down the slope they made their way with one Frenchman taking the lead and the other bringing up the rear.

They came to a narrow stretch of sand and then they were crossing to the rowing boat.

Suddenly Rhona knew a strange sense of desolation. Her wonderful, exciting journey was over.

Her prince was going away, and it was very unlikely that she would ever set eyes on him again.

Somehow she had never imagined that her parting from him would be as abrupt as this.

Quickly she chided herself. She told herself she should only feel glad that the prince's troubles were over.

He was going away to safety—no longer would men hunt him. No longer would he be forever in danger of arrest.

The two Frenchmen pushed the boat into the water, and still they urged the prince to hurry.

So all he could do was to hold the hands of Rhona and Flora for one fleeting moment.

'It seems I have no time to thank you,' he said, 'but I leave you with a very full heart. All my life I shall remember you and both your names will always be dear to me.'

Then Prince Charlie smiled very tenderly at them both.

'And some day in the future I will send a messenger to you—a messenger who will tell you all the things that I now have in my heart, but which I have no time to tell you now.'

There were tears in Rhona's eyes as the prince clambered into the boat. And at that very moment the moon disappeared behind a thick bank of cloud, and it was pitch dark again.

She just caught one glimpse of the prince's waving arm and

306

then the gloom had swallowed him up and he was gone.

Flora spoke quickly then, and it was all Rhona could do to bring her senses back to the present.

'We must hurry to the cottage, Rhona,' Flora said. 'Long before this the English captain may have reached his friends and given the alarm. Fast horses may already be speeding towards us.'

She clenched her hands nervously.

'I shall not breathe easily now until we are safe aboard our boat and the sails have been set for the Isle of Skye.'

Hand in hand they went across the beach to where a small square of light shone from the cottage window.

And then—when they were almost upon it—a voice came to Rhona that pulled her steps up dead.

In that moment every bit of colour drained from her face.

Her fingers closed tightly over the arm of her companion as Flora steered her towards the lighted window.

'Make no sound,' Rhona whispered. 'I fear danger.'

There was no glass to the window and standing alongside the square opening Rhona peered into the cottage.

She saw the angry weather-beaten face of the man who was sitting bound to a chair. He was unable to speak for a cloth had been tied round his mouth.

Rhona, feeling that her heart had suddenly stopped, leaned forward a little more. Only then did she see the figure standing just inside the doorway—a figure that stood with a drawn claymore in his hand.

Rhona began to tremble. So she had made no mistake! It was Wild Geordie from Tannock Isle who guarded the cottage door!

Then he had been rescued from the sea, as she had thought. Somehow he had managed to swim to safety.

But how did he come to be at this fisherman's cottage?

Rhona felt her heart go colder still.

The two Frenchmen had told them to go to the cottage—they had said that the fisherman was waiting there to take them to the boat in the next cove.

Then—then the Frenchmen must have been enemies after all!

And Bonnie Prince Charlie, unconscious of his peril, had willingly gone with them.

It was the sound of Wild Geordie's voice which had first alarmed Rhona. And now he spoke again.

'The Pretender is even now on his way to the ship,' he said, with a sharp laugh. 'The moment he steps aboard he will be surrounded by Redcoats. And the Redcoats have me, Wild Geordie of Tannock Isle, to thank for his capture.'

He laughed again.

'The Pretender thinks I will not oppose him again,' he went on. 'He does not know that I swam ashore just as a captured French warship sailed into the port—and that I am more determined on his capture than ever.'

An angry note came into his voice.

'I knew the plans that had been made for Flora Macdonald and the Pretender, and it was I who suggested the French ship should be manned by an English crew and sailed round to this cove. The Pretender may be clever, but Wild Geordie is cleverer. The ship will bring the Pretender into the open, as nothing else would.' · ·

He broke off to peer out of the cottage doorway.

'I sailed with the ship,' he said, 'and as you know I came ashore with the two Englishmen who were pretending to be Frenchmen. How lucky those Redcoats could speak the strange French language so well!

'While the moonlight lasted I saw them come down the slope with the Pretender walking between them. He evidently had no suspicion at all that he had given himself up to his enemies.'

308

Suddenly Wild Geordie's face became dark and he spoke to the helpless fisherman curtly.

'Any moment now,' he snapped, 'and Rhona Ross from Tannock Island and Flora Macdonald will enter this cottage. It will be good to see their faces when they recognise Wild Geordie. Once before they have been my prisoners, and now they will be my prisoners again. And this time they will not escape me—I shall deliver them safely into the hands of the Redcoats.'

A triumphant burst of laughter escaped him.

'And Wild Geordie has been offered the whole of the reward.' he exulted. 'Within a few days from now Wild Geordie will be the richest man in the Western Isles.'

But already Rhona was pulling the white-faced Flora away from the window. Desperately she tried to look out across the cove.

She was only a few yards away from the cottage when a shrill whistle escaped her—a whistle that must have carried right across the cove.

At sound of it there was a yell of anger from inside the cottage and Wild Geordie came leaping through the doorway.

But the echo of the whistle was still in the air when shouting came from the cove itself.

'The Pretender! The Pretender!' was the cry. 'He's gone overboard! He is swimming back to the beach!'

Rhona's heart started to beat madly.

The prince had heard the warning and he had acted upon it at once.

And suddenly Rhona could see the ship clearly. Now men carrying lanterns were running about its decks. Yes, she could even see that they were lowering other boats.

Wild Geordie had stood glaring about him until the shout had come echoing across the cove. Then he swung his claymore up, clenching it more tightly.

'So the Pretender swims for the beach!' he shouted. 'If he reaches it he will find Wild Geordie waiting for him.'

But no sooner had he raced away into the darkness than Rhona raced for the cottage.

She saw that Wild Geordie had evidently been making feast with the fisherman's food, for there was a dirty platter upon the table with a keen-bladed knife lying alongside it.

Rhona pulled the gag from the fisherman's mouth and she cut his bonds as quickly as she could with the knife.

He lifted himself stiffly from the chair, and then he reached out to take down a claymore from the wall.

'If our prince reaches the beach,' he said, 'he will find me waiting for him and not the traitor from Tannock Isle.'

He went stumbling out into the darkness and after that the two girls could only stand and wait anxiously, their arms tightly clasped about one another.

Then suddenly from somewhere near the water's edge came the clash of steel upon steel. Evidently Wild Geordie and the fisherman were in combat.

It was then that a shout of triumph carried to Rhona.

'Thus end all traitors!' cried the fisherman. 'To me, sire—to me!'

And Rhona knew then that Wild Geordie of Tannock Isle would never collect the huge reward upon which his heart had been set.

But there were many lights upon the cove now, and Rhona could tell that three boats were rowing towards the beach.

What of the prince?

Had he yet reached the beach?

And then Rhona's senses swam in her relief.

Out of the darkness two figures came running—Bonnie Prince Charlie and the fisherman.

'To the coach!' the prince gasped. ''Tis our only hope now!'

Rhona's heart was bursting with thankfulness as they went

310

scrambling recklessly up the slope. Her prince had escaped—he had broken free of the trap which had seemed to close about him so securely.

But Rhona knew despair as well.

Once again the prince was a fugitive. How could he possibly hope to escape from Uist now?

Farewell!

They reached the top of the slope to find the coach standing where they had left it. Looking back, Rhona realised that the three boats had only just reached the beach.

Quickly and breathlessly the prince thanked Rhona for the warning whistle which had saved him.

But there was very little time for words. Almost at once the prince turned to the fisherman.

'What of the boat that should have taken us to Skye?' he asked quickly. 'Do you know aught of it?'

'The boat lies hidden beyond Treport, sire,' the fisherman answered. 'But Fergus Macdonald, its owner, is a prisoner of the Redcoats and they are holding him at the hut just above the quay at Treport. A sergeant and three men are in charge of him.'

'Then—then we must seek some place to hide!' Flora Macdonald gasped.

But quickly Rhona stepped up to the prince.

'You still have the Redcoat officer's hat and coat in the coach, sire,' she cried.

'What think you now, little cousin?' he asked.

Breathlessly, for every second was precious, Rhona explained.

And then she was scrambling into the coach, followed by Flora and the fisherman, while the prince clambered up to the driving-seat.

When the men from the ship arrived at the top of the slope, all sound of the racing coach had died away.

Some time later the sentry on guard in front of the boat-house at Treport came stiffly to attention as an officer materialised out of the gloom.

'Your sergeant!' the officer snapped. 'I wish to speak to him.'

The door of the boathouse opened and a sergeant stepped out.

'I have news for you, sergeant,' the officer said. 'The Pretender is now in my charge. My instructions are to take Fergus Macdonald with me so that he may be imprisoned with the Stuart. Bring the man to me at once.'

The sergeant shouted an order and a burly figure clad in jersey and tasselled woollen cap was propelled out of the boat-house.

Instantly the Redcoat officer drew his sword and he prodded Fergus Macdonald with it.

'I will take full charge of him, sergeant,' he snapped. 'Do you maintain your guard here until you are relieved.'

His sword prodded Fergus Macdonald again.

'March,' he rapped.

Fergus Macdonald walked off into the darkness with the officer striding along behind him.

But they were no sooner out of sight of the boat-house than the officer drew alongside his prisoner.

'You have nothing to fear from me, Fergus,' he said quietly. 'I am your prince, Charles Stuart.'

Fergus Macdonald stared incredulously at the man in the Redcoat uniform.

At the same moment, Rhona, Flora Macdonald and the fisherman appeared out of the darkness.

'Once again a plan of yours has succeeded, little cousin,' the prince told Rhona. 'The sergeant at the boat-house had no suspicions at all. Even so we have no time to waste.'

He turned to Fergus Macdonald.

'We must get to your boat as quickly as possible,' he said. 'Men have followed close at our heels and at any moment the alarm may be raised.'

'Come,' Fergus Macdonald said, loyalty and admiration in his eyes.

But suddenly they heard the sound of galloping hoof-beats and Rhona felt her face blanch. Then the alarm had indeed been raised.

How quickly the pursuit had followed after the coach!

Fergus Macdonald spoke urgently.

'Boats are hidden far along the beach, sire,' he cried. 'It will take us a long time to reach them. We must run for our lives. If we're seen upon the beach now there will be no hope for us.'

They started to run, but at the very moment the moon appeared in the sky through a narrow rift in the clouds. It was almost as though daylight had suddenly come. And how near the hoof-beats sounded now!

Surely the prince and his companions must be seen as they raced along the beach?

It was that thought that suddenly pulled Rhona up, as she sped after the others. She let them run on, but now she herself turned back the way they had come.

The prince must not be seen. She must save him. And she had an idea how that could be done.

Quietly, using all the cover of the bushes and rocks she could find, she began to creep back the way she had come.

The hoof-beats were louder, clearer now. She was nearing the hut where Fergus Macdonald had been held prisoner.

And so were the Redcoats! All at once she froze into the shadow of a big boulder.

Just in time. A dozen Redcoats, mounted on steaming

horses, thundered by, to pull up outside the hut—now twenty yards away now!

At the sound of their arrival the doors were flung open and the sergeant appeared.

The leader of the men addressed him.

'Do you still hold your prisoner?' he demanded.

'Why, no!' he exclaimed in surprise. 'A few minutes ago the prisoner was taken out of my charge by a captain who came for him.'

Instantly there were cries of anger.

'Fool!' thundered the leader. ''Twas no captain who took your prisoner away—it was Charles Stuart himself!'

That was all Rhona waited to hear. She must not delay now if she were to save the prince. Swiftly she sped on, making now for the place where their coach had been left.

Soon it loomed out of the darkness before her. But from behind came excited voices and the restless champ of hoofs. The men were forming search plans. Before long they would be seeking the prince—unless she could prevent it.

Now she had reached the coach. Heart thumping, she clambered up on to the box. From behind her she heard the horsemen move—but she was ready now.

She caught up the reins and seized the whip. Crack! It went snaking into the air over the backs of the coach-horses.

There was a startled whinny, a jolt. With a rumble of wheels the coach thundered down the road.

And from behind Rhona came sudden, amazed shouts. The coach had been heard.

'My plan has succeeded!' she told herself breathlessly. 'Then men will follow me, thinking the prince is on the coach.'

Follow her they did. Now she heard the hoof-beats on the road behind her. But now she was urging the horses on, ever on, faster, faster.

Until, suddenly, in the moonlight, she saw the road snaking

upwards in a steep incline. A hill—and a steep one.

There it would be more than likely that the horsemen would gain on her, for the coach was heavy and the horses would have to slow for the pull up the hill.

'But they will not catch me!' Rhona breathed, her eyes shining.

They reached the foot of the hill. The horses began to climb. Gradually their speed slowed to a crawl, and as they did so Rhona gazed from side to side.

And suddenly she saw what she sought—a thick clump of heather ahead on the roadside.

Swiftly she stood up. As the coach neared it—she jumped.

She landed in the heather with a jolt, but the buoyant stems broke the force of her fall and, as she rolled over, breathless, she saw the coach-horses still plodding on, up the hill.

While behind them sounded the hoof-beats of the Redcoats, nearer now.

Rhona did not stop to see them pass, however. Gathering her shawl about her, she sped at all speed across the heather towards the cliff.

But now she had another fear. Would she be able to catch up with the prince before he sailed away? She felt she must bid him farewell and assure him once again of her loyalty and the loyalty of her people.

Meantime, down on the beach, the prince's party had stopped as the excited shouts of the men chasing the coach came to them.

'What it this? What do they pursue?' exclaimed Flora Macdonald, gazing anxiously into the darkness.

It was the prince who answered. He was looking at his companions now, and his face was white with alarm.

'Rhona!' he gasped. 'My little cousin is not with us! She must have tripped and fallen.'

The prince turned quickly.

'We must go back for her!' he exclaimed. 'We must save her. We cannot leave her to fall into the hands of the Redcoats.'

He made to start back down the beach, but the burly Fergus Macdonald reached out to grip his arm.

'We must go forward, sire!' he pleaded. 'Because of the moon, if we are not around the headland within the next few minutes, we shall assuredly be seen.'

'But—Rhona?' the prince said huskily. 'How can we desert her now?'

'She would understand, sire,' Flora Macdonald said quietly. 'She would understand why, just as any loyal Scotswoman would—just as I would. We have proof she seeks only to serve you. We have proof she thinks but of your safety——'

They went on, but more slowly now, and they all knew that, though they were doing the right thing for Scotland—for their country—to leave Rhona was a great hurt.

But the sound of the pursuit was dying away completely when they rounded the headland. From there it was but a short distance to the tiny cove.

They waited and then two men appeared out of the darkness.

Fergus Macdonald welcomed them and introduced them as two loyal supporters of the prince—two men who were being forced to flee from Uist because of the work they had done in the prince's cause.

'We must get our boats into the water at once,' Fergus Macdonald said to them. 'At any moment Redcoats may charge down on us——'

'Hist!' Flora Macdonald whispered. 'Someone comes!'

The hands of the men went to their dirks. But it was a slightly built, girlish figure that came running across the sand towards them.

The prince caught one glimpse of her as the moon slid from the clouds again and immediately a great cry escaped him.

'It is Rhona!'

316

And Rhona paused there, on the beach, her heart filled with gladness. She was in time to bid farewell to her prince. In time to wish him all speed and safety on his journey.

He came hurrying to meet her.

'My little cousin!' he cried. 'I live again now that I know you are indeed safe. I feared you would be captured and I must leave Uist, not knowing what became of you. It was the only thing that could be done, but how sad my heart was at the thought.'

Rhona was so breathless that for the moment words were completely beyond her. But then they came in a rush.

'Sire!' she blurted. 'Had I been captured aiding your escape, I should have been content. But some time will pass before the Redcoats return here——'

Quickly she explained what had happened. As she finished, the prince's arm went about her shoulders.

'I begin to think, little cousin,' he said, 'that I am more in your debt than ever.'

Flora Macdonald came up to them.

'Rhona, you are a brave lass and all Scotland should be proud of you,' she said gently. 'It is well that you have found us. We have another boat here besides the one belonging to Fergus. It belongs to two men who are compelled to flee from Uist and days ago made up their minds that they would go to Tannock Isle knowing that your father would welcome them and hide them if necessary.'

She smiled at Rhona.

'And so,' she went on, 'this must be the moment of our parting. I shall always remember you, Rhona.'

She stooped to kiss Rhona upon the cheek and then she left her alone with the prince.

The prince stood to look down at Rhona and there was a very great affection in his eyes.

'This is the hour of our parting, Rhona,' he said. 'You return

The Prince knelt. 'I owe you my life, little Rhona.'

to Tannock Isle and I start upon the last stage of my journey that will take me back to France. And I go knowing that, but for you, I would never have succeeded in escaping from this island.'

Rhona looked at him with shining eyes. For the moment words were beyond her and she made to curtsy.

Gently the prince raised her up.

'No little cousin,' he said quietly. 'Rather it is I who would kneel to you. Do I not owe you my very life?'

And it was indeed Bonnie Prince Charlie who went down upon one knee and who, taking Rhona's hand, bent his head over it for a moment.

'Farewell, little Rhona,' he said. 'Farewell.'

Almost as though in a dream Rhona found herself in the boat that would convey her back home. She knelt up in the stern facing the other boat where she could see the tall figure of the prince.

As they rowed out to sea, the distance between the two boats began to grow wider and wider. Only at the very last moment did the prince raise his hand in a final gesture of farewell.

And then the prince's boat was blotted out. She had parted from her prince forever!

Even so, there was a happy smile upon Rhona's face as she settled herself down upon the stern seat.

She was returning to her home on Tannock Isle—the same simple shepherd lass who had left it but some days ago. Yet with memories—wonderful memories—that would remain with her throughout her life.

The Girl who helped the Highwayman

by Enid Meridith

'Ah, me! How different life at Highwood House was when old Mr Hampton was alive!'

Melissa Wentworth's red-gold ringlets gleamed in the rays of the morning sun which shone through the latticed windows of the Tapestry Room at Highwood House.

Her attractive face was a trifle sad now as her thoughts drifted back to the time, only six months before, when laughter and happiness flowed through the old place. Melissa had been a maid at Highwood House, but old Josiah Hampton, its kindly owner, had treated her more as a daughter.

She remembered, her lips lifting at the corners in a tiny smile, how he had encouraged the growing friendship between his devil-may-care grandson, Laurie, and herself. Often, on wintry evenings, she and Laurie had sat together on the rich carpet at the old man's feet, while, in the glow of a roaring log fire, he told them tales of his adventurous life at sea.

'But all that is past,' she sighed, her blue eyes wandering round the four tapestried walls, each of which depicted a season.

'And why, oh why, did not Mr Hampton leave the estate to Laurie, instead of—of that horrid Roger Hampton and his family? Roger Hampton only began to come and see his father when he knew he was going to die. And now he is my new master, and I am treated as one of the lowliest servants.'

She paused, reflecting.

'And why have they suddenly sent Laurie to London to take up an apprenticeship? Oh, if only I had somewhere to go, I would leave myself, but——'

'Hey! You! Stop mooning about. We cannot afford to keep lazy servants in this house!'

Melissa swung round, pale green skirts rustling, to meet the cold grey eyes of Vincent Hampton, the new owner's son.

Vincent, arrogant and conceited, wore a well-tailored coat of blue superfine, snowy shirt, and bright yellow pantalloons, while his necktie, Melissa mused, must have taken him hours to arrange.

'I have to take the carriage to the village to meet Mr Robey, our solicitor,' he said imperiously. 'You will have to collect my father's snuff from Marson's as I shan't have time. You will go down to the village at once. Go on, girl — do as I say,' he snapped, as she seemed about to speak.

Melissa nodded. She knew it was no use arguing with Master Vincent. She still had the saloon to dust, but that must wait.

Collecting her emerald green wrap from her tiny room at the top of the big house, she slipped quietly out, noticing that the ostlers were already bringing the carriage from the stables, and harnessing two lively, high-stepping greys.

'If only Laurie were still here,' she thought as she made her way down the short drive. 'He would never treat me in the way that Master Vincent does. I wonder what Laurie is doing now——'

And then, stepping through the wide open gates on to the road outside, her thoughts trailed off. Her blue eyes opened wide, and her heart began to thump with sudden fear.

For, out of the bushes beside the gate, a huge Great Dane had sprung. Around her the dog bounded, to halt in the middle of the road, half crouched, teeth bared, glaring balefully at her as she shrank away.

'It's Major!' she gulped. 'Vincent's dog! He—he thinks I am an intruder! Oh, he—he means to attack me!'

She fell back against the wall, eyes closed, half swooning with fright.

Then suddenly a drumming of hoofs and a ringing, confident voice:

'Never fear!'

A strong arm encircled her small waist; she found herself lifted high, and, a moment later, seated firmly on the back of a horse.

She heard the Great Dane bark, and her rescuer's sharp voice as he drew rein. She opened her eyes, saw him for the first time, and, at sight of him, gave a little cry of surprise.

Slipping down from the saddle she stuttered:

'You—you're a—a highwayman!'

Dismounting before her he had gone to soothe the big dog, but at her voice he turned, a smile on his lips, the dark eyes twinkling behind his black mask.

'At your service, mistress Melissa,' he replied in a low, husky tone, and she blinked that he should know her name. 'I hope you have no objection that a—a rogue such as I should come to your rescue?'

'Oh, no! No! Do not mistake me. I—I was just surprised,' she explained. 'I'm greatly obliged to you. If it had not been for your timely intervention, I shudder to imagine what my fate might have been!'

But the highwayman was no longer listening. He had suddenly tensed, and, following his gaze, Melissa saw that Vincent, who was just leaving the house, had seen them and was waving his arm.

'Grimes! Page! Major's caught the highwayman! Quickly, both of you! We've got to get him! He mustn't escape!'

And, his men behind him, Vincent came running towards them. Melissa turned agonised eyes upon her masked rescuer.

'Oh, please, you must escape! He—he will show you no mercy!' she choked. 'Oh, do be quick, I pray you! I could not bear to see him catch you!'

She was urging him towards his horse as she spoke, and now he glanced down at her, and his eyes were smiling.

'He shall not catch me, little Melissa,' he murmured. 'I will go—but we shall meet again, I vow!'

And vaulting on to the black horse, he crashed into the woods on the opposite side of the road to vanish from sight.

Melissa spun round as Vincent and his men rushed up.

'Major! Why didn't you hold him?' he panted, as the big dog barked. 'Drat! He has escaped! But I shall get him yet!' He turned his cold grey eyes upon Melissa. 'And you, miss, should be ashamed of yourself, hob-nobbing with a rogue like him! I shall inform my father of this incident. Now—get on your way,' he ordered her. 'And hurry. You have wasted too much time as it is.'

Melissa felt her blood boiling. She would have liked to defend her rescuer, but Vincent swung away, his hand gripping the collar of the big dog which he kept specially for scaring away poachers and intruders. She returned, with a wry smile, the sympathetic glances the two men flashed at her, and continued on her way.

She passed through the toll gate farther down the road, waved to Old Ned, the toll gate keeper, then stepped briskly down the hill towards the village.

At one point she had to jump hastily aside as Vincent, driving the two fresh greys, clattered past in a cloud of dust, ignoring her completely.

She collected the jar of snuff from Marson's, and set off along the uphill road back to Highwood House pondering as to the reason for the solicitor's visit.

It was warm, and Melissa felt hot as she trudged along.

'If it had been Laurie, instead of Vincent,' she mused,

'he would have brought me with him to the village. But Vincent would consider it beneath his dignity to be seen with a servant.' She sighed. 'How utterly unlike each other Laurie and Vincent are——'

And there she stopped, stepping aside once more as the carriage from Highwood House came up behind her. But, to her surprise, instead of passing, it stopped.

'Mistress Melissa, would you care to drive with us back to the house?' asked a kindly voice. ''Tis a hot day, and you must be tired. Come, child. Sit beside me.'

It was Mr Robey who spoke. Melissa glanced towards Vincent. At his curt nod, she smiled at the solicitor and with his help climbed into the carriage, stepping carefully over the strong box which lay at his feet.

Once past the toll gate and out on the pike road, Melissa found her thoughts wandering to the highwayman again, and wondered what had been his purpose when she had encountered him.

'I could not think ill of him,' she reflected. 'He—oh, no?'

For, even as the thoughts of him chased through her mind, there came a thunder of hoofs and a black-clothed figure, riding a jet black horse, bore down on them and brought the carriage to a skidding halt with a jerk on the horses' reins!

A moment later they were menaced by a gleaming pistol.

'The—the highwayman!' she stammered. 'But——'

Just for a surprised second his gaze met hers, and then he was turning upon the solicitor, his eyes grim.

'Mr Robey, I would be greatly obliged if you would hand me that strong box you gave brought with you,' he demanded.

'Rogue!' grated Mr Robey, his arm protectively around Melissa's shoulders. 'What can you want with my papers?'

'Enough! Time is short! The box, please!' clipped the highwayman, and sliding to the ground he approached their carriage.

Still covering them with the pistol, he opened the carriage door and bent as if to pick up the box. Melissa stared at him. What could he want with a box full of papers? Surely a highwayman stole money, jewellery—valuables?

And then she heard him gasp, and her gaze jerked up as from round a bend in the road, a party of cottagers appeared. In a flash they had taken in the situation, and came running.

Her heart leapt again in fear that her highwayman rescuer might be caught, but already he had turned towards his horse.

And it was at that moment that Vincent acted. Standing up in the carriage, he swung his whip. It whistled through the air to wrap itself with a stinging crack around the highwayman's ankle.

While Melissa cried out, she saw the highwayman falter, then he was astride his horse and away, disappearing amongst the trees.

The Promise

That night Melissa retired to her room, but unable to sleep for thinking of the highwayman and wondering how badly Vincent had hurt his ankle, she sat at the latticed window staring down over the moonlit gardens.

'Why should he want that strong box?' she murmured, and then gasped, for down below something—moved!

The moon reappeared from behind the scudding clouds, and a figure was momentarily illuminated. Melissa choked.

"'Tis he! 'Tis the highwayman! But—what does he here?'

Even as she asked herself the question, she was making for the door. Speeding down the stairs she slipped through a side door and stood shivering in the night air.

She moved across to the shrubbery where she had seen the figure and halted, listening. From close beside her came the sound of heavy breathing.

''Tis I, Melissa,' she whispered. 'Please, tell me where you are! I—I am your friend.'

There was a rustling. The bushes beside her parted, and a masked face peered out, eyes questioning. She stepped into his hiding place. He moved to let her pass and caught his breath in a short gasp of pain.

'Please, let me look at your ankle,' she said softly.

After a quick examination, she tore a strip from one of her petticoats, and bound it. Then, aware that he was watching her, she sat back.

'Now, won't you tell me—why are you here?'

He paused, gazing at her for a moment, then spoke slowly.

'There is a certain letter in Mr Robey's strong box that concerns me deeply. I have lately learnt that a great wrong will be done if I cannot read it, and—and forestall my enemies. I came to obtain the letter tonight, but can go no farther. But—I must have it—by noon tomorrow. It is vital.'

'The letter means a great deal to you?' Melissa asked him slowly. 'It—it will right a great wrong?'

'Yes, but—'

'Then I will help you,' she told him impulsively, and saw his head jerk up in surprise. 'I trust you,' she added simply. 'Now, tell me, where and how shall I know this letter when I look for it?'

'What? You do not surely think I will allow you to—to attempt such a dangerous——'

'Oh, fudge!' she interrupted, and now her eyes were sparkling. 'Tell me, what does it look like, and where shall I bring it?'

'It is in a green envelope,' he told her reluctantly. 'A distinctive green envelope. Bring it to the Toll House. Ned knows my story, and is hiding me there.'

'I will be there at half past ten o'clock tomorrow morning,' she promised. 'I will bring you the letter, but what is that?'

'I will find the letter for you,' Melissa promised.

She swung round, pulses racing. A voice echoed through the night air, a voice she instantly recognised.

'He's in the grounds, somewhere, I tell you! I saw him. This time we must catch him—before it's too late!'

'Vincent!' Melissa gasped. 'He—he mustn't catch you—'

'It is no use,' the highwayman sighed. 'I have no chance. They will find my horse by the gate, and I know I cannot escape.'

Melissa's blue eyes gleamed. She stood up.

'Quickly—give me your hat,' she commanded. 'I will lead them away—you must escape when Vincent has gone!'

'Melissa! No! I will not allow it!'

'You cannot prevent me!' she retorted. 'Never fear—I can ride a horse better than Vincent. He will not catch me. Now—' she was ramming his black hat down on her head, and tucking her red-gold curls out of sight. 'Give me your cloak, also. That is right. Now, I will away. Your horse I will leave at the Toll House. Goodbye!'

And before he could protest further, she was gone, flitting soundlessly through the bushes, towards the gate. She found the horse as he had said. It moved restlessly at sight of her, but after a few soothing words, she was on his back, cantering from cover. Shouts came. She was being pursued. Her ruse was working.

Melissa evaded her would-be capturers by sitting quietly in a small copse while they thundered by.

Then, breathing a sigh of relief, she took a short cut through the fields, and leaving the horse and clothes with a startled Ned, she returned to Highwood House by a devious route, her thoughts busy with the problem of the green envelope.

She knew that on his arrival at Highwood House, the solicitor had taken his strong box to the Tapestry Room, and she remembered on previous visits that the key to the strong box had hung on a hook in that room.

Her best chance was to get it while the house was asleep, but when she tip-toed breathlessly down to the Tapestry Room, to her dismay she discovered the door securely locked.

The following morning, after breakfast, believing the room to be empty, she decided to try again, but pushing the door open, she recoiled with a gasp as her eyes beheld Roger Hampton busily writing at the desk.

'Well, don't stand there like a sap-head!' he rasped, sensing her presence. 'What do you want? Where's your tongue?' And without giving her time to answer:

'Where's that snuff you were supposed to collect for me yesterday? Bring it to me, at once!'

Melissa had forgotten the snuff. She turned. Oh dear! How could she hope to get that envelope now?

She went to her bedchamber and absent-mindedly picked up the jar of snuff she had left there. The jar tilted, the lid flew off, and Melissa went into a violent fit of sneezing, her eyes watering painfully.

'How can he partake of such horrid stuff?' she choked, wiping her eyes. 'I—but of course!' she gasped next moment. 'Maybe *that* would make him leave the Tapestry Room! But—dare I?'

Blue eyes agleam, she picked up the jar again and returned to the Tapestry Room. Roger Hampton indicated the desk and, heart pounding, Melissa stepped forward, the snuff jar held tight in her hand.

Reaching over his shoulder, as if to place the jar on his desk, she held her breath. Then, swiftly, she tilted it. Once more the lid flew off, and as Mr Hampton's head spun round, a great cascade of snuff drifted down over his face.

She had succeeded! While Melissa fell back, Mr Hampton snatched at a lace handkerchief and held it to his eyes, choking and sneezing as he did so. Then, to her relief, he staggered blindly from the room.

330

Two Problems Solved

Melissa moved fast. She snatched the keys from the hook and swiftly opened the strong box, flipping rapidly through its contents. She found the green envelope, and tucked it away into her bodice. Then, relocking the box, she replaced the key.

Not a moment too soon. Even as she stepped out of the room she came face to face with Roger Hampton, returning, his face red.

'You—girl!' he cried. 'You did that deliberately! You shall leave this house! You will remain in your room, and pack. When Mr Robey leaves this afternoon, you will accompany him to London. Now—to your room, girl!' — and he stamped into the room, slamming the door behind him.

Melissa's face turned white.

So, in helping the highwayman, she had lost her own position. She was dismissed—and she had nowhere to go!

She drew a deep breath and cast aside her own worries, remembering the task she had set herself, whatever might depend upon it.

'I must get out!' she determined. 'Whatever my own troubles, I cannot break my promise to the highwayman! I must see him—somehow!'

But by eleven o'clock she was becoming desperate, for several attempts to leave the house had been thwarted.

Then, heart pounding, a daring idea entered her mind, for looking out of her bedchamber she saw a tumbril loaded with hay.

'The tumbril!' she gasped. ''Tis my way of escape!'

A moment later she was skimming down the stairs. Pulses racing, she stepped through a side door, and keeping under cover of the bushes beside the house, worked her way round it to a spot only five yards or so from the tumbril.

Though there was a horse between the shafts she could see no one was in sight. She ran.

Seconds later she had pushed her way amongst the warm, tickling hay; and lay there, quiet, waiting.

With a quickening of heartbeats, she heard the driver approach. Then the jerk as he climbed into his seat, and another jerk as the loaded tumbril set off.

Heart in mouth she lay there until at last they reached the toll gate.

With a sense of relief she heard the driver call to Old Ned, felt the jerk as he climbed down, and listened to his receding footsteps. Then, peering out to make sure the coast was clear, she jumped down and hid behind the Toll House until the tumbril had gone.

Old Ned started at sight of her.

'Lawks, missy, but where you bin?' he cried, eyeing her dishevelled appearance in surprise and curiosity.

'I had to hide in the tumbril to get here,' she explained. 'But, where's the highwayman? I must see him—I'm late already!'

'He ain't here, missy.' Ned shook his head. 'Got worried for you when you didn't come. Went off to look for you.'

Melissa knew a sense of foreboding. What had happened to the highwayman?

She withdrew the envelope from her bodice and on a sudden impulse opened the flap, drawing out the single sheet of paper. Her blue eyes scanned it eagerly.

The letter stated that the writer, Josiah Hampton, mistrusting some of those around him, had made a second will. Fearing someone would destroy that new will, he had hidden it, and 'only the Snow Rose' would reveal its whereabouts. Sould the will not be found, his original will would become valid six months after his death.

Melissa stared at it, trembling.

'But—where and what is the Snow Rose?' she asked. 'And what has this to do with the highwayman?'

She frowned, eyes darkening, thoughts incredible.

'Ned, I must return to the house—quickly!' she cried.

'His horse is still here, missy,' offered Ned. 'Take it.'

Melissa nodded, already running for the stables. On the fleet-footed horse she reached the house in a matter of minutes, and went flying up the stairs to the Tapestry Room.

She pushed open the door, then halted, breath caught, eyes widening at the scene which met her gaze.

Mr Robey, his face grim, was standing behind the desk. Before it stood an equally grim-looking Mr Hampton and a grinning Vincent. They held between them——

'The—the highwayman! You—you're caught him!' she gasped.

'Yes—we've stopped his tricks!' gloated Vincent, giving the proudly erect highwayman a vicious dig in the ribs.

'And now,' Mr Hampton declared, 'I think the time has come to learn the identity of this rogue. And then,' he paused, 'I think he should learn the fate that awaits him!'

Melissa almost stopped breathing as Mr Hampton's hand shot out. She saw the highwayman stiffen as the man's long fingers caught at the edge of the disguising mask. A second later it was ripped from the outlaw's face, and Melissa found herself staring into the familiar features of——

'Laurie!' she choked! 'Then—then it was you! But—but I understand it all now!' She swung round on the startled solicitor. 'You must listen to me, Mr Robey. He—he isn't a rogue—he only wanted to see justice done. He wanted to see a letter which you carried with you, and this disguise provided his only means of getting it. But I——'

'Silence, girl! Leave this room at once——' broke in Roger Hampton, and Melissa saw that his face had suddenly paled.

'I will not be silenced,' she retorted, and bringing out the envelope once more, thrust it towards the solicitor.

With a frown he took it from her, opened it, read it, and folded it again.

'You stole this letter from my strong box,' he said slowly, and his voice was cold. 'That is a serious matter ——'

'I know I did—I had to,' Melissa interrupted. 'But—but the letter says there is another will—a second will—'

'Surely, child, you do not think I have had that letter all this time and do not know its contents,' he chided. 'But even so, I must continue my business with Mr Hampton. I attach little importance to the contents of that letter. I understand that Josiah Hampton was given to odd ramblings during his last few weeks of illness. Will you please retire to that seat by the window, young lady, and calm yourself? I will deal with you later. Now'—he turned to the Hamptons—' 'to finish our business.'

Dejected, Melissa moved across the room to the window-seat.

She looked at Laurie; how much older he suddenly seemed. Involuntarily her mind raced back to the times when they had listened together to his grandfather's stories in this very same room. It seemed an age ago.

She recollected the first time his grandfather had shown her the Tapestry Room, of which he was so proud. Suddenly he had laughed; had asked her if she could find—a mistake! She had examined each wall carefully, but had to admit defeat.

And then, smiling, he had led her to the wall depicting winter with its tones of white, grey and brown. He had pointed to a minute patch of colour amidst a bleak hawthorn bush—one wild rose, blooming in the mid-winter scene. One—

And now she was springing to her feet, brain awhirl.

''Tis the answer!' she cried. ''This the Snow Rose.'

In a fever of excitement, she rushed across the room to the Winter wall. There, in the bottom right-hand corner she found the thing for which she was looking—a tiny pink rose!

Her fingers touched it, moved along the tapestry, and found it loose at the edge. Carefully she probed. Yes—there was something there!

"Tis the will!' she cried. 'The missing will—hidden in the tapestry beneath the Snow Rose!' Her eyes met Laurie's, her cheeks glowing now. 'And—and it is still five minutes to noon! The second will is valid! It has been found in time!'

.   .   .   .   .

The new will disinherited the Hamptons, and established Laurie as the new Squire, and owner of the estate. The letter which accompanied it revealed how the Hamptons had turned the old man against his grandson, causing him to make his previous will, leaving all to them.

Vincent and his father left the house that afternoon, and Melissa, not at all sure of her position now, went to her room. She had been dismissed—she had even begun to pack her few belongings!

'I'm so glad all has turned out well for Laurie,' she mused, her eyes misty. 'I knew the highwayman was really not a rogue——'

There was a light tap at the door. She opened it, to fall back in surprise to see a stern-faced Laurie outside.

'What means this?' he demanded, taking the situation in at a glance.

'I—I was dismissed,' she faltered. 'And so——'

'Oh.' He was silent for so long a time that she turned away, to hide the tears welling in her eyes. 'I imagine you have nowhere to go?'

She nodded dumbly, and drew a trembling sigh.

'Then you may remain here—but I will eventually have to find someone else to fill your post.'

Her head jerked up, and she looked at him, but he had crossed the room, and was staring out of the window. So—

now he was the new master, he would dismiss her after all! She choked.

'Melissa——' his voice was soft now, and he had turned back to face her, 'when—when that time comes, there is another—a more important post I would like you to accept—'

She blinked back her tears bravely, not comprehending him for the moment.

'Melissa, this post would mean that you would never leave Highwood House any more,' he went on, and Melissa, meeting his twinkling eyes, understood and felt her cheeks begin to burn. He paused. 'As its mistress, you couldn't very well, could you?' he added.

'No, I—I couldn't, could I?' she agreed, and now her eyes were sparkling and all was suddenly right with her world. 'But I'm afraid,' she said mischievously, 'I shall never forget the gallant highwayman who rescued me!'

Happily she smiled at him as he held his hands out to her.

Votes for Women

by

Evelyn Day

Everyone has heard of my grandmother, Dame Virginia
Allerson. Until recently she was a Member of Parliament;
and her opinions are eagerly sought by newsmen and television
interviewers on important topics of the day; but if most
present-day young readers and viewers were asked what sort
of person she is—at seventy-six years of age—they would
probably describe her as very serious, gravely spoken, worldly
wise; so they would find it hard to believe that once, before
the First World War, she threw stones through plate glass
windows, and helped to throw a male Member of Parliament
into a pond or played a barrel organ to break up a political
meeting. But when she was nineteen she did all these things
—for she was a militant Suffragette in the days when hansom
cabs went clip-clopping around the streets; when buses were
still pulled by a pair of straining horses, and when women's
skirts touched the ground and were rated immodestly short
if they revealed the ankle.

Fascinated, I have listened to my grandmother telling me
about those far-off days, which now must be rated as history.
It was a completely different world from ours, when men were
men, and women were women and never the twain should
meet except when legally married or accompanied by a cha-
perone.

How did it happen that Grannie, niece of Lord Stunforth,

and cousin of an earl, most carefully brought up, became a law-breaking, window-smashing Suffragette? Her father was killed in the South African War; her mother remarried, and lived in India, leaving my grandmother at home in the care of first a nanny, then a governess, her education being completed by being taught hockey at Roedean, and having the rough social edges sand-papered; and as she said, French-polished at a finishing school in Paris. The final object of this preparation was not, she assured me, to guarantee that she threw a good hard stone or could wrestle with policemen and win, but that she should marry well—which meant she should become dependent on a man of title and substance, and agree to take orders from him, until death did them part.

So how did Virginia Allerson become such a rebel, you may ask! It has taken many evenings sitting by the fireside talking to her, to find out the whole story—and now a full picture of her youth is forming in my mind. I remember the first evening when I asked that all-important question...

'How did you come to be a Suffragette, Grannie? And is in true that you went to prison and nearly died while hunger striking? How terrible it must have been. Why *did* you do it?'

'Terrible it certainly was,' she replied, 'but well worth the long hard battle. We were inspired, fevered; each and every one of us was a Joan of Arc, even if we didn't hear voices. We were one with the Spartans, except that we would have modified their last testimony to read, "Here in defiance of our country's laws unjust, we lie".'

'But does it now seem worth all that fighting and striving?' I asked, perhaps doubtingly.

'That is a question, that you, our beneficiary and a free girl, must answer!' she smiled at me.

Then her thoughts grooved into the right channel. She lay back and remembered, while I listened, enthralled...

First, I must make it clear that the breaking of bonds and striking off of shackles was very much in the air, quiet apart from the question of female suffrage; for the end of one century and the start of another had had a quite remarkable effect on social order. I know it seems silly to suggests that the mere chance of a date—the writing of nineteen hundred instead of eighteen hundred could have a dramatic consequence on social change — yet it did. There was a general feeling of changing gear, and I don't mean the wearing of cycling bloomers instead of long frocks, nor the unpinning of hats and hair, symptomatic though such changes were. I mean that there was the belief in an expanding world. H. G. Wells was writing of War of the Worlds and other science-fiction fantasies. He believed and others believed that soon we would all be flying in aircraft, that there would be moving pavements and other scientific devices. All that we had thought permanent was to be changed; and already was changing.

Perhaps the greatest change was in the status of women who were no longer content to be just wives and mothers; more and more were going into offices, adopting careers. Women were beginning to demand liberty of action and thought; we wanted to throw aside the constraints of false modesty. Women were starting to smoke openly. There were 'New Women' taking long strides instead of mincing steps, who spoke even when they were not spoken to and sometimes without even waiting for some man to finish what he was saying! Such changes, just as is the case today, were more obvious in the young than in staid middle-aged matrons. It is always the young who create the break-through in fashions, and change tradition.

Of course, only some girls were in the front line of change— many of my friends and contemporaries were not; but I was always a little fiery and high spirited so I surf-boarded, one might say, on the rollers of the incoming tide of Time that was breaking on the shore. And my being a member of the Suffragette movement was a part of it.

But how did I *become* a part of it? You'll laugh. I followed in my own grandmother's footsteps. She was a rich woman and left me one hundred thousand pounds when I was nineteen, in the last year of the Edwardian Era—the year King Edward died, nineteen hundred and ten.

Grannie in her last years was a Suffragette. She left me the money to help the Cause, having already converted me to fighting for it.

'Virginia,' she said to me on the last occasion I saw her. 'Fight the good fight! For the Vote!'

She was in a wheel-chair, having twisted her ankle jumping from a Black Maria in which she was being taken to prison. We were in the grounds of Kelpick Castle, which had been in the family since the first or second Lord Stunforth had battle-axed the previous tenant.

'Votes for Women!' I said.

'It is not a matter for jesting, my gal,' she warned me. 'You must be completely dedicated. When I see the mess that men have made of this country I shall die an unhappy woman unless I can feel that you and others like you will not rest until you have siezed or shared power!'

Poor Grannie! She died of pneumonia after marching bare-footed in the snow in a column of militant Suffragettes that same year. She was given a magnificent funeral, the coffin draped in our colours, heliotrope, white and green; and in the procession were women doctors, nurses; in general a host of 'New Women'.

Shortly afterwards, having the means, although her estate was not then settled, I rented a flat in London, a daring and desperate thing to do for a girl of my age and social standing. For the first time, I was on my own. Just for the fun of it I took a hansom—alone—and was delighted when the cabbie opened the little door in the roof to speak to me, just to make sure that when I said 'The House of Commons', I did know where I was going. They were lovely, the hansoms with the folding-out front doors, even if hard-sprung and uncomfortable by many modern standards.

However, I soon bought myself one of the new motor-cars, and learned to drive it, so when I had a sudden summons from Uncle Henry to go to the Castle at once, I drove there.

My arrival caused a sensation. Cousin Cuthbert, heir to an earldom, was in the stable yard with his new white automobile, and his jaw actually did drop when he saw me.

'Where's the driver, Virginia?' he asked.

'I am the driver.'

'You—you're a woman!'

'I know. I've known for quite a while' I said.

Cuthbert was always a bit dim, and he frowned in a puzzled way. 'I shouldn't be too reckless, throwing money around!' he warned me.

I bridled. 'The days are over, when women had to be told when and how to spend their own money,' I told him. 'I am free. I will spend my money as I please.'

There was a strange glint in his eyes, I noticed.

'*Your* money? Your have not heard, apparently, that the will is being contested.'

'Contested? On what grounds?'

'On the grounds that Grannie was not of sound mind when she made it. That's why Uncle Henry sent for you. No one who goes about throwing stones at windows and getting themselves thrown into prison, can be sane!'

I contested Cuthbert's statement, in no uncertain terms, then I strode indoors, head in air, swinging my sable muff on the end of its delicate cord, not actually designed for that purpose.

On the way up the main staircase I saw Humphreys the

butler, and for his benefit I went up the stairs two at a time, hauling up my semi-hobble skirt to do so, well earning his shocked disapproval.

'Uncle Henry?' I said curtly.

'In the library, Miss Virginia. His lordship is expecting you.'

Furious, I pushed open the heavy studded oak door. Uncle Henry was in the armchair behind the desk. His head was resting on the back of the chair and over his face was a copy of the *Pink 'un*, which rustled and trembled when he snored. A soft whistling noise followed the awful reverberation.

Arms akimbo, I stood confronting him. Uncle Henry! The senior member of the family. His lordship, snoring at home for a change, instead of in the House of Lords! The library . . . he had never read a book at all since leaving school, except the *Racing Guide*, and his favourite racing and sporting journal, the *Pink 'un*. The only reason he sat at the large desk was because he could spread out his newspaper. There was a low bookshelf behind him, filled with *The Laws of England;* but they were only dummy copies, and comprised a simple door, behind which he kept a bottle of whisky, and glasses.

Behind him, too, were the family arms, emblazoned, and in colour. On either side were gleaming arms of war—swords, spears, knives, and a wonderful battle-axe I had once tried to carry as a girl. The moment I saw it I was tempted. I crept beside him, undid the buckles and not without considerable effort, lifted down the weapon.

'Old battle-axe-that's what she is,' he had said of Grannie.

Still recalling childhood I played a nursery trick; put a finger in my mouth, the tip against my cheek, and flicked it out with a realistic 'pop'. It woke him up. The paper fell.

'A bottle of the ninety five, Uncle Henry?' I said.

'Eh? Yes... All right... Yes,' he muttered, rubbing his eyes. 'Got a glass here somewhere.' Then he saw me, frowned, and looked around vaguely, not noticing the battle-axe.

'I was told by Cuthbert that you propose contesting Grannie's will and depriving me of my fortune,' I said coldly, resting my forearm on the top of the axe which rested upright before me. For the first time, Uncle Henry saw the axe, and his almost purple face paled slightly.

'Gad!' he said. 'Virginia ... what ... I say! My dear gal, have a thought — you Suffragettes — good gracious me!'

'Uncle Henry, fear nothing! I just want you to tell me whether Cuthbert, as one might readily suppose, has completely misunderstood what is going on, or whether you have the uncommon nerve and brazen effrontery to say that Grannie was out of her mind.'

He fumbled for his monocle and stuffed it into his right eye.

'Your grandmother,' he said, 'if I can say so without giving you pain of offence, was nuts! She threw a stone through Cartier's window and set fire to a golf club-house.'

'She did it for the Cause,' I told him, 'and that does not make her crazy. Or do you think all Suffragettes are crazy?

He looked at me, then at the axe.

'Have some tea,' he said. 'I could do with some myself. Actually, this is a matter for lawyers. Lot of legal diffledaffle. No need to trouble your pretty head, gal—'

'Pretty head nothing! Stop addressing me, please, as if I were an animated doll,' I said in fury. 'You would not like me to remind you of your thick head?'

'Don't,' he replied, pathetically stroking his shiny bald patch. 'It must have been the port. Oh dear! These lawyers—'

'If you contest the will successfully, then I shall not get the hundred thousand.'

'Mmm... yes... You could say that,' he admitted.

'So who *will* get it?'

'Well—ah—Cuthbert.'

'Cuthbert! So all is revealed — I thought as much!'

The door opened and Cuthbert himself entered.

'Yes, I will,' he said. 'The money is really family money, and should not be squandered in mad enterprises that can bring nothing but mischief ... What are you doing with that axe?'

I raised it.

'This is a symbol of embattled womanhood. If I could fix staves to my car's hub wheels, I would. Boudicea rides again; or if I had armour, I would wear it like Joan of Arc.'

I saw from the side of my eyes Cuthbert tapping his fore head, looking at Uncle Henry. So I turned, and with the battle-axe on my shoulder, marched—and I mean marched—to the door, almost as if the drums and fifes were ringing in my ears.

'Fight ... contest if you will,' I told them. 'But I will fight, too. For if what you say is true, then all Suffragettes are crazy. That means that when, collectively, they are certified and locked up, and only then, will it be true to say that Grannie, for that same reason, was crazy.'

I raised the axe — what a weight — in a vague half-military salute and almost fell over Humphreys who was listening outside the door with a loaded tea tray. Humphreys lost his balance, tottered, and clung to a suit of armour which collapsed with him; the tea tray went downstairs like a toboggan and I, eager to be gone despite my new semi-hobble skirt, slid down the glossy banisters, skidded on the mat across the hall, and unwittingly frightening a housemaid into a dead faint, departed.

We had been warned against losing our tempers. Mrs Pankhurst had warned us against it. When a temper goes, so does judgment; and I realised I had gone a good deal too far. I had been carried away, as one ought not to be. For if Uncle Henry's lawyers were treated to an account of my recent behaviour, they might decide that if I did inherit the estate the expenditure would need to be in the care of the Commissioners in Lunacy! For there were no women solicitors, or barristers then. It was a man's world.

By the time I reached London, I was cool again—in fact somewhat chilled in spirit. I had grown used to the idea of that hundred thousand pounds, I suppose, and was shocked and not a little bewildered; moreover the Movement was urgently in need of funds and I had made large-scale promises of support in all good faith that might have set in motion projects that could not otherwise be afforded.

First, I drove to my flat in Piccadilly. It was a Saturday, and there were more people about than usual, for it was always a gay day, infected with the holiday spirit; but the traffic was light enough for me to park. Even thought there were so few cars, leaving a car unattended was not lightly regarded, and one could be fined a half-guinea even if the car was the only one parked in an otherwise deserted street.

It surprised me at first glance to see that the newly-installed electric light was on in my flat, but then I remembered that Cynthia was staying there. When I entered, I found Cynthia and four other Suffragettes holding an intense meeting. The meeting, I quickly learned, was planning to spend the money I might not be able, after all, to provide. But I could, and did, provide sherry when I had told them my troubles; it seemed an act of independence, doing so uninvited by a man.

Mrs Glazier was the one most deeply affected by my sad warning, and seethed with indignation. She was in her early forties, lean, sharp-tongued; a widow left to fend for herself.

'So you will be driven out of the Movement?' she cried.

'Certainly not. It would be a betrayal of my grandmother,' I said.

Sybil Larking put her hands to her pale cheeks; her chocolate-brown eyes burned.

'How scandalous to suggest insanity. Why, if she were

insane, then so are we all!' And she looked apprehensive.

'Absurd!' scoffed Sarah Giles. 'Lot of rot! Your uncle, miss, is an old dunderhead, begging your pardon, even if he is a lord! Fine thing! If we do anything on our own like, without asking their by-your-leave, they say we're dotty. Until we get lady judges, that's what the judges might say, likely as not I shouldn't be surprised.'

Fat Mrs Cudthorpe literally shook with indignation.

'They could not prove it,' she said. 'It's political cause, and we fight with the only weapon we have. What we must decide is how this alters our plans for Monday's demonstration. Are we to march into the House of Commons or not?'

There was to be a special speech by the Prime Minister, Herbert Asquith, and we meant to interrupt it in a new way. There were now bars in the gallery, placed there as a consequence of the Suffragettes' habit of throwing things at Members. What we planned was to take into the gallery instruments hired from one of the German bands that then paraded in London, dressed in blue and silver uniforms. How to get them in was our problem. Such a demonstration would ensure publicity, and free advertisement for the Cause; it would also demonstrate that we had resource and daring.

'We may be arrested,' said Mrs Glazier.

'Hope so,' cut in Sarah. 'My Dad will beat me up if so, but it'll be worth it. Better me than you, miss. I had an uncle went to clink, and Ma was once done for shop-lifting. I'm no lady, you see, so it don't matter.'

We assured her it did matter, but we could never cure her of the habit of calling us 'M'am' and 'Miss'. We were sisters under the skin we told her, and quoted Kipling. But although she accepted it in theory and principle, in practice it gave her comfort to think that she was in the care and protection of girls with money and power, and influence.

'Your uncle is in the House of Lords, Virginia,' said Mrs

Glazier suddenly — we called her the Admiral because her father had been one.

'So?' I asked.

'You could pretend to be acting on his behalf. The policeman would treat you with respect. I was thinking of a furniture van. We could crowd into it.'

'A Trojan horse?'

'Exactly. It would take us to the door—no—farther—'

'Quite so. One of us with a trumpet draws the attention of the police and messengers in Palace Yard—perhaps with some friends creating a disturbance at the railings. Mildred has threatened to chain herself to them ... and then..'

'And then, with the policeman and messenger drawn off, open the Trojan horse; then up the stairs we rush barring ourselves in—and play!'

The House had voted against a Franchise Bill that might well have given us the first stage towards a vote, so we were retaliating by playing out a Bill dear to Mr Asquith's heart. We would drown his voice for him, as he had tried to drown ours. In prospect, it was exciting. We talked through a light supper which my cook provided—she would not join us, although sympathetic, because it was not her place to, she said. Sarah said she understood.

'I work in a fish and chip shop as you know, miss,' said Sarah, when the meeting broke up. 'I only joined you because I saved Mrs Glazier from a copper, knowing the way down an alley and over a fence, although I'm glad I did and can help. But as my Dad says, it's really for ladies, which is why he is agin it because he says, if they got the vote, all Suffragettes would vote Conservative, so why should the Liberals give it to them — or Labour if it comes to that? Ah well — got to get my bus.'

'Let me run you home in the car, Sarah,' I said, an idea in mind. 'We need more like you. We need some East End supporters to show how wrong your Dad is. After all, they're women too and can use plenty of freedom.'

Sarah thought it a grand idea, but she warned me not to press my luck. I thought of putting on some old tweeds but she argued against it with sound reason.

'If they think you're an ordinary working girl they'll just say: "Shove off! Sock 'er!" You wouldn't last on a soap box for a minute before some yobbo shoved you off and likely as not kissed you to quell you and prove something. But if you're poshed up, and any way they'll know you're a lady because of your voice, it'll be different. They may not agree but they'll lift their caps and listen, and touch a forelock when you've finished, too. And if you buy drinks all round they'll vote for you, if there's an election before they're sober again!'

It did not sound encouraging, but I knew I had to try.

So off we went, and arrived in the High Street, Walthamstow, armed with our pamphlets, banners, badges and our free and lashing tongues. I parked the car off the High Street, and tried to appear calm and collected. In the road where I parked the car, a piano-organ was being played by a man wearing a khaki jacket, a left-over from the South African war. On top of the organ was a monkey with a red cap, while around it — even at that late hour — pranced some ragged children, hopping and skipping.

'Shove a tanner in the cap — shall we? asked Sarah.

But I had a better idea; the piano-organ was what I needed to collect a crowd so, taking out a sovereign from my purse I approached the organ grinder. He was English, so I mentioned the monkey as I showed him the sovereign.

'A monkey? I thought only Italians had monkeys?' I said.

'Eh? S'right. I got it off a Wop. Itie to you, lady. It wanted feeding proper. That a sovereign, miss? Bit heavy for a lady to lift up to the cap? Allow me ...'

I held the coin back from his rough hand, and was half

afraid he would snatch it. But he had a friendly if unshaven face, watery blue eyes and a cockney grin.

'I want to hire your piano-organ,' I said, 'for half an hour.'

'Eh? Want a grind? Help yourself, lady.' He stood back.

'I want it down the High Street—somewhere where I can—er, stand on it ...'

'Stand on it! Blimey!' But his tone changed when I affixed my Suffragette badge and then wrapped a heliotrope, white and green scarf round my throat. 'Wunner them! Mmm. Suppose the organ was to get bust up? Who'd pay me?'

'I would,' I said, and dipped into my bag. 'Here is my visiting card — my adress, and ...' I added with a touch of brag, 'my telephone number. Suppose I give you a deposit of five pounds, returnable when the organ is returned?'

He removed his cap especially to scratch his head, and excite thought, and that having been done, replaced it.

'Well, I know you ladies — wild cats, meaning no offence. You give me the five pound note, and the sovereign. Hand me back the organ, and back to you goes the fiver. I don't fink,' he added more softly.

The monkey had climbed on to me, gibbering a bit. I said he had better stay as I wouldn't be responsible for him. The cockney was grinning and winking at Sarah, but he was a good sort and offered to wheel the piano-organ, saying that he would stay and watch to see that no harm came to it. He was a Boer War victim, he told me as he pushed it down the street, and if I liked proof I could see his bullet wound in the calf. Sarah told me in an aside that people usually paid him a bob not to.

The High Street staggered me. In my sheltered life I had never seen anything like it. On both sides of the street were stalls at which almost everything was sold; men were shouting out their wares and on almost every stall was a large paraffin flare that sent out much light and more heat to the accompa-

'Suffragette!' went up a shout, followed by laughter.

niment of a fierce tiger-cat hissing noise. The din was terrific; for the street itself was thronged with jostling people through which Fred, as Sarah called him, had to push the organ. I felt much as an actress does on a first night!

It was almost as if I were dreaming when Fred halted, parked the organ, and said, 'Your turn, lady. Good luck! You'll need it.' Then he showed me the organ's trick.

I turned the handle, and played Yip I Addi I Ay? and was thoroughly enjoying myself until Sarah nudged me, and pointed to an orange box she had found. I stood on it.

'Suffragette!' went up a shout, and there was laughter. Someone booed; someone cheered. The swaying crowd surged forward, eager for fun and frolic, I guessed.

'Ladies and gentlemen,' I began, and there was a roar of laughter.

'I have come,' I cried, 'to bring good news ——' It brought an expectant hush.

'She's got tickets for the Cup Final!'

'Very soon justice will be done,' I went on. 'The long years of martyrdom for women will be over; the years of servitude will be in the past—'

'What's she talking about?' A burly man pushed forward, a cloth cap on at an angle, a red scarf at his throat.

'You mean you want the vote, eh? Well, you've come to the wrong place. This is a Liberal stronghold. If you get the vote, what'll you do? Vote Conservative!'

'Booo!'

'Are you married?' I asked him.

'Yes, I am. Are you?'

'No,' I admitted, 'but—'

'But always hoping! Any offers?' called someone.

'Shut up,' said the burly man, elbowing him aside. 'You tell me, lady, one good reason why the likes of you should have the vote?'

'So that we can get the vote for the likes of your missus. You won't let her have a voice in government; she can't speak for herself. If she could, she would vote Liberal, wouldn't she?'

'She'd certainly better!'

'All right then. So not all women would vote Conservative! And how about your daughters, if you have any?'

'Five!'

'And don't you want *them* to get as good a job as men, so that you don't have to keep them? They have brains; they have unused abilities ...'

'And do us out of jobs!' shouted a man. 'Shove off!'

There was commotion in the crowd; someone form behind pushed me off the soap box. I fell on hands and knees and it was the burly man who picked me up. He demanded to know who pushed me and without waiting to find out for certain, hit the man just behind me on the chin. There was shouting and more scuffling. From nowhere. Fred arrived, and said: 'Hop it. Quick!' He and Sarah urged me through the crowd and a minute later I found myself in a dark alley, climbing on to a dustbin lid — pushed by Sarah!

Over a fence we went, surprising sleeping cats, and then back to the road where I had parked the car. There were shouts of 'Here comes a copper!' But the copper was standing by my motor-car, round which a group of small boys were crowded. They had climbed inside it, too! One was tooting the horn; another was jumping up and down on the seats; two had opened the rumble seat and were sharing out the tools.

'You can't pump up the tyres till you've let 'em down,' bawled one, holding my tyre-pump. 'How do you let 'em down?'

The policeman said 'hopit' every now and then in the intervals between writing things in his book. He was middle aged, bearded and solemn.

'How do you spell motor-car?' he asked me. 'E-r or O-r?'
'O-r,' I suggested.

'That's what comes of being eddicated,' he said resentfully.
'Not right your being a lady wot don't need it, getting eddication, instead of a man like me wot could make proper use
of it. Not right. With your eddication I could've been an
inspector.' He paused as I did not commiserate with this
unfamiliar line. 'Your car, miss? Left unattended obstructing
the highway. No lights ... well, if you left 'em on they've
blew out. You can get electric ones now. I've seen 'em.
Pinched a bloke yesterday. Turned the switch wrong way.
I got your number, miss — now your name.'

I gave him my card and he decided to copy it out later.
Then he cuffed one urchin, put his boot behind another, and
sent them all packing in the rough justice of the day without
need of a juvenile court. Luckily, no lasting damage had been
done and the policeman lent me a match and actually lit the
lamps, while Sarah told him about the row going on down the
High Street.

'It'll burn out if no one interferes,' he said calmly. 'I'll go
along and make sure it's all quiet presently.'

My scarf had gone and I now bore no outward signs of
being a Suffragette.

'Suffragettes perhaps?' I said.

'Could be. They'll cop it if I get near 'em,' he told us darkly.
'Proper pests. One of 'em kicked my shins. Hunger strike.
Forcible feeding! Let 'em starve I say! ... You'll get a sum-
mons, miss.'

I drove Sarah as near to her street as she thought advisable.

She wished me goodnight and got out of the car slowly.

Sho looked to be near to tears, and loitered, obviously
reluctant to walk away into the darkness, and I sensed that
she was afraid. At first, when I questioned her, she said,
'Nothing's wrong'; then, under pressure, she blurted it out.

It was Saturday night, and her father would return home the worse for drink. It would be awful. Her looks told me how awful, so I opened the door to the car. There was room for her at the flat.

I was tired when I steered the car through the West End. People were streaming from theatres and restaurants. Hansom cabs were jingling in all directions; horses' hoofs clacked busily. Beautifully bejewelled women in exquisite furs waited for doormen to summon cabs, cars, carriages or taxis. It was a busy night scene that would quickly fade, yet fascinating for the short while that it lasted. But as I pulled my car into the kerb in Piccadilly I had a shock. In front of me a large, high Rolls-Royce was parked; the bonnet was as low as the roof was high, and the windscreen had a likeness to a shop window. At the wheel, nodding in plum-coloured livery was Johnson, the chauffeur; beside him was Herbert the footman.

'Uncle Henry,' I breathed, and together Sarah and I peered into the partitioned-off passenger quarters that used to be called the tonneau. There, dozing, was Uncle Henry, so I opened the door.

In front of him the walnut cabinet was open. In his hand, supported by his thigh, was an empty glass.

'Unsle Henry ... time to get up,' I called softly.

He stirred, and struggled up. We helped him out and the cold night air hit him a blow in the face that made him reel.

'Virginia!' he said. 'Battle-axe!'

'Please! Don't be personal,' I urged.

'Come, come! I mean to say—the battle-axe! Where is it? I have been horrified, thinking of you at large like your poor grandmother with this terrible Urge of Cause, whatever it is, brandishing a battle-axe. I have come to collect it. It should never have been taken from the castle. I have been picturing you at large with it, smashing windows, decapitating policemen. Rushing around the House of Commons — attacking Lewd

George. Indeed to goodness, what a terrible thought!'

'Lloyd George, you mean, surely?' Sarah asked gently.

'He's Welsh. That's the way they pronounce it,' corrected Uncle Henry. 'Lewd George.'

'Clued George is nearer.'

'Clued nothing. He never had a clue! He wants to fill the House of Lords with butchers, bakers and candle-stick makers — and, if you have your way — women, too. He might as well buy a Rover ticket for the Empire!'

'Shush!' I warned. 'Wait — I will get the battle-axe ... Get in the car and keep him company, Sarah,' I whispered.

'After you,' said Uncle Henry, gallantly clinging to the door, and then when Sarah had stepped into the tonneau, he butted his top hat against the roof and pushed the rim down over his ears. 'Cars should be higher. Damn Liberals,' he muttered.

I fetched the battle-axe and raced back with it, to find that Uncle Henry with his concertina hat removed, had fallen asleep in a corner and was snoring.

'The National Gallery,' I told Johnson who had been trained to obey without question. 'Trafalgar Square.'

I had brought one of my summer panama hats, and with a Suffragette ribbon on, it seemed to suit Uncle Henry very well. It did not take long to reach the National Gallery, which was shut of course, and in pitch darkness; but Uncle Henry, roused again suffered himself to be led out of the car — after which I told Johnson to drive on a few yards and wait.

Together Sarah and I helped Uncle Henry, wearing my hat and carrying the battle-axe, up the several flights of steps.

'Not my club?' he said.

'Change of address,' I told him.

'Always changing ... everything,' he grumbled.

'Knock them up,' I said. 'You've got the battle-axe.'

He carefully turned the blade round away from the door, unaware that on the other side was a spike. To arouse the place, he slammed it against the door with a loud thud.

'Shout!' I said. 'Votes for Women!'

'Votes for Women?' asked Uncle Henry.

He tried to unstick the axe and tottered, but we saved him.

'We're in luck — a policeman! This should mean prison,' cried Sarah in glee.

'Now then. What's all this?' asked the policeman.

'Votes for Women!' both Sarah and I shouted in unison.

Uncle Henry turned, blinking — his panama hat with the 'Votes for Women' colours twisted sideways.

'Votes — Women?' he echoed, bewildered.

The policeman looked at him.

'You drunk?' he said, sniffing. 'Port?'

'Port? Doe min' if I do,' said Uncle Henry. 'Thanks. What's all this — Votes f'Wimmen—'

'And what are you doing with that battle-axe?' asked the cop, wrenching it from the door.

Uncle Henry glared.

'That's mine! Been in my family hundreds-v-years. Give me my battle-axe!'

'Banging down the doors of the Gallery, were you? Going to chop some more masterpieces, eh? Caught in the act,' said the copper. 'I know your games, you Suffragettes.'

I suddenly seized the battle-axe from him and went down the steps with it. He chased me while I shouted 'Rolls!' to Sarah. Of course the policeman caught me, and of course Sarah came to my rescue and knocked his helmet off while Johnson and Herbert ran from the Rolls, rescued Uncle Henry, deposited him in the tonneau and drove him off.

Possibly Sarah's booting the policeman's helmet along the pavement was a bit much; but my playing hockey with it, using the battle-axe as a stick, was no better. So the magistrate said later. But it kept the policeman's mind off Uncle Henry.

'And who?' I was asked, in the police court next day,

'was this mad-man accompanying you at the National Gallery, trying to axe down the doors?'

'He was taking us to the pictures, Your Worship,' I said.

'To the *pictures*? At the National Gallery? Those pictures don't move.'

'With Your Worship's pardon, they do with assistance,' I said. 'In a suitable barrow.'

He told me, when we were unrepentant, that the community must be protected from Suffragettes. It was a pity that our male accomplice had not also been taken into custody, especially as the constable's evidence suggested he might be weak in the head and in need of mental care and treatment.

It was all very scandalous and shocking, although not so shocking, Uncle Henry agreed, as if the newspapers had carried headlines and his photograph armed with the battle-axe. Obviously I had no intention of giving him away, as I told Cousin Cuthbert when he came on visiting day.

'Of course,' he muttered, 'we shall no longer contest the will. I mean to say — er, Uncle Henry might be cross-examined. Johnson could be subpoenaed as a witness, and under oath ...'

'Quite!' I said. 'But we can convert him. If he says he was a militant Suffragette, no one will think him barmy. If, on the other hand, he is an enemy, he might very easily be thought to have been potty — or even the worse for drink, behaving in that manner.'

'Yes,' said Cousin Cuthbert, which about summed it up. Being a Suffragette was clearly an acceptable and preferable alternative!

I was given six months for my disorderly conduct, disturbing the peace, and assaulting the police, so my name was written in golden letters at headquarters. As was my duty, I went on hunger strike. To refuse food, to suffer true hunger, is agonising and requires a terrific effort of will; but even worse is forcible feeding. One day I might describe the effects in greater detail, but they are gruesome, and a memory one prefers not to dwell on. But you can understand that it was not just a dramatic stunt; we wanted to make real difficulties for the sluggish Government, and also to be set free. It cannot be denied that the focus of interest made thousands think about the franchise who otherwise would not have done so. Of course, Sarah endured it all with me, and there is a photograph somewhere showing us in our prison clothes and aprons with the broad arrows on them.

Strangely, enough, Uncle Henry suddenly joined us as a sympathiser, but before he could be enrolled officially, war came; and the war brought a truce. In the midst of it, in nineteen seventeen, the Electoral Reform Bill was passed, giving votes to all women when they were thirty. It became law in January nineteen eighteen. As the Poet Laureate had said in nineteen ten to an assembly of women, 'You have proclaimed for the first time that the old rule of sex is dead; and that the next rule of human beings, of comrades, may begin to make this world like a star.'

ACKNOWLEDGEMENTS

THE WRECKERS, VOTES FOR WOMEN, A LAMP FOR ELI-
ZABETH— THE HAMLYN PUBLISHING GROUP LTD, 1968.
THE PUBLISHERS WISH TO EXPRESS THEIR THANKS
TO FLEETWAY PUBLICATIONS LTD FOR PERMISSION
TO INCLUDE ALL THE OTHER STORIES IN THIS BOOK,
© FLEETWAY PUBLICATIONS LTD 1968.